dear ~~Bailey~~

RANDOM
&RARE

Dig Forever !

CAT PORTER

xx Cat Porter .

CONTENTS

PROLOGUE

I'M DEAD.

I know, trust me. But it doesn't matter. Well, maybe to you it does. There's a point to all this, though. There has to be. I'm trying to figure it out myself. I want to shake this off, leave this mire. I do.

But I can't.

I can still feel her—her smile against my back, her warm breath on my neck, her arms squeezing my middle, her legs at my sides, her whispers in my ear. Those sensations will be forever indented on my soul and imprinted on my heart. Just like the rhythm of my engine, they vibrate together. And that's the way it should be, because Grace was my once-in-a-lifetime good thing. And I like to believe that's what might move this redemption of mine along.

Is her unhappiness keeping me here? Oh, it's there, way deep underneath. I can hear it, pinging inside her soul, tripping through her heartbeat. She hides it well. Can't hide it from me though, because I caused it.

Promises made, promises broken, promises glued back together. None of it means much now. The time for regrets is over. But they still mean something to her—just like her happiness does, and it should. Unlike me, she's alive in the living, breathing, bleeding world. The lack of that joy in her life has kept me tethered and burning all these years. I want that back for her. She deserves it.

I took that away, didn't I?

We men have big dreams. Some of us aim high, too high from time to time.

Grace never let go, always believed. She made me believe in that hungry emotion called love. She held my bounty in her fists. I'm glad I went first. I don't think I would have made it alone, brotherhood or not. Without her, I would have become an even nastier, more brittle soul than I already was.

I might not be breathing and bleeding anymore, but I've felt her pain, her hurt, and her disappointment since it all went down. Then that fucker sent her on an odyssey, sent her spinning out on her own Greek fucking tragedy. That shit had started with me, and he made my old lady finish it. Great fucking legacy I left my wife. That's not what Grace was made for, yet she has proven that she's made of sterner stuff. She's a survivor.

Yeah, yeah, I know. If she hadn't gotten involved with me, she probably would have moved on and lived a better life, a clean life. She would have gone to some swanky out-of-state college; gotten a fancy job where she wore designer skirts and high heels every day; married some intellectual, white-collar metrosexual asshole who barbecued on the weekends, drank white wine with her while they had great conversations where they dissected current events in the backyard of their McMansion; gone on Caribbean vacations every goddamn year; and had two to four kids and a Lexus hybrid to ferry them around in.

I could have left her to that.

With me?

With me, she got drug deals, strippers, shootings, drunken brawls, nasty, selfish, filthy men, and a whole lot of wondering where the hell I was late at night while saying a prayer or two that I'd come back home to her in one piece. But she also got brutal honesty, the back of my bike on runs through glorious country, fierce love, sweet fucking, friends who would kill for her, die for her; and promises I still burn to keep.

But no, I have no regrets—despite the pain I caused, despite the heartache, bitterness, and scabs I left behind. Fuck no.

My Grace. Yes, she's someone else's now, and he's a good man. And I'm glad, because I left him behind, too. But a patch of her heart will always be woven with mine.

From the first moment I laid eyes on her, I knew I didn't deserve her, but a part of me needed to try, needed to believe that I was worthy of breathing that air, of claiming the brass ring that could be us. I took my shot and won big. I'm paying my penance for that, if that's what this is called. But she doesn't owe a thing to anybody. She came back and created a bright new life over our ashes, and I'm glad because she deserves to soar.

Is there more for me to give her? I honestly wish there were, somehow, instead of being that gash in her soul.

Once, I loved her, really loved her.

And she loved me, and it was so fucking beautiful.

Once.

Is time fluid?

How can that rare beautiful be rendered irrelevant, intangible when I still feel so damn much? Does all that energy, that glory, that significance simply dissolve? Turn to smoke? To nothing?

It can't. It just can't.

PART I
DIG

PAST

ONE

THAT TOOK GUTS.

Running up to a bunch of dope-dealing bikers, begging for help, her eyes wild, long light-brown hair flying. What color eyes were those? Green-brown? Green-gray?

It'd been a boring night at a high school keg party on a ranch outside of town. We had just been killing some time, selling bags of weed before we were going to head on to another party in Spearfish anyway. Slapping around some smug high school football pricks who were assaulting a girl would be a good time. That shit didn't fly any way you sliced it, not for me.

I recognized the girl when I clawed one of the assholes off her. I'd seen her in Pete's Tavern in town plenty of times. The girl was fearless and in your face, looked you straight in the eyes and smoked you.

This one?

"Thank you. Thank you so much!" She clung to her big sister.

"You keep out of trouble, you hear?" I said. "And get her to do the same."

Her big eyes shone with relief, brimful of gratitude, full of fucking sincerity.

This girl melted in my mouth.

"Yeah, I know. Thanks again."

I let out a huff of air, masking it with a chuckle. "I bet you don't get into much trouble though, do you?" came tumbling from my lips.

Her forehead wrinkled. "Uh, not really, no."

"Didn't think so." I grinned.

I took one last look at her, that grin still plastered on my face. I got on my bike, put Fresh Young Thing out of my head, and dove in between someone else's legs later that night.

But when I finally woke up the next day, before I even opened my eyelids, the first thing I saw were those shimmering eyes of hers.

Hazel. That was what they called that fucking color.

"My little sister's not like me. In fact, she's not like most girls."

"You think I haven't noticed?" I chugged on my longneck. It had been fours years since I first laid eyes on Ruby's little sister at that keg party. Fours years of keeping my distance.

Pete's Tavern was crowded tonight. Another cascading ache surged through my skull. I didn't have my pills with me, so I'd moved to sit at the bar by myself to get a glass of water and another beer, away from the brouhaha at our table. Unfortunately, Ruby had followed me.

"Good. You noticed," Ruby said. "But also bad."

"Huh?" I tore my gaze away from her sister serving a pitcher of beer to a cowboy.

Her curvy hips were plastered into faded jeans frayed at the ends, her legs encased in scuffed brown leather cowboy boots, her full, round tits were covered by a stretchy white tank top with Pete's logo, and the base of her throat displayed a tiny necklace.

"You noticed her, Dig."

"Yeah, I noticed her. I'm a man. My blood's pumping, and my dick gets hard on a regular basis. You know how that goes, don't you?" I set my beer bottle back on the bar top and swiped at the corner of my mouth with the side of my hand. "She's cute, and she's got a hot little body that goes real nice with that cute. Heads-up—I don't think I'm the only one who's noticed either. But I also know that her kind of cute is way too fresh for me."

"Fresh, huh? You sure?" Ruby narrowed those same hazel eyes as her little sister's, but hers were unyielding and sharp. Actually, no. Tonight, Ruby's pupils were pinned, like almost every night recently. The bitch was speeding—again.

"Oh, I'm sure," I said. "Why the hell do you think I haven't been over to your little den of sin to party all this time? Staying out of the line of fire."

She let out a hoarse laugh. "Oh, ho—fire, huh?"

I made a face. "You know what I mean."

She crossed her arms and leaned on the bar. "I do, Dig, and I appreciate it—seriously."

"Aren't you the protective older sister? Who would have thought? She's not that young, for Christ's sake. She must see all sorts of shit at your house. You're a fucking contradiction, aren't you?"

"She doesn't mind. 'Live and let live' is our family motto. It's just that we aren't the same kind of girls, me and my sister."

No shit.

"I mean, if that's what you think, if that's what you're hoping for," Ruby said. "Grace isn't that."

My eyes riveted on Ruby. "Grace?"

"Yeah. Her name's Grace."

A groan escaped my throat. I'd never asked about her, never inquired. Best to stay away.

Grace. Perfect. A secret wish or hope. Something poetic, elusive.

Fuck me.

I rubbed my mouth with my hand. In another lifetime maybe. The one that had been taken away, the one I'd turned my back on.

I rapped my knuckles on the bar top. "Pete, hit me with a tequila, would you? And one for Ruby here." I straightened my shoulders and glanced up at the football game on the television overhead.

Who the hell was playing tonight anyway?

Ruby smirked and shook her head.

"What?" I asked, my focus remaining glued on the screen.

She leaned in closer to me. "Grace has dreams and brains. She's going to college now, and she's working to save money to keep herself there. I'm helping her with that. I want her out of this nowhere town, and so does she. She just won't admit it, though, because she thinks I need her or some shit like that."

I glanced at Ruby.

Yeah, smart girl. A fucking good sister, that Grace.

Ruby definitely needed backup. The woman was in over her head most times, yet she seemed to always enjoy the ride. Some chicks were built that way. Grace didn't seem to be, but you never knew what still waters hid.

"She really doesn't give you any shit for all the high living you do?" I asked.

"Lately, just a bit. But she doesn't know about my dancing at the Tingle yet either."

"Why not? You afraid you gonna disappoint her?"

Ruby's eyes tightened. "Yeah, maybe." She shifted her weight against the bar.

"Well, she's right, you know—about keeping an eye on you. How many times I gotta tell you to slow it down?"

Ruby shrugged and looked away, her hand brushing over her arm. Those track marks and bruises were still evident to me, makeup or no.

"I'm sober and good to go on the nights I have to work. You got any complaints about me on that score?" she asked, a hand sifting through her long blonde hair.

"No. But you know, using junk cuts you out of the club. It fucks everything up. Everything."

"I just tried it a couple of times. I'm sticking with the ole favorites, no worries."

I tilted my head at her. "You know, I think your sister's got a point. Maybe you should respect that she's sticking around for your sorry ass."

"I do."

"You realize, you're lucky you got her?"

"Yep, I do," Ruby replied, her jaw set.

"Don't fuck that up."

"I won't. But I also don't want someone like you fucking her up—getting in her head or in her pants and messing with her. She isn't cut out to be a Saturday night toy for a guy like you."

"Yeah, Rube, 'cause a guy like me is only good for one thing, right?"

Ruby let out a laugh. "You're having your good time, same as the rest of us, and that's great. It's you—right now at least. You and me are realists and make no bones about it. But all that isn't Grace. And, FYI, it's never going to be."

"And what is Grace? What does she need? Some fairy-tale bullshit?"

"No, that's not her either. She's a realist at heart—more than me in some ways. But she needs a guy who'll bring her flowers once in a while, just for the hell of it."

My gaze fell on Grace once more. She leaned over a table, wiping it down.

Ruby followed my gaze. "She's not the dozen-roses kind of girl either. Grace is something less flashy, more…sincere, like handpicked flowers."

A blond guy with a cocky grin splitting his face came up behind Grace and swept his hands over her ass and up around her hips. The blood shot to my head, my skin heated. She flinched, her eyes darting up at him. Then a smile suddenly brightened her face, and her body relaxed in the motherfucker's long arms.

My scalp prickled. "Like Prince Charming over there, you mean?"

The blond jock laid a kiss on Grace's mouth and pulled her close, talking in her ear. His hands descended to her ass again.

Fuckwad.

She was smiling, her fingers curled into his University of Missouri T-shirt.

"Hell no," Ruby said. "That kid's an asshole. Told her too. Trey Owens. He's been banging everything in sight all summer. Grace is just next on his hit list. I've seen him at the Tingle a lot. He's a cheap asshole. Daddy's allowance money must not stretch far enough for all the trips he makes to the titty bar."

We both stared at them as they laughed and talked, their arms wrapped around each other.

I drained my beer. "You could eat him for breakfast, Rube."

"I'd love to, believe me. But Grace thinks he's sweet and really cute, and she wants her shot. I had to back down. She's got to live and learn. He's just recycled bullshit, and she might as well sharpen her radar. On the other hand"—she turned and eyed me—"she also doesn't need an outlaw asshole like you entertaining himself with her. She's off *your* radar is what I'm saying."

Who would have thought that Ruby had a soul?

She'd been around the club for the better part of a year now—partying, hanging out—and she was a great lay from what I'd heard. A couple of months ago, after her impressive debut dancing at Tingle, she'd almost made it onto my cock in the office, but she'd had a thing for Jump, and he'd finally set his sights on her that night. She'd gotten on his cock instead, and they had been hanging together ever since.

"She is not on my radar."

Ruby smirked. "Right."

"Did you not hear me just now when I said I made that decision a long time ago? You think I'm stupid?"

"Dig Quillen, if there's one thing I'm sure of, it's that you are not stupid."

"Relax your ass. I just like admiring her from afar once in a while. That okay with you?"

She grinned. "Yeah, that's okay."

"Good." I swallowed the shot of tequila Pete had slid in front of me. The liquid burned down my throat.

"You're not sweet and cute anyway," she said before downing her own shot. We laughed. "What you are is one sexy motherfucker, and you know it, too."

"We done with this fascinating conversation now?"

"Oh, yeah." She pushed back from the bar. "Thanks for the drink."

"Hey, you ready for this thing with Vig?" I asked.

Ruby was running a little recon for me and Jump with Vig, the VP of the Demon Seeds, a club in northern Montana. For a long while now, we'd been trying to coordinate delivering our meth and weed inventory with the Seeds, but Vig would always change the rules at the last minute. This was pissing me off, really pissing me off. I had people depending on me, and new clients in Wyoming were waiting. The asshole was fucking with my trade. And for what? For the hell of it.

Ruby had snagged his attention last weekend at Tingle, and whip-smart woman that she was, she'd caught my eye, and we'd concocted a silent plan. With a nod from me, she'd given him a memorable lap dance. He'd kept in touch, and she'd showered him with all sorts of attention.

The result—tomorrow, Ruby and Vig would be headed for a weekend rally up north. Jump would be taking some new girl, Alicia, and they were all going out to the Seeds' club in Montana so that Jump could get the lay of the land and get the show on the fucking road. Jump could be very diplomatic in a tight squeeze. In a couple of weeks, I'd meet up with them at another rally just outside of Rapid City.

"Yeah, all set." Ruby smiled and clinked her empty glass with mine.

I hadn't taken it lightly that Ruby was putting herself out there in the lion's den for the club. She wasn't even Jump's property. Unlike most of the women who hung around the club, Ruby had made it clear from the start that she wasn't interested in any such ties that bind. All the better—although I could tell that Jump had been ticked about her sharing her wares with Vig for over an hour in a VIP room at the strip club. He hadn't stayed ticked for long, though, as usual.

Ruby had once again proven that she could see the forest for the trees, and I'd gladly taken her up on her offer to help with Vig. The woman had shown herself to be a quick thinker in several other tight situations that could have gone south. Just last month, she had smoothly stepped in—much to my relief—and played the role of the sexed-up bitch, creating a distraction to the hilt with a guy who'd been lingering on the street in his car, giving me, Jump, and Dready time to reset an alarm system and get out of an auto parts store in the middle of the night without a hitch.

No, Ruby was anything but dumb. She'd come through for us. The only thing that concerned me was her mighty serious love affair with coke and speed and God knew what else.

"I appreciate this," I said.

Ruby winked at me. "Good to know." She glanced over at Grace once more and lifted her chin. "And I appreciate *this*." She turned and stalked off on those unbelievably long legs of hers in boots, her tight ass peeking out of her cutoff denim shorts. *Lucky Jump. Lucky Vig.*

I stretched my lower back. Suddenly, this barstool was a pain in my ass. I drained my beer bottle, licked at the last traces of brew on my lips, and swiveled around on my stool. Like they had a will of their own, my eyes searched the cavernous dark interior of this old bar that the town had practically been built around over a hundred years ago.

I couldn't help myself.

There.

She was leaning over a table, taking an order, her long hair shining like thick waves of satin under the spotlight hanging overhead. She grinned and nodded at the two gray-haired ranchers who were chatting her up. The balding guy in glasses said something, and she suddenly knocked back her head and laughed.

A spark raced up my spine. *How sexy could a woman's throat be?*

I looked away as if my eyes had been pricked by a blaze of sunlight.

TWO

"YOU GONNA BE OKAY, MAN?"

"Honestly?" Wreck asked.

His heavy eyes rested on his little brother, Miller, who was packing up his gear into Wreck's truck in the front yard of the club. Miller pressed a hand down over a layer of rolled-up khaki and camouflage T-shirts as he dragged shut the zipper on his duffel.

"Always," I said.

"I don't fucking know." Wreck tugged his fingers through his short beard. "It was one thing, sending him off to basic training. But this is a whole other hill of beans. Hell, I'm not the one shipping off to some civil war halfway around the world though, am I? He's the one who needs the support here, not me."

"Face it. You're like a great big mama bear sending her cub off into the wild forest." I slapped my hand over his bulky shoulder squeezing it. "He's your boy, man, our boy."

Wreck nodded as he sniffed in air, jamming his hands into his jeans pockets.

I leaned into him. "Miller's a good kid. He's not some newbie out of the suburbs. He knows how to handle a weapon. Hell, he's comfortable with a whole range of weapons. We made sure of that. And he's been around the block. The kid can sense trouble a mile off. He's smart, careful. You gave him that. That came from you. He will be fine, just fine."

Would he be? Fuck, I hoped so. Miller was Wreck's half brother via their rodeo slut of a mother. He had tracked the kid down for years before he finally found Miller, beaten up and bruised in the basement of his drunken father's shack of a house on the Pine Ridge Reservation. Wreck had punched out the old man, grabbed Miller and brought him home, raising the kid himself.

Now nineteen years old, Miller was taller than Wreck and just as tough—on the outside at least. The kid's darker than dark eyes hid a swarming world in their depths.

I slung my arm around Wreck's shoulders. "He wants this, right? You gotta give it to him. Shit, you're the one who put the idea in his head anyway. Get some living under his belt before he decides on patching in or not? He ain't the college type, so all that discipline and obedience he's gonna be swimming in now will only forge his character. Make him a man to be proud of."

"He already is that man," Wreck breathed, his eyes on Miller.

"Yeah, he is," I said quietly. "Don't make this harder for him though."

Wreck held my gaze, his mouth stiffening.

"All set," Miller said, a lopsided grin on his tan face. His guarded eyes darted between me and Wreck. "We good to go?"

"Yep." Wreck nodded and headed for the driver's side of the truck.

Miller gestured at Wreck with a flick of a thumb. "He okay?"

"He will be—eventually." I grabbed him by the scruff of his neck and hugged him.

Miller thumped my back. "Thanks for everything, Dig."

"Shut up, and make us proud."

He released me, his black eyes holding mine, his jaw tense. "I'm gonna miss everybody."

"We're going to miss you, too, kid." I ran a hand over his freshly buzzed hair. "Still can't get used to you buzzed. Sucks."

He let out a throaty laugh and swatted my hand off his scalp. "Yeah, me neither. I don't know if I'll ever get used to it." He rubbed his sheared head of hair as a half smile lit up his dark eyes. "But I gotta say, it does make life easier."

"It's too harsh a look on you. Grow it right the fuck back the minute you're out."

"You kidding? No question." He glanced over his shoulder at Wreck sitting in the truck, lighting a cigarette for Boner, my best friend, who was leaning against the vehicle. Miller's features sobered. "Dig, keep your eye on him for me."

"Always do." I lifted my chin. "Don't worry about him. You stay focused and get the job done. And don't fuck anything over there. You might get your dick cut off."

He rolled his eyes at me. "I'm not going to the Middle East, Dig. They're sending me to Europe."

"Well, you never know, man."

Miller let out a small laugh. "Yeah, I'll keep that in mind." He strode toward the truck, and as he climbed inside he shot me a grin.

"You're the little sister, right?"

As if I fucking didn't know.

The pounding loud music along with the rumbling of the Saturday night crowd at Pete's made it next to impossible for her to hear me. She leaned in closer. A magical fragrance of orange blossoms filled my nose. Florida in early spring. Heat, sun, freedom.

Jesus.

She narrowed her eyes at me.

Good, she was nervous. It was the first time I'd talked to her in years—since that keg party in fact.

She struck a pose and mouthed off about my patches.

My cock jerked to attention once the words, "Oh, an officer? Are you a gentleman, too?" sparked out of that sweet hot mouth as she threw me an I-could-give-two-shits-who-you-are look from her usually innocent face.

My entire body tightened. I held her fierce gaze. "Sit down."

Grace moved quickly and finally settled. I explained the situation in very simple terms.

Ruby had fucked up the Vig setup on the last day. According to Jump, everything had been going perfectly until Ruby decided she needed more blow to help her through her post-weed low. She'd scored some cocaine but gotten in the guy's face about his customer service when he tried to stick his hand down her shirt. Meanwhile, Vig had meth and a couple of unregistered guns on his bike, and Jump's pockets had been lined with weed.

All this had happened at a truck stop with two highway patrol cruisers present. Police involvement had been inevitable, and a quick escape had been a fantasy. Jump had Vig get rid of his unlicensed guns, and he'd stockpiled all their goodies into Ruby's designer backpack while she was having it out loudly and wildly with the frisky dealer. It was a good call, and it sucked. We would either throw Ruby under the bus, or Vig, if he didn't want to play ball our way.

"She got herself arrested today with one of my brothers."

Grace only took a deep breath and pressed her lips together. She didn't look too surprised or upset, but not shocked either. No yelling, shrieking, crying, fainting. No accusations, only asking one question after the next.

"Calm down, Peanut."

Where the hell did that come from now?

Her being all frazzled, looking like a lost little girl trying to hold it together and determined to make sense of it all was something to behold. Her hair swished off her shoulder as she spoke. I couldn't resist touching it, and I twirled a soft lock around two of my fingers. It was a richer color than I'd originally thought. Brown with streaks of dark gold. A sun-kissed nymph.

The second I told her I needed her to do something for me, she squeaked, and her eyes popped open like one of those old-fashioned baby dolls. I had no idea why the fuck that had set her off, but I'd had enough. I pulled her into my lap and held her against me. That was good, too good. In fact, it was bad. I knew this, but now that I had her on me, I was like a sinking ship that had stalled just before it got sucked down in that final nosedive toward the abyss of the ocean.

I stroked her back, my other hand squeezing her thigh. I went in closer to that sexy throat for another whiff of that fresh-but-not-too-sweet scent, now mixed with girlish panic. Why was that such a turn-on? I usually liked the experienced ones who never needed much direction from me in order to suit any mood and appetite. Kept things moving nicely along.

This girl was not that. She was...

Christ. What the fuck am I doing?

Back to business.

I needed her to visit Ruby in jail and convince her to take the fall for possession. I had to keep Jump clean and Vig clean, showing good faith and brotherhood so that Vig would be in my debt and finally cooperate in the way I wanted him to. If not, I'd throw him under the bus instead of her. It was a good opportunity. Just a shame about Ruby. But I'd make a deal with her. I wasn't going to let her or her little sister flap in the wind over this clusterfuck.

"We'll look out for you, too," I said.

She fidgeted in my lap, her eyes narrowing at me. Her ass rubbed against my very hard dick, and I grinned. Her eyes went round as saucers as my erection enjoyed itself against her. That seemed to shut her up right quick, and she lost her concentration for a moment. I pulled her even closer, my hand moving up her tight thigh over her velvety soft jeans. My thumb flicked between her legs, and her breath caught in her throat.

Fuck, what would it be like to get in there, pound into that, pull moans out of her over and over again, hear that mellow voice cry out my name?

I fingered the hem of her T-shirt, grazing her soft bare skin. "You still got that pissant boyfriend, peanut?"

She was at a total loss for words and only shook her head.

My fingers slid up along her warm skin, and she shivered. They slipped under the thin cotton fabric of her bra strap, and her breath hitched again.

Oh, yes, Peanut. That little bra is coming off, and soon—with my fucking teeth if need be.

"How about I take you to breakfast tomorrow and explain it all then?" I asked.

Yeah, that, and give her another taste of playtime with Dig. God, I'm such a dog.

I was in a haze of lust and in the iron grip of an overwhelming urge. Was it to protect her or devour her? Hell, it was both. There was a first time for everything.

The hulking figure of Pete stood over us, his hands slung on his hips. "You want to let my star waitress get back to work, Dig? I got a business to run."

I let her go. She swallowed hard, grabbed her serving tray, and sprinted off.

I only grinned.

"I thought you meant something else when you said you needed me to do something." She glanced out the big picture window by our table at a small diner two towns over from Meager where I'd told her to meet me. Her gaze followed the lone elderly man wandering down Main Street with a newspaper under his arm. No rush hour in Pine Needle on a Sunday morning. Her eyes rested on my Harley parked right out front, next to her old Jimmy truck.

"Why? What did you think?" I asked.

Grace's cheeks turned beet red as she concentrated on swishing her waffle around in a puddle of syrup. A wavy lock of hair fell out of her ponytail and swung in her face, hiding her eyes, and I stifled the urge to reach out and wipe it away.

"Hey, tell me." I trapped one of her legs between mine under the table and squeezed it.

She blinked up at me. "That, um…I was going to have to come to the club and, um…"

"Yeah?"

"Do stuff."

"Do stuff?"

"I mean, do *things*…for you and the rest of the men."

I swallowed my coffee down fast before I spit it up. "No, Peanut. That ain't gonna happen, not ever."

"But that happens, right? Pete's told me—"

"I don't know what Pete or anybody else told you, but I'm telling you that is not happening." Not with her at least. "Is that what your sister told you?"

"She's never told me much about the club. But with the few things I saw and heard at home when everyone used to come around, I figured…"

"Well, shit happens, not all of it good. But the women who hang with the club are there because they wanna be. Look, you just concentrate on talking to Ruby today."

"Okay."

"I wish I could take you into Rapid to see her, but we got to play Ruby's club connection a bit loose here—or at least try to. Our lawyer hired another lawyer for her, so she's all set. You'll meet him eventually. He'll walk you through everything. Until her sentence has passed, I'm gonna be out of touch. I'll be around if you need anything, though. I'll be watching out for you, but it won't be a good idea for us to have any contact for a while."

Hell, isn't that the truth? I sank back in my vinyl seat and gulped the lukewarm coffee in my mug.

Golden sunlight poured through the large window, filling the tired small luncheonette with warmth. The only other patrons were an elderly couple sitting side by side, silently chewing their food. In about an hour the place would be jammed with the good folk who had gone to church services this morning. The heavy smell of bacon grease and singed toast hung in the air.

Grace chewed on her last piece of waffle, staring at me.

I grinned. "What's so fascinating, Peanut?"

Her cheeks flushed. "Nothing."

"Spill. Come on."

"It's, um, your hair."

"My hair?"

"Yes." A slight smile swept her lips.

"Do I have dandruff or something?"

"No! It's just in this light, the color—"

"No one's ever been able to figure out this color—light brown, gold dirt, dirty honey, dirty blond—you name it, it's been…"

"Your hair is the color of whiskey and wheat."

Her eyes melted with mine and something shifted in my chest.

"Well, no one's ever said that before."

"That's what I see." Her face broke out into a shy grin, and she brought a syrupy fingertip to her lips as she swallowed.

I took in a deep breath, my grip on my mug tightening. "You like waffles, Peanut?"

"When they're homemade, not the frozen ones. My mom used to make them for us every Saturday morning when we were kids. There's nothing like eating one fresh off the waffle iron. The butter melts in all the deep nooks, and if you've got really good syrup—the real-deal maple, not that fake-colored corn-syrup crap, well…" She let out a sigh.

I stretched my legs, grazing hers again. "You know how to make 'em?"

A sudden image of her puttering in a kitchen, concentrating those beautiful eyes over gloppy batter in a steaming electrical appliance as that piece of hair fell in her face, had me enthralled.

"Oh, yeah. It's not exactly rocket science. But I haven't had the chance in a long time. My mom trashed the waffle iron a while ago in a fit of anti-domesticity." She yanked a couple of napkins out of the metal dispenser at the edge of our table.

I laughed. "And what exactly is a fit of anti-domesticity?"

"When your husband and the father of your children leaves you one day after twenty years of marriage and takes off, never to be heard from again."

"Oh, that." I toyed with the handle of my coffee cup. "Yeah, that does suck."

She wiped her lips with a napkin and balled it in her hand. "Where's your family?"

"My family?"

"Yeah. Are you from around here?"

"No. Came up from Colorado years ago with Boner, kicking around on our bikes. We met Wreck at Sturgis, came down here to Meager with him and hooked up with the club."

"You still have family back home?"

"No. Nobody's left in Colorado." I swallowed more coffee.

"No brothers or sisters?"

"The One-Eyed Jacks are my brothers." I drained my mug and shifted in my seat.

She put down her fork, and her eyes rested on me. She was probably waiting for a story, but it was a story I wouldn't tell.

I swiped the bill from next to my dish, the paper sticking to my suddenly damp hand. "You finished?" I shot up from behind the table, not caring for her answer. "I'm gonna go take care of this."

The words *family* and *home* in connection with blood relatives hadn't been a part of my personal vocabulary for over a decade.

"Fifteen dollars, please."

I handed the cashier a twenty. She handed me the change, her manicured fingertips lingering in my palm just a fraction of a second longer than necessary. I glanced up at her. Blonde, blue-eyed, pouty willingness filled my gaze.

She arched a pierced eyebrow as she slammed the drawer of the cash register, her chest jutting out. "There you go," she said softly, leaning on the counter, her tongue swiping the corner of her mouth.

Yeah. There was this. This was what I knew well. This was easy, comfortable. This was all the time. This was, *I don't have to think about it at all the next day—or even the next moment after I zip my jeans back up.*

I glanced back at the table. Grace put her fork and knife neatly in her plate as she smiled up at the waitress who leaned over to clear our dirty dishes. Grace slipped her faded jean jacket over her arms and wiped back that stray piece of hair once again.

I let out an exhale. What I needed to be doing was concentrating on business—keeping the little sister safe, keeping the bitch in jail on an even-keel and protected, and smoothing the way with the Seeds.

I turned back to blondie and grinned. "Thanks, sweetheart. How are you doing today?"

THREE

"SHE DOESN'T LIKE ME MUCH, HUH?" Jump asked, his voice straining over Alabama blaring from the old jukebox in Pete's.

"Who? The sister?"

"Yeah," he said. "Can't say I blame her."

"She'll get over it. Does it matter to you anyway?"

"Nah."

Yeah, not much mattered to Jump outside of the club and his immediate needs. Efficient way to live, I supposed. His quasi-girlfriend was in the slammer on a trumped-up charge of his own making, but he was out partying and sleeping like a baby every night.

As for me, I had been staying on the straight and narrow for weeks now.

Along with the business at hand, I kept my focus on making sure the Peanut was okay—from a distance. She was all alone in that house, working long hours at Pete's, and trucking to some college in Rapid. Nowadays, I would go by Pete's a lot, more than I ever had before. I wanted to see for myself that she was okay, and I'd make sure she got home all right by having one of my prospects follow her.

"How's it going, Little Sister?"

"Stop calling me that."

"Why? It fits. That's how we met, ain't it? 'Please save my sister…'"

"Oh, God, help me."

"Give me a smile, Peanut."

"I'm busy, Dig. Get lost."

"You're not a very friendly waitress, babe. Your tips must suck."

Grace let out a laugh. "My tips are amazing, *babe*." She charged off, her arms straining under a tray full of dirty glasses and overflowing ashtrays.

Many times, I'd shoot by her house on my way home a few hours before dawn to make sure that piece-of-shit Jimmy of hers was in the drive. I'd send Butler, my new prospect, to Rapid to hang out whenever she had classes, and then he'd follow her home. I wasn't taking any chances.

A fresh beer landed on the table in front of me. "Here you go, Dig." Mandy, the other waitress, leaned over me, trying to get me interested in her tits yet again.

A crash and a shriek erupted a few tables over. Boner's hand slammed into my chest, and my head shot up. Grace's ex, the Blond Fuckwad, had her in his lap, an empty serving tray teetering on her hand, her shirt wet, her face stamped with shock. His hand gripped her bicep, and he tugged on her, his tense mouth moving, spitting out smack at her. Sister remained tight-lipped. His friends were laughing, hooting.

My head exploded, and I dived out of my chair.

Boner yanked Little Sister out of Trey's grasp, and I snatched the shithead out of his chair, ramming my fist in his face. Blood gushed out of his nose, over his teeth, and on my hands. I jerked him close shaking him.

"You don't ever fucking touch her again, you hear? You even look at her, I'm gonna slice your balls off and fry 'em, you got that? You got that?"

He warbled something, choking, and I dropped him on the floor, kicking him once in the ribs.

My gaze shifted to his frozen gang of pals. "Get the fuck out, and don't come back."

They scrambled, jerked the idiot to his feet, and hustled him out.

"Dig?"

Grace's sharp breathing rose up behind me. I turned to her. Her eyes were wide, her lips parted. My heart was pounding with adrenaline. Fuck, just the sight of her being handled had made me crazy—not her, not fucking ever. I ran my knuckles down her cheek, leaving behind a smear of blood on her silky pale skin, and my eyes flared. That was wrong. This girl was clean, unmarked, and she should stay that way.

A chill swept up my back. I would kill anyone who tried otherwise.

I took in a breath and rubbed the blood off her cheek with my thumb. We didn't say a word to each other. I planted a quick kiss on her forehead and then got the fuck away from her. I had to get the hell out of Pete's.

"We off?" I asked Jump.

"Fuck yeah. Bringing Mandy and these other two back with us." He pointed at the two dark-haired girls laughing at a joke Boner was telling them.

Good. I needed a distraction—badly.

"Butler, you stay here till closing. Get Little Sister home safe. Watch for that asshole."

Butler raised his beer bottle and slid back in his chair, a grin lighting up his face. "No worries."

"Why should I believe you?" Vig asked. "At the end of the day, that cunt's your property. She's gonna do what you and your club want her to do, not what's good for me."

"Ruby's following orders on this, or she's gonna get hurt, and she knows it," I spit into the mouthpiece of the pay phone at a gas station on Route 44 just outside of Rapid. "She's cutting a deal with the DA as we speak, taking the fall for you and Jump. Ain't that good enough for you?"

"Nah, it ain't. Until she gets sentenced, it ain't good enough."

"You're just going to have to wait it out. A few more weeks now."

"I don't like waiting, Diggy."

God, I hated this asshole.

"I'm thinking I need some confirmation here," his voice sneered at me.

"Oh, yeah?"

"I think I need a better guarantee than your word."

"Thanks for the insult. Like what?"

"I hear the bitch has a sister."

Sparks fired in my veins. "And?"

"Think I'm gonna check her out."

That familiar tense rhythm pounded through my head. "I told you before, man. Ruby's not our property, so why would I care?"

"Ruby might care though. And I want to guarantee that she *really* cares where all this is headed if she doesn't come through for me. Bitch is crazy, and now, she's going through a forced detox in the slammer. How do I know she might not lose it and change her mind at the last second for the fuck of it?"

My vision went red. I squeezed my eyes shut, my grip tightening on the plastic handset. Mick, my president, was relying on me to resolve this shit. If I didn't come through…

"Our business is hinging on this, Vig. Don't you think I give a shit if the outcome is in your favor? Don't you think I've put a lot of thought and effort into making sure that this rolls the way we all need it to?"

"Maybe what you need and what I need are two different things, Diggy."

The line went dead.

I slammed the phone back in its cradle. "Fuck!" I took in a deep breath, popped in another quarter, and punched in the number for Butler's beeper.

A few minutes later, he rang.

"Hey, what's up?" he asked.

"Where's Little Sister?"

"She just walked into the supermarket."

"Are you on her, for fuck's sake?"

"Yeah, of course, I am. I'm on the pay phone by the barbershop next door, Dig. What the fuck?"

"Stay put. I'm sending Boner over. Stay on them the rest of the day—at a distance, you hear? You see anything out of the ordinary—and I mean, anything—you let him know."

"Yeah, okay. What the hell's going on?"

"Just fucking stay on her!"

"I'll stay on her. Actually, I like staying on her, so no problem."

I gritted my teeth. "Shut the fuck up, and keep your eyes open."

I beeped Boner next. "Keep her in the supermarket for a while until I beep you the all-clear. I got to check out what Vig is up to. Then you take her home and stay with her. I don't want to freak her out by bringing her into the club, but I might have to."

"Anything you say, bro. I got her. Don't worry."

I trusted Boner with my life. We had been through hell and back together as teenagers.

"You keep her safe, man."

"Dig, I got this."

Jump and I went over to Ruby and Grace's house with the cracked siding and the rusted swing set in the yard. Jump let us in with the key he still had from Ruby. We searched the small house for signs of a break-in. Faded and worn furniture from another era filled the living room. A small television with a thickly upholstered lounge chair sat in the corner, begging for a weary grandpa to fill it. A couple of framed photos were propped on the wood table by the chair. *Jesus, not a speck of dust in sight.* I picked up a photo—two little girls in frilly dresses, arm in arm, with a smiling little blonde boy in front of them.

I pushed Jump out of the way in the small hallway and found her bedroom. Pinks and yellows, like a leftover preteen dream. Country-style white curtains, a full-sized antique brass bed, and a quilt with fucking flowers on it. My spine stiffened. Had she ever fooled around with the blond fucker on this bed? Taken off her top for him and let him feel her, suck on her? Had she squirmed for his hand between her legs or moaned for his hard dick to be inside her? Had his cum gotten all over this goddamn daisy quilt?

My teeth raked across my lower lip. That sting started tearing through my stomach.

Several fashion magazines were piled on the dresser. Makeup and bottles of girl stuff and a couple of hairbrushes were organized in a long plastic container. The only evidence of a recent inhabitant was a crumpled pale green blouse and a pink bra dumped on the smoothly made bed. Someone couldn't decide what to wear this morning.

I picked up the pink bra by the thin strap, my eyes drinking it in as if I had made an important scientific discovery beyond my wildest dreams. I brought it close to my face and inhaled. *Fuck me.* Pink, all right. All girl-woman—baby powder, a warm hint of skin, and a delicate touch of that goddamn orange-blossom perfume. A flare of heat seeped through my chest. I rubbed the bra against my lips, and my stubble caught on the satin, scraping it.

"Things cool in here?" Jump asked, standing in the doorway.

I dropped the bra back down on the bed and nodded. "Yeah, seems all good."

"Doesn't look like anyone's been here, except Little Sister."

"Good," I muttered, brushing past him and out the door.

A couple of hours later, Boner called me. "Get your ass over here, and bring beer. Sister's cooking homemade mac and cheese.

You believe that shit? I didn't know you could make it from scratch, bro. Did you?"

I rubbed my eyes as I shook my head. "Be prepared," I said, letting out a laugh. "It's not going to be that orange color you know and love so well, but I'm sure it will taste a fuck of a lot better. She good? She suspect anything?"

"Everything's good. Get off the phone, and bring the beer."

"I'm on it."

By the time I got there with two icy-cold six-packs in hand, Grace had a pile of sautéed chicken breasts on a platter, a casserole dish of bubbling mac and cheese, and a huge spinach salad with a couple of bottled dressings to choose from. I grinned as I tore off my jacket, quickly washed my hands at the sink, and then settled into a chair next to Boner, who cracked open three beers. A small smile swept over Grace's lips as she scooped creamy macaroni and cheese into my dish.

I leaned back in the chair. Matching silverware, matching dishes, clean clear glasses. A complete meal.

I smoothed my hair behind my ears and took in a breath.

"You okay?" she asked, sitting across from me.

"Yeah, just hungry. This looks great."

"Tastes better," Boner said through a mouthful of chicken.

Grace smiled at me from across the table, and that surge of heat spiked in my chest again. I tucked into the golden mac and cheese.

A few hours later, Jump called the house and confirmed there was no sign of any Demon Seeds in the entire county, let alone in our little Meager, South Dakota. I glanced at Sister and Boner slouched on the sofa next to each other, their feet up on the coffee table. The young lady and the crude pirate. They laughed over yet another episode of *The Brady Bunch* on some cable-channel marathon.

"We should go," I said, clicking off the remote control for the television as I hopped up from the lounger.

Boner lifted Grace in his arms and planted a fat kiss on her forehead. "Thanks, hon. Great dinner. Let me know when you're up for cooking for me again."

"Whenever you want. Just let me do the shopping next time?" She let out a lazy laugh.

Her messed-up hair, drowsy eyes, and half smile were completely adorable. An urge to take her in my arms and squeeze her myself overwhelmed me. An urge to lick that soft throat like a melting ice cream cone and hear her breath catch for me were even more overwhelming.

Nope, not going to happen.

Things were good as they were. Leaving her here, alone, in this worn-out house tonight made my gut heavy, but we'd be taking turns doing drive-bys through the night. I didn't want her to worry. Boner strolled over to his bike while I stood in the doorway, running a hand through my hair and chewing on my lower lip like a fucking teenager.

"Dig? What is it?" she asked.

"Hmm?"

One last touch.

My hand reached out, and my knuckles stroked her cheek. "Nothing, baby."

Her eyes softened.

I pulled my hand back and plucked my keys from my pocket. "Lock up, okay?"

"Yeah, okay," she said quietly.

She closed the door behind me and left me standing outside, alone in the darkness. The door's lock bolted into place, and I turned and headed for my chopper. Out of the corner of my eye, I noticed Boner waving at her. She must have been standing at the window, holding back that thick curtain.

"Let's go," I muttered.

"Yeah, yeah." Boner settled on his saddle.

I got on my bike and lit her up. I forced myself not to look back, and instead, my eyes snagged on a vintage Chevy Nova in the driveway next door. I took in the car's familiar curves and breathed again.

We sped off, our engines exploding in the silence of the night.

FOUR

"SHE'S THAT CUNT'S LITTLE SISTER, AIN'T SHE?" Vig's grip sank deeper into Grace.

He wrenched her closer into his thick body like an ape clutching its prey. Grace gasped, her arms straining against his bulk.

"She ain't house pussy," I said, my voice low, tight. "Now, let her go."

"Why should I? She's here, ain't she? Why do you give a shit?"

Damn it, what the fuck was she doing here?

The party was jamming at the clubhouse, more crowded and crazier than I had seen in years. We had finally reached an agreement with the Demon Seeds and successfully coordinated and completed that run through Wyoming. We'd invited them to stick around for the weekend to party before they headed back home to Montana. With the Seeds bullshit finally resolved—at least for now—we all had extra change in our pockets and hope for plenty more in the coming months.

Tonight, there was lots of food, booze, weed, and girls to go around and then some. Our clubhouse was an old go-kart factory building, long since renovated, with a one-mile asphalt track, sitting on three acres of property on the outskirts of town. We never had to worry about causing a disturbance to our neighbors because we had no neighbors. We shot our guns, played our music loud, revved our bikes hard, and raced around our track.

Tonight, things had gotten raucous fast. It felt good to cut loose and not have all this shit hanging over my head for a change, and I had taken full advantage. I had just buttoned up my jeans after an enthusiastic blow job from one of the many eager young things here tonight when Boner shouted out for me. My head had snapped up, my senses recognizing that edgy tone in his voice. My sweet, easy high had gotten zapped real quick.

Wreck, his lips smashing together, had pulled me through the noisy crowd. "Sister's here," he said.

Fuck.

My insides had snapped like overloaded circuits at the sight of her struggling in Vig's big hands, his nostrils flaring like a beast in heat. *Not her, not fucking ever.* She'd raised a bottle over his head, but I'd grabbed it in time. Grace had jerked her head to the side, and her burning wild eyes had found mine, ripping my breath from me. She'd winced and gasped as he twisted her in his arms again and again. My muscles had strained against my skin.

Did Miss Pink-and-Yellow Daisies come here to party with her girlfriends after I'd told her to stay away? Idiotic bitches.

I took in a deep breath and squelched the pounding war drums in my head and the delicious visions of skinning Vig alive, shooting him in the kneecaps, biting off his fingers. I handed the tequila bottle to Boner. "Let her go, Vig," I spit out through gritted teeth.

Vig's laugh boomed through the crowd. He was enjoying this. Oh, he was determined to fuck with her, fuck with me. I could see it in that diabolical glimmer in his eyes, echoing that unforgettable ugly voice grunting from my past—

"Fuck me. That was good shit."

Vig licked her neck. My pulse slammed into hyperdrive.

"Hey, excuse me, but I'm Dig's woman!" Grace blared out. "We got into a major blowout last week, and I took off so, of course, he's been banging everything in sight! He does it to get back at me, like all the other times we've broken up. He's a man-whore, and I'm a mouthy bitch, but I'm back now, and I'd like to fuck my man tonight, show him what he's been missing, if that's all right with you?"

Holy mother of fuck. A speech worthy of an old lady.

I stared at her, every word out of that innocent mouth sparking a nerve ending. A flash of adrenaline blazed through me, yet I willed myself to still.

Vig froze, not making a sound. Laughter and snickers rose around us. He cursed under his breath and dug his filthy fucking hands into her once more. She flinched. Turning her head, her shining eyes found mine.

Aut viam inveviam aut faciam, baby. Here was my Latin mantra come to life. Grace was finding her way by making one.

My hands tightened into fists, my thick pistol ring digging into my finger bone, and I pulled in a deep breath.

Oh, Dig Quillen, this is your smoking lucky day.

This girl had just roared in the jungle, and it resounded in my ears. She'd made a call. She'd made a choice.

And now, there was no longer any choice for me to make.

My eyes slid back to Vig. "You heard her, man." My voice was loud, firm. "Get your hands off my property, and there won't be any trouble."

Her eyes went round.

That's right, babe. Excellent play, and I'm making it official.

"You wait one more second, and there's gonna be a shitstorm, motherfucker," said Wreck.

Under the glare of his president, Cowboy, Vig—the fucker supreme—finally let Grace go, shoving her into my arms.

Amen.

My eyes slid closed for a split second under the fantastic pressure of her body against mine. She planted kisses on my chest, the side of my face, my lips, her fingers digging into my back. My pulse hammered in my throat and my arm slid around her back and pressed her closer.

"I'm sorry, baby," she said. "It's all my fault."

Sister threw her arms around my neck and hopped up into my embrace, legs around my waist. My arms hooked her tight, and my one hand dug into her perfect little ass under her jean skirt.

Oh, yeah, lucky fucking day.

And she didn't stop there.

"You know you're the only one for me, the only one I need," she said just loud enough for everyone around us to hear, like a humbled girl begging for mercy. "I'm sorry Dig, I'll never leave you like that again. I was looking for you just now, and I bumped into him by mistake, and he got pissed. I came back for *you*, babe. I missed you. God, I missed you and your mouth. And that tongue. I can't live without that tongue on me. You know what else I missed, don't you? I need you, and I can't wait to show you how much."

Jesus H. Christ. My dick stood at attention.

"Oh, man." Boner let out a groan from somewhere behind me.

Cowboy and Vig took off. The crowd around us finally thinned out. I set her down and let her have it for showing up. The panic and the tears began. Her sister had been sentenced this afternoon, and reality and shock had finally set in. Grace had come here pissed at me, at all of us, for putting Ruby away. That and the knowledge that, for the first time, she would truly be on her own.

Something in my chest squeezed hard.

I congratulated her on her little role-play performance.

"It's a damn good idea. It'll make you totally hands-off—for a while at least."

She was speechless, frozen to the spot. She blinked. "Excuse me?"

I laid it out for her. She was now mine for the weekend, and she needed to act the part. She rocked back on her boots. I needed to nip any tears, whiny pleading, or protests in the bud. Fast.

I grabbed the sides of her face and kissed her hard. That sweet mouth immediately gave way to me. I drove my tongue inside her and staked my claim. I sucked away the traces of tequila in that mouth along with all the questions, doubts, hazy maybes, and blurred lines that had arisen between us over the past months.

That mouth now belonged to me, and so did the rest of her.

Well, at least for this weekend.

"Would it be that difficult, Peanut?" I said against her lips.

Her gaze darted to my mouth.

Yeah, that's right. You're in. And so the fuck am I.

"I didn't think so. Play along, baby. You've been around us long enough to know the drill."

Her eyes bulged. She mouthed off in a panic.

"Relax!" I grabbed her, pulling her in close again. I licked around her small ear and then slid my tongue down the side of her damp neck. She tasted of salt, that insane perfume of hers, and a mystical brew of pure fear and arousal. A small cry escaped her lips. *Oh, yeah, just as beautiful as I knew it would sound.* My hand cupped a firm round breast. Her breath caught, she froze.

"Can't you pretend you want to fuck me, Peanut? That you can't get enough of me? Can't you pretend you're hungry for me, baby?" I tripped on this glorious new high.

"I'll try."

My spine stiffened. That only spelled disaster. "No, Sister. You fucking do it. We put on a believable show, even make my brothers believe it. You got that? There'll be no room for anyone to make a move on you as revenge against Ruby or the club's decision for her to take the fall."

She settled down. I lightened the mood with a couple of flirty comments, and she blushed.

"You ready?" I asked.

"Sure."

I smacked that ass.

Oh, fuck yeah.

"Hey!" Her eyes glittered.

"I need enthusiasm, babe."

Her jaw set. She moved in closer and slid her hands over my ass, pulling my body into hers. Her tongue stroked my bottom lip and slid into my mouth where it danced with my tongue. A groan built in my throat as I sank my fingers in her hair. She slowly sucked on my lower lip, nipping it with her teeth.

I willed myself to remain steady, like a TV reporter trying stay on his feet in hurricane force winds.

"I can work with that," I said against her mouth.

She tried to sass me, brush it off, but I jerked her into reality with a few choice words. With her silent nod and steely gaze, she agreed to play the role of my personal Pussy Candy for the weekend. I took her hand in mine, and we stalked toward the bar to get drinks. She needed one as much as I did.

My thumb rubbed over her fingers. This was the harsh big boy leagues, and Grace had now descended into our stinky pit to get dirty with the rest of us.

"Two shots of tequila."

"Comin' up," said Butler. He did a double take at the sight of Grace, and a grin split his face. "Hey, what are you doing here, Little Sister?"

I let go of her hand and slung my arm around her neck, brushing the side of her face with my lips. "Just pour the fucking drinks," I ordered.

"Yeah," Butler muttered, grabbing a bottle.

The party was going strong. It was the witching hour—that point deep in the night when no traces of threats or apprehensions remained. Everyone was riding the high, galloping blindly, and guzzling more. No thinking. Just rolling. The music drove its relentless harsh beats through every one of us, releasing our brain cells from duty. The smell of burning wood and weed filled the air. All these bodies moving, humping, fighting, laughing—all of it generated tremendous heat despite the fact that it was an unusually cool night. The smut playground by the shed was still attracting a throng of participants and onlookers. A handful of idiots were racing their bikes on the small track we had on the property. Screeching rubber, harsh smoke, and shouts rose in the distance.

Grace slid her arm around my waist and dug her fingers into a back pocket of my jeans. She pressed into my side, her hand squeezing my ass.

This could get dirty.

Sister and I made the rounds, making sure a wide cross-section of Seeds and Jacks saw us and got the message.

Nothing like a visual.

She kept up with me, move for move. She didn't flinch or glare at me—even when she was sitting on my lap with my hand under her skirt, stroking up her bare thigh, until my fingers finally landed between her legs. All the while, I was discussing a winter bike run to Florida with a couple of Demon Seeds. By that point she had melted, her flesh quivering at my touch over the damp fabric of her panty. Her little breaths were coming in fast against my neck, her head slumped on my shoulder. It was a heady mix of her obedience, submission, and raw need. I wanted to get in there bad. It was all I could think about, but I had to get business done first.

My gut was stretched tight. My dick pounded in my jeans. Sweat trickled down my back. Touching her, palming her, kissing her hard all night with her tongue daring mine to go further each time, her little hands roaming my body for hours—I loved it. My blood had backed up in my veins, threatening my sanity. She was different, way different, from all the other women here tonight. And I liked it. Most of them weren't happy about me and Sister, and they were making it obvious. It didn't seem to bother her much. It definitely didn't bother me.

Shit, I hadn't felt this kind of need in...I couldn't even remember when. Immediate gratification had been my way of life for years now. I never really gave a lot of thought to desire or craving. Lust was lust, wasn't it?

This, however, was some kind of slow-burn crazy drama that had not only taken over my cock and my entire body, but my mind. I not only wanted to end this precious torture spectacularly, but I also actually wanted to prolong it at the same fucking time.

Boner handed us both fresh beers. I let the cold brew wash down my throat and chill my burning insides. Grace, her face flushed, chugged on hers. Yeah, the Peanut had it bad, too.

This was only the fucking first night. How would she hold up over the rest of the weekend? I stuck my wet icy beer bottle between her smooth thighs. She flinched and let out a gasp, her fingers squeezing my shoulders, her O-shaped lips relaxing into a grin.

Only two more days, and then I would cut her loose.

Keep telling yourself that, Quillen.

"I've never done this before," she whispered.

"What, baby? Done what?" I zipped down my jeans.

Fuck. Finally.

Grace had just come against my fingers, her body shaking in my arms. Her moans had nearly sent me shooting my wad. Now, I was finally going to slam into her.

That's it, push down the jeans.

Now.

"Sex. I've never had sex before."

I froze, my hand on my incredibly stiff, throbbing boy. "Never?"

My heart stopped in that painful half second, waiting for her answer.

"Never."

I squeezed my eyes shut, and my brain rattled in my skull. *Motherfuck.* I gnashed my teeth as I tucked my rock-hard dick back into my jeans.

On the one hand, I was thrilled that no else had gotten in there before me—like Blond Fuckwad, for one. On the other...

Ah, hell, I couldn't pop her cherry out here on the hood of my car in the yard.

Ruby's stony eyes glared at me from that night at Pete's when she'd caught me trolling her sister. Grace had obviously had opportunities to have sex, but she had made a choice not to.

Ah, shit. Whatever. My pulse dragged to a thudding strum.

"But I want to. I want to with you," she said, her eyes large, her fingers clutching my shirt.

Holy hell, so do I.

But I couldn't just fuck her out here like I ordinarily would with any of the rest of them, like I had done over and over. She wasn't another body offering me a quick high, a distraction, an opportunity to play any way I wanted to get off. Grace was beyond the daily special.

I blinked in the dark and focused my eyes on her bare chest heaving for air. That cute pink bra of hers was tangled around her waist.

Tangled.

She'd gotten tangled with me, and she was a fucking virgin. She had charged over here tonight and jumped headfirst into the pit.

I planted my palms on the hood of my Camaro.

Me popping her cherry?

This joyride was only supposed to last the weekend. I was protecting her. That was what all this was about, not taking advantage of her—blue balls be damned. Thank fuck I'd gotten sucked off earlier in the evening. Otherwise, I'd be really fucking hurting about now. My gaze fell on her parted lips and then down to her squirming thighs. Waves of heat pulsed through me again. I couldn't cut her loose now though. Until the weekend was up, Peanut and I could play. No penetration required.

I exhaled.

This could be fun—dazzling the virgin with orgasms until her beautiful eyes popped out of her head, sucking on her like my very own made-to-order lollipop. She'd be begging me to stop by Sunday morning, and I could teach her a thing or two or five about dazzling me. It would be an educational weekend for the Peanut. A seminar of higher learning. A public service. By Monday, I'd be putting an all new and improved Grace out there on the streets of life, on the streets of Meager.

My jaw tightened. *For someone else to enjoy.*

Her hips squirmed. Shit, this girl had already twisted me in two.

Shut the fuck up already and dip in.

I flipped up her skirt and finally tore off those damp pink panties.

Nothing like the heady perfume of need and lust. Magic fucking potion.

"Dig, what are you doing?"

I grinned at her pussy. I grinned at her.

Dirty it is, baby.

She got nice and loud just like I'd hoped she would. I liked this first-time thing. I tugged on her nipples for extra effect.

"Oh my God...Dig!"

I let out a low laugh. "Babe, I think we need to do that again."

"What?"

I blew air over her soaked pussy and gently hooked my fingers inside her. Her back arched up, and she writhed on the hood of my car.

Fuck me. There was something to be said for taking your time with the details.

We ended the evening with a shower in my room. Her delicate small hand slid past my snake tattoo, which wrapped around my hips, and my breath stalled at the sight. Her fingers crept over my aching dick and gently stroked it. *Paradise on earth.* I leaned against her and put my hand over hers, showing her how to work my cock hard until I blew in her hand. I turned to look at her, the cool water beating down on us. Her eyes were bright, her lips parted.

I kissed her hard and slid my hands over her sleek ass. *Kill me now.* I had to make her come again, had to hear those moans. I soaped up her beautiful body and slid my fingers in that wet silk between her legs. Her head sank back against the tile, her eyes never leaving mine. I held onto her shuddering body, as she came on my fingers, those illicit soft cries escaping her mouth.

We dried off and hit my bed. I wrapped my arms around her, pulling her into me. We fit.

What the fuck was I doing? I didn't know exactly.

I had never been the affectionate type. I only knew I wanted to hold her, feel her against me. She fell asleep right away, her even breathing humming in my ear, her breath warm and humid on my chest. My lips brushed across her nose and forehead, and then I stared at the ceiling and concentrated on the scent of my shampoo on her hair. I inhaled it as if I were standing on a bluff back in Colorado, filling my lungs with that crisp fresh mountain air. I drifted asleep on a puff of that sweet air.

Grace's mouth on my cock woke me up like a five-alarm fire bell.

"Show me how, Dig."

My eyes unglued fast. My heart raced as I showed her how. Her wet lips stretching around my dick, that moist heat taking me in, was like a slow death to everything I thought I knew and a sweet surge of a previously unknown glory all at once.

I somehow found my power of speech again. "That's good, babe, so good. You can do it harder. Just watch your teeth."

She peeked up at me as she sucked deep, her cheeks pulling in, her hand rubbing up and along the base. *Shit, was that a smile?* My mind blanked as my hips flexed toward her mouth, never wanting this sweet agony to end, counting my blessings. My entire body tensed, and I blew, groaning loudly. She stayed on me, swallowing it all. I dug my fingers in her hair, pulled her up my body, and I kissed my hot little virgin.

"Good morning," she said, burying her face in my neck.

"You bet your sweet ass." That reminded me—time to explore in the daylight.

I flipped her over on her stomach and raised her onto her knees. My hands stroked lightly as I nibbled at the smooth skin of her thighs, her ass, eliciting moans and *oh*s and the constant patter of my name tumbling from her mouth.

Good fucking morning to me.

Once we resurfaced, we were in time to join everyone for lunch in the courtyard. I took her hand in mine, and we walked out together, our sunglasses over our eyes.

"How old are you anyhow?" I asked.

She let out a laugh. "I'll be twenty-one next month. Too old for you?"

I squeezed her hand. "Smart-ass."

"And you?"

"Twenty-seven."

"Oh my gosh, almost thirty? Grandpa material! What would my daddy say?"

"Yeah, what would your daddy say if he knew you didn't have your panties on at the One-Eyed Jacks' clubhouse?"

She scoffed. "We don't have to worry about that now, do we?"

I remembered how her father had come by the clubhouse and thanked us all for saving Ruby at that high school keg party. It was a sincere gesture, and the man had been truly grateful. It hadn't gone unappreciated. How had a man like that abandoned his family? Would he be grateful if he knew that Ruby was serving time for the club? That his daughter was my personal plaything for the weekend? That I had taken away her panties as a deposit for services rendered? That I had thoroughly defiled her?

Well, not completely, but just about. We still had the whole weekend ahead of us.

Everyone turned and stared, grins hanging on their faces.

"I'd really feel better about this if I had my panties on," she murmured.

"Deal's a deal, Sister."

"If I bend over to pick something up and your brothers or the Seeds see and do or say something, I think you're the one who's not going to be too happy about it, big guy."

I pulled her closer into my side. "No bending over, no leaning, no reaching up. And you sit in my lap the whole time so you don't get any splinters on that gorgeous ass or catch a chill. I'll even feed you myself. How's that?"

She smirked. "Oh, so caring. Anything else, your majesty?"

I hooked my arm around her neck and pulled her close, kissing the side of her face. "Not just yet, but I'll think of something."

She pushed against my chest. "I think I'm going to go help out in the kitchen."

"Oh"—I tugged her back in—"one more thing?"

"Now what?"

"Watch out for the old ladies. They might be all smiles with you at first, but don't trust 'em—at least not yet. And stay completely away from the other women. Remember, to them you're the new bitch on the block."

"Right. I'll keep that in mind." She strode off, her bare legs in those heavy brown cowboy boots, her hips swaying slightly in her wrinkled skirt.

I lit a cigarette.

Within minutes, she came back out, holding a tray of sodas. She was yakking with Dee, Judge's old lady, as the two of them headed for the tables. The girl could make friends with anybody.

"How's the little romantic reunion going?" a raspy voice snarled behind me.

I rubbed my chest as I exhaled a thick stream of smoke and grinned at Vig. "Fucking amazing."

"Ain't that sweet?"

FIVE

COME MONDAY MORNING, I was exhausted.

It wasn't the late nights and hard partying. It was Grace.

Since I'd decided that fucking her was not going to happen, we had taken our time, and we had done a hell of a lot of other things that I hadn't really ever taken so much time with. Before, all these little bits had been quick snacks or obligatory fixes on the way to the main event. But with no main event on the horizon, we'd spent a lot of time exploring each other's bodies with our mouths, our tongues, our fingers. I'd really enjoyed every nerve-jolting, blood-rushing, skin-blistering moment. I'd begun to enjoy the biting sensation that I was going to explode out of control, and when I had exploded, it had been fucking good.

Grace had become an expert at reading me and taken care of me every time, never hesitating, sometimes asking for direction. We'd sixty-nined it, played with friction in a lot of interesting positions—with and without objects I'd slid over her, inside her—and I'd found her special quiver-spot up in that beautiful pussy. She'd opened her legs high and wide for me on command, gotten on all fours for me, raised up that fantastic ass, trusting me with previously unmarked territory. She'd trembled in my arms, her range of moans and cries becoming my favorite soundtrack of all time.

"Can we take a break?" she'd sighed from the pillow.

I'd swatted her luscious ass and then bit it hard. She'd let out a shriek.

"Famous last words," I'd said in a melodramatic menacing tone against her skin.

She'd laughed, and I had gone back to licking her and nudging my fingertip inside her rear, my other hand stroking her clit to distract her. She'd been helpless in my hands.

That was beautiful.

She'd come hard—yet again.

Fuck, I'm addicted.

"Dig!"

The way she'd gasped my name filled me with pride and a surge of joy as she curled her body into mine and plastered my chest with kisses. We'd talked in hushed tones about what we liked most and why. She'd experimented on me, on herself, her eyes searching mine for approval. I had given Grace plenty of fucking direction and plenty of approval, telling her in dirty detail how it all turned me on. That had turned her on even more. She'd shown me how much, and I'd shown her right back. The girl had an appetite.

Yes, I loved knowing that I had woken her up to it; that she'd found it with me, her body coming alive with mine. Did that make me a selfish, self-centered bastard? Maybe. But I was a man hot for the woman in his bed, and by Sunday morning she had stopped blushing altogether.

Her hands clutched mine as they kneaded her breasts. "You always keep your rings on?" she'd said, her voice low, throaty.

"Always. You like 'em?"

Her head had fallen back against my shoulder. "I like everything about you, Dig."

That blazing heat had flared inside my chest again, and I'd slid a hand between her legs. She'd jammed her face into the pillow. I'd stopped what I was doing and smacked her ass hard, my own hand stinging. She'd turned her face to me and blinked, her lower lip jutting out.

"You think we're the only ones getting busy under this roof?" I'd asked. "Can't you hear all the groaning and the shouting? You want me to take you out to the main room right now and show you? I promise you, none of 'em would even notice we were naked."

Her eyes had widened, and she'd wiped the hair from her sweaty face.

I'd rubbed her ass where I'd hit her. "You wanna stop?"

"No," she'd whispered.

"You gotta give it to me loud, baby. I need to hear it." I'd rolled her over onto the mattress and raised myself up, my hands planted on the bed, my dick pressing into her clit, stroking it back and forth. "You loud makes me hard. You want me hard for you, don't you?"

Her lips had parted, and she had taken in a deep breath. She'd angled her hips against mine, and a moan had heaved from her.

She'd kept her eyes on me and expressed herself freely, easily, loudly.

"Fuck yeah," I'd muttered.

My hips rocked against hers until she had blown, and I'd shot my cum all over her stomach. *Fuck, what a sight.* Marking, claiming in the jungle.

I'd never wanted to watch a woman come before or look her in the eye while fucking her. Never even occurred to me. With Grace, I not only wanted to watch her. I wanted to learn how every kiss, touch, or angle I offered her affected her pleasure. Even when she had me in her mouth, I was compelled to watch. I wanted to know.

I needed to know.

We'd laughed a hell of a lot together on that bed, too. And she wouldn't take five hours in the bathroom, and she wouldn't mind when I opened the door without knocking and took a leak while she washed up or brushed her teeth. Some women freaked about that shit. Not Grace. She would just keep yakking, picking up a previous conversation. She'd even pulled me into the shower on one occasion.

The fatigue had started wearing on me the more thought I gave to the fact that Monday was fast approaching, and I was going to have to take her home and leave her there and all *this* behind. I would continue watching over her just as I had promised Ruby I would, but this little sex adventure—*or non-sex adventure, I guess*—had to be done with. I'd really thought if I had her all to myself for an entire weekend, I'd get over my fascination with Little Miss Fresh. I had done everything I could, short of putting my cock inside her, to do that, to take my fill. But it hadn't worked. My fascination had only grown, intensified, harshened.

But I needed to focus on business, and she needed to focus on school, her job, her house, her friends. She had the real world. I was on the fringe of all that, and we both knew it.

She had experienced a slice of club life when her sister brought it into their house. She knew what we were about, and it wasn't all good. It wasn't good for a girl like Grace. Now that connection to us, to me, was about to be broken.

She shoved the key in that old bolt on the front door of her house and turned the knob. The door creaked open, and a whirlpool went off in my chest, spinning there.

The Seeds had left. Vig's hostile stares and the Ruby bullshit were all finally resolved. The Jacks were headed to the Hippie Hole for a daylong swim and a picnic to relax after the crazy weekend. I didn't mention it to Grace because her gig was done, and that was for the best.

The masquerade ball was over. Everyone eventually went home to take off their costumes and then closed the door behind them. The end.

I could breathe easy now, right?

But I had barely been breathing the whole seven-minute ride over to her house from the club. Her arms squeezing around my jacket, her legs brushing mine—Jesus, it'd felt right, solid.

She had gotten off my bike and ambled to her front door.

Shit.

I'd followed her. *What a fucking gentleman.*

She had taken out her key.

The one thing I wanted to cling to at this very moment, which suddenly seemed more important to me than even my own bike, was about to shove through a portal of no return, seal it closed behind her, barring me forever. Grace took that one step up, past the front door, into her house, and an ache twinged in my chest.

My last chance at this fix to my new, all-consuming addiction was fizzling before me.

"Get your bikini. We're going to the Hippie Hole for a swim."

Just one more day. Just one.

Now that the pressure was off, now that it was just us and my brothers and we no longer had anything to prove to anybody, would things between us be different? Would they be better?

She stilled, turned her head, and smiled at me, those beautiful hazel eyes brightening for a moment. "Oh, okay." Her breezy voice hung in the air.

Christ.

I stepped inside her house behind her and let go of the breath I hadn't realized I was holding on to. We moved past the kitchen to get to her room.

I froze. "Peanut, what the fuck?"

A tornado had blown through the kitchen. I stepped in the center of the room, my feet crunching over thick shards of broken glass and plastic on the frayed linoleum. What was once a clock dangled from the wall, mangled and destroyed. Cabinet doors had been flung open and were now gaping wide. Most of the shelves were empty. Icy needles pricked my spine. Had someone broken in over the weekend—that someone being Vig?

"Oh." She shrugged and let out a sigh. "I had a spaz before I came looking for you at the club on Friday night."

I stared at her. Her lips were pursed, her fingers tugging at the hem of her blouse, as her eyes darted over the mess she had created. Yeah, there had been thieves here. Rage and despair were the thieves, and they had had their way in this house, a house now broken into and broken. A house where she could break. Her instinct had had her fighting back, and she'd refused to give in. Damned if I was going to let those thieves have their way with her, change her, take control of her—like they'd had with me.

No fucking way.

I'd gotten out, and so could she. I knew I couldn't leave her here, all alone. I was as sure of that as breathing. I wanted to make it better for her.

Had to.

Here she was, hurting inside, but a fucking realist through and through. She'd wallowed, she'd raged, she'd spoken her piece, and she'd moved on. Standing there, across this field littered with empty shells and casings, she kicked the debris underfoot with that little shrug she gave me. She was me. My pulse hammered in my head and screeched to a grinding stop.

If I hadn't invited her to the Hole, if I hadn't walked in here right now—

But I had.

I had been kidding myself all weekend by not fucking her. Her cherry had been a convenient loophole, a way to duck out. I'd been convinced I was being a responsible stand-up guy, not marking her, not taking from her for her own good. But she and I were linked. It wasn't DNA, but a chain of pain and a molten core of resilience. I recognized the smell. Here we were, standing on her insides, and it reflected up at me like the hot glare of the summer sun on the surface of the lake.

I was done playing, sidestepping, pussyfooting.

Done.

"What?" She swallowed. "What is it?"

Her eyes were round and glassy. I only wanted to take her in my arms, protect her. Get lost in her sweet scent once more. The scent of certainty sprinkled with relief, hope.

"Come here," I said, my voice tight, low.

She closed the distance between us, crossing the kitchen, her eyes on me, her boots crunching over her debris. I took her in my arms and lifted her, and she easily hooked her legs around my waist, wrapping her arms around my neck. I gently kissed her, and a small moan escaped her lips, making my heart thunder in my chest.

My thumb rubbed across her lips. With that kiss, I brushed my boot over the line I had drawn in the sand between us and erased any trace of it. The taste of her mouth and the perfect press of her body into mine only confirmed what I had known deep down inside for a long time but had denied.

I was hers.

"This shit's over for you, baby. You're with me now. You got that?"

A slow smile lit up her face.

And she was mine.

We messed around in her room. She wasn't shy or hesitant with me anymore, and we were both pretty damn enthusiastic. I almost did her right there on that goddamn daisy quilt, and she wanted me to, but no, I had a better plan in mind. I intended on blowing her away for her first time—today, within hours.

Riding through the Black Hills to the Hippie Hole with Grace on the back of my bike was an unexpected pleasure. Both of us were riding on a new route on the same old road map. It was a road I had driven thousands of times, but now, I rode it with a degree of relaxation and self-possession I hadn't been conscious of before. Handling the smooth curves through the dense green and rocky woodland made me fucking smile at the rush filling my veins.

We ate up the road, the stony sloping hills stretching out before us, thick with tall evergreens flashing by, taking us in. My blood pumped through every cell. I felt alive—not tied up, not tied down. I did a mental check, and nope, no traces of buyer's remorse. It felt damn good—Grace scrunched up behind me, pressing into me, holding on to me. *How could being attached set you free?* It did for me right then, right there. It sang in my blood. I decided not to question it but to trust it.

Once the gravel road ended, we parked and dismounted. Grace was speechless, caught in a high, a goofy smile on her face after her first long ride on a quality bike. She curled her fingers into the belt loops of my jeans, and we hiked to where I knew our group would be. The steep trail started downhill but eventually turned flat. Two red-tailed hawks flew off the branches they had been perched on and soared in the sky above us. A white mountain goat appeared on the jagged rocks across from our path, curiously observing us, and then tracked away. We continued along Battle Creek until we got to the Hippie Hole, a rock wall with a waterfall dropping into a deep pool.

Everyone was a little surprised to see Grace. Boner gave her a kiss on the cheek and took the bag of food we'd picked up on our way here out of her hands. He grinned, jerking his chin at me. We swam, acted like idiots, ate, got high, and fell asleep on our blankets in the shade. Now, it was time for my plan.

"Grace is something less flashy, more…sincere, like handpicked flowers."

I took Ruby's advice. I didn't want to have sex with Grace for the first time back in my room at the club where so many others had come on that mattress. My own hole in the wall in town was a mess, and I didn't want her first time to be in her broken house that was full of other memories.

I wanted it to be somewhere new and sweet for her *and* for me, where we could take our time. *Since when had I become such a fucking romantic?* All I knew was I wanted to give her something unique, something that would make it worth her waiting, as if I were offering her some kind of long yearned for and very deserved prize. She was giving that part of herself to me, that part she had never given nor shared with anyone else, and it mattered to me. I was determined to make it good for her.

Over the weekend, our bodies had gotten into a kind of wild sync with each other. Her body was fucking calling to me right now as we lay in the late afternoon sun, trying to take a nap. I couldn't get any sleep if I tried. I was too worked up. Earlier, while swimming, she had let me suck on her tits, her legs hooked around my waist, her body rubbing against mine. Her laughter had drifted over the water. That detonating sensation of wanting her drove through me now, making me hard as hell.

I woke her up, packed up our blankets, and dragged her on another hike. We arrived at the spot I had scouted earlier where the trees hung like a green canopy, and there were a ton of wildflowers. The blue ones. *I liked the blue ones.*

"What's all this?" she asked.

I took off her bikini and then my cutoffs. I thought she was going to cry, but instead, she threw all that emotion into kissing me hard. I laid her on the blanket, and like some sort of jackass, I tore off the flowers from their stems and threw them over her naked body—every inch, bottom to top. So beautiful, like a fucking nature goddess. She was all laid out for me, my Black Hills nymph, twisting with need for me. All for me. A feast for a hungry man.

We kissed. A greedy wild kiss. I licked a trail down her body to her thighs, her legs falling open for me. I ate her pussy as if it were the very first time—great big licks, hard sucks—making her come for me, getting her ready and desperate for my cock. I held her gaze as I positioned myself and eased into her as gently as I could.

Holy shit. Fucking finally.

I inched in deeper. A frown passed over her face, her brows furrowed, and she clenched up. I couldn't move. I was going to explode.

"Open up for me, baby," I whispered against her skin.

I touched her in all the right places, and she got excited all over again, her body relaxing once more. I thrust slowly and finally buried myself inside her. We watched each other, moved together, clutched at each other, moaning, whispering. New sensations marked her face. I got her there again, and she came, crying out my name. Something new seared my insides and took over, rendering me speechless.

Grace murmured words and phrases I could barely understand through her erratic breathing. But I knew what they meant.

I knew.

SIX

"WHY DO WE ALWAYS HAVE TO SIT IN THE BACK?" Creeper shoved his chair to the side of the table, his greasy fork and knife clattering on his ketchup-smeared plate.

"I like to see what's going on, who's coming in and out at all times." I scanned the restaurant filled with families and couples and waitresses bustling between their tables, carrying huge trays of burgers, steaks, and potatoes.

Not having eaten earlier, we'd stopped for a big lunch in Sidney, Montana, before crossing the border into North Dakota.

He stretched his legs. "What the fuck are you so paranoid about?"

"I'm not paranoid. I like to be aware and prepared. Maybe, one day, you'll learn that lesson."

Creeper snorted. "I just want to get there already, man."

For some of these assholes, it was the partying that drove them, not their bikes. But being a member of a motorcycle club *was* about your bike—riding it, taking care of that metallic extension of your soul, and being one with whatever road you chose. Not just getting your ass to the next party to get drunk and nail some tail. Partying was a good thing, but it wasn't what was at the core of the life for me or for those closest to me.

Not Creeper though.

I let out a breath and shook my head. "You're an idiot." I stuck a toothpick between my teeth.

"Fuck you. Let's get outta here already."

Fall and winter had quickly come and finally gone, leaving trails of wetness and mud in their wake. It was terrific to be back on the road, my chopper cutting through the wind. It was just a real pity that my first spring run had to be with this asshole. I didn't know what Judge ever saw in him, recruiting his ass. Creeper was a good worker bee when called upon, but otherwise he was a whiny bitch in my book. I couldn't wait to drop him off at our North Dakota chapter on my way home from a spot of business in Montana.

"I'm gonna hit the john," he muttered.

"Hey, your turn to pay, asshole." I tapped on the check.

He grimaced as he took out his wallet. He flicked a twenty on the table, and I signaled the waitress.

She grabbed the money along with the check. "Be back in a minute, hon." She took off.

I heard an unusual tinkly laugh as I stretched my back in my chair. Turning to my left, I saw him.

Ray Hastings, Grace's father.

I had seen them come in earlier, but he'd been wearing sunglasses and a baseball cap, and the two of them had settled quietly in a corner. His arm was thrown around a woman, who was maybe a few years older than Ruby. She fed him a piece of steak as she whispered in his ear. They both laughed, and she dabbed at the side of his face with a napkin.

My entire body heated like a furnace that had suddenly been switched on to full power.

Years ago, when he had shown up at the clubhouse, thanking me and the boys for saving Ruby from those football players, it had impressed me. Grace had shown me a photo of him and her mom at her house. And now, here was Mr. Abandon My Family Without a Word, canoodling with some giggly young woman at a hole-in-the-wall restaurant in Sidney, Montana. Not too close, and certainly not too far away after all.

I pushed my chair back—loudly. He noticed. His eyes flicked over my colors, and an eyebrow jumped.

Hidey-ho, old man.

I couldn't resist confrontations.

I crossed over to their table. "Ray Hastings. Remember me?"

"Should I?" His forehead creased, his shoulders stiffened. "You're from the club in Meager?"

I smirked. "One-Eyed Jacks."

His eyes darted over my colors once more. "Dig, is it?"

"Yeah."

"I'm sorry, but...I can't recall..." His arm tightened over his girlfriend.

She sat up straighter and eyed me up and down as she swallowed her food.

I let out a dry laugh. "Do you remember your two daughters?"

He frowned and raised his chin. "I remember you now."

I nodded. "You living up here? Working?" My gaze lingered over the woman in his arm. Her lips parted. "Enjoyin' yourself?"

Why is it that I slip into bad English every time I talk to one of these upstanding-citizen motherfuckers?

"Do you need something? You're interrupting our dinner."

I planted my hands on their table and leaned over. "I'm just curious, is all. You been up here all this time?"

"How is that any of your business?"

"I say it is."

"Really?" He put down his fork. "How so?"

"Your daughters have been my business for quite some time." I turned to his girlfriend. "He's got two gorgeous daughters right around your age, sweetheart."

She bit her lip as she sank back into her seat. "Ray?" she mumbled.

I leveled my gaze on him. "I wasn't looking for you, man. I would never have looked for you anyhow. I'm just passing through, heading back home. Home to Meager. South Dakota? You know where that is? You get on Route 200 into North Dakota, and then you—"

"Are the girls okay?"

"Dandy. Ruby was working for me as a stripper for a good long time. Got herself into jail on a drug bust. Now, she's out and in rehab in Colorado. She's got a tiny little cocaine, speed, and maybe heroine issue."

The girlfriend gasped.

Ray's eyes flared, his jaw tightened. "Grace?"

"In my bed."

His eyes widened, his lips stiffening into a long white line. The silence between us thick, thrumming, wired.

I leaned in closer. "She's all mine now, old man. Mine to protect. Mine to take care of. Mine to keep happy. And I know how to keep my woman happy."

His free hand tightened into a fist on the table. "N-no, she…she…"

"Hmm…she finished college, hung on tooth and nail while she had a job and kept up your house. All on my watch. Real special. Pity you don't know that—what makes both your daughters so special. I don't think they even know. I figure you were the one who put that mental block in there for them. It's embedded in them like a slab of fucking concrete. I've been workin' on loosening it for a good long while now. Almost got it."

"I'll just bet you have," Ray replied, sliding his arm off the girlfriend.

She shot him a worried look.

I tapped on the table with my knuckles. "Grace is my woman now, Ray. She don't need you no more. You're a sorry-ass excuse for a father anyway. Other parents sacrifice for their families, die for 'em. You just fuckin' walked away."

Ray's multicolored eyes hardened. He had Grace's eyes. "You've said quite enough. I think you should go now."

"Oh, I'm going. I'm on my way home to her right now. She's waiting for me. I wanted you to know—here, now, while you're having your good life—if you ever do see her again, know that you had nothing to do with the beauty, that goodness that is Grace. That smile on her and that generous, wise soul of hers are all her own making, and now they belong to me." I rose up. "I'm not gonna tell her I saw you, 'cause if I tell her, she's gonna want to come find you herself, and I ain't gonna let that happen. You know why? You don't deserve that, and I'm positive Ruby would agree with me."

Ray's chest expanded, his face tightening.

"If it ever happens that you two run into each other by some chance, you're gonna be the one to grovel at her feet. You. I'm not gonna let one tear fall down my woman's face over you. No way in this hell or the next." I plucked the toothpick from my mouth and tossed it onto his steak. "You two have yourselves a good din-din now. Don't forget dessert, darlin'."

I winked at the bitch, who was now staring at me, open-mouthed. I strode out of the restaurant and headed for my bike.

I got home, and that night, I held Grace in our new bed in our new little house. Boxes and garbage bags full of our crap were piled everywhere—some half-emptied, some still full—but not in our bedroom. Grace had put all her energy into making it clean and ready for us. She'd surprised me when I got home with soft new sheets, big pillows, and a matching comforter as well as thick new towels in the john, all of it washed and ready for us to use.

Her eyes had sparkled when I first entered the room earlier, but I hadn't known what to say. Our very own little nest. I had taken her in my arms and held her without saying a word. Could she possibly know how important this one simple thing that she had done was? Maybe if I'd told her, but my brain couldn't form the words. I was one big whirring mess inside.

She slept with her head on my chest, the weight of her lax naked body pressed into mine. I couldn't sleep, which was nothing new, but here with my woman in my arms—in our own home, a home we would fill with our own way of life—something lightened inside me. My fingers traced patterns over her bare skin as I listened to her even deep breaths filling the quiet of the room. I knew there was so much more to lose now, but for the first time in a long, long time, there was so much for me to hold on to.

For years, I'd been daring Death to come for me, laughing in his face. It was a desolate dance of arrogance since I'd left Colorado behind. I was sure he would come for me sooner rather than later, but I really liked *this*—this quiet stillness right now. No sirens, no engines gunning, no shouting, not even a dog barking. Simply skin on skin, heat against heat, the soft fragrance of fabric softener laced with the odor of fresh paint and satisfied flesh. I inhaled it. I wanted this—us, our normal. For me this normal, mundane crap was totally sublime, my fucking sacred. I kissed the side of her face, and her head shifted over my chest, the minty scent of her shampoo drifting over me.

"I love you, Wildflower," I whispered in the dark against her damp forehead, my fingers brushing through silky pieces of her hair.

If anything could combat my deeply embedded hatred and dread of the come-what-may-and-it-will, I was very sure my love for her and our life together would be the thing. A tiny part of me hoped it would redeem me somehow in this life, and maybe even the next.

I let out a gust of air and stared at the ceiling while her heart beat against mine. "Always loved you, always will. That's a promise."

SEVEN

"Don't ask questions. Just do it, damn it."

Grace pressed her lips together. Her eyes narrowed as she pierced my torn skin with the threaded needle in her hand.

"That's it, hon," said Wreck. "Don't look at him. Ignore him. You focus and keep breathing. Now, nab the—right, good. You got it."

Grace stitched my skin together, sweat beading on her forehead. Her puffs of warm breath settled over my upper chest where she worked. Wreck stood close at her side, his eyes following her handiwork.

"You gotta learn this shit sometime," Wreck said. "You never know what trouble you'll get in, riding with this asshole."

"Ain't that the truth?" Butler handed me a fresh bottle of whiskey.

I glared at him through my blurry vision, gnashing my teeth. "Shut the fuck up."

"He's right, man," said Wreck. "That's why I'm getting her on a bike. She's got to be able to ride and take care of basic shit if something happens to you. Sister just starting your engine up for you like a good old lady ain't good enough. Not to mention knowing how to use a weapon."

I stared at Grace and Wreck, their faces tight in concentration over my wound. Two unlikely peas in a pod. The girl next door and the sage elder. Grace shot a quick glance at Wreck and then at me. She went back to her work on my chest, her needle tugging on my flesh, her lips pressed together.

"Fine. Teach her to ride. I'll take her shooting."

Butler grinned, shaking his blond hair off his face.

He had patched in the same night I'd made Grace my old lady several months after being together. Another excuse for a party. Each one of us had taken turns thrashing the leather—riding our bikes over Butler's colors, peeing on them, even. We'd done anything to make the leather look worn and lived in, experienced— not that eager smooth shine of a newbie. Afterward, I'd taken my old lady—yeah, I liked the way that sounded—on a run to

Spearfish, all on our own, for a couple of days of hiking, camping, and fucking in the great outdoors.

Wreck continued to coach Grace on stitching me up, and an odd sense of contentment eased my aching body, along with the warmth from the cheap whiskey sliding down my throat. What he'd said to me the day I made her officially mine drifted through me once again.

"You sure about this?" Wreck asked me.

I folded a new leather jacket and a denim vest with the club property patch on it. I would be giving them to Grace in a few hours.

"Are you shitting me, man?"

"She's a good kid. She's young. That's all."

"Not that young," I replied.

"Young enough."

I laughed. "You think I'm robbing the cradle or something?"

Wreck frowned. "Don't be an idiot. What I'm saying is, do you think she's ready to be your old lady? Be a part of this club? Maybe this is just hormones and enthusiasm for both of you, huh? This life ain't for everybody."

I pushed the jacket down into the bag. "What's this now? I thought you liked her, man."

"No, Dig. I love her like she's my own little sister. That's why I'm asking you this. Hear me out. Are you sure of her? Are you sure of your own self with her? It's one thing to have a regular woman in your bed. It's another to make this kind of commitment because that's what this is. Heartbreak and disappointment will rip you, is all I'm saying. And it will especially rip a girl like her. The way she looks at you...you're her world, brother. At the end of the day, that's a responsibility you have to bear."

"I've never been more sure of anything. It's the same feeling I had when I prospected under you here. That sure."

"All right then." Wreck grinned, dragging a hand through his beard. "Go claim your woman."

Now my old lady was sewing a gash a couple of inches long on my upper chest that I had gotten in a standoff at a bike rally up north.

Wreck scowled at the wound. "Why didn't you have this taken care of earlier? It's deep."

"Didn't think it was that bad. Wanted to get home." I stared at Grace's concentrating face.

"You rode for five hours like that?" Butler asked. "Jesus!"

Grace smashed her lips together again until they were pale under the strain.

"Don't even say it," I said to her, my voice low.

Her eyes didn't leave my wound. "Oh, I won't—not now at least." She hissed in air.

There had been four of us—me, Jump, Clip, and Judge—and ten of them. The surprise on their faces that there had been men who simply refused to live their lives in fear had cracked me up. The four of us had stood together in a way that we covered each other's backs, and we'd invited them to come and get it. They had gotten their courage from their beer and each other and the false belief that there was strength in numbers. There wasn't. In a true brotherhood, strength came from unity. And that, we had.

"You got it, hon." Wreck held scissors in his hands and snipped the thread off. "Here. Give it to me now."

Grace let out a heavy exhale as she took the whiskey bottle from me and took a long glug.

She popped the bottle back from her lips, winced with her final swallow, and sank a hand into my hair, lowering her face to mine. Our lips touched. Shit, I'd missed her. Her tongue stroked mine, and the woodsy warmth of her whiskey surged in my mouth. I savored her taste, but she pulled away suddenly, taking in a shaky breath.

"Baby, the thing is, I don't look for trouble. I don't need to. It always finds me. Comes with the territory," I whispered.

My old lady snaked her arms around my middle. I inhaled the orange blossom scent rising from her neck.

I was home.

Wreck finished with me, and she led me into the back hallway and opened the door to my room. Grace had gotten my room organized and cleaned up with a fresh coat of white paint on the walls, a framed photo of us on my Harley, and extra pairs of our boots all in a row against one wall. She'd even sanded down and varnished the old dresser. Next to it was a new fucking laundry basket that she'd finally trained me to use—when I was in the mood, of course.

"Lie down," she said.

I lay down on the blue-striped comforter and sighed. Shit, my back was unhappy with me. Grace pulled off my boots and socks. I swallowed some more whiskey from the bottle.

"Fuck, it's good to be home."

Grace unbuckled my belt and tugged down my jeans. My cock bobbed at her, and she smirked as she continued pulling the jeans off my legs.

"You ever gonna get used to me going commando?"

"You always go commando. I like it. A lot." She threw the jeans in the basket and fell into the bed at my side.

My fingers tangled with hers. "Sucks when boxers ride up my ass while riding. Hate that."

"Now you know how I feel, wearing those stupid thongs, baby."

I chuckled. "Ah, but I like those."

She only grinned at me, her lips brushing the side of my face. "Dig, what happened?" she whispered, her fingers stroking my scalp.

"Bullshit happened. On the way home from the rally, we stopped at a truck stop. Boy toys were checking out our bikes. One touched Jump's chopper, didn't apologize for his transgression, and the rest was history. Messed up the wound from the rally throw down some more." I squeezed her hand. "Much better now."

Grace let out a huff, but she didn't push it. She knew better than to ask details about business and especially business at a brothers-only run.

"Glad you're home." She snuggled into my side.

"Me, too." My eyelids drooped.

"Baby?"

"Sorry, hon. I'm wiped."

"It's okay. Get some sleep. You never get enough sleep." She turned on her side, and her hand smoothed over my chest in slow circles.

Sleep would be nice. In fact, I didn't think I had gotten a good night's sleep in years unless it was drug or alcohol-induced. But then again, I wouldn't call that sleep. I'd call it a mindfuck coma. Sleep was better with Grace next to me, but it would still elude me.

"Don't go," I murmured.

"I'm right here."

Her lips nuzzled my cheek, and my fingers uncurled in her hand. The weed and the whiskey took over, and I let them.

And I drifted.

The sirens wailed on and on.

Are they finally coming for me?

That clipped voice kept murmuring while his radio bleeped on and off. His hands gripped my shoulders, and his stiff wide-brimmed hat moved in my face as he spoke. His lips pulled in tight. I couldn't tear my eyes from the splashes of blood on the road. The battered sneaker, laces soaked red, the white sole splashed with muck. The lifeless eyes, the long blonde hair twisted around her face that was lying at a ridiculous, revolting angle on the asphalt. The torn body splayed in the hallway, flooding the tile floor with blood. His eyes were open, still searching, still…the chopped buzzing of the walkie-talkies.

"Horrible things sometimes happen to good people, son. Can't explain it. It's part of life. This sort of thing is a very rare occurrence. I promise you, we will find them. We'll catch up with them. I'm real sorry. You go with this nice lady now. She'll take care of you, okay? She's going to take you to the hospital and make sure you're okay. Don't look anymore, son. Don't look."

"Dig."

Part of life.

"Dig!"

Rare.

"Dig, honey, you're hurting me. Baby, please. Honey, stop. Stop!"

Choking, gurgling.

Gracie. My wildflower.

Pounding at the door. A burst, pushing. Heavy voices.

"Fuck. You okay?" Boner shouted.

Heaving breaths.

Who the hell is yelling?

Shit, it's me.

My eyes peeled open. My body shook. A cold sweat had doused my face and chest. Grace's strained eyes pleaded with me from the safety of Boner's embrace.

"Oh, shit. Fuck. Again?" I buried my face in the damp pillow.

"Yeah, bro, a-fuckin'-gain." He turned to Grace, his hand cradling her head. "You okay, babe?"

She nodded, blinking.

"Should I stay?"

"No, it's okay. Go," she mumbled. "Thank you."

Boner stroked the side of her face, glanced at me, and left the room, closing the door behind him.

"Baby, I'm sorry." I licked at my dry lips.

"Shh…it's okay." Grace wrapped her arms around me.

I pushed her away, but she wouldn't have any of it. She folded me in her arms and held me tight, wiping the matted wet hair from my face.

"It's over now. Honey, shh…"

This wasn't the first time Boner had intervened. Grace had stopped asking me what my nightmares were about months ago because I'd refused to tell her. I'd refused to tell her how my life had gotten blown to bits at thirteen years of age.

I sank my face in her neck, the adrenaline pumping through me at full throttle, my heart pounding in my chest. I could still see—

No, shut it down, Quillen. I rubbed my face against her chest. *Get it together.*

"Baby, I'm sorry. You okay?" I finally managed. My hand stroked her throat as if it could caress away the pain and terror it had inflicted earlier.

"I'm fine. You haven't had one of those bad ones in a long time. What the hell is it?"

"Nothing. It's—"

"That was not nothing."

I didn't want to share it, discuss it. I only wanted to use the electricity charging through me. I pulled her down over me, smelling her sweet warm skin. "I need you, baby."

My fingers went to her panties, and her lips pulled in for a second. She rose up, stripped them off, and straddled me.

"Give it to me, Grace," I breathed, clutching her hips.

We both guided my throbbing cock inside her, and I thrust deep into my oasis.

My head arched back. "Oh…fuck."

"Jesus…Dig…" Her palms pressed into my chest as she moved over me.

"Fuck me, Wildflower," I let out on a groan.

Her hips rolled into mine, quickening our pace. I strained to keep my eyes on hers, to concentrate on her beautiful ones swelling with feeling.

"Talk to me, baby. Tell me..." I spit out.

"I'm right here for you, baby. Right here...oh, Dig, your cock's so hard, that's the way I like it, all for me...oh yeah...harder, baby..."

I growled as I gripped her flesh and slammed into her. This sweet, kind girl was still here—still taking me in her arms, offering me refuge, dousing me with relief in her body's embrace, like the cascading waterfalls in the Hills we'd stand under in the heat of summer. What I felt for her was bigger than those three words, the ones we said to each other over and over, could ever express, but I knew she needed me to say them, and I would. I fucking needed to say them, too. It had taken me a while to realize that.

The tension exploded in my head and zapped through my body, making it intent on one thing only. I wanted to get her off with me. I stroked her clit, fast and hard, and her cries sharpened and grew more urgent. That raunchy squishy, slapping sound of our bodies sliding and jamming against each other only drove me on. The call of the wild; raw, animal instinct.

Forget, forget. Just let it fucking go. Obliterate the soul-searing eyes of a dead body. Obliterate the piercing wails of desperate, hopeless crying.

But I knew—no matter how hard I blocked it, fucked past it, drove through it, ignored it—it would always be there. I wanted to break into two or two-thousand pieces, not sure which would be better, which would give me more relief.

But right now...right now, I thrust inside her as fast as I could, my chest wound burning. I grunted as I raised my hips just a bit more and squeezed her clit.

"Holy shit!" she cried out.

Her body clamped down on mine, her insides gripping me to hell and back, and I finally shot off, my entire body shaking with it. I groaned loudly as my head fell back into the mattress. Grace leaned forward and kissed me down my throat, curling up on me but avoiding the wound. My fingers trailed through the sweat trickling down her back. Fuck, I wanted this feeling to last, this high-wire connection. I needed it like a drug, and Grace was the only dealer. My fingers sank into her hips, and I moved inside her once more.

"Give it to me again, Wildflower." I rolled her over and pushed both her knees up high. "Come on," I whispered, my hair hanging in her eyes. My lips trailed over her wet cheek.

Wet.

I opened my eyes and focused my vision on her. She didn't make a sound. Her jaw was tight, and her gaze was zeroed in on the opposite wall, tears silently falling down her face.

"Babe, what's wrong? What is it?" I gently lowered myself over her.

My hand swept her hair from her damp skin. She looked away from me.

"Baby, tell me."

She only shook her head.

"Babe?"

"Why do you do this?" she whispered, her breath hitching.

I exhaled, forcing out a chuckle. "Was I too much of a beast?"

Her lips trembled with the unspoken. Her tight gaze flitted over my face.

Jesus, what the fuck?

"The way you make love to me is brutally honest. And I like it. I love it, Dig. But you have to give me that back in return. I feel like I'm out there on my own half the time, and I hate that. That's not why I'm with you."

"Look, I know, I've been leaving you here on your own a lot…"

"That's not what I'm talking about."

"What the hell are you talking about?" I snapped.

She took in a deep breath. "I trust you, baby. I trust you with my life. But you don't trust me."

"You're my old lady. Of course I trust you! I didn't get you ready, right? Too rough? Selfish?"

"Oh my God, it's not the sex!"

I was lost. Men were stupid that way, especially right after coming like a train wreck. My happy buzz was transforming into a traffic jam.

I rubbed my eyes. "Babe, give it to me straight, would you?"

"You're suffering, and I don't know why!" Her face crumpled. "You won't let me in where it's dark for you. I need to be in there to help you."

My hand stroked the side of her face. "What are you talking about? You don't have to help me."

"Dig—"

"I don't want you there. You're my wildflower, baby. I need you outside in the light, in the air."

"That's not how it works. We're supposed to help each other."

"You do help me, Gracie. Obviously more than you know."

She only averted her gaze.

"Baby, look at me."

She turned her head to face me. Her eyes were red, her jaw clenched.

"I love you. You know that, right?" I brushed my lips with hers.

Her muscles instantly relaxed all around me. My dick settled inside her. Her hips flexed up, and I rocked in again. Her tightness took my breath away for an intense split second.

"I love you, too," she whispered, wiping at her face.

"I know."

I closed my eyes and slowly rocked in again as I took a deep breath. Her hips tightened, their movement stalling. My eyes blinked open.

"Who the hell is Eve?" she asked.

"What?"

"Eve? You kept calling out to her in your sleep. I thought you said you never had a serious girlfriend before. Why are you dreaming of a girl named Eve, and it's making you miserable and freaking you out?"

I exhaled roughly as I pulled out of her. Frowning, she adjusted herself on me.

"Is she your long-lost first love?"

"Ah, for fuck's sake. You're my goddamn first love!" I covered my eyes with my hands.

"Great."

I raised my hands in the air. "Great? Holy shit!"

"So why are you dreaming of her?" she raised her voice.

I snapped. "Eve's my sister."

"Your sister?"

"She's dead."

"Oh, I'm so sorry, honey." She got off me and rolled into my side, planting a kiss on my shoulder, her arm snaking around my middle. She didn't say anything more.

I leaned my head against hers. My breath evened out as I focused on her soft strokes along my side.

"She was killed," I said.

Grace let out a little breathy gasp and said nothing more, only raising herself over me just a bit to dig her fingers through my hair. That soft numbing feeling flowed over me, and I welcomed it. Yes, no more talking, thinking, forming words, explaining feelings. I was fucking drained.

My hand went up her T-shirt, desperate for the feel of her bare tits in my hand. She knew what I needed and managed to get her shirt and then her bra off in seconds flat. I nestled my face in her smooth, full curves, enjoying her baby-soft skin, her powder scent. I kissed her breasts, fondling them, sucking on her nipples until they were hard and wet. Grace always used baby powder after a shower, and I had grown to love that delicate fragrance. It had become my quiet breathing space, my piece of comfort during all these months together.

All was right with the world again.

She let out a sigh, her legs squirming, rubbing against mine. I focused on her silky skin, the drum of her heartbeat until my own began to finally slow down, and I drifted asleep on a cloud of velvet promise, her arms wrapped around me.

"Coffee smells good, babe." I sat up in bed and grabbed the steamy mug she had left for me on the side table. I swallowed the hot unsweetened black brew.

Grace glanced up at me from the edge of the bed. She was writing on something.

"What are you doing?"

"Doodling."

"Oh, yeah? Show me." I nudged her lower back with my knee.

She bit her lip as she held up my Ray-Ban case. She had written her nickname in ink, decorated with a little flower over the I and one on either side. "Artistry, huh?"

I grinned. "I like it."

"So you don't forget about me when you're on the road, which is most of the time."

"I always think about you. Never forget you, baby."

She propped the case and the pen on the dresser and turned to me. "How do you feel?"

"Fine."

"Fine, huh?"

"Yeah. Why?"

"Fine?"

"Babe—"

She glanced up at the ceiling for a second. "You're going to have to do a better job of lying to me, *babe*. First, you get attacked, or you attacked, and not once, but twice on one run, which in itself is nothing new to write home about. Then you have another horrible nightmare that freaks you out and makes you a mess."

"I scared you. I'm sorry."

"It's not that, Dig."

"I said I feel much better. I managed to get some good sleep. The cut looks okay, right?" I poked a finger at the bandage on my chest.

"Yes, it looks better. But you don't get good sleep consistently, if at all. You haven't been eating either. I'm worried about you."

"My stomach's been acting up again. Got that burn going on. I don't want to eat anyway. Well, no, I'd much rather eat you."

She didn't even crack a smile as my finger tracked up her leg.

"Oh, come on, baby. Give me a smile, a little one... come on..."

She swatted my hand away. "It's not funny, Dig. You can't keep up like this."

My eyes pierced hers. "I've been doing it long before you came along."

She raised her chin. "Oh, okay. Right. I'm in your way then? Pain in your ass?"

I let out an exhale, my one hand dropping on the mattress, the other putting the coffee mug on the side table. "I didn't mean it like that, Grace. What I meant was, you can quit your worrying."

She crossed her arms and legs and scowled at me.

"Why don't you get over here and let me show you how grateful I am that you didn't let Jump make the coffee?"

"There's something else I need to talk to you about."

I slid back down on the bed, my hand over the sheet outlining my enormous hard-on for her. "Okay. Talk, if you're still able to at the sight of this magnificence."

She rolled her eyes, and we both laughed.

She wiped a hand across her forehead. "I had a scare the other day."

"What the fuck are you talking about?"

"I was late. My period. I was late two weeks. I'm never late."

I sat up higher against the wall, my heart thudding in my chest. "You're still on the pill, right?"

"Yes."

My eyebrows jammed into my forehead. "What are you saying? Are you pregnant? How can you be pregnant?"

She looked me square in the eyes, her spine stiffening. "Would that be so bad?"

"Yeah, actually, it would. Baby, I'm not…the way things are with the club right now…"

"Other guys have kids, families."

"Yeah, but—"

"But what?"

"That ain't me."

Her eyes flared into a darker shade of green-brown. "Oh. Well, I guess we should have had this conversation a lot sooner then."

The hairs on the back of my neck stood at attention. I grabbed her arm. "Are you pregnant?"

"No. It turned out to be a false alarm." She pulled away from me. "Would you have told me to get rid of it if I were?"

I leaned my head back against the headboard and let out a breath. "Doesn't matter now."

"It matters to me. What are we doing here anyway?"

My eyes snapped at her. "What the fuck is that supposed to mean?"

"When you say things like that, what am I supposed to think? "

"Hey, you're my old lady, Grace. You're mine. My responsibility in this club. We take care of each other, in and out of this bed. We make up a unit."

She nodded at me, mentally ticking off my laundry-list definition but not very impressed. "And a child doesn't fit into that unit? *Our* child?"

"Babe, I'm on the road a lot. We spend most of our time at this dump—"

"We can make adjustments."

"Wildflower—"

"You're telling me you don't want a kid? Ever?" Her eyes suddenly pooled with liquid as she drew in a breath. She was waiting for my answer.

Oh, I wanted a kid. A kid with Grace. Our child. A few in fact. A family. Our family. I wanted it so bad that I didn't need to think about it or weigh pros and cons. I knew this as a fact, deep in my gut. But the thought of being powerless to protect them—that was an insane kind of vulnerability. That blade twisted inside me. No, not ready yet. Soon.

I grasped her hand in mine. "I didn't say that. Babe, you just finished college. You wanna start with babies already?"

She bit her bottom lip. "No, that's true. Not right now. But if I were to get pregnant now, I wouldn't get rid of it. Just so you know."

"Understood."

"Good." She nodded and swept her long hair behind her ears.

"Okay." I got back to breathing again.

"Anyway, I got a job,"

"What kind of job?"

"Pete wants to retire from running the bar. He's not ready to sell, but he wants to cut down on the hours he spends there. He asked me to manage it. Full-time."

"You want to do it?"

"Yeah, I do."

"Do it."

"You don't have a problem with me being there almost every night?"

"We're practically there every night, hon. Works for me. You running the place? Big win all around."

"Good."

"Good." I ripped the sheet off my body, and my aching cock greeted her, begging for her attention. "You wanna manage *me* now?"

She glanced at her watch, making a face. "Shucks. I'm a little pressed for time. Maybe later."

"Get that ass over here—now."

She frowned. "You're going to have to make it quick though."

"Babe."

"We've got to make it fast, honey. I've got to meet up with Pete," she whispered. "But, tonight, you will be making up for it in detail. You got that?"

"Get rid of the clothes."

She stripped off, and I brought her down on her side and turned her, molding myself to her body from behind. I immediately drove my desperate cock inside her, grunting like a greedy, hungry beast. I plunged deeper, holding her upper thigh open, my fingers biting into her flesh. Her head rolled back, and she let out a harsh moan. I slowly pulled out of her slickness and then thrust back in deep.

"I'll make up for it tonight. I'm good with details, aren't I?" I said through ragged breaths. "Always make good on my debts, don't I, babe?"

My fingers dug into her thigh as I rolled my hips, pumping into her fast. "Good morning, Wildflower."

"Shut up already!" she gasped, pressing her head back against me.

I sucked on her earlobe, and she shivered in my tight grip.

Thrust.

"You like that?"

Thrust.

"Yes."

Thrust.

"Oh, Dig, dammit…"

She forgot about making it fast. It was all in the details.

EIGHT

"YOU WANNA DANCE WITH ME?"

"Nope."

"Ah, c'mon, Dig." Lissa's lips twisted into a pout, her hips jutted to the right, and she stamped her feet together.

Brat.

The lead singer of a country-hits cover band was crooning on the small stage at Pete's, wishing he were Tim McGraw, and I could barely hear what Lissa was saying, not that it mattered. It wasn't as if I didn't know what she was after.

"I don't dance. You go on. I'll watch."

She laughed. Her eyes were pinned on me as she leaned in closer. "You do that, baby. I'll be dancing just for you." She planted a kiss on my lips, her black roots glaring at me in the spotlight over my table. She sprang off me and hopped down toward the dance floor, grabbing one of her girlfriends as she went.

I nabbed my pack of cigarettes from the table. A lighter flicked open for me as two long legs stretched next to mine. I grinned at Miller as I took in a long drag.

"Thought you had an old lady," he said, bringing the lighter to his own cigarette.

I eased back in my chair and grinned at Lissa while she swiveled her hips and shook her incredibly round ass at me on the dance floor in those fuck-me platform shoes. "Yeah?"

He took a long drag off his cigarette. "Where is she?"

I trained my eyes on him. "Why?"

Miller shrugged, holding my eyes, waiting for a reprimand or a laugh. I wasn't sure which.

"It'd be a first, is all. Seeing you with an old lady. Wanted to meet her. Wreck's told me about her." He ran a hand over his closely cropped hair. "You know, I think I knew her in high school."

I eyed him as I expelled the smoke from my lungs.

"Not like that, man. I mean, I knew who she was from far away. Very far away." He shook his head at me, his hand sliding down his abs, as he laughed.

"She was in Denver, visiting her sister. Now she's on her way down to Florida with Jump's old lady to get some sun."

He made a face. "Fuck. You sure that was a good idea?"

"I set Alicia straight before they took off. Anyway, we'll be heading on down ourselves next week. This snow ain't letting up anytime soon."

"Neither is she." Miller gestured toward Lissa showing off for me on the dance floor, kicking up her legs, shaking her loose platinum-blonde curls.

I shifted in my chair. Miller's gaze settled on me as he took a swig from his beer bottle and then let out a laugh.

"Yeah, you know the way this shit goes," I muttered.

"It's a story as ancient as time. Just make sure you don't bring any STDs down to Florida with you."

I swiped a hand across my mouth. "I don't plan on fucking her. She's just another fucking groupie, man. You like her? Take a stab."

"Nah. Not my type."

"Who gives a shit about type? A willing female, young man, is a willing female."

He snickered. "Old habits die hard, eh?"

"I'm not stepping out on my old lady, Miller. It's definitely a discipline not to. But when there's purpose behind it, it's all good."

"Purpose?"

"Yeah."

A slight grin warmed his face as he raised his beer bottle at me. "Well then, I look forward to meeting your old lady when I get back."

"Oh yeah?"

"Yeah, I'm fascinated to meet Dig Quillen's great purpose in life."

We laughed.

I tapped the ash off my cigarette and glanced at Lissa dancing, shaking those curvy hips. "Sometimes though, you're in the candy store, you want to smell the flavors, check out the colors, so you crack open the packaging just for a peek, a whiff, and then you pop it back on the shelf. No calorie intake. No harm done to the waistline."

"Ah, but the shopkeeper's gonna be after you to pay for that candy, if you opened the package."

"Shut up."

Miller raised a thick eyebrow. "There will be plenty of man-candy for your old lady to check out on a Florida beach this time of year. That's for sure."

I glared at him. "You aiming to piss me off tonight?"

"What's the point of candy if you've got a full dinner waiting for you on the table at home?" He smirked at me and guzzled more beer.

"What is it? Go on, say it."

He wiped the side of his mouth. "You're full of shit. How's that? What did you teach me once? There's shit that's random and shit you can control. It's up to you to choose what you'll react to and how to make your mark. What do you choose to control?" Miller's black eyes bore down on mine.

He never would have talked back like that to me before. He used to squirm in his seat when he had something to say, that blunt jaw clenched, his gaze intense, heavy. Being a soldier had stiffened his spine. Our boy had grown up.

"You weigh in and control the important shit, young Skywalker."

He raised his chin. "I figure, if you finally got yourself an old lady, a woman who's worth calling your own, then what's the point of this...willing female?"

Our eyes slid to Lissa and her girlfriend gyrating on the dance floor with their tits bouncing in their fuzzy tight cropped sweaters. They bumping into other men as they laughed uproariously.

Miller let out a small huff of air. "She's as fuckin' random as a pinball whizzing by."

I rubbed at the side of my head with my thumb, trying to relieve the sudden wave of pounding. "How much longer do I have to put up with your ass?" I asked before taking another drag on my cigarette.

"I just got into town, man. Isn't that why we came out tonight?"

"Yeah, but you're already ruining my mojo."

Miller let out a hearty laugh. "Forgive me my transgressions, master."

"I'll think about it. Why don't we go shooting tomorrow? You can show me what Uncle Sam's taught you."

"Sounds good. Not much else to do in all this snow anyway."

Lissa bounced into my lap. The weight of her body was like a load of bricks. A sweaty arm slid around my shoulders, her heavy breaths hitting my face. The odor of stale cotton candy rose between us.

Holding my gaze, Miller blew out a stream of smoke. "I stand corrected." He gestured at Lissa's back with his cigarette. "There's another snow-time activity for you."

"Huh?" Lissa grinned at me, her face shiny. "Did you like that, babe?"

"Yeah, fucking fantastic," I replied.

"Love it when you watch me like that."

Miller chuckled, and I shot him a glare.

"Why don't you go put that soldier-boy charm to good use and find some tail?"

"Ah, there's an idea. Why didn't I think of that?" His dark eyes stayed pinned on me as he rubbed his cigarette out in the ashtray between us on the table. Grabbing his beer bottle, he strode toward the crowded bar.

Lissa giggled as she wiggled her ass in my lap, running her fingers up my arms. My dick responded, but my erection rush was not the usual invitation to roar. It was an annoyance, making me uncomfortable. I pushed her off me, dumping her in the chair the kid had just vacated. I drained my beer bottle and banged it back on the table. Lissa stared at me as she flicked strands of her dried-out hair away from her flushed face. I stood up, shoving my near-empty pack of smokes in my jacket pocket.

She licked at her lips. "You gettin' me a drink?" Her voice was on the edge of shrill.

"Uh, no." I stalked toward Wreck, Boner, Miller, Dready, and Clip at the bar.

"Dig! Di—" The blare of music drowned out Lissa's shriek.

"A bacon cheeseburger, two chili dogs, two fries."

"That it?" asked the waitress, still scribbling on her pad, straining to hear over the roar of the long lines of bikes motoring in around us in the huge parking lot of Dead Ringer's Roadhouse.

"That's it, hon," Jump replied.

The waitress nodded and took off, weaving in between the endless rows of motorcycles.

"Is that for both of us or just you?" asked Alicia, her hands on her hips.

"Have no fear, babe. You'll get what you need," Jump replied.

Grace snorted. Alicia narrowed her eyes at her old man as she wrapped a hand around his bulging bicep, pressing herself into his side.

There was nothing like Bike Night at the Roadhouse, over an hour northwest of Rapid, to break up our week. With warmer weather in full swing, the hunger to get back on our bikes and eat the road had finally been satisfied. The parking lot was a sea of colored shiny metal, jammed full of long, long rows of bikes.

After our arrival, we had spent the first hour checking out the brand-new Harleys the yuppie posers were showing off, them eyeing us, us smirking at them and admiring quite a few beautiful hogs and plenty of women along the way. Other clubs had shown up with their choppers, which inspired our respect for their inventiveness and audacity.

I handed Grace a big plastic cup of draft beer from the passing waitress.

"Thanks, baby," she murmured.

"Pizza?" asked another waitress, bearing a platter of Sicilian squares in her hands, nudging it in my face.

I flinched at the stench.

"No, thanks! He's allergic to the oregano." Grace pulled me away. "Geez, I guess Biff is spiffing up the menu."

"Great." I swallowed down the acid at the back of my throat, clenching my jaw.

"Honey, Cruel Fate is setting up. I'm going to go over and say hi to Eric, okay?"

A frown escaped my control at the name of the band and its lead guitarist rolling off her lips.

She scowled at me. "Dig, I want them to play at Pete's. Better in person than over the phone. I need to make a good impression."

"Yeah, you'll make an impression all right."

She rolled her eyes and stood on her toes, sticking her tongue in my mouth.

I squeezed her ass in return. "You're evil," I whispered. "Who's gonna protect me from the fucking pizza?"

"Geez, you and your sensitive allergy. Relax, I'll be back in a bit. Oh, no, wait."

"What?" I gulped at my cold beer, enjoying its icy slide down the back of my tense throat.

"I'll be back after I register for the wet T-shirt contest." She tugged at her black T-shirt with the One-Eyed Jacks skull under her denim property vest, her tits popping up over the V-neck.

I gave her the full-on threatening frown.

"What? I'm wearing my club T-shirt. This is good promo for the club—especially since last week's fundraiser for Cheryl Devere's chemo, thanks to *moi*, and then the club replacing those old windows on Mrs. Chibbet's house. You got in big with the Rotary Club there. Don't forget that. You do want the club to stay in people's minds, don't you?"

"Yeah, baby. The club, not my old lady's tits."

She lifted an eyebrow. "My tits wouldn't do the club proud?"

"Your tits do *me* proud. Nobody else. Are we clear?" I readjusted her shirt. "Hate to disappoint you, but I don't think any members of the Rotary Club are here tonight anyway."

"Bet their horny teenage kids are though." She gave me another kiss and slid her arms around my middle, pulling me close, as she grinned. "Oh, for God's sake, I'm just teasing you! Alicia said they canceled it tonight anyway. It got too crazy last time." She shook me. "What's wrong?"

"Nothing. Just a little wound up."

"What is it?"

"Nothin'!"

"Quillen, we came to have fun tonight. I don't see any enemies around."

I wiped strands of her hair from her eyes and exhaled. She still wanted to believe in the good in everyone. Would she always stay this positive, eager, and generous after years with me? I didn't want Grace to be naive, yet I also didn't want her to transform into the dog-eared, gnawed-on soul too many of us were, especially the women.

"They're always around, babe."

"Right. Well, get unwound. And I'll help you get even more unwound later on. How about that?"

I swatted her ass, and she grinned at me. She strode toward the small stage in the center of the lot, and I rubbed a hand across my jaw as I watched her walk away from me.

Grace called out to a tall guy with a ponytail, holding a guitar. He turned and smiled huge at her. She stretched out her hand, and they shook. He leaned over further and pulled her up onstage.

Motherfucker.

She laughed, and he kept grinning at her as she talked on, her face beaming, her free hand gesturing in the air.

I shoved Boner in her direction with my shoulder. "Go hover, would you?"

"Uh, yeah, sure, bro." He grabbed another large plastic cup of beer and headed toward the makeshift stage.

"The Blades are here, huh?" Butler asked at my side.

"Yeah, saw Zed the minute I got off my bike. What's up with that? He hasn't been up here in a while. Not that there's anything wrong with that."

"Nope, nothing wrong with that." Butler folded his arms across his chest and leaned back against a table. "Always nice to have visitors from Nebraska. I have a feeling though. This whole relaxed and easy approach is bullshit."

"Oh, yeah." I flicked on my lighter and lit my cigarette.

"We gonna go say hello, or wait for him to make a move?"

I turned to my right. Jump, Clip, Dready, and Judge were devouring their food like they hadn't eaten all day. Our president, Mick, and his old lady were checking out bikes. Creeper was plodding along at his side with some older woman in tow who was dressed like a twenty-something.

"We wait."

"Hey, guys. How you doing?" a babyish girl's voice chirped at our side. A sexy tall redhead in a tank top advertising a bike repair shop chain that had an outlet in Rapid dangled key chains in front of us. "How would you like a key chain from our store? We offer a full range of services you might need." She smiled, one hand on her hip and the other holding up a key chain with a photo of a guy doing a wheelie on a scooter.

"Oh, yeah? What kinda services?" asked Butler, his fingers rubbing across his chest, a dirty smile curling his lips. "'Course you can fully service me anytime. I always need that."

She only laughed and tucked the key chain into the front of his jeans, planted a kiss on the side of his face, and sauntered off. He smirked and pulled out the key chain, stuffing it in his jacket. "Let's get some food, bro. I'm fuckin' starvin'."

"Let's check out the rice burners first. I need a good laugh."

"Aw, did you see that mess of Hondas and Yamahas pulling in ahead of us?"

I nodded, and my eyes darted across the lot to the stage where Boner had an arm slung around Grace's shoulders while she kept talking to that guitarist fuck. The band's drummer had taken an interest, too. He hung over her, his eyes on her chest. His sticks were at his side, tapping out a rhythm against his leg. He laughed at something Grace had said and leaned into her, filling her ear with some sort of bullshit. Even though my woman wore my patch on that denim vest and had Boner glued to her side, it still didn't make any sort of difference to those two assholes.

Fuck, men are dogs.

"You comin' or what?" Butler nabbed a cigarette from the pack in my front pocket and tapped at my chest.

I swiped his hand away. "Yeah, let's hit it."

An hour later, we had checked out the flashy bikes, both American and Japanese, brought by the yuppies who only took out their fancy name-brand machines on nights like this and then popped them right back in their garages or trailers.

Shit, I wouldn't trade my custom-built 1967 Panhead for the world.

Wreck and I had built that bike around a new motor that I had bought off a guy in Ohio who had once worked at a Harley store. Months later, it was built, and I'd taken it through the Badlands on its first long run, roaring through that desolate stone terrain, the blast of the pipes and my humming pulse weaving together, centering me. I'd never felt such a rush, such a fucking high. It was a clear high, glorious and humbling all at once.

Cruel fucking Fate was playing a blaring cover of "Devil Woman."

God help us all.

Where the hell was Grace?

If she were in the front row, dancing and singing along, I was going to bust a gasket. The migraine surged in on both sides of my skull.

"Dig, long time no see, man. Hey, Butler. What's up?"

A beefy inked arm clapped me on the shoulder, and my eyes shot up.

Ronny, who had a choice tattoo parlor in Deadwood, let out a belly laugh. His long silver chains, hung with oversized crosses and skulls, clattered together with the rolling movement of his big body. "Haven't seen you in a while, pal. How you been?"

"Good. Good to see you. I've been meaning to come by. I've—"

"What do you boys think of Lissa's new rose?"

Fuck.

Lissa stood next to Ronny, wearing a pink cutout one-piece bathing suit, which only really covered her nipples and pussy at best. Big gold rings attached all the strips of fabric. High heels topped off the getup. A '70s wet dream. She chewed on gum and trained her gaze on me, one bleached blonde eyebrow arching higher than the other.

Ronny's thick index finger traced a trail from the edge of her left tit where the red flower tattoo was in full bloom down her side, running along the tattooed stem dotted with smaller roses, complete with thorns and drops of blood. Butler let out a heavy exhale as Ronny's finger circled over a tiny rose low on her hip just near the swell of her round ass. Ripe fruit, plump and juicy for the picking.

I shifted my weight, begging my cock to lay low.

"Nice, huh?" Ronny said.

"Very." Butler grinned, his blue eyes glued to Lissa's full round ass cheeks separated by the thong of the suit.

Ronny laughed. "You two know where the store is. I don't need to give you a business card."

Lissa punched out her other hip, a hand landing on her waist.

My gaze met hers. "Nope."

"Good to hear. Better make the rounds while the going's still good. Where did Stacy get to again?"

Lissa shrugged, and Ronny wandered off.

Lissa took two steps closer to me, blew a bubble with those bright red-painted lips and popped it, her tongue lashing the pink goop back into her mouth.

A girl in a Confederate flag bikini top bounced next to her. "Lissa, come on. These guys want to take pictures of us on their bikes. They got us Jell-O shots and everything. Where's Ronny?"

Lissa smirked at me, her eyes narrowing. She got even closer and slowly ran her hand down my chest, spanning over my abs. My cock argued with me. She tugged at my belt buckle and then let go of it and nabbed the cigarette from behind my ear, holding it between her fingers. I snapped out my lighter and flicked it on. Her plump red lips held my cigarette in between them, sending my brain messages of doom and chaos. Lissa inclined her head closer to me, her hand over mine on the lighter, and inhaled until the cigarette inflamed. She lifted her face at me and grinned, exhaling a long trail of smoke just to my side. I grinned back at her. Licking her lower lip, she turned and sauntered off on her platform heels, her friend in tow.

Butler let out a hiss. "Shit, that was calling my name."

"Go for it. Get her off my fucking back."

"You don't want a piece of that?"

"No."

"Oh, man. You already had a piece of that."

"No, I did not. Have not. Will not."

Butler laughed. "Whoa. Okay, bro. Your loss, my gain." He stalked off after Lissa.

I drained my beer cup and tossed it in a trash can. *Where the hell was my old lady?*

The lot was filled with people laughing and yelling, clapping and hooting, singing along with the band. Vendors hawked riding accessories, studded and fringed saddlebags, all sorts of T-shirts, while others were offering Jell-O shots and hot dogs and fucking pizza. Everyone was taking photos of themselves in front of bikes, on bikes, of girls kissing each other on bikes, girls licking each other on bikes, chicks posing with their asses in the air on bikes. The sun had long since set, and the huge overhead lights were glaring down on us.

My eyes strained, searching the crowd by the band—no Grace, no Alicia, no Dee. I pressed my fingers into the sides of my head and rubbed. The piercing burn behind my eyes only flared. I needed another beer.

"Hey! Is there a wet T-shirt contest tonight?" I asked the waitress.

"No, we decided against it this time. There was so much trouble the last time we had one. Forget that!"

"Right." I handed her a few bills and grabbed the beer.

"Dig Quillen. How you doing?"

I squinted through my increasingly blurry vision. Zed, the president of the Broken Blades from northern Nebraska. He scratched at his neck, which was stamped all over with tats heralding his time in the Marines. He had a huge Z down one arm. Zed had a long, complicated Polish last name that was too hard to pronounce, and everyone had settled on calling him by the first three letters.

"Hey, man. Good to see you. What brings you my way?"

"A beer, hon." Zed threw bills across the narrow counter of the temporary bar set up outside, leaning his hairy forearms against it, fingers dragging through his long mustache. "Been wanting to talk to you for a long while now. Came through town, especially for you."

"For me? Or the Jacks?"

He snorted. "You. Your prez and me just don't see eye-to-eye on most subjects. I thought it might be smoother if we did it this way—bumping into you at a social event." He waggled his eyebrows and snorted.

"He's here, you know."

"Yeah, I know. We said our hellos."

"What's up, Zed?"

"Demon Seeds are on my ass."

My eyelids sank for a second. I put down my beer and grabbed a cigarette. "What the fuck is their problem now? They reaching out to you?"

"*Reaching out* would be kind, brother. More like threatening, torching. They even handled a brother's woman last week. Making statements left and right."

My goddamn piece-of-shit lighter suddenly wouldn't light. Third try. Fourth. I tossed it. Zed flipped open his lighter for me.

I bent my head, lit my Marlboro, and took in a deep drag. My eyes raced round the lot. *Where the fuck is Grace now?* I exhaled a stream of smoke as I rubbed my forehead. "What do they want?"

"Want us to patch in. I've had my ear to the ground for a while man. On Vig. He's making moves with the Russians out west, Washington State, even California. They want access to the Midwest through the quiet that is us. Fuck that. I've got my own game in play. So do you. Am I right?"

"Yeah."

"We give one inch on this, and they'll only be back for more. I don't want to give that up to play ball with these goons. I don't care what kinda cash he's talking. I don't trust these Russkie assholes. Can barely speak English, some of 'em in their fancy suits. What do these motherfuckers want with my corner of Nebraska anyhow?"

"They just want it all. Vig's all about the squeeze. Squeezing to get his way. He wants a toll-free road through Colorado, too. Colorado is ours."

Zed held my gaze. "That's why I came through here, Dig. Glad I did." He shifted his formidable weight, a hand smoothing down his gray mustache. "Tell me, he squeezing you?"

"He tried. He's all about this *brave new world*. But I saved his hide in a drug bust a while back, and he's been laying off us for a while now."

"Don't count on it for too much longer."

"Oh, I agree. The Jacks and the Broken Blades have worked together in the past, shared, had each other's backs. Ain't no reason why we can't do so in the future." I leaned closer to him. "Frankly, there's all the more reason to do so right now, but that's just my personal opinion."

"Feel the same way. Fucking Seeds don't like the long-standing relationship our two clubs got. And they don't like the truce we've both managed with the Flames of Hell either. That was hard won, and they want to fuck with that balance. A balance that's worked real good for all of us."

If I could keep Zed and his Broken Blades on my side of that balance and forge a relationship with the Flames of Hell, a very independent and formidable 1% club just over the border in Nebraska, then things would be more than good. We could form a hard wall against the Seeds and beyond.

Zed drank from his beer. "Look, we're heading to Wyoming for that poker run. Wanted to stop by though and touch base with you. Play nice with Mick. For now."

"I will. Much appreciated."

He eyed me. "I'm standing firm. You standing firm?"

"Fuck yeah.

His huge coffee-colored eyes flashed as he clapped a hand on my shoulder. "Got to start watching out for those tacos, too, you know?" He sighed. "Fucking Mexicans."

Hissing and hooting rose among a group of leather-clad men and women to our right. One-Eyed Jacks were having a standoff with members of an amateur riding club from Rapid. Clip, his eyes full of fire, was in the face of one of the men, as a girl pulled on his arm, her mouth running. Two of Zed's brothers stood in the center. Clip pushed one of them to the side, and the Blade's eyes bulged.

Zed groaned. "Ah, fuck. Now what?"

I let out a laugh. "All's right with the world, man."

"Yeah. Last time we got together, same ole shit."

"This is the *good* shit. This gives me a sense of pride," I said on a laugh, stamping out my cigarette.

Zed roared with laughter. "Exactly! I don't even remember what the last one was about, do you?"

I shrugged. "Who fucking does, man? Let's go keep the balance."

"Hey." He pulled on my arm, lifting his chin. "Know you got my support," he said, his voice low, "should you ever sit at the head of your table, when that time comes."

My chest tightened. A bid for the presidency. I'd been thinking about it, biding my time, stepping carefully, judiciously. Boner and Jump and I hadn't even discussed it out loud, only in subtle looks and movements over the table.

My eyes held Zed's assessing ones. Knowing that I had a club like the Broken Blades behind me, ready to work with me, coexist with the Jacks, was huge.

"Appreciate it, man."

"Dig, months ago you shared with me when my club needed it. It made sense for you to make adjustments, and you didn't fight it just to be a prick. You made those adjustments. You didn't tick me off your list out of spite, and you didn't bullshit me either. Kept it uncomplicated. Ain't typical. I respect that. Just trying to do the same." He hiked up his jeans. "Gotta kick some ass tonight. Promised my boys. You in?"

I grinned. "Here's to keeping it real."

"That's right. See you on the road, brother." Zed stalked in the direction of the swell of jeering and hooting.

Boner came up next to me. "A couple Blades kicked this pansy's Honda, and the idiot thought it was Clip. All Clip was doing was necking with this chick who was hanging out by the bike. I think the stare down has just about hit its limit."

I grabbed Boner's collar. "Where the fuck is Grace?"

He pushed off my hands. "She went inside to the restroom with Dee. They're around."

"Around is not here, bro!"

He wrapped a hand around my neck. "Hey, man, easy. The women are fine. They're inside. Listen, Jump and Judge are already in the mix." The grin splitting his face was unmistakable.

I took in a deep breath. *Power in unity.* Yeah, despite our president, Mick. Despite his divisive tactics. "Let's get in on it before the cops get here."

Boner and I stalked off toward the brouhaha to the left of the stage. I'd recognize that hair anywhere. Jackhammers went off behind my eyes. Grace's long brown waves shook over her shoulders as she talked. Talked with Butler. No, she was laughing with Butler. Both of them, relaxed, listening to the music, their bodies moving to the beat as they spoke. Their eyes were half on the band, half on each other. Her shirt was soaking wet, outlining her tits. She had it knotted and pulled tight, her bare midriff showing, her curves on display. Her one hand held a beer cup, and she hoisted it in the air, cheering the band on.

Grace leaned her head closer to Butler's and put a hand up against her mouth, her eyes opening wide with every word she uttered.

Is what she has to tell him that important?

A slow smile lit Butler's face as he dragged his white teeth across his lower lip. Gone was his usual smug grin. Gone was that air of boredom he cultivated so well. He now wore an expression I'd never seen on him before. He wasn't charming the panties off some bitch with that surfer-boy grin and those light-blue eyes he knew how to work. No, he was *listening* to whatever Grace was saying. Listening and interested.

He leaned over her and made some remark, that long blond hair of his covering his face, and she threw her head back and laughed, her one hand clutching his arm. He laughed, too, his eyes never leaving hers, soaking in her reaction. He swept his hair out of his face and took the beer cup out of her hand, gulping down whatever was left. She jumped up and down, clapping for the band. He cheered alongside her, the two of them laughing.

I sucked in air. The searing ache in my head shifted. A burning knife dragged its poisoned hot tip through my brain. Fuck, I had to deal with testosterone first before I could deal with my woman. At least she was with a Jack and away from the brawl.

I scanned the crowd and spotted each of our brothers, except for one. "Where the hell is Creeper?"

"He left with that kinky rich bitch he's been banging. We won't be seeing him again tonight."

"Jesus."

We charged to the end of the lot where the Blades had taken up position, and a wave of people pushed and clamored, shouting and cursing at each other. A tall thin guy was in Zed's face, talking trash. Judge was at his side, shoving a Blade out of the way.

"Bring it on!" Zed smirked at the man.

Alicia stood behind Jump with an empty beer bottle in her hand, ready to use it. I had to hand it to the woman. She was always prepared and ready to defend her old man. Being vicious or sweet, she always had his back, no matter if the enemy was male or female. She'd used that old bike chain on her belt many times, doing just that, not to mention her rings or the odd shot glass. She caught my gaze and narrowed her eyes at me.

"Go get Sister and Dee!" I spit out, pushing her out of the way, as Boner and I lunged into the brawl.

The blur of pounding and shouting took over, and I forgot everything else. Zed let me get in a few good shots on the tall thin guy he was holding onto, and then Zed went to town on the him, hooking high with a powerful right, slamming his knee up into his chest. I distracted another civilian who had come up behind Zed and gave Jump a chance to get his licks in. Luckily, none of us were stupid enough to bring guns to this little local hoedown. Maybe a knife or razors were concealed in a boot or two, but that was all.

You could get hurled down that road of no return in the blink of an eye.

Police sirens stung the night air, peeling me out of my bloodlust. Jump, Wreck, and I pushed through the yelling citizens and good-time bitches scattering all over the lot. Yeah, they wanted to fuck you and climb all over you, but the minute the going got tough, they would be screaming and running in the opposite direction. Stale beer, grease, and exhaust fumes filled my nostrils. Bikes were gunning and twisting out of the Dead Ringer's lot, one right after the other. The knot of people loosened, and the crowd thinned and receded.

A sudden wave of nausea had me wavering, and I crouched down on the asphalt to fight it. I took in several deep breaths and swiped at a cut on my forehead, wiping the sweat out of my eyes. The burn in my belly spiraled. Two legs in faded tight jeans, capped off with brand-new Harley boots that I recognized, stood before me. I raised my bleary eyes, my head falling back.

Gracie.

"You okay?" My voice came out in a rasp.

She only stared at me, her eyes hard, her hands on her hips.

"Answer me." My tone sharpened. "You okay?"

She offered me her hand, and I reached out and clasped her lower arm, raising myself up.

"Where the hell have you been?"

Her eyes darted over the dwindling crowd. "Listening to the band."

"Right. Was it a good time?"

She made a face at my sharp tone. "Very," she replied. Her cool fingers touched my forehead. "Are you okay?"

I brushed her hand away, and her lips pinched together.

I yanked on her tucked-up damp T-shirt. "Why is your shirt wet?"

"Some jerk in the crowd spilled his beer on me."

I let out an exhale as I wrapped my bloodied sore hands around her neck and bent to kiss her. She shifted her face, and something inside my chest prickled. It was a slight movement, a few degrees at most, but it was a move. I lifted her chin in a tight grip and took her mouth hostage, my tongue storming inside her, leaving no questions as to who owned it and how. Her hands dug into my middle, and I pulled her into me, keeping her face close.

"Go start my bike, babe," I said against her parted lips, my voice tight.

She pushed back from me, taking a step away, scowling.

I clenched my jaw against a new wave of nausea. There wasn't time for this shit now. "Bike."

"Yeah, I heard you," she muttered. She pivoted away from me but stumbled and crashed right into a cop.

He grabbed her by the arms and steadied her on her feet. She pulled her arms out of his grip.

"Watch it, Grace."

Trey fucking Owens.

Since that dick-brain had become a cop in Rapid, if he ever spotted us riding through, he'd find a reason to stop us, make a remark, insinuation, look over Grace. He towered over her now, talking down at her, with a stone-cold look etched on his face, his mouth stiff as it moved. I stormed towards them.

I slid an arm around my old lady's waist. "What's the problem, officer?"

He scoffed and slung out a hip. "You're kidding, right, asshole?"

"Grace has nothing to do with all this. We were jumped, so figure it out. I got to get my old lady home now, so if—"

He raised a hand in my face. "Mr. Sergeant at Arms, you're a part of this little disorderly conduct drama tonight, so back it up," he said, his eyes glinting in the dark. "Feds are going to be really interested in your little chat with a club from Nebraska."

I glanced at Grace. Her hands were jammed in her back pockets. She was chewing on the inside of her cheek like she did whenever she was anxious. Tonight was supposed to have been a bit of fun, the two of us hanging out, enjoying ourselves with our friends. Once again, it hadn't quite turned out that way. Not very surprising.

I held out a hand to her, and she looked down at it. Taking in a breath of air, she untucked one of her hands from a pocket and curled her fingers into my palm. I tugged her closer and squeezed her hand, but she still wouldn't look at me.

Hours later, we paid our fines with no one pressing any real charges against us, certainly not Biff who owned Dead Ringer's. Biff knew which side his bread was buttered, and Bike Night always made him a tidy mint of cash every month from all the bike clubs in the area as well as a long line of local vendors and a number of citizens who lusted to get down and dance with the illusion of their liberation.

Finally back home, I set on a course of bedroom redemption, armed with a combination of skill, flair, and unyielding determination.

Some time later, Grace moaned, her face half-buried in the bedding, "Oh my God. That was...oh, just...oh...ah...geez."

An arm hung over the edge of the mattress. Her eyes were closed with her mouth slack, and her body still quivering as I settled beside her.

Unable to let her be, I licked a trail across the salty damp nape of her neck as her breathy gasps quickly evolved into the long deep breaths of sleep. I sank back onto my pillow, my hand lingering on her ass. She had moaned for me, yelled out loud for me, but for the first time, she hadn't cried out my name.

Not once.

NINE

"THAT WAS AN INTERESTING MEETING," said Jump.

"He just doesn't fucking get it," I muttered.

Boner shrugged. "Mick's got his own way of doing things, Dig."

"It ain't my way. He's got Creeper for a lap dog now, too." I slammed an open tool drawer shut. The repair shed was empty, except for us and Willie and Wreck.

"Everyone in power needs one, I guess," snorted Willie.

"You got to keep your cool, man. Don't think he hasn't noticed your attitude," said Boner.

"Trying. Trying real hard." I kicked at an old swivel desk chair, sending it flying across the room, the ripped vinyl of the seat shuddering. "Suddenly he's all about working with the Demon Seeds full time? We had agreed we'd had enough of their bullshit. That was done. Now he's doing a 180 on us? What the fuck? Mick keeps shifting shit, ever so little over time. Like we won't notice? Just go along with it? The Seeds are after one thing. And one day, before you know it, we ain't gonna be calling the shots on our own club any longer. And that is just fucking insane."

"Things ain't what they used to be around here," said Willie, a scowl on his face. Willie and Mick were the last remaining Vietnam vets of the Jacks. "And they're only gonna get worse if you don't stand up for what you believe in, for what's right."

"Do something about it," said Wreck, tearing off the bandana from his head before wiping his forehead with it. "That shit's not what this club is about."

"You should be the one holding that gavel, and you know it," I said.

"Nah, I shouldn't." Wreck threw a can of beer at Willie and, cracking another open, took a swig. "I hate this political shit. Hate it to the bone. I like making decisions for the better, though. It's a responsibility as a member of this club. The last major one I made was finding this property and settling our asses here after years of trashing through shacks and flophouse after flophouse. Dig, you don't hate the political shit. You get off on it. 'Cause when you feel strongly enough about something, you want to deal with it. You come up with plans, strategies. That's good. I respect that. I admire you for it."

Jump crossed his arms. "What? You don't care enough?"

I shot Jump a look. If there was anyone who cared too much about the club, it was Wreck.

"Of course I fucking care." Wreck tossed the bandana on his workbench, tilting his head at Jump. "But I don't have the desire or the patience to hassle and haggle and posture. I don't feel the need to compare my dick to the next guy's. In the end, most of these assholes at the top are out for the spotlight."

His hands settled on his waist. "Yes, I'm a part of a club, a voting member, but I'm a part of this club to keep the passing lane clear for my brothers when they need it, keep our formation on the highway tight, make sure we can deal with our own mechanical problems ninety-nine percent of the time. I'm proud to ride a machine that I built myself, and I'm damn proud of having like-minded brothers all over the country who would welcome me in and go out of their way to make sure I have that good time. That's my creed, and I would defend it with my life if it were threatened. And that's all I gotta say on the matter."

"Amen!" Willie raised his beer can at Wreck.

I grinned. "Comes time to vote, and it might be months from now, maybe longer, how you two gonna go? I need to hear it."

"Yeah, you can count on me," Wreck muttered.

"Yep." Willie nodded.

"We gotta be ready," Jump said. "Mick's been agreeing with you for a while now about keeping the Seeds at a safe distance, but obviously, he's been playing nice with Cowboy lately. Real nice. He's got himself a sweet in with 'em now."

"You did good, working shit out with the Seeds a while back, Dig." Wreck's eyes held mine. "But I've been around this track before with Mick. Once he's got the in and he starts playing nice, he'll slip in his own agenda and then present it to the club as a done deal." Wreck crushed the beer can between his hands and tossed it in the huge trash can.

"Wreck's right." Willie wiped the side of his mouth with his sleeve. "Watch for it. Only a matter of time."

"That can't happen," I said, lowering my voice. "Things are solid with the Broken Blades, and Flames of Hell threw me some business this morning."

"No shit," muttered Jump.

"Nothing big, but I'm gonna take it. First steps. But the minute Mick makes a move toward the Seeds, those bets are off. Flames of Hell does not work with just anybody, and they play straight up and do not forget wrongs. I figure this small business today is a test that we need to pass with flying colors. I'm gonna get the details and bring it to the table."

"You sure?" asked Jump.

"Very. It's got to be handled right. If they get a whiff that other shit is going on behind the scenes with the Demon Seeds, we can kiss this and any future deals, along with their backup in our region and beyond, good-bye." I rubbed my eyes and let out a breath. "That just can't happen."

My ass was on the line. I had set up this entire steel-cabled yet delicate network between us, our Colorado chapter, and Zed's Blades in Nebraska. I was hoping on working in the Flames of Hell. No matter what, I was going to have to pay homage to them somehow. Flames of Hell was the outlaw elder club of the Great Plains; their reach was national. I wasn't about to let my creative collaboration collapse into dust at the foot of Mick's ambitions with the Demon Seeds.

"I have no doubt." Wreck frowned, his fingers trailing down the dented tank of a '79 Lowrider he'd been working on. "I got work to do. Get the hell out of my shed."

"What do you want? I'll give you anything you want," my mother said. Her voice was high-pitched, panicked.

"You bet your ass you will, lady. Move it."

"Please, you're hurting me!"

"Shut the fuck up!"

My mouthful of cold pizza was stuck in my throat like bunched-up plastic. I swallowed the chunk down and darted to the kitchen door, hiding behind it. A tall man pulled Mom up by her hair, dragging her into the living room across the hall. My heart jammed in my chest, my lungs stalling. He threw her onto the floor where she collapsed on the beige carpet. A high-heeled shoe flew through the air, tumbling against my mother's favorite antique Chinese urn at the corner of the fireplace.

She wailed, and my throat closed at the horrible sound. Something queer spiraled in my chest and sent my heart hammering so hard it hurt. The huge beast of a man with shaggy dark hair and a stubbly face was wearing a dark blue workman's uniform.

Is he the plumber? An electrician?

"Don't move. Me and your little girl will be right back."

I moved barely an inch. He grabbed Eve by the arm and pulled on her. She was still wearing her cheerleader uniform from practice. She was as pale as porcelain and just as stiff, paralyzed, her eyes wide. He pulled on her, and for one moment, she faced me, her huge blue eyes locked on mine, her mouth hanging open. A blur of blonde hair flying, and she was gone, her shriek filling the space she'd once occupied. He tromped down the hallway, dragging her with him. Drawers and doors were flung open as he talked to himself, trudging through our house, polluting it with his presence.

I bolted into the living room and landed on my knees at my mother's side. "Mom?"

Wet brown eyes held mine. "Jake," she whispered hoarsely, barely moving a muscle.

Oh God, did he hurt her?

"Get out of the house, honey. He'll be back any second. You go. Go and call nine-one-one. Go! Now!" Her blouse was ripped, her chest was scratched, blood staining her white skin.

My head was fuzzy. My chest pressing on my lungs, I could no longer breathe right. I couldn't control anything.

I reached out to grab her arm. "Get up, and come with me. Please, Mommy!" My mouth was so dry that I could barely get the words out.

"Go, Jake. Go across the street to Mrs. Gordon and call the police. Now, Jake. Now!" The whites of her eyes exploded.

I jerked up to my feet. Heavy footsteps dragged down the stairs, scornful laughter bouncing off the walls. There was another voice joining his. I froze. Someone else was here, too.

My mother's perfectly manicured fingernails dug into my arm. "Jake, go!"

But there was no time to make it to the front door or even back to the kitchen. They would see me. I darted to the closet in the hallway and crammed *myself in between winter coats, old sneakers, rain boots, umbrellas, and a vacuum cleaner, leaving the door ajar several inches.*

I'm safe. My mother and sister will be safe.

They have to be.

"Nice house, huh? Knew it when I spotted them."

"You know how to pick 'em, man."

My head sank against the wall, the stifling darkness pressing in on me, but my mother's desperate short breaths, even Eve's silence, seemed louder in here. The gummy flavor of mozzarella cheese festered in my mouth, the sour taste of tomato sauce and the bitterness of the oregano lingering.

I flexed my gloved fingers over my handlebars and released the breath I hadn't realized I was holding on to. I blinked, my eyes stinging, but there was nothing in my eyes. It was all in my brain, spewing on endless replay. My eyes strained to focus through my goggles on the winding dark ribbon of road ahead of me, snaking through the Black Hills. I sucked in a breath and listened to the hum of my engine.

In. Out. In. Out.

Those twisted memories still crawled in front of my eyes at the most ridiculous times. Even though I had built my barriers years ago, those demons still scaled my walls, still threatening, still demanding my surrender. But I refused.

Keep breathing.

Under my gloves, my swollen fingers clenched the handlebars, throbbing against the hard silver of my rings. I welcomed that discomfort. It was a constant reminder I had tagged myself with years ago.

I relaxed my grip and concentrated on the dense thickets of towering evergreens blanketing the rolling peaks, the jagged granite formations, as we whipped past heaven-sent pockets of blue lakes.

In. Out. In. Out.

I sucked the quiet ease of the Hills into my lungs, into every pore. A weight adjusted at my back, pressing into me. *My Wildflower.*

My left hand stretched back, landed on her knee, and rested there. I let out another exhale, expelling any trace of those fucking voices in my head, forcing out that icy-cold dread that enjoyed shearing my veins. Grace's legs squeezed my sides, and that ease and warmth dipped through me.

I'd never really noticed the intensity of the tension before. It had been my status quo for as long as I could remember. With Grace, however, had come the difference—quality sleep, moments of deep relaxation. My inner brooding had become less ferocious. The inevitable migraine and that burning acidic sensation in my belly still came but not as often. My back straightened as I slid my hand down her jean-clad leg and then brought it back to the handlebar, a grin stealing across my lips. I knew how fucking lucky I was. Down to my bones, I knew.

Traffic up ahead made me cut my speed, my brothers gliding ahead of me, beside me, behind me. Butler raised a fist in the air at the road sign that Crazy Horse Memorial was just a few more miles away. Grace's hands squeezed my middle.

Every year, we would make it a point to have a run to a nighttime blast on that immense granite monument dedicated to the Lakota Sioux warrior chief, and I was looking forward to it tonight before we would go to the campsite outside of Mount Rushmore for a music festival. Grace had made sure that we all brought plenty of canned food, which was the price of admission to the monument complex, as a donation for a local food drive.

As a transplanted Dakotan, I was damn proud of the fact that from its beginning, this largest in-progress sculpture in the world—along with the Native American Cultural and Education Center at its base—had never been funded by the government but by private donations only. God only knew if the sculpture of the great warrior chief and his horse would ever be finished, but hell, it was still an extraordinary, improbable thing worthy of our admiration.

Luckily, we got there in time for Grace to see the Native American dancers doing their thing. We'd been here several times together, but each time, Grace would go to a show.

Jump, Clip, and Creeper only laughed.

"This is born and bred South Dakota and about as ethnic as we're going to get around these parts. What's not to love?"

"It's totally primal," Boner muttered at her side. "You shits just don't get it. Let's go, Sister."

I winked at her as Boner took her hand in his, and they tore off through the thick crowd toward the deck where the dancing was going on. The striking feather headdresses and costumes were visible from here, their bold colors shuffling in the wind. Heavy steps stomped out that harsh ancient rhythm and suspended over us in the crisp air.

"I'm gonna hit the john. You guys go on," I said as I walked off.

Butler nodded at me and joined the rest of the bros walking toward the café. I headed for the restroom and waited. I checked my watch again.

"Hey."

My head jerked up at the carved and scarred grim face of Finger, the VP of the Flames of Hell. He was here. He'd come. My spine straightened as I reached out my arm. He grabbed it, and we shook. Both his middle fingers were missing from his large hands. I held his piercing gaze. We headed back outside behind the building.

"Good to see you, man."

"Talk to me." His voice was low, throaty, barely audible over the scratchiness.

"I want the One-Eyed Jacks to work with the Flames on a few special projects. I have a new deal in the works with—"

He crossed his arms. "You need our protection."

Straight to the point. My kind of negotiation.

"That and your kind of cooperation. What I don't like is the Demon Seeds variety pushing everything out west, making me the little guy in the equation. I'm not a bug to be squashed."

A slight grin cracked Finger's mouth.

"I'm not into razzle-dazzle and big-name glory either, like some. That's not who the One-Eyed Jacks are. What I'm into is good business. Business that grows, has a future, and isn't at the mercy of the egos of a select few. The Jacks and the Flames could hammer out a deal within our region. Our Colorado chapter is doing well, and so are things here. I'm looking to beef up activity in North Dakota. There's a huge influx of people now with the oil-drilling going in full swing. I'd like to think we can do it on our own, but with the Demon Seeds and all sorts of other idiots hovering, it's not very likely."

"And what will you do for the Flames?"

"Bring the Broken Blades in on the deal. The three of us form a velvet network in our region through our territories. A network no outsider is going to want to fuck with and never will."

Finger took in a slow long breath through his nostrils. "We don't work with other clubs long-term, Dig. You know that."

"We like our independence, too, and want to keep it that way. Our clubs been coexisting peacefully for years, respecting each other from afar. Why can't our organizations work together if it's mutually beneficial? We could keep it simple. Offer you a specific service at a discount, of course. I've noticed a few glitches here and there between you and the Blades. I could help."

"I'll bring this to my prez."

"Thank you. I appreciate the meet, Finger."

His eyes narrowed at me.

Was he amused at my good manners? "See you at the campsite later on. Should be a good time."

We tagged fists.

"Should be." Finger gave me a curt nod and stalked off into the crowd.

I leaned my head back and took in a breath. Finger had shown up and had listened without cutting me off or refusing out of the gate. God only knew what that meant, but it was a start.

The Flames were notoriously unfriendly to outsiders. If they wanted something, they would take it. No deals, no compromises. Finger and I had bumped into each other a few times over the years, and I always took care with each instance. Jump hadn't wanted to know, hadn't wanted to have anything to do with the Flames. But my gut had told me that if the One-Eyed Jacks wanted a strong path, we were going to have to lay the tracks of alliances sooner or later.

I preferred to do it with like-minded brothers who had a fearsome reputation, not with a club like the Seeds who had leaders like Vig at the helm, willing to work with lunatics. Oh, I knew it was all relative, the level of lunacy, but with the Flames, the playing field would be more level than with Russians and Mexicans and fame-whores like Vig deejaying the party and making the rest of us dance to their eccentric playlists at gunpoint.

The grinding tension in my upper back finally eased as I caught up with the guys, the orange sun setting in the sky. Grace and Boner met up with us later, and we strolled through the museum. The women poked around in the gift shop, and we had a few beers.

We finally found a good spot to watch the night blast. The night blasts only happened twice a year, and as it was September, this one commemorated the death of Crazy Horse and the birth of the memorial's sculptor. The laser show up first was entertaining, but didn't do it for me the way the blast did.

An hour later, with Grace in my arms, her hands gripping my biceps as she pressed back against my chest, the show finally began. She flinched with the first popping blast that boomed in the cool night air, signaling the beginning. An orange ball of fire detonated and bloomed against the stone mountain and then another and another and another. The detonations went off with a slow deep cadence, a subtle tempo. Each and every bam was perfectly timed and balanced, lighting up the mountain, a ribbon of fire trimming its edges. Around and around, each blast exploded until it reached the top, leaving puffs of smoke in its wake.

The contours of Crazy Horse's ninety-foot-tall face erupted from the granite mountain, fierce in the flickering orange shadows, steadfast in the center of the fireballs. The pyrotechnics continued winding their way around the carved mountain with a heavy solemn grace, like a ceremonial drumbeat, an incantation, a ritual born of these very rocks. It was noble, and yes, it was primal, just like Boner had said about the dancing. In comparison, traditional fireworks were only superficial high jinks.

I glanced at my brothers, their arms slung around their women, their faces still, relaxed, touched with loose smiles. Not a care in the fucking world. You wouldn't see that often when they weren't riding, especially if they weren't high or drunk. Here in the darkness, under that infinite star-filled sky, an immense wedge of clouds shifting overhead, all was indeed right with the world in this split second of quiet. The last exploding drumbeat faded, and the final fleeting blaze was swallowed up by the darkness.

Applause and hollering burst up around us, and we joined in. Grace pressed her head back against my chest, smiling up at me. I leaned over and planted a kiss on her lips and then her nose, and she giggled softly.

"I love you," she whispered, her fingers pulling on my hair.

I cradled her beautiful face and slid my tongue between her parted lips, my one hand feeling up the swell of a breast through the mesh of her cotton sweater. All was right with my world.

Not for fucking long.

Once we made it to the campsite just south of Mount Rushmore, we set up our playground on a plateau on a high wooded hill where the burning leaves of autumn had already made their startling debut. It would be easy to secure and defend our spot if necessary. Always had to be ready for the unexpected. Every club parked their bikes like old-time frontier wagon trains, in a circle so that strangers would keep out. The vibrating drone of all those Harleys running together gave me a buzz.

A couple of clubs were here from Wyoming, as were the Broken Blades from Nebraska. Flames of Hell was here from Nebraska as well, commanding respect with their military-style riding formation, causing most of the common folk to stop what they were doing and watch. It was an intimidating ominous sight. I fucking loved it.

Other than my wanting to continue making inroads with Finger, the only thing on my mind and everyone else's was having enough whiskey, beer, weed and all sorts of chemical entertainment to get us through the night of partying and live music.

Within an hour, the party was in full session. The crowd was screaming for Alicia in her bid to be crowned wet T-shirt queen yet again. Of course they were. The woman had an impressive rack and an attitude to go along with it.

Two men splashed her with a large bucket full of icy water, and the crowd roared. She raised her hands high in the air, her eyes smiling, as her thin white T-shirt plastered to her body, her hard nipples blaring through the wet cotton fabric. Only a pair of red Western boots were visible on her bare thin legs.

She started dancing along with the music, jiggling her tits, with a porn-star grin on her face, swishing her long blonde hair. She squeezed her tits together and paraded up and down the stage, hips swinging, like an experienced super model. The crowd went wild. Alicia twisted around and leaned over, wiggling her small ass up in the air, the strap of a red thong barely visible. Jump, Clip, and Boner hollered for her, and Grace and I whistled loudly. She waved good-bye as the presenter introduced an overweight woman in jeans and a T-shirt who took center stage, waving and laughing her ass off at herself. Grace hopped up and down next to me, cheering her on.

I pulled her close. "Babe, your girl is gonna lose if you keep that shit up!"

"Alicia won't lose. No way. Anyway, this woman deserves our cheering more! Woo!"

I laughed as I brushed the side of her face with my lips.

"Next up, ladies and gentlemen, is—what did you say your name was, hon?" The emcee bent over a short blonde and then popped his mic up once again. "Right, folks. Next up is Lissa!"

I shifted my weight. On the other side of me, Butler and Clip cheered and howled like desperate wolves.

Lissa strode to the front of the stage and whipped up her American flag T-shirt, flashing her perfectly round, perfectly new stiff plastic tits to the roar of the crowd. She laughed and jumped up on her toes, clapping, as two men tipped the bucket of ice water over her. She whooped out loud and then launched straight into shaking those tits at us. Damn, her nipples were huge and hard as rocks under the wet fabric now slicked to her skin. She twisted her body around, hands planted on her waist, and flashed her very round ass at us, her tiny denim cutoffs a second skin, swinging her curvy hips left and right. My insides tightened along with the crowd's screams. She strutted up and down the small stage, her gaze suddenly spearing mine.

Don't fucking do it.

She winked and wagged her tongue at me. Smiling huge, she shimmied her body like a practiced stripper dedicating her moves to her special client. Her hands skimmed her sides and then dragged through her platinum hair as she gave her tits one last shake. The crowd went wild.

My jaw clenched as Grace stilled at my side. Alicia shot Grace a look from the stage. Jump thumped my back, whooping loudly. Boner groaned, his teeth dragging along his bottom lip.

Twenty excruciating minutes later, Alicia thankfully walked away the winner, a hundred bucks in her hand.

"I'm not giving my prize money to you this time. No way, asshole," she muttered to Jump.

He lifted her in his arms, rubbing her bare ass. "Come on, babe. I told ya, I'm gonna sock it away for that house-renovation thing Sister is putting together next month."

"You know he's just going to take it and fucking drink it," Grace snapped.

Jump glared at her. I touched her elbow and pulled her away from them. She flinched back from me, and my shoulders stiffened.

"Of course I know," said Alicia, her eyes gleaming.

He roared with laughter. She grinned and tightly wrapped her arms around him, kissing him, and then biting his lower lip. I shook my head and slung an arm around Grace's waist.

"Need a drink," she said, peeling out of my arm, striding off toward the kegs.

My old chain, which was hooked on her jeans, flicked against her hips with her every long stride.

"Grace!"

She ignored me as she marched off into the crowd.

"Alicia, do me a favor."

Her heavily made-up eyes flared at me. "Are you shitting me?"

"I don't want her out there on her own," I retorted, raising my voice. "And I think she'd rather talk to you than me right now."

Alicia only made a face at me.

Jump smacked her ass. "Go on."

"Hey, I'll go, man." Butler clamped a hand on my shoulder. "We'll bring back more beers." He jogged after Grace, catching up with her, and my jaw clenched.

His hand skimmed her arm for just a second. She jerked back and then relaxed, bumping her body into his, both of them laughing.

Fucker.

"Dig!"

Zed and four Broken Blades strode toward me. I had business to take care of.

As usual, this entertaining two-day getaway run was hardly about being an entertaining getaway. It was an opportunity for business to get done, and there was no way around it. Grace had accepted that, but she also hated it. Deals needed constant tending-to. Even the most sincere agreements often got unexpectedly violated with too much booze, pussy, and drugs in the mix.

"Brothers, good to see you."

We shook, tagged fists.

Zed's eyes settled on Alicia—or rather on Alicia's knockers. She took in a slow breath, her heavy tits rising and falling slightly, as she slid up to her old man. Zed, wearing a faded old Boot Hill Saloon T-shirt that stretched over his bulky muscles, congratulated Alicia on her win, and she rewarded him with a million-dollar smile. He rattled on about the weenie contest earlier and how we'd missed such a good time.

What a fucking shame. I did not want to see Grace roped into that shit again. The memory from a barbecue last year up in North Dakota of her standing up on the back of Jump's bike with Alicia driving, Grace's open mouth reaching for a jumbo hot dog hanging on a laundry line shot in front of my eyes.

"They had the chicks do it topless for the final round. You should have seen this one bitch go at it. What a mouth! She deep-throated those hot dogs right off the fuckin' line. Reminded me of the old days. Shit."

Yeah, that would be the way good ole days before AIDS had come ripping through the party that was our never-ending good time.

Alicia and Jump laughed, and I nodded, grinning like an idiot. I definitely wasn't drunk enough yet to appreciate a discussion about the finer points of a weenie suck.

Angel, Zed's old lady, sidled up next to him, wrapping her hand around a thick bicep. She smiled at me, but I immediately shifted my eyes away. Her gaze cut to Jump, who smiled back at her. She thoroughly studied him from head to toe as if he were the hot new boy in class. Jump only smirked, his eyes lingering on her black leather property vest. Barely held together in the front by a loose silver chain, it gaped open to reveal the curvy swells of her bare tits underneath. Angel glanced at Alicia, and the two of them grinned at each other.

I knew where that was heading.

Zed's heavy hand landed on my shoulder. "I like your weed best of all, Dig. You bring what I wanted?"

"Yeah, 'course I did." I took out the large bag of homegrown he'd ordered special from me.

He slapped a fifty-dollar bill in my hand and took the bag. Nothing like a discount. We continued on with small talk. My eyes darted over the crowd once more. No sign of Grace and fucking Butler.

"Who wants to smack some ass or suck a titty?"

Notch, the VP of the Broken Blades, a cigarette dangling from his mouth, pulled a young brunette behind him by the hand. The girl couldn't have been more than fifteen, sixteen years old at best. She had a lot of makeup on, a high ponytail, and wore a bikini with tennis shoes on her feet. A stuffed nylon fanny pack was slung over her hips. The girl smiled at us, her pupils pinned, her gaze drifting. She was high and not on weed alone.

"Whatcha doing, Notch? Giving your piece a tour?" Zed laughed.

Angel smirked, an eyebrow arching.

"'Course I am. This here's Peaches, y'all. You can either suck the peaches up front here"—he swiped at a breast—"or these ones back here!" He smacked the girl's ass hard, and she jolted forward, squealing. He grabbed on to a handful of her flesh, jiggling it. "Yeah, those are my favorite."

My scalp prickled as several Blades snickered and moved forward. The girl's eyes widened as two Blades grabbed at her behind, one smacking it, both of them muttering their approval. Another one palmed her tits, squeezing hard. The other then leaned over and bit her ass, and the girl cried out, her body jerking into the other Blade who was gripping a tit and licking it into a firm peak, his unusually long tongue fluttering grotesquely over her brown nipple. He sucked hard and loud as if her tit was a baby bottle, and he was a mighty thirsty toddler. The girl gasped. Laughter and grunts erupted.

The blood rushed to my head, swamping my brain with cold venom. "Don't you think she's a little young for this shit?" I bit out.

"Stupid sluts. They come looking for it," Angel muttered.

My eyes pierced hers. "Look at her. It's obvious she doesn't get what's going on."

"She's getting it all right!" Zed spit out, snorting loudly.

Notch shook with laughter. He held the dazed girl up by her upper arm and took a swig of his beer.

"And if she don't get it now, she will soon," said Angel, grinning.

More laughter, especially from the other Blade women. The girl struggled in Notch's hold, her face fell, and she let out a cry tinted with that helpless tone.

Bite marks and red blotches seeped over the girl's pale skin. Her lips trembled, her shoulders twitched.

My mouth dried, and I licked my lips. "She's too young."

Zed scowled at me. "This place is crawling with these pretty things, Dig. Go find your own, and fuss over her if you want."

My lungs slammed together, every muscle wired, coiling tightly. "I think you should let her go."

Notch's dark eyes narrowed at me. He pulled his rolled cigarette from between his lips. "Fuck off, man!"

"She's a kid. Not your pet. Look at her." My pulse throbbed in my neck.

The girl wavered in their hold as they pawed her, her limp smile fading, her eyebrows squishing together.

Notch's face contorted into an ugly scowl. "Oh, I'm looking at her all right. What am I? Fucking stupid?" Laughter rumbled all around me. "Hey, she found me, bud, wanting some fun. She don't know any better, not my problem."

One Blade yanked at the front of the girl's bikini bottom. "Whatcha got down there, huh?" He stuck his hand inside her bikini, down in between her legs, and hissed as she twisted in his rough hold. "Aw, it's sweet and fresh down here, y'all. Yeah." She struggled as he rubbed harder at her pussy. "You like that, don't you, bitch?"

The other men pressed in closer, their weight shifting, tongues dragging across their teeth, snorting, mumbling to themselves and each other. All their attention, all their raw hungry energy focused on the girl. The Blade bent over and stuck his tongue in her mouth. She stopped squirming, her hands dropping to her sides. Suddenly, her body went rigid, and she gasped as his hand dug up inside her.

Notch cackled. "Yeah, not every day you find 'em uncooked, huh?"

I saw red. I lunged at Notch, tearing him from the girl, pounding at his face, his chest. My fist slammed against bone, jaw, paunchy flesh, taut muscle. All of it a blur of sensation—pain, rage, the girl's face.

Her face.

"Dig! Dig! Stop it, man! What the fuck?" Wreck's voice boomed from somewhere behind me.

His large hands on my shoulders pulled at me, heaving me to the side. His dark blue eyes flared at me, inches from mine. "Get it together, bro. What the hell you doing?"

My body shook, and I shoved at Wreck, but his hands were fisted in my shirt, holding me tight against him, his silver eagle ring glaring at me. His mouth moved sharply, sounds bobbed around me.

"You can't do this. You cannot get in between that shit. You hear? You can't save 'em all, Dig. Let this one go."

My head shook on its own, and I stumbled in his grip. Couldn't form words or connect thoughts. Pain slammed through the left side of my head. My breath cut short.

A warm hand slid around my neck, rubbing the corded muscles there.

Boner's green eyes held mine. "Brother, he's right. Can't do this with the Blades right now. We need them in our corner. Let it go."

Let it go.

If only I could. Goddamn, if only I could. I'd be a saner man. A man who could sleep, eat, and unwind like any normal man. A man who could fall into his bed content at the end of the night. I wasn't that. I was corroded.

Boner and Wreck shoved me backward, away from the Blades, several of whom had their knives out, their hands at their guns. Their faces were red, their nostrils flaring.

"No harm done. We've all had a lot to drink, right?" Wreck's one hand stayed glued to my chest.

I stumbled back, shivering, gnarled.

"But that's what we're here for, isn't it?" Wreck said.

"What the fuck is wrong with you, man? You insane?" Zed's voice thundered. "Attacking us like that over a two-bit bitch and a little fun. Fuck no! Fuck no! You gonna tell us how to be? Fuck no!"

I forced air into my lungs, and it stung there. The pounding in my head surged through my skull. Hands grabbed at my shoulders, others at my torso, pulling me back, shoving me behind my brothers.

My eyes focused on movement. Jump had his hand on Zed's shoulder, Alicia standing between them. Zed's huge dark eyes pinned me to the spot. Several Flames of Hell members stood to his side. Finger, his chin tilted down, a scowl on his face, turned and strode away.

Fuck.

A blur of movement blocked my view. Two faces. Four hands holding cups of beer.

"Baby, what happened? You okay?"

My body recognized her warm voice before my brain did. My shoulders dropped, and my head sank.

Wreck leaned his face against Grace's, whispering in her ear, his hand tight around her arm.

"Have a drink, man." Butler put a tall plastic cup in my hand. "Go on."

I drank the lukewarm brew in one go. Sour piss water. I spit it out on the ground, wiping a hand across my lips, choking for air. Grace swept an arm around my middle, pulling me close, her hand stroking my back. My gaze lifted to her greenish-brown eyes, and the numbness retreated by degrees. The young girl whimpered as Notch and his brothers dragged her off.

Grace's warm hand cradled my face. "Baby, you okay?"

I nodded as I sat back on my chopper.

"Dig?"

"I'm just fine, goddamn it! Okay? Jesus." My unsteady hands scrubbed over my face.

She stood before me, not moving a muscle. "All right, honey," she murmured, her arms rising around my shoulders.

I adjusted Grace in between my legs, hooking an arm around her waist, my one hand sliding down her thigh. I buried my face in the side of her neck, inhaling her light flowery scent like it was the antidote to all my ills.

She lit a cigarette for me and put it between my lips, and I inhaled hard on it.

Let it go.

Grace rambled on about the friends she and Butler had bumped into when getting beer as she pushed my hair back, lightly stroking the sides of my face. I focused on the rhythm of her speech, the bounce of her voice, as she told her story.

"Dig, tell me about the VP of the Flames of Hell."

"Finger?"

"Yeah, we saw him. He's pretty damn scary with those scars on his face and his two middle fingers missing."

"As a prospect, he got caught in a war with a big national outlaw club out in the Midwest. They cut up his face with two letter Fs on each cheek and chopped off his middle fingers as a lesson for his club to stop giving them the finger and heel to what they wanted."

Her body tensed. "Oh God."

"What bands are playing tonight?" I asked, suddenly desperate to change the subject.

Grace told me the lineup. Eventually, her voice mellowed, slowed, matching the pace her hand stroked down my middle. We smoked some weed as the party rolled around us. Night fell. The humid air clung to our skin and our clothes, and then it lifted just a bit with the light breeze, which sifted through the tall trees against the star-filled black sky. Booming bass and screeching guitars rose in the distance.

"Do you want to go hear the band play?"

"No, baby. Sorry." I still felt like shit, and I also thought I should stay away from any Broken Blades for the rest of the night. Not to mention Finger. *Shit, shit, shit.* "My head is still...you go."

"No, I want to stay here with you," she whispered, her fingers sweeping through my hair.

At the edge of our group, Alicia, her eyes trained on Zed, sauntered over to the Blades president. Zed slung his arm around her neck, bringing her body against his. They walked off together in between the curve of bikes winding all over the field. Angel sank her fingers into Jump's long braid, tugging his head back, as he watched his old lady in the grips of another man. He immediately hooked a finger on the chain of her vest, yanking her close. Grinning, he leaned down and took her mouth in a rough deep kiss.

"Here we go again," I whispered against Grace's hair.

She giggled softly. "The funny thing is, Alicia doesn't get jealous when they do that. She likes swapping."

"They fucking do it often enough. Keeps shit *un*stale for them, I guess."

"You want to do it?" Grace asked.

I stared at her. "What?"

"I mean, Jump and Alicia have been together about as long as we have. Are things stale for you?"

I turned her around in my arms, my hand cupping her jaw. "Is that what you think?" My breath tightened in my chest.

She shrugged. "It's just that, everywhere we go, there are women you've had, ones I know of and plenty I don't. And there are more that just want to have you in any way they can." She raised her chin out of my hand. "It'd be easy for you to…"

"Yeah, it'd be very easy. But that doesn't mean that I'm going to do it."

She swallowed. "You used to be impulsive. You didn't have to think about it. Now—"

"Now I got you, and that's what I want." I filled my chest with air and gratitude. "You think I remember them all? That I recognize them even? A few, but definitely not all." My lips twitched.

"Oh, don't be an asshole." She poked me in the stomach. "No, I don't think you remember all of them or give two shits actually."

"I don't."

"But there are always new ones all the time."

"Always will be."

I tucked her hand in mine, and she stared at our clasped hands.

"What's goin' on, babe?" I asked.

"I just feel like you've been holding back from me."

"Babe, I just need some sleep."

"You always need sleep! What was that all about before? Why did you attack that Blade?"

"That girl he had with him, she's young. She's got no idea what she got herself into."

"Sometimes, they do, though, Dig. I stopped feeling sorry for them a while ago. Some of these girls put themselves out there and do stupid things just to get your attention, and you idiots eat it up."

"Well, I don't usually give a fuck either. It's their choice to do the shit they do. But she was different, really young and all doped up. Did you see the fanny pack she had on?"

Grace nodded.

"That's the Blades' goody bag for the evening. Some other little girl is probably carrying the rest of it. If the police come, they can't search minors like they can the rest of us. She's a safe bet for the stash."

"Multitasking brilliance. Fuckable, stashable...an endless source of entertainment for so many. All-purpose party female." Grace let out a dry laugh.

"Yeah." I nibbled on her neck. A fierce hunger for her flared through my every muscle at the sound of that laugh, my fingers digging into her flesh. "Fuck 'em. Come here, baby," I breathed against her skin. My tongue ravaged her mouth. "I like being impulsive with you."

"I guess everyone handles it differently, like Jump and Alicia do," she murmured in between kisses.

My hands ran up her sides, under her halter top, and palmed her full round breasts, which were free of a bra today. My thumbs rubbed over Grace's hard nipples, smooth pebbles under my touch, and she let out a soft moan. I kissed her again, but her eyes remained in the distance. I glanced in the direction of her gaze. Jump and Angel kissed and groped each other. Suddenly Jump threw her over his shoulder, and they disappeared down the hill.

"Jump could never keep it in his pants" I said. "He wants what he wants, and Alicia handles him her way." I pushed up Grace's shirt and released a breast to the cool night air.

Fuck, look at that. A handful of pert silk all for me. My cock stiffened against my jeans.

"I still can't figure out if she likes it or if she's just doing half the shit she does to keep up with him," I muttered as I bent over and lapped at her nipple with long swirls of my tongue.

She let out a cry, her fingers raking through my tangle of hair. "A little of both, I think. It's their thing."

"Yeah, whatever gets you hard."

Fuck, there was a lot more to being in a relationship than I'd realized. Attentions wandered, and passions drifted over time. Seemed natural. But they'd drift back if the core was quality, wouldn't they? Drifting raised dust clouds though. You could easily get lost in the haze, get distracted by the debris.

My fingers tugged on her tit until her nipple got pointy and stiff. I let out a groan. "Aw, baby, look at that."

She hissed in air as my head dipped to hers. I nudged at the seam of her lips with the tip of my tongue and stole inside her mouth. She sighed all around me, and a hush settled in my chest. My fingers brushed over her other nipple, and she jumped ever so slightly in my arms. She pressed against me, her bare tits crushed against my shirt, as my tongue slid against hers. My wildflower maiden of the woods held me tight, wanting more from me. Liquid heat seeped through my veins.

"You feel how hard I am for you, Wildflower?" I whispered in her ear, rocking my erection up between her legs.

My headache finally relented, and that pounding ache manifested itself in a new way. She hugged me tighter.

"I need you on my cock, baby."

Her hands slid around my back, under my shirt, slipped down the gap in my jeans, and over my bare ass. A shiver raced through me.

"Let's go to the bonfire, find a spot, and see who else is sharing and swapping," she whispered, letting out a soft giggle.

"Baby, you like watchin', don't you?" My hand kneaded her breast, tugging on it.

She let out a tiny gasp and nodded, biting her lip.

I laughed. "You wanna watch while I do you?"

"So articulate," she whispered against my lips.

I grinned. "I knew my college girl would appreciate that." My hands left her skin and reached out to the metal latch at the end of my bike, releasing the silky nylon of our sleeping bag into my grateful hands.

She moaned loudly, and her head rolled back.

I glanced up at her riding me, her bare skin lit in the shadows of the moon, her nipples wet and hard from my sucking, her fingertips digging into my shoulders.

Oh, yeah, almost there. Al-fucking-most.

I loved watching her come. I loved listening to her come. I loved that she thought it was funny that we were sliding all over the goddamn sleeping bag.

Grace fell off of me letting out a yelp. "Oh, shit. Damn it! Baby?"

We both erupted into laughter.

"Wait…" I repositioned under her and pulled her down over me. "Here. Oh…ah, yeah…" I thrust inside her again, groaning. "Yeah. Oh, yeah. Baby, that's it…shit."

The trees whispered over us as I jacked up into her harder, keeping her hips close. My thumb rubbed over her slick clit as she got lost in the frantic rhythm of her movements, taking me with her, higher, harder.

"So fucking wet…oh fuck, that's it…yeah…"

She let out a tight cry, her neck stiffening, her eyelids jerking open even wider. Her hands slid higher on my neck and tensed there, her mouth slackening just a tiny bit more. My balls tightened, ready to explode, but she had lost our rhythm again.

I lifted my eyes to hers, but her gaze was trained elsewhere, across the trees. Where we had watched Butler and Clip getting it on with a couple of giggling tourists, stripping them of their clothes and making them kiss each other, as I had fingered her, while rubbing myself up against her ass. Clip had then taken his chick a ways off, but Butler had pushed the other one to her knees and fucked her face. That was when I had turned Grace around and positioned her over my lap.

My brain cells scattered and tightened all at once.

I raised myself up a few degrees, my bleary eyes straining in the dark. There he was, Butler, with his eyes on my woman. My woman who had my cock inside her, making her come. Or maybe I wasn't making her come. Maybe her pussy was gripping my cock at the thought of Butler fucking her?

"Things stale for you?"

Obviously, I should have asked her the same goddamn question. Obviously, I hadn't wanted to hear the answer.

Heat simmered through my body, and my every muscle strained not to crush her in my hands. I took in a gust of air, and holding her tight, I bit into the side of her tit. She yelped, her attention disengaging. I licked over the bite and took the tip of her breast in my mouth, roughly sucking on it. Grace winced as I tucked her ass closer into me. She ground down once, twice more, and I fired off inside her, her body shuddering over me. I tightly gripped her ass in my hands, and she sank her face in my neck, murmuring, trembling.

Soft laughter, deep moans, and rhythmic grunting rolled through the woods.

"Look at me." My voice came out harsh, clipped.

Her lips brushed over my chin as she tried hard to focus on my eyes, her breathing erratic.

"Look at me, baby," I said through gritted teeth.

She raised her head, level with mine, and I wiped the hair from her face and off her shoulders.

"Yeah, that's it."

She adjusted herself over me, rising up, but I kept her down over my cock. Her eyebrows lifted, and I ran a thumb across her swollen lips.

"I love you, Wildflower."

She smiled in the shadows and kissed my thumb.

"You know that, right?"

She nodded. Her shoulders dropped, and she sighed, taking my thumb in her mouth.

Goddamn it. Nothing better than watching her do that.

Well, now, that isn't true, is it?

"Now you're gonna suck my cock, baby."

Her mouth stopped moving, releasing its suction on my thumb, as her fingers tightened their grip around my hand.

"You're gonna get me ready," I whispered, taking my hand back and squeezing her tits together.

She winced, her body stiffening.

"Then you're gonna get on your hands and knees, hold on to this tree over here, and I'm gonna fuck you hard till you shout my name out loud for everyone to hear. 'Cause you're my old lady, aren't you?"

She blinked, thoughts registering on her face. It broke my heart.

I didn't think Grace would ever act on her attraction to Butler, but something must be missing from us for her to be open to him. She was getting something from him that she wasn't getting from me. This could go from random crush to Something Else really quickly, and that was Not Going To Happen. Butler and Grace's little mutual fascination society was going to come to an end.

"You're full of shit. How's that?"

Miller's biting words, the accusatory tone in his voice from the last time I had seen him, flashed back at me. Yeah, I was full of shit. This applied to me and my little fascinations, too, didn't it? Got to clean that dust and debris away.

I took a swig from the bottle of Jack at my side and pulled her off my cock, none too gently, and she grunted. I kissed the side of her face, but she stiffened against me. Her heartbeat raced under my hand, her muscles tense.

"I'll take care of you baby, always do, don't I?" I whispered in her hair, my voice hoarse.

She only nodded her head, her breathing choppy. My fingertips dug into her ass cheek, and a sharp intake of breath escaped her lips.

"Get to it, woman."

She grabbed the Jack from beside me and tipped the bottle back, taking a long swig, her hard gaze never leaving mine. She licked her lips as she shoved the bottle in my chest.

Grace wedged herself between my legs, and she got to it.

TEN

THE REST OF THE RUN that had started at Crazy Horse continued on smoothly for me and Grace, but the tension my outburst had created between the Jacks and the Blades never broke. That truly sucked, and it also pissed Mick off.

A week after we'd gotten home, Grace had told me she wanted to get her first tattoo, my name somewhere on her body. I'd chosen her ass, of course. She chose the blue wildflowers I'd used when I deflowered her at the Hippie Hole. She held my hand the whole time Ronny inked her, my chest tightening, as our names slowly rose on her skin, linked in the leaves of that blue flower.

"Hey, you doing okay?" Alicia stood in the doorway.

"Yeah, it's good," Grace said. "Ronny is truly a master of his craft."

"Yes, he is." Alicia eyed Ronny as he cut his ink gun and adjusted his glasses.

His lips tipped up. "Hey, chickie. What's up?"

"Hi, hon. I want that tat you told me about for my back. The lotus flower with the dragonfly?"

Ronny's eyes narrowed at her. "Oh, yeah? You sure?"

Her blue eyes flared. "Definitely! I know Jump took off with that dancer, Monica, for the weekend. On a run to Hound, my ass."

She glared at me, and I only shook my head. She was right. Jump hadn't gone up to our North Dakota chapter. He was in Deadwood, holed up in some hotel with Monica, fucking and gambling all weekend. But I couldn't get in between a brother, his good time, and his old lady.

"Well, baby, I'll be done here in ten minutes." Ronny winked at her. "You pour yourself a drink in my office, and I'll be right there, and we'll take care of you," he said slowly.

Alicia's face softened. "Okay, honey. See you guys later." She spun out of the room, her heels tromping down the hallway of the shop.

Ronny glanced up at me, his glasses low on his nose. "I'm gonna give her that beautiful one-of-a-kind tat with my signature on it, and that son of a bitch is gonna know when he sees it on her bare back that when he was getting it from his lousy whore, his old lady was getting it from me. Each and every time. Years, I've been telling her to drop his ass, but she won't listen. That's all right, though. That fine woman comes to me to make it feel better. Who am I to say no?" The ink gun buzzed back on, and Ronny got back to work on Grace's wildflower, a smile on his face.

I had no doubt that Alicia wouldn't let any opportunity go by to put her long hair up and show off Ronny's colorful masterpiece wearing a bikini or tank top, not to mention insist Jump fuck her from behind as often as possible. Jump had fucked up, and his old lady had found a way to make sure he never forgot it.

Grace only grinned at me, and I kissed her hand.

Jump and I stood in the open doorway of the shed, motionless.

Butler laughed, holding Grace in his arms, spinning her around the shed, not a care in the goddamn world.

Carefree newlyweds about to cross the threshold.

Except Grace was grimacing, punching his shoulder.

"Please put me down, Butler!" she pushed against him, letting out a yelp. "Please!"

Something flashed behind my eyes. I blanked.

His hands on her.

Holding her.

The fucker was convinced he was God's gift to womankind.

I was done.

I ripped her off him, gripping her wrist. Grunts and shouting filled the shed, Boner and Wreck rushing behind me. Butler held his hands up in the air, bullshit tumbling out of his mouth.

"She's my old lady. She's mine, goddammit!" I smacked Grace's ass to make my point to him, to her, to everybody. "She's got my mark on her. I'm the one in her day and night. Not you, not ever."

"I wouldn't fuck your old lady, man. You're my brother. That shit just isn't done."

After a quick tribunal where Butler whined and moaned, Wreck got Grace out of the shed, and I beat Butler down, punching him senseless, finishing him off with my knife. But I didn't feel any better.

"Enough, man!" Boner pulled on my arm, ripping me off him. "Enough!"

I kicked the bastard's shaking bleeding body, and he rolled over on the concrete, a groan heaving from his bloodied mouth. I wiped his blood off my knife on his colors and stalked out of the shed to my bike. I swerved off the property, my Harley screaming.

I tore through the Badlands. The Lakota rightly named their sacred land *mako sica* or *land bad*. Grim and bleak to some, but to me the eroded canyons, steep slopes, and rugged peaks were a kind of Zen meditation which I needed, craved. *Right the fuck now.* I was no passerby here. I was a traveler being taken on, accepted, and I was respectful in turn of its irascible beauty. Beauty scratched and battered yet stunning and untouched, telling the story of time.

The road wound me through textured layers of colored rock—sandy brown, clay red, charcoal gray, dull black, muted yellows—their tones transforming in the shimmer of the sun. My heartbeat tuned into the rhythm of my engine, my muscles eased one after the other. My mind let go.

Let go.

The unrelenting stone pinnacles—whispering an ancient quiet, eerie and inexplicable—dominated the wide-open Dakota sky. It was my holy and my thrill. Riding through this blunt, magnificent desolation my whirring thoughts, my rage, my stifling memories released their sinister grip on me.

Two hours later, I ended up at Dead Ringer's. I slammed through the Old West-style panel doors and threw myself at the bar.

"The 15."

Biff only nodded at me and placed the bottle of Glenlivet 15 Year Old French Oak Reserve in front of me. I stared at the label, the familiar shape of the bottle.

My dad's favorite.

I poured the amber liquor in the glass Biff had slid toward me. The Doors were playing low over the speaker system. Biff fucking loved the Doors.

119

With my full glass, I saluted his prized poster of Morrison against the side wall. "Long live the king!" I mumbled and knocked back the whiskey, absorbing its warm, almost sweet smoothness down my throat.

"Hey you," a voice rose up next to me.

Spicy perfume clogged my nostrils. Carly, one of the older waitresses, stood at my side, a hand on her waist, a small smile painted on her red lips.

She lifted an eyebrow. "Must be bad this time."

I drained my glass. She raised the bottle and poured me another. I swallowed it down.

She eyed me. "Hmm. Real bad."

I glanced up at her. Her small brown eyes were heavily lined with black like some sort of Cleopatra, long dark hair down her curvy thirty-something body. She was sexy. She was offering. I could take her now, grab her by the arm, and fuck her in the restroom. Hell, we could probably get away with it right here against the bar. There was no one around. Bar wasn't even open yet. Biff had disappeared into the back. I stared at her tits rising and falling rapidly under her Aerosmith T-shirt. Jump and Clip had fucked her together a couple of years ago. She was always willing. I'd just never gotten around to it.

It would be so easy, so very easy, to take out my anger and desperation on Carly instead of Grace. But that would be incredibly stupid. That would push this whole mess into different territory, hellish territory.

My gaze darted up at my reflection in the mirror behind the bar. My eyes were haggard, my hair, barely touching my shoulders, was a stringy mess after my long ride.

"Your hair is the color of whiskey and wheat."

I drank.

Carly's fingers trailed under my sleeve. "Hey, Dig," she murmured.

I studied us in the mirror as she leaned in closer to me, her cigarette-laced breath mingling with mine, her lips parting.

A sour taste rose in my mouth. I didn't want to touch or smell or kiss anybody but Grace.

Grace. Grace. Grace.

I squeezed my eyes shut. Her face marred by a wash of shame earlier in the shed passed before me. Shame and guilt from the out-in-the-open acknowledgement before the whole club that whatever was going on between her and Butler wasn't right. Rage no longer had me in its grip, only frustration that Grace wouldn't open her mouth and just say no to Butler. And disappointment that I was less than her everything. A strange sense of longing I didn't understand lingered. The thought of losing her gripped my insides tighter and tighter like the slithering tentacles of a foul monster from the deep pit of my blackest fears.

Why don't I just break this whole thing off? Right now. Perfect out. The Ruby of my past nodded her head at me.

Carly's purple-painted fingernails dragged down my arm, a smile breaking over her full lips, and that heavy perfume wafting between us. The siren's call.

This would be the easy way.

I'd done it so many fucking times before. Cheating, indulging, shrugging my shoulders, skipping stones over the surface of that water, dipping in a toe. But that sort of easy had been over for me now for a very long time. And I didn't want an easy out now. Fuck, I didn't want an out at all.

My fingers clenched the glass.

I only wanted in deeper, more in than ever before.

Getting that tat on her the other day was a part of that, wasn't it? That wasn't just boyfriend-girlfriend shit, like my grandfather having given his college ring to my grandmother as a sign of going steady when they were first dating. Grace's tat was a promise, sinking deep in layers of skin and emotion, just like mine was. I laid my left arm down on the bar and tugged up my sleeve. The word stained over my skin pulsed on the inside of my wrist.

Wildflower

They weren't just a bunch of letters or some clever motto inked on my skin. I didn't get tats for the fuck of it. Tats were engraved on my body from experiences I bore in my soul. Right there, right over my throbbing vein, was a vow. A declaration that my reality was now rooted in her, in the same rocky soil, and nothing and no one was going to take that away. I wouldn't let that happen.

I shoved my cotton sleeve back down my arm. Sucking in air, I stared at myself in the mirror once more. I rubbed a hand across my jaw. The silver of my pistol ring glinted in the overhead light.

I will either find a way or make one.

I made my own choices in this sea of inconsequential madness. I remained at the tiller of my ship. And I had chosen Grace over and over again.

There was only her.

A hand slid over my shoulder.

Not Grace's hand.

A breathy voice rumbled in my ear.

Not Grace's.

"Nobody's here, Dig. We could—"

I dug my fingertips into her arm and slammed it onto the bar, pinning her there, her body twisting.

She let out a loud gasp. "Hey! What the—"

"Don't fucking touch me. Ever."

I released her, ripped bills out of my pocket, and tossed them on the bar as I shot up from my seat. I got out of there and got on my bike—my brain clear, my body tight—and I raced toward Meager.

I could only see Grace ahead of me on the road, not the signs or the traffic lights, not the cars and trucks giving me free rein. I stormed back into the club, into my room, and found her there, folded up on the floor, staring up at me. Awaiting judgment? Awaiting exile? She surrendered to my anger, and I made her strip. Her naked body was in my arms, arousing me, enraging me at the idea of her sharing it with anyone else. She was mine. I was her Sergeant at Arms.

I lectured her about not letting anyone take advantage of her. I gripped her jaw, taking in her every reaction to my gunfire of questions. "You want Butler? You liked having his eyes on you?" My blood screamed in my veins. "You curious? You've only been with me. You bored already?" I shook her in my hands as I went down the list. "You like him? You want to fuck him?"

"He's..."

The sting burned through me as I waited for her to spill her liquid fire.

"...I'm attracted to him. But I don't want his hands on me, his mouth on me. I don't want him inside me." She put her hand over mine on her tattoo. "Your mark means everything to me. You're everything to me, Dig. I wouldn't throw away what we have for...I love you."

The sting burned through me. I only wanted to punish her and smother myself in her at the same time. I pushed her hand aside and squeezed her ass. "Yeah? You sure about that?"

Her gaze hardened. "What about that bottle-blonde who keeps showing up everywhere we go?" she asked, her voice low, steady, her eyes flashing.

Lissa.

Oh, any of them. All of them. All the fucking Lissas in the world.

"You want her? You want inside that cheap ass? You want to fuck her? Come on, say it!" Her hazel eyes hardened and burned right through mine.

She was pissed, disappointed, like I was.

"Yeah, I do."

It was the goddamn truth, wasn't it?

I believed that telling the truth, no matter how uncomfortable it was, robbed a hidden thing of its power. Grace and I were usually frank with one another. Yet this time, we'd gotten stuck.

I gripped her hard, her eyes swimming in the same hurt, anger, sadness in which I too was spattered.

My forehead slid to hers. "She ain't got what you got, Grace. None of 'em do. And I need you, need you to fucking breathe. Everything comes back to you. Always you."

We fell into each other, and I repeated that chant with every hard thrust inside her.

We made a mess of my tiny room at the clubhouse, devouring each other for the better part of the afternoon and night. Each of us was punishing, each of us demanding, each of us begging. The damp sheets were half torn off the mattress, pillows dumped on the floor, both of us sweaty, exhausted, satisfied. My fingers outlined the fresh ink on her ass cheek. I sucked on the soft curve of her skin below the tattoo.

Goose bumps erupted on her skin. "Are you giving me a hickey on my butt?"

"I think I'll make a ring of hickeys around this leg, like a garter belt." I let out a laugh as my hand slid up her thigh, grazing her wet pussy.

Her flesh quivered under my touch, her breath caught. Yeah, she was sore.

"Shh." I sat up, raised her hips high, and gently licked her slit all the way up to her ass, the tip of my tongue teasing the puckered flesh, swirling round and round. My hand smoothed up her torso until it found a full breast.

Another moan. She raised her ass higher.

My fingers skimmed down her thighs to the backs of her knees, and I sat up. "Grab the ointment, babe."

Her hips squirmed at the loss of contact, and I grinned. She handed me the small tube from the table within her reach. I squirted it out over her tat and smoothed it over the flower, our initials glistening up at me.

My mark.

Our mark.

"Grace?"

"Hmm?"

"Let's get married."

She shuffled her head to the side, over her arms, one round eye staring at me. "What?"

"Let's get married."

She dropped to her side. "Why?"

I quirked an eyebrow and fell back on my haunches. "Why? That's great, baby."

"I mean, why now, all of a sudden?"

"Because I love you. Because you're my old lady, and I want to make that permanent."

"What's the rush?"

"Rush? Babe, we've been together for a year. You consider that rushing?" I tightened the cap on the tube and tossed it on the table. "Unless you don't—"

"It's all I've ever wanted." Her eyes searched mine.

"Okay. What's the problem?"

Her face softened. "There is no problem. I just didn't think—"

"Good. How's next week for you?"

She shrieked, "Next week?"

I laughed. "What? Did you want the diamond-ring, register-for-shit-we-can't-afford-and-we'll-never-use, lacy-white-dress, and limo-to-the-church thing?"

She let out a heavy exhale, her eyes wide.

"My wordy girl is speechless?" My fingers slid up the back of her thigh. "But if you want it…"

She hissed in air. "You're all I want."

My fingers stroked the flesh of her behind and slid between her legs, nestling in her wet heat. Her lids grew heavy. My cock twitched to life once more.

"Anyway, I hate lace," she murmured, her voice catching, her hips moving against my hand.

"I'm getting you a ring, though," I whispered as her flesh vibrated against my fingers.

"You'd better," she breathed.

I smirked against her damp skin. My fingers slid deeper. "There's my wildflower."

"Oh…Dig." Her legs gave way, and she let out a cry as I buried my tongue inside her again.

 ELEVEN

"BUTLER JUST TOOK OFF," Jump said.

"What?"

"You didn't expect him to stay after what you did to him?"

"He fucking deserved it."

"Yeah, he sure as shit did. But he's not sticking around. Mick gave him an option. He's heading to North Dakota to solidify things up there."

"Shit."

"Shit is right. We needed Butler. Now we lost his vote." Jump rubbed the back of his neck. "This is what getting your dick in a twist over a piece of pussy gets you."

My hand shot out to his throat. "Watch what you say, motherfucker!"

His eyes shone. "It's the truth! Bitches start getting in between brothers, there are big problems, no matter what. She may be your old lady and all, but she's no better than any of the rest of 'em. This is all on her."

"What the fuck is your problem, Jump? Butler's been on her ass for months. I was the idiot who didn't nip it sooner, too fucking busy to look after my own house."

"Yeah, whatever."

"No. No. Not one of your whatevers. She got attention from him, attention that should've been coming from me. Of course she liked it. He's a flirt, and he ain't rough on the eyes."

"Right."

"I don't have to explain my woman to you. You've known her since she was just past being a teenager, for Christ's sake. She didn't have a hell of a lot of experience with men before we got involved."

"Okay, yeah, Sister was always a good kid. I'll give you that. But pussy is pussy, and this shit don't change. Ever."

My throat tightened, a freight train blowing between my ears. "You need to shut the fuck up!"

"She blew this for you!" He shoved his finger toward me in the air. "For us. She did this! That's what I know."

"Fuck you, man. I don't piss on your old lady. Don't you dare piss on mine."

He only shook his head, his eyes darting down the dimly lit long hallway. "By sending Creeper up there with Butler, Mick's solidifying shit in the North Dakota chapter to his benefit. And after your little blowup with the Blades on that run, they're not so eager to play ball with you and me no more."

"I will fix it," I said, holding back a snarl.

"How?"

"First of all, Butler and Creeper are definitely not best friends. I'll give Butler some time to lick his wounds, and then I'll reach out to him."

"Yeah, Creeper is not your biggest fan either. You think he's gonna let that happen, you're dreamin'."

"We'll see. I'm a good negotiator."

"This is gonna take a lot of sit-and-wait now. Damn it. First things first, you start making nice with Zed. Find a way. Throw some free product his way. Do something. Make it right."

I nodded, running a hand through my hair, and yawned. "I'm gonna get back."

"Your dick hasn't fallen off yet?"

"Not yet, asshole."

It was our wedding day.

Grace and I had gone to Rapid, gotten registered, and gotten the marriage license. Matt, a guy I knew who did weddings at Sturgis during the rally every year, was going to officiate. I wore a new pair of black jeans, even a long-sleeved white shirt that Grace had ironed for me, and my colors. My formal look.

There was a beer truck along with the pig that we'd set to roasting hours ago. A fake wedding cake towered over the big table because inevitably some drunk asshole would knock it over. Alicia and Dee had overseen making the huge sheet cake, which stood ready in the fridge along with the other food.

All the chapters had shown for our wedding. Butler was there. He paid his respects and kept a safe distance from us. Grace's cranky best friend from high school, Tania, was there too. She didn't like the club much, but I knew she had Grace's back, had had it for a long time, so I'd put up with her, and she'd put up with me. It was a silent understanding between us, and it worked.

"Oh, bro, look at her," murmured Boner, his hand squeezing my shoulder.

Grace held a small bouquet of white roses in her hands. Mixed in the blooms were a few of those blue wildflowers she'd gone and picked early that morning. Her alarm had shrieked in our bedroom before the sun had even risen and she'd sprung from our bed. I'd tried to pull her back under the covers, but she'd pushed me away.

"No! No! Don't start. I have to have those flowers! I have to!"

I'd only buried my face back in my warm pillow and grinned.

My heart banged against my ribs at the sight of Wreck with one arm wrapped around my woman, both of them moving toward me together down the long proud aisle of the brothers' parked bikes. Everyone gunned their engines as Grace and Wreck swept past.

Oh my God, she was beautiful. *All for me.*

She wore a long white dress with a slit up the side and the new black boots I'd just bought her. That lacy black garter belt I picked out yesterday adorned the thigh showing through the slit. Hanging down her chest was a silver One-Eyed Jack's medallion with one diamond chip in the skull's eye and our names engraved on the back. I had given it to her the night before. She'd had a diamond chip inserted in the one eye of my club skull ring as a wedding gift.

I took in a breath of air and savored the pressure in my chest. I was so fucking grateful I'd managed to get here in one piece. Well, maybe a few pieces, but I was here. Here in this moment with Grace, Wreck, and Boner. And without having been maimed or having a prison term on my record. Not yet at least.

And those who weren't here?

I squashed the riot of faces and voices simmering in my insides and the what ifs and the could've-beens. Maybe I wouldn't have had Grace if…yeah, I would've been someone else entirely, somewhere else.

My eyes were riveted on my bride, letting the radiance beaming from her face steady me, root me to the very ground, to the dry wind blowing at our hair, to the tall grasses sweeping in the distance. To Wreck's face-splitting grin.

Boner, my best man, standing at my side, was unusually serious. His lips firmly sealed, his piercing green eyes bright. He and I had come so far together. From two straggly, dirty teenagers running away from a group home, looking to rip off before we were ripped off, scraping change together to eat or just plain stealing to survive. We'd learned about bikes together, made raw confessions to each other from under the cloak of darkness, only the rasp of our voices mingling in the night air on the side of a road.

Boner and I had cleaned up each other's messes, even now, and righted each other's wrongs over and over again. We were two patched-up souls who'd finally found purpose in brotherhood and a dented sense of peace here in a corner of South Dakota, and we'd accomplished that side by side.

Wreck planted a gentle kiss on Grace's cheek and then put her hand in mine. He covered them both with his. He let out a heavy breath as he squeezed all our hands together. He raised his gaze to mine, his sapphire-blue eyes shimmering. "She's your woman. Shield her heart and soul with your own." He turned to Grace. "He's your man, yours to support and keep strong when he's not able and when he doesn't know how. You take care of each other, and you do it right. Do it well. Be fair."

A shiver raced up my spine at the emotion in his voice, at Grace's sharp intake of breath. That was ceremony enough for me, but Matt waited behind me to make it all legal and official for the State of South Dakota. Wreck released our hands, his wet eyes holding mine, as he stepped back.

"You all ready for a wedding?" shouted Boner, his voice tight.

Everyone hollered. I wrapped my hands around Grace's neck and kissed her right then, official pronouncement be damned.

"How you feeling, baby?" I raised my voice over the blast of Pearl Jam's "Even Flow" booming through Pete's.

Grace glanced up at me as she rubbed down the bar top, her lips tipping up at the sight of me. "Oh, hey! What? What do you mean?"

"Being an old married lady."

She smirked. "Mr. Quillen, I'm a married old lady, not an old married lady."

I threw my head back and laughed, and she threw her spongy white towel at me.

"With you, Dig, I think I'm going to stay young forever."

"Sounds good to me."

I threw the towel back on the bar, and she grabbed it and folded it.

"What are you doing here, baby?" Grace asked. "I thought you had to be at Tingle tonight? You need something from me?"

Alicia and Dee laughed over their shot glasses at the crowded bar. Cruel Fate was setting up on the small stage in a corner of Pete's. They'd been on tour through the Midwest and down to Texas for months, and they had gained a solid following. This was their first gig in the Rapid City area, and they had chosen to play at Pete's to promote their first single. There was already a line outside.

I planted my hands over the bar. "Wrong question. I always need something from you."

She made a face at me. "Oh, brother. That, we know."

The women snickered over their kamikazes and clinked glasses.

"Asshole's jealous!" Alicia laughed.

I shot her a glare.

I turned around and leaned back against the bar, surveying the noisy crowd and the hustle of the staff. I didn't think Pete's had seen a crowd like this in decades. It had been a real hippie hangout in the '60s and '70s. Plenty of folk singers and country balladeers had stumbled through it along with a number of garage bands in recent years, but tonight, it would turn into a rock 'n' roll house of worship.

"I wanted to be here to show my support for my wife on her big score," I said. I also wanted to show my face and get the lay of the land. Two of our prospects were here running security outside.

Eric, the lead guitarist, and Teddy, the drummer, caught my eye and nodded at me, stiff half grins on their faces. I raised my chin and flicked two fingers in response.

Mission accomplished.

But I couldn't stay.

"Hey, Grace. That soda gun is sputtering again!" a bartender shouted.

"I'll be right there!"

I turned around. "I'll take a look at it."

"Oh, would you, babe? That would be great. Thank you." She leaned in and kissed me, her fingers tracing through the stubble on the side of my face. The driving guitars of "Hold On" flared over the speakers.

"What's with all the Pearl Jam tonight?" I asked.

She grinned. "That's in your honor."

"I don't get it."

"You're my Eddie Vedder, baby." She leaned in close to me once again, her hand curling into the trim of my jacket, as she fluttered her tongue against my lips. "I keep you close to me, even when you're not here."

"Oh, man." I laughed hard, my hand clasping her bicep. "That's the most romantic thing you've ever said to me, Grace Quillen."

"Aw, is it? It's true, honey. You're my fantasy and my reality all rolled into one fab man package."

"Does that mean you're gonna worship me like a dedicated groupie when you get home tonight? You'd better not fall asleep on me like last night, is all I have to say, or I'm going to have to rethink this whole managing-a-bar-full-time career choice of yours."

Her lips pulled in, her cheeks flushed, and her shoulders pushed back. "Oh, really? Let's see. You manage a strip club. Should I rethink that, babe?"

The women broke out into hard loud laughs.

"Have I ever fallen asleep on you, darlin'?"

"Oh, no. Really?" Dee laughed, her eyes wide. "Grace, that's not good, hon!"

"Ah! That only means his techniques need a makeover!" Alicia squawked as she slammed a hand on the bar.

Grace's eyes flared. "You can plan on a full worship session tonight. Just get moving on that Sprite gun, would you?"

The women whooped and cheered.

I threw my hands in the air. "Fuck this marriage shit, I swear."

Dee and Alicia raised yet another round of kamikaze shots toward Grace.

"Set your old man straight, Sister! That a girl!" Dee laughed.

Grace grinned from ear to ear and stuck her tongue out, wagging it at me. I winked at my wife as she strode past me and directed two of her waitresses on setting up several extra tables. I let out a breath. I wished I didn't have to go to work tonight. I wished I could stay here and have a plain ole good time with my wife, but business was business.

"Dig?"

Behind the bar the bartender pointed to the soda gun in question.

"Got it."

"Hey you." Lissa's voice piped up behind me stopping me in my tracks.

Ah, fuck.

"Hey."

"Haven't seen you around in a while."

"Busy. Got married. Life."

Glasses thunked on the bar top, and stools shuffled behind me.

Lissa's thin eyebrows shot up for a second. "Oh. Right."

"Yep."

She punched out a hip and smirked. "And how's that going?"

"Who wants to know?" Grace suddenly stood next to me, her eyes piercing Lissa.

"Uh…"

Grace inclined her head. "Who are you?" she slowly uttered the words.

Oh, she wasn't asking for Lissa's name. She was asking a deeper metaphysical question.

"I'm Li—"

"And I don't care," Grace practically snarled. "This is my old man. He's not yours. Not yours to touch, kiss, lick, suck, strip for, dance for, tease, nor does he light your fucking cigarettes or buy you a drink. Ever."

Lissa gulped, her eyes wide, her body motionless.

Grace turned to her BFFs standing on my other side. "Did I miss anything?"

"No, honey," Dee replied. "You got it."

Grace turned back to Lissa. "Did that register, or should I go over that one more time for you to make sure?"

Speechless.

I was transfixed.

"No, I-I got it," Lissa mumbled.

"Let me know if you need a review of these basics because you cross those lines again, any of them, in any fucking way, large or small—ever—there will be serious repercussions for you." Grace leaned into Lissa. Her stance wide, my old lady looked larger than life. My cock stiffened against my jeans.

"Did you hear that, bitch?" Alicia said, her face twisting in a nasty sneer.

"Got it. Yeah, sorry." Lissa glanced at me.

Mistake.

Grace leaned in closer, her hand gripping Lissa's chin. "Honey, I get that bikers do it for you. But this particular biker is mine. All fucking mine, head to toe, inside and out. So fuck off. Got that?"

Grace released Lissa's chin, and Lissa stiffly and slowly nodded her head, like a toy robot on its last charge of battery power.

"Yeah, that's right." Dee let out a throaty dark laugh.

"I know you've been trying your damnedest for the longest time. I've been watching. But he is not going to be tapping that ass of yours. Not ever. Get the fuck out of my bar, and do not come back." Grace was still, focused like a stealthy cobra calmly waiting in between strikes.

"Okay," Lissa mumbled as she teetered away.

"Tommy!" Grace shouted to one of her bouncers at the door.

Tommy's bodybuilding bulk towered before Lissa. His eyes flicked over her. "What's up, Mrs. Q?"

"This girl needs to be escorted out of our bar, and she's not allowed back in. Got that?"

"Got it." He glared at Lissa. "Let's go."

Lissa plodded after Tommy toward the front door.

"Lissa?" Two girls screeched and bustled at the other end of the bar. "Lissa? What's going on? Where are you going? Wait up!"

Grace scowled at me, her hands digging into her waist. "Sprite!" she snapped.

I nodded as I rounded the bar top. She grabbed my arm as I brushed past her.

Her big greenish eyes flashed at me. "My office when you're done, and be prepared to get on your knees."

My breath stalled.

I fixed that soda gun within four minutes, strode into the office, and made sure the door behind me was locked.

"Dammit, that mouth." Grace sighed, her fingertips brushing through my hair, her one booted leg sliding up my back.

I grinned as I gave her pussy a final long lick, my fingers sliding out from inside her. My eyes stayed on hers as her hips rose slightly, and she let out a soft moan. Her tang melted on my tongue, and something twinged in my chest.

"Grace?" I planted kisses along her damp, inner thigh.

"Hmm?"

"Baby, you happy?"

She sat up straighter on the desk, her brow furrowed. "Of course I'm happy."

Here I was, on my knees, eating out my old lady in the musty back room, which called itself an office, of a two-bit bar in a two-bit town. Piles of old photos and town notices, bills and orders, dotted the floor and the old desk under Grace's fantastic naked ass. She remained determined to make a dent in organizing the mess Pete had left behind. Here she was, in all her sensual bare beauty, splayed out on this battered metal desk just for me. Downright majestic. I fucking loved it.

"And you just made me even happier." She giggled. "That was extremely satisfying, Mr. Quillen."

"Glad to hear it. We like a satisfied customer in these parts, ma'am." I laughed, standing up, adjusting the painful erection in my jeans.

I exhaled as my fingers went back to trailing over her hot skin, teasing her drenched pussy one last time, and then tracing wet circles over her tummy. She sighed and stretched out on the desk once more.

We'd managed it, hadn't we? Made a new life, here in our little spot in the world, me and Grace. We had pledged loyalty, commitment, and truth to each other just a few months before. We regularly worshiped each other's bodies, shared our good times and our sorrows—well, not all of them, not mine. That wasn't her burden to bear, though, and it didn't matter right now.

My hand stretched out over the warm skin of her stomach. Grace's body was our temple, our bit of holy, where both of us connected and exploded together in some sort of glorious, furious symphony. Her skin was still flush with the pleasure I'd just given her, and my mark stained the skin on her sweet ass. Forever.

Her fingers traced lines up and down my arm, and a shiver raced over my flesh.

"What is it, honey? You okay?"

I stared at her. "I—"

Her eyes darted up at the large commercial clock on the wall, and her fingers gripped my arms. "Shoot, I need to get back out there and see what's going on with the band!" Her body jerked up on the desk. "Baby, I promise you big payback tonight when I get home, no matter what."

I stroked her side. "I don't need payback from you."

She only grinned and swung her long necklace around from her back where it had fallen during our stolen little sexcapade. The silver One-Eyed Jacks medallion now settled over her middle. I flipped over the shiny pendant, my fingertip smoothing over the engraved words on the back.

DIG & GRACE

Yeah.

This two-bit bar, this worn-out town, just a speck in the middle of a lonely grassy prairie with the stony hills beyond, the small fix-it-yourself house I'd bought for us—that was all ours, our world, our high life. It wasn't name-brand, shiny, or white picket fences, but none of that mattered. As long as we were together, it was good, it was clean, it was ours.

She lifted up.

"Wait," I said, my two hands pressing down over her middle.

She blinked up at me, propping herself back on her elbows once again. "Dig, I need to get dressed and get back to work."

My lips tipped up as I reached down on the floor and grabbed her panties. She held out a hand for them, but I raised an eyebrow and shook my head. I guided the strip of blue satin carefully over each boot and then slid it up her legs. She raised her hips and let out a sigh, as I kissed her pussy one last time. I brought the panty up, smoothing the waistband over her hips.

My hands stroked her middle. "I want to make that baby you were talking about a while back."

"What?" Her abs tensed under my touch.

"Let's do it."

Her eyes searched mine. "Really?"

"Yeah."

Her face tightened, her lips pursed.

"What is it? I thought you'd be jumping up and down."

"I am." She sat up on the desk. "It's just that...well, now that I'm working full-time, I think I'd rather wait on the baby thing a little while longer, so I can throw myself into this for a bit more. Is that okay?"

I grinned. "Can't do both, huh?"

Her face fell. "Not the way I'd like to. With the hours we both work and how we work? I don't think so, Dig. Could we give it another year or two? Is that okay?"

A piece of my heart shrank. "Sure. You're still a fresh young thing." My hands stroked her thighs.

"No, really. Is that okay?" Her fingers curled in my belt.

"Yeah, baby. That's fine. You just let Mr. Peckerwood here know when he's needed, is all."

We both laughed as her hand rubbed over the stiff bulge between my legs.

"Aw, don't listen to him, Mr. Peckerwood. You're always needed."

She kissed the bulk tenting in my jeans as I cupped a breast, letting out a deep sigh.

"I love you," she whispered against my middle, her arms tightening around me.

My hands sifted through her wavy long hair, and I planted a quick kiss on the top of her head. "Love you, too."

Grace released me and hopped down from the desk. She peeled two receipts and a bill from the back of her thigh, making a funny face as she smacked them back on the desk. "Geez."

She smoothed her skirt down over her gorgeous legs. I would never get tired of that sight. No, that anxious teenager I'd first seen over a bonfire at a high school keg party a century ago was now a confident, sexy woman. My woman.

I grinned at my old lady. "I've got to get to work myself. Dready will be here at four on the dot to get you home. He's not here by then, you call him, and then you call me."

"Okay." She smooched my cheek and then rubbed her face against the damp scruff on my chin. "Hmm...I like my perfume on you, especially when you're going to Tingle for the night." She let out a little dry laugh.

"I like it, too." I kissed her one last time.

Smiling, Grace pushed back from me and unlocked the office door. Her short skirt twitching over her ass, she strode out into the wild Meager night, live music blaring.

TWELVE

"Sister, it's going to look sexy! Come on, my treat."

"Caitlyn, what the hell are you up to with my old lady?"

Butler's old lady only smiled that shit-eating grin of hers. It had been just over three years since Butler had left Meager, and Grace and I had gotten married. Years of relative quiet and good times. Butler and I had finally made peace, and we had been able to meet, make plans, do business. Since Butler had hooked up with Caitlyn a couple of years back, things had been even smoother between us. In fact, Grace and I would go up to the club's North Dakota chapter in Hound once in a while and spend time with them since our women actually enjoyed each other's company. That was what we were doing this weekend.

"It's a surprise for you, Dig. One of the first of many, I'm hoping." Caitlyn's blue eyes cut back to Grace. "Right? You wouldn't want to disappoint your old man now, would you?" She made a face.

Grace burst out laughing. "Stop! I told you I'd think about it."

Caitlyn slid her arm through Grace's. "Time's up. Think about it at the tattoo shop. Let's go."

Butler only grinned and handed Caitlyn their car keys, and they kissed once, twice, his hand fisting in her long blonde hair.

"See you boys later." Caitlyn waved at us.

I planted a kiss on Grace's mouth and tugged at the sides of her trapper hat. "You getting another tattoo without me?"

"No." She rolled her eyes. "Caitlyn has other plans for me today."

I smirked and squeezed her waist. Some kind of body piercing no doubt. Grace, however, was not a fan. "Whatever it is, honey, I will suck on it and make it better later."

"Oh, goody," she said. She brushed my mouth with hers.

"Don't be too long, you two. We're gonna be heading out to the cabin by four," Butler said, glancing at me.

"We know, babe. We'll be here," said Caitlyn.

She and Grace crunched over the snow on the ground and climbed into Caitlyn's SUV. They took off down the gravel road leading out of the North Dakota clubhouse, which was now lined with high mounds of shoveled ice and snow.

The fact remained that I needed Butler in my corner. I was now VP of the Meager chapter with Jump as Sergeant at Arms, and Judge was now the President with Butler the VP of the One-Eyed Jacks of Hound, North Dakota. Butler had risen the ranks over the years, having proven his quick thinking and smarts time and time again, unlike Creeper, who seemed to hang in the background like a rat burrowed under the brush.

Creeper gestured at me with his cigarette. "Hey, got a question for you before we head inside. How do we know what kinda cut you're keeping from that deal with the Blades?"

"What's that supposed to mean?"

Zed had finally accepted one of my many overtures over the years, and last month we had worked together on a complicated shipment and delivery through three states in the Midwest to our mutual benefit.

"It's just that you're out there, doing business on your own. A lot of business."

"Any business I do is club business. Should I bring an accountant with me on the road next time, have him print out reports, and fax them to you to keep you informed?"

Creeper only eyed me through the smoke trail that he'd exhaled.

"Dig's always come through for this club, man," said Butler. "What the fuck?"

"Just saying. He's built up quite a reputation out there for a quality product, but only he gets to move it, nobody else."

Butler smirked. "What business *you* running for this club?"

"Come on, B. I work at the chop shop, same as everybody else."

Butler shook his head. "That's what I mean. No creativity, no business-enterprising brain cell in your body. Stop complaining like a jealous bitch because Dig's wearing fancier clothes than you are or some shit."

Creeper only took a deep drag on his cigarette and then swiped his tongue across his teeth.

Butler crossed his arms and leaned into him. "I get that you were a big shit out there in Desert Storm, man. But that was a while ago, and this isn't Kuwait. This is fucking North Dakota.

This ain't the U.S. Army either. This is the One-Eyed Jacks, and you chose to be here. Here, you're under our president's command and then mine. This club makes decisions together, but I make sure those decisions get carried out. You need to pay your dues. They're late. Again."

Creeper sneered and raised his hands in the air, his fingernails edged in dirt, his fingertips yellowed. "Hey, I was just makin' a suggestion, man."

"Sure you were. Great." Butler's aqua-blue eyes glinted like stones in the heat of the sun.

"You're just never willing to listen, is all I'm saying."

"Oh, I listened all right," Butler said on a hiss. "I didn't like what I heard. Get your dues in."

Creeper shook his head, his nicotine-stained teeth showing in his warped grin. "That's nice. The two of you defending each other. You wanna be prez of your club so bad, you can taste it, can't you, Dig?"

I snapped my head at him. "My only objective in my club is to run the club the right away."

"Objective, huh? Yeah, see? That's what I'm saying. You ain't the one holding the gavel, man. And I don't think you're showing too much respect for the man who is."

"Mick has my respect. He knows that. I'm here, supporting his decisions, his directions. You, however, do not have my respect. At fucking all. But you already knew that."

Creeper snorted. "Not very brotherly, man."

"You're right. You know, I'm not feeling the loyalty from you that a brother deserves. A club survives on that loyalty, that commitment. That's what binds us together. This isn't no free-for-all party, like some seem to think it is."

Creeper nodded his head and flicked his cigarette butt outside the open screen door of the clubhouse. "Nothing's for free. That's for damn sure." He turned away and sauntered inside.

Butler frowned. "Man, you gotta watch it with him."

I turned on my heel. "You serious?"

"He's got Mick's ear, Dig. Don't think I don't know he's feeding Mick everything that goes on around here. Judge ain't happy about it either, but there ain't much we can do about it at the moment. Things are getting tricky. Anyway, you want Mick to start looking at you differently, suspecting you of shit?"

"He already is."

"Yeah, and I'm sure Creeper will be reporting all this back to him. You gotta tone it down. Not good for any of us." Butler's gaze shifted around the small yard. "Look, I got your back, man. Always will. You brought me into the One-Eyed Jacks. That means a lot to me despite—"

My legs stiffened, and I held up my hand. "B, I need you with me on this. I ain't looking to score votes. I just want us to make the right decisions. Flames of Hell is upping their production and distribution. We have to get on their good side. Show them we don't want to play with the Seeds or Mexicans or Russians or whatever the fuck. We need them. Things have been better with Zed and the Blades, but still not a hundred percent. They know how to hold a fucking grudge, like a sour mother-in-law."

"Shit, you're so damn lucky that you don't have one of those," Butler muttered. "Look, I'm totally on board with working with the Blades and making nice with the Flames of Hell, but I don't know if all our brothers are. Flames of Hell has not been too friendly to us in the past."

I shrugged. "They've got sharp boundaries. That's a good thing. It's time to get in the sandbox with them."

"Well at least Finger's talking to you again."

"Exactly. My outburst cost us big. Years worth. But we've been respectful, and they've been showing their appreciation little by little. That's how they operate. No grand gestures. Like the Demon Seeds. I'm telling you, B, if we don't get our shit together now, the Mexicans are gonna march right in and call the shots in a few years, and then they'll take it all. If I don't like what I'm seeing from Mick or from Creeper, I'm gonna open my mouth. Our club needs to prepare."

"You gotta watch your step. That's all I'm saying. Just a whiff of backstabbing around here could land you in the shit pile."

"Yeah, don't I know it?"

We both stood there in silence in the empty yard, staring at the open stretch of prairie now covered with thick drifts of snow, an icy wind wafting over it creating an otherworldly vapor.

But Lady Luck smiled down on me a few weeks later when, one night, my solution to Creeper and Mick strolled through the doors of Tingle and handed me the key on a silver platter.

"Hey, it's the ball-and-chain parade, bro." Clip hollered over the boom of a Toni Braxton song.

I made a face at Clip and turned in the direction he was facing. Grace trailed behind a pretty damn drunk Alicia, who was stalking through Tingle, undoubtedly on another hunt for her old man. I jerked my head at Clip, and he sprang toward the office where Jump was fucking the new dancer.

Tonight was supposed to be boys' night out while the ladies had spent all afternoon shopping and doing girl crap before going out for dinner and drinks. Grace grinned as she kissed me, and that taste of us rushed through my mouth, filling my insides with a slow heat, a base concoction of ease and need, comfort and raw lust.

I licked my lips. I'd brought this girl from her mother's kitchen, her pastel-colored bedroom. And where had we ended up? At a seedy strip joint. But here she was, smiling at me still, her fingers digging into my waist, eyeing the naked dancers grinding around us without any traces of alarm or too much irritation. I wiped a strand of hair from her cheek as she wrapped her arms around my waist.

Alicia stormed toward the office. Clip and a dancer lunged at her. I waved over one of my new prospects to join in the fun as I pulled in a deep breath. Alicia started shouting as she slapped and punched Clip in the chest while the dancer held on to her, trying to talk her down. Grace's weight pressed into me. I planted a kiss on her temple and drew her closer into my arms, my chin rubbing the top of her head.

An image of my dad sniffing that first glass of expensive wine the sommelier poured for him whenever we went out to dinner snaked in front of my eyes. That particular slow, confident smile would deepen his face as he would glance at Mom, and she'd smile back. I'd never understood how smelling a drink could offer him so much pleasure and satisfaction or what that confident, knowing smile they shared was all about, but I used to wait for it each and every time.

Now, over twenty years later, I finally fucking knew that kind of intricate satisfaction deep down in my heart right here, right now in the middle of a seamy strip club. The edges of my lips curled up. I knew Grace trusted me, even here at Tingle, surrounded by naked women dangling around me with a variety of illegal sexual acts going on throughout the building. My chosen profession was under the radar and over the edge of the law. The improbability that was my reality was fucking exhilarating.

Jump finally emerged from the office, gripping old lady's arms, shaking her. No, he would never understand.

I kissed Grace. She smirked at me, misinterpreting my surge of affection as my being horny and teased me about the dancers, my wedding ring, my dick, and I teased her right back about my wedding ring being around my dick.

I clasped her hand over my heart. "This little muscle right in here, wiseass. It's got your name burned on it, and you know it." I kissed her, softly this time, and glanced down at her. *Fuck.*

Tonight, she had paired a short skirt with new high-heeled black boots. Sultry. So damn sexy. Yeah, I wanted to drink from this bottle of wine. *Right the fuck now.* Some happy-go-lucky Will Smith rap tune flared over the speakers, urging on my enthusiasm. Clutching her hand in mine, I dragged her through the club.

"Dig?"

We charged up the stairs and barged into an empty VIP room as a dancer was leading in a client. Wasn't the first time. Would definitely not be the last.

We'd barely gotten started when Grace threw me with a piece of lacy lingerie hiding under the clothes that she was slowly stripping off for me.

Oh, my wildflower.

She didn't care for lace, but she knew I loved it.

Grace straddled me, and my cock surged against my jeans. I filled my hands with her, pressing her warm body closer against mine, as I inhaled her warm flowery scent and smiled.

Fine wine.

"I'm going to stop taking the pill tomorrow, like we talked about. I want us to start making a baby."

My chest tightened. "You do?"

She nodded at me, a small smile playing on her lips, her fingers rubbing the back of my neck.

My pulse sped.

"I want this. Let's do it," she whispered.

Yes.

Yes.

It had been several years since we first talked about it, and I was ready. So fucking ready. The horizon was pretty damn clear. Nothing we couldn't handle. We'd settled into our life together.

We kissed, our tongues flicking and diving against each other, her hands groping me. I slowly finger-fucked her, and with my free hand, I stroked her boot-covered leg at my side, my fingers sliding over the silky leather. The blood rushed to my head as I watched her groan and grind over me, my cock pounding mercilessly. She begged me to talk dirty to her, and I gladly complied. Her lips parted, her breathing got urgent. My chest thumped with a million different sensations.

Suddenly, the urge to fuck her fizzled as I thought about possibly making our kid on this red vinyl seat that had seen years of action that I didn't really want to think about, in this closet of a room of the Tingle. Yet here was Grace—unruffled, unbothered—wanting me any way she could have me.

"I'm not fucking you here."

"What?"

She teased me about my lack of knowledge about the pill, about not wanting to have sex in here. Grace's fingers worked my belt buckle, the metal scraping and clanging. We laughed, and I buried my face in her throat, in that silky skin.

A gunshot exploded and then another. She froze, and I heaved her from my lap.

"Get dressed." I buckled back up, my dick painfully protesting.

I took my gun out and slowly opened the door as Grace crouched behind me. My eyes strained, peering down on the club floor over the banister.

Jump and Boner held a Demon Seed by the arms.

"Get off me, man!" The Seed's rough voice boomed through the club.

Grace squeezed my arm. "I love you," she whispered.

I glanced at my wife. Her hand gripped my arm and her jaw clenched in her attempt to take this shit in stride.

She knew I had to go.

"Love you, too, babe." My lips brushed hers. "You keep that thing on for when I get home later, yeah?"

She only grinned at me, and with that piece of light in my chest, I headed down the stairs to the bullshit that never ceased to rear its ugly head around me.

"Get our women home," I said to Clip.

"Sure thing." He charged off.

My shoulders pushed back, I charged toward the Seed. "What's the problem, man?" I leaned into him. "Why are you shitting in my club?"

He squirmed in my brothers' grips. "Got something you might wanna hear—about one of your brothers."

I stilled and shot a look at Jump, who nodded, his lips twitching.

I turned to one of my bouncers, who hovered at my side. "Clean this mess up."

The busboys and the waitresses scrambled to right the overturned chairs and table, sweep away the broken glass.

"Office—now."

Jump and Boner led the Seed away.

I turned to the jostling crowd with a tight grin on my face. "Round of drinks for everyone!"

The music blared again, a few cheers rose up, and people shifted back to their tables once more.

I followed the boys to the office in the back, and a used full condom greeted us on the floor. I shot Jump a glare as I shoved the Seed down on the couch. "Fucking clean up your shit, man!"

Jump grumbled as he scooped up the condom and tossed it in the trash.

"Did you leave her panties behind, too?" The Seed laughed as I scanned his colors for a name. *Hobbit.*

The guy was way the hell over six feet tall, and his feet were fucking huge.

"What you doin' here, asshole? Got no strip clubs up in Montana?" Jump asked.

"Yeah, sure we do. But I like this girl you all got here. Crystal. Fucking beautiful name, right?" His head rolled back, and a dazed smile swept over his lips. "Fucking amazing ass."

"Crystal had to leave early," I said. "Did you get to see her dance?"

"Yeah, I did. Wait, I think I did. Fuck, not sure." He laughed again.

"Why did you shoot your gun off?"

"A One-Eye Jack was in my face!"

"This is a One-Eyed Jacks's business, asshole," Jump said.

"Yeah, asshole. Aw, Crystal's got this amazing asshole. I fit right in."

"Congrats. That's fucking great." Jump rolled his eyes as he clapped a hand on Hobbit's shoulder. "Outside, you said you had something for us."

"Yeah, I do. About a brother up north."

"Who?" I asked, glancing at Jump.

"Creeper. He's been hanging with us. Now *he's* a real asshole. Fuckin' smells like ass half the time."

"Hanging with you, huh?" I asked.

"Yeah, hanging, partying." Hobbit held my gaze. "He took my girl."

Jump leaned against the desk. "Really? You got a girl?"

"Yeah. Jade. Creeper took her back to North Dakota with him. Motherfucker."

"Oh, that sucks, huh?" Jump grinned at me. "How did that happen?"

"Cowboy gave him Jade as a thank-you gift. He did it to piss me off, too, warn me. Fuckers were enjoyin' themselves."

"Why would your prez do that?"

"Me and Vig go way back. He's been Nomad out west for a while. Cowboy sent him. I'm sure he sent Vig on purpose. But I got my brother's back, ya know?"

"That's the way it ought to be," I agreed, shifting my weight.

His jaw jutted out, and he held my gaze. "Right. We're nothin' without our brothers." He shifted in his seat. "I came down here to find his girl. Although, gotta say, don't know how he gets any bitches to fuck him."

Jump laughed. "Creeper's got lots of charm to make up for his looks. And a huge cock."

Hobbit made a face.

"You came down and found Crystal, huh?" I asked.

His head snapped toward me. "Yeah, that's right. He's talked about her a few times, how she was his, the hottest dancer at Tingle, blah, blah, blah. I found her here last night. Spent money on her. We had a good time. She promised she'd be here tonight, but she ain't." He shook his head. "Not happy."

"Yeah, she's got a kid. He got sick. She left early. What are you gonna do, right? Don't take it personally, man."

"You're lying to me."

"No, I'm not. She was scheduled to work all night." Jump patted his shoulder. "You were looking for a bit of payback, huh? Maybe we can help."

Hobbit's eyelids sank and then opened again. His red eyes darted around the room. "Oh, yeah?"

"I'm a little confused, Hobbit. What's Creeper doing with the Demon Seeds?" I asked. "He come over to play checkers with you guys? A little game of softball maybe?"

"Nah, he don't hang with us. He's always talking to Cowboy, talking to Cowboy." Hobbit's gaze drifted.

Jump's eyebrows jammed together. "To your prez?"

"Yeah, fucking One-Eyed dick, Creeper."

"Maybe they're just talking about football or the weather report, huh?"

"Fuck no. They talk business, always the two of 'em alone, behind closed doors."

"We could help you ease your pain with Creeper," I said.

"Yeah?" Hobbit's head bobbed and then suddenly straightened. "That's good."

"All right then." Jump licked his bottom lip.

I crouched down before Hobbit, my eyes level with his. "You find out what him and Cowboy are talking about, you feed it to us, and we'll make sure Creeper gets what he deserves. A brother crossin' over ain't no brother at all."

Hobbit focused his glassy eyes on mine. "That's shit, is what that is."

"That's right," said Jump. "How about we give Crystal a call and see if she can come by just for you? In the meantime, another girl will keep you company till she gets here, huh? On the house, man. We'll put you up for the night, too. How's that sound?"

Hobbit's face perked up.

Jump called Crystal and offered her an extra five hundred to come back to work and make all of Hobbit's dreams come true. I sent another dancer to her place for the rest of the night to stay with her son, who thankfully had gotten over his fever and was finally asleep.

Jump sat on the desk. "All set."

Hobbit only grinned and blinked. "That's mighty nice of you all."

I slapped a hand on his massive shoulder. "Anything for a brother."

THIRTEEN

"HERE, HON." I held out a beer bottle to my wife.

"No, I don't want any."

"You want one of those fruity wine coolers Alicia brought?" I frowned. "I don't know how she drinks that shit."

She only shook her head at me.

"That's all we got, baby. There's soda, which you don't like. There might be bottled water leftover in the other cooler." I brushed her lips with mine and then unscrewed the top of my brew.

It was a glorious early summer day, and we were taking full advantage of it at the Hippie Hole. There'd been plenty of snow this past winter, and we were thrilled to find active waterfalls unlike last year. The water was high, and Boner and I had dived off the rocks and plunged into the icy pool below the minute we arrived.

I shook the water from my hair, and Grace blinked as cool drops splattered on her face. The heat of the sun warmed my skin and the sparkling glare from the surface of the water had me squinting down at my wife. I flicked her nose with my finger and laughed. She got up on her toes, her arms snaking around my middle, and sucked in a tiny breath as she leaned in closer to me.

I cupped the back of her head. "What is it, babe?"

Her mouth tickled my ear. "We're going to have a baby."

My heart bounced in my chest. I clasped her face close to mine. Grace's greenish-brown eyes were filled with water.

"Say it again," I breathed.

"We're going to have a baby, Dig. I'm pregnant."

The world stopped.

Shifted.

Slid out from under me.

And shoved back into new pegs.

A jolt went through my spine, rendering me immobile and filling me with adrenaline all at once. Only Grace's eyes made sense, their warmth pulling me back down to earth.

And I flew apart.

"Woo!" My heart pounded against my ribs.

"Dig!" She grabbed the beer bottle from my hand as I lifted her up high in my arms.

"What the hell?" Wreck laughed.

"We're having a baby!" I shouted.

Wreck's face broke into a huge smile and he howled, clapping a hand on my shoulder. Jump hooted loudly.

"Oh my God! Wait! Hold on! Hold on! You guys! Look over here!" Alicia shouted.

My eyes stayed glued on my woman's. The harsh glare of the sun bouncing off the water and the jagged rocks made my head ache. That green smell of the swimming hole mixed with Grace's sweat and the scent of her suntan lotion filled my lungs. I squeezed her tight, and then I squeezed her even tighter. She only laughed harder. Grace suddenly turned her head toward Alicia, and my lips ended up on the side of her sweet face.

"Great shot! Got it!"

Oh, I've got it. Got everything. Right here in my arms.

We had each other.

My brothers. Our friends.

Ruby sober and getting on with her life.

My bikes.

Our house.

Grace wrapped around me every night and me around her.

Now…now, this kid who we'd made was finally here, taking root inside her.

Our kid.

Yeah. That was all we needed. Everything else could be handled.

Fuck everything else.

Fuck it all.

I lifted Grace even higher in my hold and spun her around. She laughed, her fingers twisting in my hair, her head swinging back.

I shouted out loud. Shouted to the owls in the tall trees, to the hawks soaring overhead. Shouted to the sky, the clouds, the sun, the moon, the stars.

Dreams do come true.

What I didn't realize in the grip of my euphoria that afternoon was that the universe didn't differentiate between good and bad dreams.

Wish fulfillment came both ways.

FOURTEEN

"DON'T THINK I'M EVER GONNA LET THIS GO, DIG. You been trying to make nice for a long time now, and Zed was happy to suck it up. Not me. Not happy. Not sucking."

Zed had succumbed to a massive heart attack a few days earlier, and Notch had been voted President of the Broken Blades. The One-Eyed Jacks had come to Nebraska for the funeral to pay their respects.

My efforts at reaching out, apologies, a second-chance-at-love thing had not gone ignored by Zed over the years. After our recent successful collaboration, the first in a long time, a couple of months later, I'd helped out when his old lady got arrested for a DUI in South Dakota, and he'd been grateful. Real grateful. Things had begun to get comfortable once again, but then he'd upped and died.

I was fucked. Again.

"I ain't buying your shit," said Notch.

Really fucked.

"You have a *thing* with little girls," Notch continued. "I have a thing *for* 'em. Got me a new bitch all of fourteen. She don't look it. Sure don't act like it. My dick gives it to her good 'cause it likes fresh meat." He eyed me as he exhaled a long stream of smoke. "Gonna bring her a Barbie that she can play with while I fuck her ass. What do you think of that?"

I smiled. "Domestic bliss at its finest."

He nodded at me, smirking. "That's right, and you got no say in my plans to play ball with any other club."

"You know something, Notch? It's been years since our little bust-up. I've apologized. I've bent over backward for your club."

"Zed ain't here no more. Don't give a shit. Gotta say, I'm impressed you're VP now."

"I get the job done. I deliver. That's why."

"Well, I'm rethinking all of Zed's ideas of cooperation and partnership."

"That's your decision to make."

He raised his chin. "You got that right."

"Baby? Can you hear me?"

I was on a pay phone outside a bar in Fort Worth. Grace and I had planned a time when I would beep her, and she would call me from a pay phone outside of Meager.

The Flames of Hell had invited us to join them on a run down to Austin as an experiment in cooperation and cohabitation. I had kept in touch with Finger, had done a few minor jobs for him off the radar and free of charge. It had paid off. I'd wanted to show my brothers the possibility of working with one of the most formidable outlaw clubs in the Great Plains, that there was a future to be had for us alongside them. Mick had not been impressed, just as I'd expected, but he'd known it would be stupid to say no to the Flames.

I was determined that Mick's slippery bullshit was not going to get in the way of this opportunity. Unfortunately, he'd gotten a bout of nasty food poisoning, thanks to Clip's well-timed cooking at the club, and was unable to lead the Jacks on this run. Real shame. Mick reluctantly handed me the reigns in between bouts of vomiting.

"This pay phone is crap," said Grace. "You still don't want me calling you from home?"

"No, baby. They're watching us. We've been stopped a couple of times already as it is. You okay?"

"I'm good. Miss you though. A hell of a lot."

I grinned against the broken plastic mouthpiece, my hand pressing into the graffitied glass of the booth. "Me, too."

"Where are you now?"

"Some disco in the Bahamas."

Grace only chuckled. She would always ask me on purpose, knowing I would lie in case we were being heard. She always enjoyed my creative replies.

"What happened with your fundraiser last night?" I asked.

Distract me, entertain me, talk to me. Just let me hear that voice.

"We made fourteen thousand dollars! Can you believe it? That's just us. The others made a lot, too."

I leaned my forehead against the booth wall, my eyes slid closed. "Shit, really? That's amazing."

"Yeah, new record. Me and the girls are heading to the hospital in the morning with an official bank check to rub it in the hospital's face. We called the *Rapid City Journal* and everything. This insurance thing is really awful. I'm so relieved Bobby can finally have that leg operation."

The week before, when I'd brought Grace into Meager to the post office to send a package to Ruby, ten-year-old Bobby Greene's leg had gotten crushed by a delivery truck backing up over him on Clay Street as we were getting off my bike. We knew his mom from Marla's Eatery down the block where she waitressed. I'd held the kid's bloodied hand, covered him with my jacket, as he plummeted into shock and Grace ran into the diner for his mom.

"Bobby! Bobby! Look at me, Bobby. Stay with me!"

I'd talked him down from the fear and panic overwhelming him, face pale, eyes huge, moans escaping his small mouth, as we waited for the ambulance.

Bobby hadn't let go of my hand or stopped staring at me as I talked, talked, talked a blue streak, choking back the bile burning the back of my throat. So much fucking blood from one little boy. Bobby's mom had begged the paramedics to let me come in the ambulance with them. Grace had followed us on my bike. The hospital had set his shattered leg, but refused to operate because his single mother had no insurance. Grace had stepped in immediately and spearheaded a three-day fundraiser at Pete's and at five other businesses in town.

The townsfolk liked my woman. She was one of their own, after all. They remembered how she had lost her little brother to a hit and run driver years ago. They trusted the sincerity of her smile and her words, knew her intentions meant action.

My insides tightened as I listened to her excited voice recount the mud-wrestling match she had set up at Dead Ringer's last night, featuring the dancers from Tingle, to cap off the three-day series of events all around town.

"Of course, Alicia had to get in there and challenge the champion. I took pictures for Jump. I'm sure he'll get off on it."

I let out a low chuckle. "Ah, I miss you." I took in a deep breath. "How's our little rascal? Still making you puke?"

"Not so much anymore. Much better this week."

"Perfect, baby. Oh, are you still going to check in at Tingle for me tonight, make sure the payroll got done right? Swear to God, I'm gonna kill Clip if he doesn't get it together."

"Yes, I'm on my way there now. Don't worry. I'll let you know."

A roar went up behind me. My head swerved. The crowd in the parking lot rolled like a black wave, ready to crash on the bikes parked there. A wall of jeers and curses rose toward me. Punches were being thrown. Shouting rose in the air.

Shit.

"Gracie, gotta go."

"Dig? What's going on?"

"Jump might've gotten the wrong girl to suck his dick. Fuck if I know. I gotta go, hon. Be ready for my next call."

"I will. I love you"

"Love you." I jammed the phone back in its cradle, my eyes narrowing on the fight breaking out in front of the bar where our bikes were parked side by side. A group of citizen onlookers were spooked and caught between watching and getting out of the way fast.

I ran. Boner's loose hair flew, his grunts rising in the distance as he shoved a member of the Vicious Horde, a local Texas club. Flames of Hell hung back in a semicircle—for now. Wreck jumped the Vicious Horde who was on Boner and managed to throw him off. I lunged at Boner, who was getting whaled on by another asshole, shoving Boner out of the way. A heavy ring-loaded punch smashed into my gut, and I pulled back for a moment, gasping for air. Dready grabbed Wreck from behind and shoved him to the left of me.

Wreck's eyes held mine, eyes wide open, teeth bared, blood running down the side of his face. The glint of a blade flashed across his throat.

"No!"

"Back the fuck off!" The abrupt slide of metal. A Vicious Horde trained a rifle at me.

I stood still, barely breathing, my fingers flexed.

The crush of silence.

The chaos of men hollering, women shouting, rubber screeching. Like a cresting wave, the pressing crowd suddenly fell away. Wreck slumped against Dready. Wreck's eyes widened even more for a split second. A thick spill of blood gushed down his front.

I froze, my mouth hanging open, as we held each other's gaze.

"We're gonna rebuild this Indian Chief together. You'll see. It's gonna be the best thing for Miller. I know it will."

"Sister's a sweet thing. You sure she's for you? 'Cause if you play her, I'm gonna bust your ass and find someone else for her."

"Never ride drunk. Don't be an asshole. Gotta have respect for your machine and yourself."

"I love you, man. Fuckin' love you."

"That ain't how you use a torque wrench. Jesus, get out of the way and lemme show you."

"Sturgis ain't what it used to be. You boys want to see what it's really all about?"

Fading. Fading. Dull. Dazed.

Wreck's eyelids sank a few degrees.

Wreck. Richie. Richard Tallin.

Wreck.

His knees buckled. Still clutching him, Dready fell back against two bikes parked behind him. The machines lurched. Metal and chrome collapsed, crashed, both large men tumbling back with them.

Screams, shouts, pipes roared. Blood surged in my head, my pulse beating a hole through my heart.

The blood.

So much fucking blood.

There was the bloodied living room sofa where they'd destroyed Eve.

My mother's twisted body on the staircase, an arm hanging through the spindles.

My father's white dress shirt shredded, splattered in blood, his lifeless eyes staring up at me in the foyer.

The asphalt with pieces of my sister on it.

That never-ending river of blood seeped down the sides of Wreck's legs, his chest, all the way to my own boots, gluing me to him, to this moment.

Forever.

And in that glue was the confirmation I didn't need.

Because I already know.

My boots scraped through my brother's blood, and I dropped down on the asphalt next to him. I held his head up, the gash across his throat so deep I saw bone.

"This sort of thing is a very rare occurrence. I promise you, we will find them. We'll catch up with them. I'm real sorry. You go with this nice lady now. She'll take care of you, okay? She's going to take you to the hospital and make sure you're okay. Don't look anymore, son. Don't look."

I took Wreck in my arms and cradled his upper body with my own. His almost severed head slumped back against my arm. I shuddered, a sob escaping my lips.

"Dig, keep your eye on him for me." Miller's solemn voice from years ago bore a hole in my chest.

Yes, Miller. I'm watching his soul leave his body.

My fingers shook as they touched Wreck's eyelids. They only drooped under my touch. I wiped the dampness from his cool face, sweeping back his hair, and held him.

There was nothing else left to do.

The swell of sound and screaming around us melted into nothing.

There is no escape.

This will always be the way for me.

Always.

My life was not meant to be filled with tenderness or beauty or joy. Some of us were marked with tar. Creatures of the swamp. That was all. No way around it with pretty words or sentimental ideas stringing together the illusion of hope.

Because words and ideas weren't real.

This is real.

This.

My brother's body pumping its last in my arms, cold creeping over his drained, lifeless flesh.

This is hell.

This unrelenting raw gutting is mine. For others, these things were random events occurring rarely in their normal world, like the policeman had told me on my street that morning over twenty years ago. But everyone else's random would never be rare for me. My random was a demon that kept attacking me, gorging itself on my entrails like the unsatisfied feral beast it was, dancing his grotesque dance on the road before me.

Inevitable.

No matter what I did. How I fought it. With whomever I aligned myself, even men who had my back. With whom I shared an identity, a commitment, a name. Nor with my perfect, imperfect beautiful wife.

It didn't matter how much I fought, how I planned, maneuvered.

Doesn't make a damn bit of difference. Never has. Never will.

Burning rubber, exhaust, and the stench of copper filled my lungs.

"Dig? Ah, no! No! Fuck! Fuck!" Boner's ragged voice dragged me back to the parking lot of a bar in a corner of Fort Worth, Texas.

Sirens blared. Red and blue lights flashed across Wreck's ashen still face, across my bloodied hands.

Battered hands soaked in blood.

Soaked.

No. No escape. Not ever.

My lips brushed Wreck's cool forehead, and a choked wail heaved from my chest as I rocked him, rocked him to and fro.

To and fro.

To and fro.

I would never make that scheduled phone call to Grace the following day. In fact, I didn't say another word until we got back to Meager, over two days and a thousand miles later.

The ride back to South Dakota was a deafening blur. I kept my aching eyes trained on the road, on the van in front of me that carried Wreck's precious 1969 Panhead back home. We'd had to leave his body behind in Texas until the authorities would release it and we could get him home.

Grace lunged at me the second I got off my bike at two in the morning at the clubhouse, but I had nothing to give her. She only kept her hand on my back as we all trudged inside. I sent her to my room and stayed up all night in the lounge with a bottle of Jack in one hand and Pearl Jam's "Once" on endless repeat on the stereo.

The next day, Grace, Boner, and I all stared at the phone sitting on the bar as if we were willingly waiting for a grenade to explode any second.

Grace touched my arm. "Baby, are you sure you don't want me to talk to him?"

I shook my head, my hands scrubbing down my face. I lit another cigarette.

I had put in a call to the Army about talking to Miller. Told them why. The kid was on some sort of special assignment though. They got back to me and set up this call. I glanced at my watch. He would be phoning in one minute, thirty seconds.

"Dig—"

"Grace, stop! I have to do this."

She bit her bottom lip and settled back on her stool. Boner only stared at me, his hand gripping Wreck's colors, which lay across the bar in between us.

The phone rang. The three of us jerked to life like puppets being wrenched by our strings. I squashed the cigarette in the ashtray, took in a shallow breath, and picked up the fucking phone.

"Private Flies as Eagles speaking."

"Miller?"

Boner's head sank over his hands. Grace fingered the frayed stitches of Wreck's Road Captain rocker.

My brain and mouth managed to coordinate an explanation for his brother's death. No, wait, there was no explanation. Bar. Fight. Punches. Knife. Dead.

Miller sucked in a deep gust of air over the telephone. A horrible silence filled the five-thousand-three-hundred-something miles between us.

"I'm so sorry, man. So very sorry. We're all destroyed here. They already told me they can't release you. They got you in deep over there, and..."

Only silence from Miller. I clutched the phone even tighter, but my hand still shook. My arm shook. My body shook.

"Mill?" my voice cracked. "He died like he'd lived. We're gonna give him a good send-off, man. Just what he deserved. Better."

Horrible silence.

"He was our rock."

Wreck's colors blended into one watery swirl before me. Grace murmured somewhere in the distance. The phone was peeled from my cold grip. Two rough hands went around my wrists and held them there.

"Hello?" Grace clutched the phone. "Hello? This is Grace Quillen. I…oh, damn it." The cordless phone clacked on the bar. "He hung up," she whispered.

I wrenched my hands out of Boner's grip and lit another cigarette. "Get me a fucking drink, would you?"

Boner turned and grabbed a bottle of something. Anything. What did it matter? I swallowed deep, and it burned down my throat like sweet acid on fire.

A large platter of pizza slices was shoved on the bar right by my arm. My pulse skidded.

"I thought you guys would like something to eat." Somebody's new bitch smiled at us, rubbing her hands together.

The splayed pile of red-and-yellow triangles stared at me. That foul taste seared my mouth, the greasy odor infiltrating everything. Oregano, salty-sweet tomato, chalky mozzarella.

My lips curled, my burning stomach heaved. A lead weight pulled me down, dragging my flesh with it.

Grace swooped in. "No! No! Take it away!"

I jerked up and sent it flying through the air, crashing on the floor. Melted cheese and greasy splotches of red splattered everywhere around the girl, on the girl, the broken pieces of the platter at her feet.

"Oh my God!" Her whiny voice cut the air.

"Clean this shit up! Now!" Boner shouted.

"He doesn't like pizza?" she shrieked. "Who the hell doesn't like pizza?"

"Dig, you okay? Honey?"

"Get the fuck out! Get out!" I yelled. I yelled at the bitch with the pizza. I yelled at myself. I yelled at Wreck. I yelled at Miller across the endless miles of land and ocean separating us.

Miller.

Those mournful dark eyes stared at me.

I failed you.

Mom.

Eve.

Dad.

Wreck. I had failed to keep one of the finest men I had ever known, my mentor, safe on my watch.

I had failed my brother.

"Dig?" Grace's hands swept up my arms.

I stared at her. Her hazel eyes wide open. Deep lines I had never noticed before now etched her skin, altering her face.

I wouldn't let this touch her. It just couldn't. I would surely die if it did. Fuck, I would end it myself.

I held her gaze, focusing on her eyes, as her fingertips stroked my arm. I swallowed.

"What the hell's going on?" Alicia screeched from across the room.

My glare shut her up. Her eyes widened, and her body froze in place—a body swollen with her unborn child. She was five months more pregnant than Grace.

Grace would look like that soon, wouldn't she?

Budding, round. Full.

Full of sweet expectations. Full of useless dreams.

Full of our kid.

Vulnerable.

I peeled Grace's hands off my cold skin.

Her eyes filled with tears. "It doesn't have to be like this. Honey, please let me help you. Please, please let me help you." Her voice hitched, and she threw herself at me, her hands flying around my neck, her wet face sliding against mine. "Don't shut me out now. I miss him, too. I'm hurting, too. Dig, please. Please!"

I shoved her off and inhaled the pizza-saturated air. I gagged, vomit rising in my throat. God, it reeked.

It all fucking reeked.

"No."

"Don't do this!" She was crying, shaking.

Crying for us, crying for Wreck, for Miller, for me.

For our kid.

She should be crying.

"Hey." Boner's eyes pierced mine like daggers, his hand grabbing my shoulder.

I shoved past him and charged outside. As I got on my bike, my gaze automatically lifted to the shed as it had done thousands of times before, thousands of times a day for eons.

Wreck's Repair.

The hanging rusty sign creaked and groaned in the cold wind over the padlocked metal doors.

I squeezed my eyes shut as I turned the ignition over.

Another haunted fucking house.

It was a classic funeral.

The long procession of motorcycles. Clubs from all over the west and Midwest came to pay their respects. We took turns at the shovel. We filled in the grave.

I emptied out my insides in that pit of dirt over his box.

I didn't hear from Miller again. None of us did.

"You sure you're okay? This is so fucking horrible. But it ain't nothing new, is it?" Butler rested a hand on my shoulder. The send-off party at the club had finally wound down.

My gaze fell on our old ladies hugging in the yard. Caitlyn smiled as she rubbed Grace's belly.

"She's so excited about your baby," said Butler. He let out a gust of air. "We've been trying, but it ain't happened so far. Caitlyn wants us to go get tested, but I ain't jacking off in no cup in a doctor's office."

My gaze met his. Crystal-clear aqua, so different from mine. Uncluttered.

Butler shifted his weight. "Hey, look, why don't the two of you come up to Hound, get away from here? We can head up to Caitlyn's brother's cabin in our trucks. He's fixed it up pretty sweet since the last time you came up, all the creature comforts. It'll be good."

"Maybe. We'll see."

"All right." His mouth screwed up tightly. "Darlin', let's roll!"

Caitlyn waved a hand at him, her pretty face breaking into a grin. She and Grace hugged tight, saying their good-byes.

"Gimme a call, all right?" Butler and I embraced, and he thumped me on my back. He turned and mounted his bike.

"Bye, Dig. Take care of my girl." Caitlyn smiled up at me, adjusting her leather jacket. All those fucking silver hoops on her ears and in her one eyebrow glinted in the sun. She got her lid on and swung herself on the back of the Harley, her spike-heeled boots settling on the pegs.

Butler's pipes roared. He raised his chin at me, and they spun off the property.

That night, like every night since we'd come back from Texas, I gripped Grace from behind, raised her hips, and thrust my cock into her. I didn't want to look into her eyes. I didn't want her to look into mine. I didn't want her to hold on to me. I only wanted her to take me in, to endure my self-punishment. And she did, my one hand sinking in between her legs, her breaths coming hard and fast as I fucked her with short, quick strokes. Her sharp moans pleaded with me, her insides pulsated around me, trying to milk me of my bile. After, she nestled back against me, wrapped my arms around her body, and fell sleep. The illusion of comfort was good enough for her. I rested my head against hers on the pillow, the thick waves of her hair in between us, and I counted the hours, the minutes until morning.

For morning would surely come. It always did.

FIFTEEN

"THIS MUST BE SPECIAL. I don't get a call from my favorite One-Eyed Jack very often. It's been years in fact."

"Yeah, it's a special occasion." I hung my helmet on a handlebar and removed the bandana from my head, shaking out my hair.

Loud laughter jerked our attention to the front door of the burger joint where we stood in the parking lot. A family of four ambled out the door into the sun-filled lot in eastern Montana. I rolled my stiff shoulders as they stared at us as if we were the new acquisitions at the zoo—vintage Harleys, dirt-covered leathers, thick boots, dark sunglasses, wild hair. The little boy, his mouth hanging open, waved at me, and I wiggled a finger at him. The teenage daughter's eyes widened, her pace slowing. The mother pulled on their arms and led them to their Ford Explorer where the dad slammed his door shut and started the engine.

"Let's hear it," said Vig.

I ran my fingers through my damp hair. "I think we share some common ground, Vig. Funny, isn't it? You want play out there in the big wide world with new playmates, but Cowboy wants to be an isolationist. I don't want play out there, but Mick wants to."

Vig chuckled. "Let's you and me switch colors and call it a day, huh?"

We laughed.

Vig shrugged. "Hey, we all got different ideas about what works for our clubs." He wiped the edge of his mouth with the back of his hand and crumpled the foil wrapper from the burger he'd eaten while waiting for me.

I wrinkled my nose at the stench of pickles and onions. "Different ideas is one thing. Different vision is another. You and I have different visions, Vig, but in a fucked-up way, we're the same. We each want what we think is best for our clubs."

"I agree with you. For once. I've been out west cultivating a few opportunities for the Seeds. But in order to follow through on them, I gotta build things up. I'm not interested in keeping things backwoods anymore."

"That's where you and I differ."

He laughed. "You like backwoods, don't you?"

"Low-key has its merits."

He laughed. "Mick sure don't see it that way."

I eyed him. "No, he doesn't. He wants a bite of the drug-cartel action that's sweeping the edges of our states. I think that's quicksand. It's shit you can't get out of once you start. There might be money in it, but these people are a twisted side of fucked up, and I don't want to introduce that sort of hell into our area or deal with it for-fucking-ever. Those contracts are signed in blood."

"Ah, it's all relative in the end, Diggy. Only a matter of time before they sweep the entire U. S. of A. It's time to play ball."

"Not playing ball, man. What I want to do is solidify what we got. A few different clubs working together to forge our own network. We'll own our own territories, but coordinate production and sales and distribution and be a stronger force together rather than separate."

"How long do you think that's going to last, Dig? Things are good now, but then again, every Tom, Dick, and Granny are producing their own meth out in their cornfields or in the back of their pickups and selling. You think the Feds aren't going to cop on to everybody going from pharmacy to pharmacy to stock up on material?"

"Of course they will. Everything's going to be computerized soon enough, and then they'll even know what brand of toilet paper we're buying and when. But when that happens, we'll be ready."

"When that happens, the Mexicanos are gonna move right on in. Then you'll see what's gonna happen to our cash flow."

"That's what I mean, Vig. The time to forge alliances between us is now."

Vig leaned over and spit to the side of his bike. "So, this is all sweet to hear and warms my insides to no fucking end, but why did you want to meet me? I haven't been home in months. You're lucky you caught me on my way in. Glad I invested in a cell phone."

"I think I can help you out with your vision thing."

"Oh yeah? Okay, I'll bite."

"Cowboy's tired and old and not in line with your progressive, forward way of thinking, right? You've mentioned that once or twice over the years. Yet he's still holding on."

A crooked grin split Vig's features. "Idiot had to have a knee replacement last year after a bike accident. Stubborn bastard hasn't kept up with his physical therapy. Ain't no way that fat fuck is gonna be walking let alone riding the way he should be anytime soon."

No riding equaled no club membership. Definitely no presidency.

Vig's eyes gleamed at me. Yeah, he could taste the presidency, could already feel the hard length of the gavel in his grip.

"Your boys eager for change, too?" I asked. "What would you say if I told you, Mr. Vice President, that your prez has a new vision for his club that he intends to make real before he steps down?"

A shadow crossed Vig's face as he raised his chin at me. "How do you know my prez's new vision?"

"You wanna hear it or what?"

"I'm listening."

"Joining forces with the Jacks. He and Mick have been meeting up north. Creeper's been playing go-between."

Butler had been keeping me informed of the goings-on for a long time now. Things had heated up the last few months though, and I'd gotten my details from Hobbit. Secret meets, secret payouts between the alleged competitors. Mick and Cowboy, the illicit besties.

Vig stared at me, his bulky body perfectly still. "No."

"Yes. You've been gone a good long while, haven't you?"

"Cowboy sent me out west to play footsie with the Russians. Things got a little complicated, had to tie up a few loose ends. Took longer than I thought."

I lit a cigarette. "Great timing on Cowboy's part, sending you Nomad while he got down to other tricks you wouldn't like. Maybe he was hoping you wouldn't survive your Russian vacation?"

Vig's face contorted. "What the fuck?" He hissed in air.

I ran my fingers down the worn leather of my saddle as I exhaled a stream of smoke. "Mick wants the Seeds for a bigger, better One-Eyed Jacks future. He's playing nice with Cowboy till he gets what he wants, and then all bets are off. Like one of those nasty corporate takeovers on Wall Street. That's my little theory at least."

Vig tore his gaze away from mine and rubbed a hand over his mouth. "Motherfucker."

"You want the presidency of your club, don't you?"

His eyes burned a hole through mine. "Fuck yes," he rasped.

"And I want my club left in peace."

"You don't want nothing more?"

"I got plenty for now, Vig. What I want is for my club to be left alone from those big corporate organizations you seem to favor and do its thing, first and foremost."

"Why tell me? If this all goes down the way you say and Mick patches us in, you would have it all."

"That's the difference between you and me, I guess. I don't want it all."

Vig crossed his arms and took in a deep breath. "Where's this leading?"

"There's a meet coming up between Cowboy and Mick. I might be willing to give you the info on the when and where. You could swoop in and catch your prez and Mick sucking on each other. Play it up, piss off your brothers, gather support for your cause. Have a little *coup d'état* while you're at it."

He made a face. "A what?"

"A takeover, man. It's all in how you play the big drama, your big reveal. Play it any way you like, but bottom line, we ruin it. For both of them. Then you and I clean house."

Vig's eyes narrowed, his lips rolled.

"You have the support to make it worth the effort? You been gone a while."

"Fuck yeah. I got my boys."

I was sure he did. I knew Hobbit had been stoking the fires of revolution all this time.

I flicked my butt to the side. It fizzled and hissed in a puddle. "Good."

"What do you get out of it?" Vig asked.

"Exposing lies and broken promises. Creating a rupture. Cleaning house, like I said."

He smirked. "Sounds all noble. You ain't gonna stage your own takeover, too? Although, you're a man down—with Wreck gone. Gotta say, they don't make 'em like him no more. He was a good man. Old school all the way."

"Yeah." I glanced down at my scuffed boots. "My club, my concern. You'd better confirm the support at your end. Notice, I had to fill you in on your own prez's doings."

Vig rubbed his chest. "Don't worry your pretty head about me, Diggy."

"I won't. You just be where I tell you, when I tell you."

Vig smirked. "All right. I'll keep playing up our little hostility thing to set the stage all proper."

"I'll return the favor."

I zipped up my jacket and turned to get on my bike, but Vig remained motionless.

"There something else?" I unstrapped my helmet.

He leveled his gaze at me. "This was easy."

"What's that?"

"Dealing with you," replied Vig. "You've always been such a fucking self-righteous pain in my ass. Today we were able to talk, understand each other, agree, set a plan in motion."

"We've both got the same objective, and it's very clear." I settled on my saddle. "And so you and me are extremely clear. There is no blood to be shed. That goes without saying as we're all brothers and we're talking about our presidents. Or am I asking too much of your ambition?"

He slowly shook his head, twisting his lips once more. "Nah, I don't want that blood on my hands."

I pulled my bandana tight over my head. "I hope so. According to Shakespeare, that kind of bloodbath comes back to haunt you, bites you in the ass."

He made a face. "Shakespeare?"

"Yeah, you never read *Macbeth* or *Hamlet* in school? Things get way fucking bloody after you kill a king. Big tragic mess."

Vig shrugged. "I liked reading *Hägar the Horrible*. Still do." He let out a roll of laughter, his thick belly quivering, as he put on his gloves.

Was it a gift that Vig could move forward in his shabby, dirty little life without being tainted by a memory or stunted by a regret?

"I'll be waiting to hear from you," he muttered as he adjusted his glasses.

What must it be like to glide forward, to only consider what you want now, in this moment or a little later on? Was Vig ever affected by a thudding on his heart, a reverse pull in the flow of his blood?

"Dig—"

He didn't have to say anything else. I had noticed the Kawasaki with the suited-up rider at the gas station on the other end of the lot when I first got here. He had to be tailing Vig.

"Lucky for you, I'm in the mood to lend a brotherly hand."

"I'd be much obliged," he muttered.

"Is this what you meant by loose ends?"

"Yeah."

I put on my helmet. "How you want to play it?"

"You stay here. I'll take off, him on my tail, and you come up from behind. We'll get creative from there."

"All right. Nothing like a little game of cat-and-mouse to break up my day."

Vig got on his bike and started up his engine. He swerved out of the parking lot and got onto the road.

This was no major highway though. It was a narrow country route in between towns in eastern rural Montana, away from the Bakken oil traffic, that we had chosen specifically.

The Kawasaki followed.

Game on.

I counted to twenty and got my bike onto the empty road.

A few miles later, there was Kawasaki man on Vig. Vig drifted to his left as I accelerated, shooting forward, until I was on Kawasaki's ass. He jerked his bike to his right, tearing ahead on the road.

"Let's go, motherfucker."

Vig broke out, thrusting forward on the road, on the rice burner's tail, me keeping tight on him on the other side. We burned through the ice-cold wind, gaining on him. I motioned with one hand to Vig to keep on. He nodded, and I eased up on my speed, hanging back. I checked my mirrors. Checked again. My hand went to my Kimber 1911 in my holster across my chest as my eyes darted to my side mirror one final time.

An SUV came up the low hill behind me. My hand went back to the handlebar again. I squinted at the reflection of the vehicle in my side mirror.

Was that the family from the restaurant? Did they get lost and turn around? *Fuck.*

I pulled back from Kawasaki and kept to my right to let the Ford Explorer pass. The little boy peeked at me over the backseat through the rear window, his fingers gripping the edges of the headrest.

Go. Go. Go.

Kawasaki picked up speed, putting a long bite of road between him and me, and he shot toward Vig. The Explorer swerved slightly to the left to avoid Kawasaki. I hung back. The Explorer's left blinker flashed.

Yes. Turn. Get the fuck off the road.

Vig weaved in and out of the road, making Kawasaki's life difficult.

I would make it short.

Explorer Dad veered to the left at a fork in the route, the little boy kept waving, and they were gone.

I sped toward the two bikes, and my right hand slid across my chest once again. Adrenaline surged through my veins, my eyes drilled holes through my visor. Kawasaki was focused on the Vig Games. I drew my 1911 out of my holster and aimed.

Squeezed.

His tire blew.

Squeezed.

His leg spewed. His head fell back, and he lost control of his sewing machine. Spinning out, the Kawasaki flew off the road. I slid my Kimber back in its holster.

I circled back to where Kawasaki was ditched on the side of the road, Vig coming up behind me. His body twitched on the rocky ground covered in pine needles and brush, moans rising from his helmet. I kicked him over onto his back.

Vig unclipped the guy's firearm and tucked it in his jeans. "Let's get him out of sight."

We lifted him, and he groaned as we dragged him into the woods. I went back, got his bike, and rolled it over.

I removed my helmet. "I'm gonna go find my casings before it gets dark." I hiked back to the road. It was a bitch, but I found them, and I brought my bike deeper into the woods. Vig did the same with his bike a few moments later. I sucked in a breath, wiping the sweat from my upper lip.

Vig had flung up the rider's visor.

"Know him?" I asked.

"Yeah. One of the dogs that I worked with. Hit man. Works for the lower-level Russian I had dealings with."

"You make friends everywhere you go, don't you? You need any information from him?"

"Nah, I know. I know." Vig slid out his gun, attaching a silencer.

A moan. "No!" A hand raised in the air from the crumpled body. A pair of brown eyes flared with anguish.

Vig blew three stiff shots into Kawasaki's belly and chest. He sniffed, taking a step back while opening his cell phone. He pushed a button and waited. "Hey. Need you to meet me. Got a situation. Drop everything else."

I stared at the lifeless body.

Situation dealt with.

"I appreciate this," said Vig. "You didn't have to help me, but you did. That's two saves in one day."

I crouched by the body, ripped back the torn fabric over the gunshot wound on his leg, poking my fingers in the charred, bloody flesh. "Does that make us best friends after all these years?"

"I'm grateful, how's that?"

I removed my skinny knife from the sheath on the inside of my lower leg and gouged it into the oozing wound, past ripped blood vessels, bone fragments until my blade grazed the hard surface of my bullet. I dug it out. I wouldn't leave any evidence of me behind in Vig's hands. I wiped my knife on the leaves and secured it, tucking the blood smeared bullet in my jacket pocket.

"I need someone I can trust right now, Dig. Someone on my outside. Now more than ever."

"What the hell's going on?"

"There's a lot to be had out there. I want my piece. I'm takin' it."

"*Your* piece?"

"For my club. And if things with Cowboy go the way you say, it's gonna happen for me. I need your help though."

"I can't vote for you, Vig."

He ignored my joke. "This guy was after some goods I stole from his boss. I skimmed a little bit more from the top than they had planned on giving me. Thought they could get one over on the dumbass hick biker."

"They were wrong, huh?"

"Fuck yeah. I need to hide them. Keep 'em safe till I need to draw on 'em. If you help me hide my diamonds, Dig, you can make your own dreams come true."

"Diamonds? What the fuck?"

"Half a mill's worth," Vig said. "I'll give you a cut. We'll figure out the details. Count on at least fifty thousand."

"A hundred."

He scowled. "What?"

"I just saved your fucking ass."

He only shook his head.

There was something to be said for a smart barter.

I crossed my arms. "Seventy-five thousand, and you keep your club off the One-Eyed Jacks and back away from the Blades."

"Don't get greedy, Diggy."

"These diamonds are a once-in-a-lifetime for you, aren't they? Notch has stars in his eyes where you're concerned. End the crush."

If Vig agreed, I could ensure my club's safety and wholeness, along with making a very thick wad of cash for myself and the club, all at the same time. Butler was doing good things for his chapter, but he could use a serious injection of funds to back it up and make his investment of time and effort really grow. Our network throughout the Dakotas and down into Colorado with our brother chapters would only be fortified. This was good. Very good. But I still needed Nebraska. If I could form a new network with the Broken Blades and have the power and the clout of the Flames of Hell behind us, we would create a firewall between all of us and the Demon Seeds and their new mafia playmates. We would be laying solid ground for our future and be fucking unblockable.

Me working with Vig? Never say never. I couldn't share this with anyone, not just yet, but it was a risk I was willing to take.

Vig took in a deep breath of air as he hooked his hands on his hips. "I'll take your offer, Dig. Not because I've changed my mind about bringing the One-Eyed Jacks or the Blades to their knees, but because I've gotta prioritize right now, and this is huge. Without securing my diamonds, I lose big." He rubbed a thick thumb across his forehead. "Okay, I'll make sure the Seeds lay off your club and the Blades. For now. But one day, one day soon, know I'm going to go back to convincing you that it's the right move, and you all need to make it." His eyes gleamed at me from behind his thick glasses. "Unless you have principles and high morals and don't want to dirty your hands with the likes of me behind your club's back?"

"Vig, my principles and high morals were blown to bits a long time ago. The only principle I have left is my old lady. My loyalty to my brothers goes without saying."

"That's what I like about you, Diggy. A dependable traditionalist."

I touched his shoulder. "Anything happens to me, there cannot be any blowback on my old lady."

"You got it, man."

"I need to know you'll have your eyes out in case something goes bad. You give me or Boner a heads-up if anything starts to fall apart."

"Young love."

I gritted my teeth. "She's pregnant, Vig."

His head jerked back. "Oh, congratulations. Yeah, I will let you know. Of course. Goes without saying." He lifted his chin. "Count on it."

I studied his face. "You got kids?"

"Yeah, I do. Two. One's in Oregon. The other's in Wisconsin. I see 'em when I can."

Vig, the fucking family man.

The throbbing in the left side of my head pounded wave upon wave of pressure all through my skull. I rubbed my fingers along the sides of my face.

Within half an hour, Hobbit showed up in a dry-cleaning van, another Seed at his side. We only nodded at each other. He and his brother bundled the body in plastic and then shoved it in the back, propping boxes and mats over it. They then loaded the ruined Kawasaki into the van, shoving it alongside the concealed corpse. Hobbit and the other Seed got into the van and waited.

"We set?" Vig asked, his eyes hard.

"Let's do this."

His lips twitched. "'Course, you know what'll happen if you don't follow through on this."

I smirked. "Oh, I know."

He opened one of his saddlebags and handed me a small duffel. "That's all of it. You hide them, secure them, and I'll let you know when and how much is needed over time. You got a place to stash them? And I don't mean under your mattress or in your clubhouse."

"I got a place, several to choose from in fact. I always plan ahead for opportunities like these."

"I think we need a handshake here, wouldn't you say?"

I let out a laugh as I took his damp thick hand in mine. We shook once and withdrew from each other. I put the duffel in my saddlebag and locked it.

"Let's move!" Vig signaled to Hobbit, and the van pulled out. Vig raised his chin at me, hit his kickstand, and slowly took off behind Hobbit's van.

I hit the buttons on my cell phone.

"Yeah?" came Butler's voice.

"Got Vig to back off."

"You're shitting me! How?"

"Let's just say, he feels compelled to show me some gratitude. You make sure our Colorado chapter is primed. Once this goes down, they need to be a lock."

"You got it."

"We cannot fuck this up, B."

We couldn't waste this reprieve Vig was offering from the Seeds blocking us or encroaching on our territory in addition to them laying off the Blades. Notch would fall in line. I could now bring more to the table with the Flames. A newly zoned map of the Great Plains was on the horizon.

"I know, man. I know how important this is. This is good news." Butler exhaled over the phone. "You heading to Nebraska?"

The shadows of twilight settled on the woods. There was no breeze, no cool air, simply stillness after all the cacophony of bullets, engines, pleading, and pipes. Raindrops haphazardly dribbled on the leaves, breaking that silence. The pattering quickened, growing louder, the cool drops tapping at my upturned face, my leathers, my bruised hands. The sky was marred with thick billowy swirls of dark and light, moving, constantly moving.

"Dig? Dig, you there? What's going on?"

"Yeah." My boot kicked over leaves smeared in Kawasaki's blood, and I rubbed the bloody tip of my boot into a mound of pine needles. The hushed glow of dusk faded, sinking into darkness.

"You heading to Nebraska now?"

"No, got to stop home first. Got shit to do for a few days, and then I'll head down." I wiped the water from my face.

I got home, took care of the diamonds, got local business done.

But I never made it to Nebraska.

And my responsibility became my old lady's burden.

Within less than a year, war erupted between the Demon Seeds and the One-Eyed Jacks without the buffer of the Broken Blades or the backup of the Flames of Hell, sending my club spinning for years afterward.

All told, it was a good thing that Vig's fucking diamonds forced Grace away from the club, out of South Dakota.

And into exile.

SIXTEEN

"I'LL TAKE THE MAMA. I don't like my pussy too tight. You take the girl."

"Fuck yeah," another heavy voice came from the living room.

I couldn't see much from my hiding place in the closet.

"No, please no! Not my daughter! Take anything you want. I'll get you more money. I have cash upstairs in a safe. Please, please, just leave my daughter alone. Please!"

He clamped a hand on my mother's jaw and shook her head like a kid's toy. "Shut up, lady. You don't get this, do ya? We call the shots, and we're not going anywhere, not for a long while. Your pretty house is now our hotel. Best kind of hotel there is. Full service." He chuckled. "You don't shut up..." He put a gun in her mouth, and his other hand wrapped tightly around her throat.

Mom struggled and made a choking sound, her eyes wide.

"You ain't gonna like it," he said in a singsong voice, laughing.

"Hey, man. I saw some pizza in the kitchen. You want some?" his friend asked.

"What pizza?"

"There's a dish with pizza on the counter."

He immediately snapped his head back toward my mother and shook her. "Someone else here? You got another kid. I saw his picture. Where's your boy?"

Icy needles prickled my spine and froze my heart to a standstill. A scream unknotted in my throat, but I wrestled it back down.

"He's at football practice," she sputtered.

He let go of her, and her head dropped to the floor.

He turned to his friend, who I still couldn't see. "Let's see that sweet little cunt, huh? Let mama here watch, just in case she thinks she can get away with lying to us."

The rip of clothing sliced through the thick air.

Eve wailed. She screamed. "Mom! Mom!"

The hairs on the back of my neck stood on end. My entire body shivered and shrank.

"No!" Her voice split my eardrums.

My heart was racing, pounding like a freight train on the loose. I rocked back and forth on my haunches, my hands slapping over my mouth.

"Shut her up already, would ya?"

Eve's cries were muffled, and the sound of choking replaced her yells. Mom cried, small wails escaping from her. Desperate to see her, I brought my face to the crack in the door once again. Her chest shuddered, but she couldn't move much as her hands were now tied over her head. The monster had his back to me. He was focused on the other side of the living room where the sofa was. Heavy grunting and the slapping of flesh filled my ears. Harsh breathing, like a horse running on a track. More slaps and a string of muttered words I couldn't make out kept going on and on and on. Vomit churned in my gut. I rocked back and forth in the dark closet. My knees hurt, my eyes stung.

"Oh, yeah. Look at that. I'm gonna have to have a piece of that later."

I couldn't blink. I couldn't move. The stale smell of plastic, metal and wool stifled me. The sky had finally fallen. Armageddon was here, in my very own living room.

"Fuck me. That was good shit." He let out a lazy laugh.

He unzipped his pants in a slow long slide, the sound echoing in my eardrums, ripping at my insides. I glued my face to the edge of the doorjamb. His pants dropped, and he positioned himself on top of my mother gripping her arms with his hands. Her head rolled to the side. The flood of tears had smudged her pale face with the makeup she had so carefully put on this morning. Her red eyes found mine and widened once again.

My pulse hammered as she stared at me. "Mom," I whispered. The word vibrated through every vein.

Staring at me, she slightly shook her head. The monster raised himself up and plunged his body into hers. Her body jerked forward, and she grimaced, her eyes squeezing shut. He shoved himself into her, faster and faster. He was talking to himself and grunting out ugly words, a mudslide of dirt and nastiness.

I clutched my hair and ground my head into the doorjamb, unable to look away. My mother's eyes opened again and found mine. I wanted to take this pain, this horror, away for her, siphon it off through her gaze like gasoline from a car. My eyes were lasers now, beams of light. I was sending her the white blue light of the Force, filling her with my love, pushing out his revolting, foul ugliness.

I'm here, Mom. I will save you!

I went to move, tumbling forward out of my hiding place. Now that he was distracted, I could pounce on him, hit him over the head with something.

Do something!

Mom's eyes hardened, warning me, stopping me. Don't move. Don't make a sound. Do not move.

A loud wail mixed with brittle laughter rose in the room. Eve's horrible sobbing filled my ears. My blood froze in my veins, my heart clenched tight. Mom's face was so red and blotchy now. Her eyes closed, and our laser-eye-Force connection was lost. I shook, all alone in the hall that seemed like enemy territory all of a sudden, not my home any longer. I scurried back into the stuffy closet. My head knocked against a cold metal rod and I grabbed it, but it was no Jedi lightsaber, only the stupid vacuum cleaner. My chest was crushed. I couldn't breathe anymore.

Couldn't breathe.

Yes, the sky had fallen. No escape.

I was trapped in that closet,

listening,

listening,

listening—

"Dig!"

Jarring movement, shaking. A small fist pounded on my chest.

"Dig! Please, baby!"

A choking sound, gurgling.

My eyes flew open. I heaved for air.

Grace's watery eyes bulged before me. My hands were at her throat, her hands gripping my wrists. Our room at the club. I'd been drinking last night, and we'd stayed here instead of driving home.

"Fuck!" I unlatched my hands from around her neck.

She gulped for air, her chin quivering. I let out a low growl as I shoved my face in her chest, wrapping my arms around her. I pulled her down under me and sucked on the side of her throat. My knee separated her legs, and I steadied my raging cock with my one hand and plunged inside her.

"Dig—"

We convulsed together.

I didn't answer. I couldn't form words, couldn't connect my thoughts. I just wanted release, relief, to forget, to be washed, to lose myself inside my wife. To make it up to her.

I fucked away Eve's yells, my mother's anguished face, my father's blood all over the foyer. I fucked away Wreck's eyes sinking closed, his blood staining my fingers, Miller's impenetrable silence.

Drilled and thrust through all of it.

All of it.

My balls tightened, the rush pulled me in, twisted me, catapulted me over. Grace gasped sharply, her body tensing and I groaned. I extracted myself from her and curled up in a ball.

Fucking ugly.

Grace's hands touched my back. "What the hell is going on with you?" Her voice creaked. "Why won't you talk to me? Since you came back from Texas, you've been…it's been over a month since Wreck died, and you still can't talk to me about it. You're dreaming about your sister again, and you were yelling for your mom just now."

My fingers dug into the pillows underneath me.

"Please tell me what's going on." Her voice was pointed now, demanding. "I swear to God, I'm going to go assault Boner and make him tell me. Because if another living soul knows, it's got to be him. You two have been together since you were kids."

"Let it be," I spit out.

"No, damn it, I won't."

I turned over and blinked up at her. Her jaw was set, her eyes ablaze, as she sat up on her knees beside me, wearing one of my old T-shirts, wiping at the cum seeping down her thighs.

"Well?"

I turned over again.

"I don't need Boner." Her voice snapped like an old branch underfoot in a quiet forest. "I did a little *digging* on my own, Jake Pence."

My eyelids shot up. *My name. She knew my real name.*

"There's this thing called the Internet now. You can do research from a computer and go all around the world. From our town library, I got as far as Denver, Colorado."

"Grace…"

"You want to hear what I found out?"

"How? How did you—"

"I was cleaning out Boner's room. I found an envelope with paperwork in it from the Welfare Department of the State of Colorado. With his real name on it. I traced him to find you."

A chill settled over my skin, my heart slowly filling with cement.

"Jake and Eve Pence, the children of Amelia Pence, a prominent lawyer, and Michael Pence, a successful investment banker living in an upscale suburban community of Denver. Their two children attended an exclusive private school, and the family lived in a very expensive beautiful house on a hill. One day—"

"Shut up, Grace!" I sat up.

Grace pushed me back on the mattress and straddled my torso, pinning me down. My fingers dug into her thighs. She winced, but she didn't budge, not a fucking inch.

"One day, Mrs. Pence and her sixteen-year-old daughter were attacked as they entered their home by two men who had followed them there. They were held hostage, raped repeatedly, and the house was ransacked. When Mr. Pence arrived home that evening, he was brutally attacked with a hunting knife and bled to death in the entryway."

My eyes bore holes into hers.

She swallowed hard. "The lone survivor was their son, Jake who had gone home early from school that day, and witnessed…witnessed everything from a hall closet where he'd been trapped for hours."

"Stop!" I fought for air.

"Mrs. Pence was choked to death on the staircase, but the two perpetrators decided to take Eve with them. They dragged her outside, but she managed to get away. They shot her and ran her over on the road with her own father's car until she stopped screaming. They drove off with thousands of dollars in cash and jewelry from the family safe. They were pursued by police and federal agents as they had invaded a house in New Mexico as well as two other houses in Colorado. They were finally caught and remain on death row."

I stared at her, my jaw clenched.

She leaned over, her hands pressing down on my chest, her face inches from my own. "Jake Pence, you remember it so well that it twists your insides, pours out of you in your sleep. That's why you can't sleep. Can barely sit still. Have a chronic stomach ulcer, suffer from migraines."

"Get off me and leave the room," I breathed, my insides simmering.

"Oh, I'm not going anywhere." She tilted her head. "How did you get here?"

Another metaphysical question.

"Here? To Meager? Or do you mean here, to being able to steal, kill. Deal drugs. Pimp. Lie without feeling bad about it or second-guessing myself?"

"Yeah, Dig. Here, to being the VP of the One-Eyed Jacks. Jake Pence was hardly a candidate for an outlaw bike club, let alone an officer."

"Like you were the perfect candidate for a biker's old lady?"

"More so than you becoming a biker, Jake."

I winced. "Don't call me that."

She raised her head. "Tell me. You and Boner both told me you met in a group home, but I figured you had done time in juvie or something before that."

I shook my head against the pillow and took in a deep breath to steady my swirling brain. "After all that, an uncle took me in. A college professor cokehead, who was screwing his interns—boys and girls—every chance he got. He was full of shit. He liked me because I came with a trust fund and the money from the sale of the house. One night he came to tuck me in and tried to suck my dick. I knocked him out. He was afraid I'd ruin his career by spreading the story, so he dumped me in the foster care system just as he came down with AIDS.

"Foster care was another barrel of laughs. I was an undesirable; an aggressive teenage boy who got tossed from home to home. Eventually, I got placed in a group home where I met Boner. We didn't last too long in the system. By the time we turned seventeen, we ran off, hit the streets, stole, got into drugs, got out of drugs, dealt drugs. We got into biking and sort of cleaned up our acts. We managed to make the pilgrimage to Sturgis one year where we met Wreck, as you know, and the rest is history."

Tears streamed down her face, her eyes wild. "Why couldn't you ever tell me? You know everything about me. Everything. But you never let me in."

"In? I don't want you in there! I don't want to be in there either, Grace. But it won't let me go. No matter what I do, who I've become, it won't let me go."

She wiped at her eyes, but the tears kept spilling. I didn't want her crying for me, not for me.

"This is why I like living poor, by the seat of my pants, in a small, nondescript house. I like living on impulse. I like the burn of gasoline and oil and metal in my lungs, the wind beating at me, as I tear down the road. Knowing it's me moving through the air, over that road. No one, nothing, holding me back, holding me in.

"Then I met you, and that kind of crazy free wasn't necessary anymore, but you were. You were another kind of necessary. Wanted you for myself. When I had no right to that sort of life and no right to pull you into my shit. But I did. I wanted you that bad. Even your sister made me promise to stay away from you, but you showed up at the club that night and tilted my world upside down, broke the axis I'd had in place, broke it in fucking two. So I destroyed that promise.

"I knew what that meant, but it wasn't putting down roots that bothered me. I like having enough money in my pocket to get by but not the fancy house, the cars, the clothes. That excess doesn't mean shit to me. That only attracts bullshit and the wrong kind of attention. They targeted my mother at the parking lot of the fancy mall where she and Eve went shopping after school. They followed my family home and salivated over our house and what was inside. It was a random pick. That's what the policeman told me."

Grace's shoulders sank. "Oh God."

"My mother came from a small mountain town in Colorado, Grace. She worked hard, got educated, and made something of herself. She could afford nice, pretty things for herself, her house, her family. Where did it get her though? Watching her teenage daughter get raped and tortured over and over again and getting raped herself over and over again. And on top of all of that, knowing her son was watching and listening to everything."

Her useless, helpless son.

My hands covered my eyes. My chest caved in.

"Dig—"

"I should've been at football practice that afternoon, but I had pulled a muscle the day before and used it as a last-minute excuse to cut out because I wanted to go home and play my new video games. I knew Mom and Eve would be out shopping."

"You must have been terrified! You didn't want to leave her."

I ran my hands up and down Grace's bare thighs. "No, I didn't want to leave her alone on the living room floor where they had thrown her like yesterday's garbage. But I was an idiot. Instead of running outside when I had the chance and finding a neighbor like she was begging me to do the whole time—I can still hear her voice in my head, Grace! Did I do what she asked me? The very last thing my amazing, brave beautiful mother asked of me? No, I didn't do it."

"Honey—"

"I held her hand. I tried to pick her up off the floor, but there wasn't time for all that. I should have gone for help. She kept begging me 'Go! Go!' She was so freaked out that she lapsed into her country mountain twang. 'Get gone, Jake!' She pleaded with me, pleaded with me to be safe so that they wouldn't see me. I was supposed to save her. Instead, she saved me. While she was suffering, being tortured, she fucking saved me, Grace." My throat stung.

"They found the cold pizza I'd been eating in the kitchen when they broke in."

"You're not allergic to ..."

I shook my head.

"Oh God."

"They asked her about me. They started looking for me in the house, but she stopped them. Stopped them with her quick thinking, her powerful words, her power of persuasion. She led them to the safe upstairs in her room, gave them whatever they wanted and more. And they kept taking more. She sacrificed herself for me, her worthless piece-of-shit son. 'Get gone!' she'd begged me. But I hadn't listened." My fingers curled in the hem of Grace's shirt.

"I'd only panicked. I froze. Fucking useless!"

"You were thirteen."

"I was an idiot! A helpless idiot. And I humiliated my mother even more by her knowing that I was watching and listening to all that shit they were doing. And Eve—" The breath burned in my lungs. "Eve killed herself that day, and no one can tell me different. Her screeching ripped me in fucking two as she tore out onto the street. Once the police finally arrived and I crawled out, I saw the pieces of her on the road in front of that grand palace we called home."

"And your dad?" she whispered.

"My dad?" My head sank into the pillow and I swallowed hard. "My dad had come home earlier than usual to surprise my mom. He had just landed a big deal account out of New York, and we were supposed to celebrate that night. That was what his secretary told me at the funeral. Celebrate his success." I inhaled a deep breath. "My mom had panicked when they heard Dad's message on the answering machine, saying he was on his way home, that they ended up choking her after doing her one last time on the stairs. Both of them. She had gotten all her jewelry out of the safe and whatever cash was in there, the silver in the dining room, and that was their big *thank you for all your trouble, ma'am.*

"They were waiting for my dad when they heard his Cadillac roll up in the driveway, his key in the door. I threw up in the closet, ticking down the seconds till I heard his key scrape in the lock, then turning it. 'Amelia?' He always called out her name the second he stepped through that door. They hacked him with a hunting knife they had and one of the gardener's tools they'd found out back. I had to walk over him to get out."

"Jake—"

"Don't fucking calling me that! Don't ever! Jake Pence died that day. He was raped by what he saw, what he heard. He was cut and hacked. He bled out, was run over, and crushed to pieces. And all those pieces were left smashed on the road in front of that fucking house. He's gone. Gone!" I roared, bucking her off me.

The door burst open.

"What the hell are you doing, motherfucker?" Boner shouted.

He darted over to Grace, who was crumpled at the edge of the mattress, crying. He ripped the sheet off the bed, wrapped it around her naked lower body, and held her in his arms.

Her sobs ripped through me and squeezed in my chest.

"Don't cry for me, Grace! Goddamn it! Stop."

"I will!" she sobbed. "You need someone to cry for you! You need *me* to do it!"

Boner's huge eyes glinted at me. He shook his head as he cradled her, tucking her deeper in his embrace "Not like this, man. Should have told her a fucking long time ago. Not like this."

My jaw stiffened. I moved to the edge of the bed near them but said nothing. All of it was a jumble in my brain, tying my tongue, mangling any sense left in me.

"How do you think we managed to buy this dump for the club and fix it up? Huh?" I asked. "For years, we'd been living in flophouses, abandoned warehouses, motels gone bankrupt, here and there, moving around the area. Wreck had found this go-kart factory, but the club didn't have the money for it. I bought it for the club with that trust fund money and we fixed it up. Whatever I inherited that evil fucking day, I put it down here and gave the rest away."

Grace's head sagged against Boner's arm, her watery gaze never wavering from mine.

"The one good thing that remains from all that was a terrific lesson, Gracie. The cop who found me in the closet told me I shouldn't worry. He said these sorts of bad things were random occurrences that happened rarely. What a fucking joke. All through our meaningless little lives, random, chance acts blow by you, or they blow at you. Just maybe, on the rare occasion, they explode in your face. Boom! Or they don't. What is sure is that you have no control over it, so the faster you learn that and accept it, the better off you'll be." I reached over to the nightstand and lit a cigarette, tossing the lighter back on the table.

I exhaled a thick stream of smoke, staring at her. "When I met you, I saw it in your eyes, that random blowback. It had touched you, too, but you'd kept your head high through all of it. Not me. I stuck mine in the gutter, in the dirt, down real low. My parents used to tell me and Eve, 'You've got a bright future ahead of you.' Yeah, me and Eve sure did." I rubbed a hand down my chest, letting out a heavy breath.

"I made a life that works for me by ignoring my shadow. I'm not even sure I fucking have one anymore." My fingertips traced over the snake tattoo circling my lower waist. "Bite before you get bitten," I murmured.

"Dig—"

"But with you in the equation, that just doesn't work. And it's not fair to you. I want it to work real bad. So fucking bad. Why do you think I never came by to party at your sister's house all those years ago? 'Cause I knew I'd get hooked on you, and that wouldn't be good for either of us. So, I stayed away, but you stayed in here." I tapped on the side of my head. "And when I finally had you—in my hands, in my bed, on my bike—I felt like maybe, just maybe, it was my turn. Finally, something good just for me."

"Why didn't you tell me? We've been together for years, Dig! Why?"

"For that look in your eyes right now. That pity, that fucking sympathy, that horror."

"That's not what I'm feeling!" She sat up in Boner's embrace, wiping at her face.

I let out a hiss of air. "Look at you, baby."

She pushed away from Boner and crawled on the bed in front of me, the sheet dragging down her body, her eyes full of water, her face red and wet. "This is my respect and belief in you. This is my deep fucking admiration." She wiped at her nose with the back of her hand. "I believe in you—Jake Pence, Dig Quillen. I believe in *you*. I believe that you would protect me with your life. I believe in the goodness that you keep squashed so damn deep inside. I believe in your loyalty and your smarts and generosity. I believe in you, and most of all, I believe in your love for me. That's what this is." She pointed to her face. "That's what gets us by, keeps us sane. That's all that matters. Can't you see that?"

I peered into those savage eyes, the stiff lines of her face and body adamant, and it zapped right through me and lit up my soul for a few brilliant seconds like forked Dakota lightning flashing against a black sky.

This is faith. This is what love is.

"What if I can't protect you? I couldn't protect Wreck. That man used to protect me, watch out for me and for Miller. I fucked that up. I broke that chain. Now we've got the baby coming. I got to be able to keep you safe."

"That's why you didn't want a baby?"

"Yeah, but I'd had enough of keeping that shit tight. I wanted a piece of the dream, too."

Her hands gripped my arms. "Yes, that's right. We're having that dream come true together."

"Oh, baby, look around you. Wreck is gone. His neck was practically ripped clean through. He was nearly empty of blood by the time the ambulance showed. And over what?" A laugh escaped my throat. "Fucking nothin'. That's what. No matter what we do, how we live our lives, this shit happens. God knows if we'll ever see or hear from Miller again."

"What are you saying?" She raised her voice, her eyes lighting up. "Should we go run and hide in a cave somewhere? Is that what you're saying?"

"No. No. The beauty of it is that we aren't *ever* going to be immune from it. At least here, with the club, I found a way to live by my rules, my way. I can fight back better, stronger, than if I were living my mom and dad's life. I don't need a Caddy or a Mercedes to feel alive. Just my bike with you on it." I held her

189

watery gaze. "None of it makes sense otherwise, Grace. I didn't think I'd ever get married, ever want a kid. But here we fucking are. I still fight it half the time and embrace it the rest."

"I know you do," she whispered.

My head tipped back, my body sagged. "You're in my bones, Grace. Can't stand straight without you, baby. Can't."

"Me either."

"Christ," Boner muttered.

Grace crawled closer to me and I dropped my head in her chest. Her arms wrapped around me, and my breath snagged. Boner stood up, tossing the twisted sheet he was still holding on to on the floor. His hand passed over my head, tugging my hair as he left the room. The door closed with a firm thud.

I buried my face in her throat, my hands sliding around her waist. "You on for that ride, baby?"

She clutched my neck, my shoulders. "I've always been on."

SEVENTEEN

"YOU MOLE? HOW'D YOU GET MY NUMBER?"

"Friend of a friend of a friend." The stringy kid standing in his motel room doorway laughed. He had the jitters, his eyes were bugging out of his head, and he smelled bad from his stained blue hoodie down to his torn jeans. "I'm a little far from home and didn't pack my suitcase right." He cackled through his nose as he bounced from foot to foot.

"Yeah. What's it gonna be?" I didn't have time for this shit, but a sale was a sale. I was on my way home when I got his call, and I could spare the time. We were just outside of Deadwood. Wouldn't take long. This shit never did.

"Whatever you got, man. Should've planned ahead better. But you know how it goes, right?" He stared at my patches.

I eyed him, and he averted his gaze. "What kind of money you got to spend? Let's start there, huh?"

He shoved a hand in his back pocket and came out with a twenty-dollar bill. His forehead creased, and he bumped the glasses on his face higher. I caught a flash of red from a familiar tattoo on his arm.

I jerked my chin at him. "You ain't a Seed. What the fuck?"

He shook his head as he searched for more money in his other pockets. "Nah, my uncle is. Me and my brother are patching in."

"Oh, yeah?" *As if.* "You a prospect?"

"Uh, soon. We got us the inside track."

Right.

This kid?

Thick eyeglasses over small-set eyes, acne spattered on his face, wiry muscles, and greasy spiky hair along with those stupid fucking plastic gauges in his ears. Real Demon Seed material.

"Never seen you around before. I don't forget a face."

His eyebrows jumped. "Keeping it on the QT, bro."

"Don't call me bro. I ain't your bro. And by the way, Mr. QT, having that tat on you ain't right. You're gonna get yourself in big trouble."

Whoever his uncle was, he had a clusterfuck in the making on his hands.

Time to get this done. "What's it going to be? We talking twenty?"

"Well, ten. I need some gas money." He snorted and scratched his middle, hitching up his T-shirt.

"You got me up here for a ten-buck deal? Are you shittin' me? I stopped dealing with punks like you a long, long time ago."

I shook my head and stepped back.

A muffled yelping came from behind him. He blinked rapidly, and his lips flattened. A moan. A thud against the wall—once, twice, three times. Another moan. My spine stiffened, my muscles tensed. My eyes slid to his.

"I, uh…got something you might be interested in, in place of extra cash." He pushed the door open further and motioned me inside his room with a jerk of his head.

I took a step forward.

There, on his bed, was a woman.

No, a girl.

A young teenage girl, raw terror on her round face. Her mouth was bound with tape, and her eyes were red and puffy. One eye was almost swollen shut. Traces of makeup were smeared on her blotchy skin. Her yellow T-shirt was ripped up the middle, her bare breasts on display. Otherwise, she was naked. Her entire body shook under my stare, even her arms and legs, which were tied to the bedposts. Her head rose slightly as I stepped closer to the bed. She froze for an instant and shook again.

"Why don't you have a piece of that while I set myself up?" Mole let out a snort. "I'm gonna need energy, ya know?"

My breath stalled, and my spine knotted.

"Be my guest, man. Have a piece. Have at it. You want, we could do her together. I'm up for that."

The girl's one eye widened. She struggled to kick her legs, legs covered in red scratches and bruises. She gave up and slumped back onto the mattress once more, her face covered in sweat, her strawberry-blonde hair in a knotty sea over her head, her chest heaving. Mole kicked two empty pizza boxes to the side of the room.

I stepped slowly toward the bed, toward the girl, toward the sacrifice.

"She sucked my dick real nice for breakfast. That's my kinda room service, right? Long as she's got my gun at her head, that is. Get on, man. Give her a go. I just fucked her tits. Hey, you know, if you want, you can fuck her first. Nothing like popping a tight cherry. I was saving that for after *this,* but I can fuck her ass, no problem. That'll do me real good. Maybe you could, um…give me another bag for that, huh? That good for you? We could do that. What do they call it when you swap? Bartering? Yeah, let's barter. We're doing business here, right? Awesome."

I heard nothing.

I heard everything—her shuddering body, the rope twisting on the headboard, her feet thumping on the mattress, her choppy and harsh breaths, an eighteen-wheeler thundering down the highway.

I stared down at her bruised and bitten body, the soiled sheets. I inhaled the stink of piss, cum, sweat, fear. My veins surged with adrenaline. My eyes went to his.

He raised himself up on his toes. "Are we cool?"

A smile flickered over my lips. I held out a small plastic baggie filled with his candy of choice.

He seized it.

Mole flung himself in a chair by the bed and got busy over the bag with a spoon, a lighter. I climbed on the bed and straddled the girl's hips as she let out a low moan. She struggled, pulling on the headboard, and it banged on the wall. My hands slowly stroked up and down her arms. She twisted and shook.

A vibrating windup toy at my disposal.

A toy.

"Yeah, man. Yeah. Go for it." Plastic crinkled and crumpled. The determined flick of a lighter. Once. Twice. A desperate inhale, a groan. The squeak of a chair.

I leaned over the girl, my face inches from hers, eye-to-eye. She squealed, twisting her head away.

Is this what it's like?

"Slap her to get her to shut up if you want." He snorted, sniffing deep.

"Look at me." My voice was low, controlled.

She opened her one good eye. Red blood vessels strained up at me. A blue eye, the same blue of…

I planted my hands on either side of her head, my left landing in a pillow, fisting there. She moaned and squirmed under my weight, her eyes pleading, begging.

Hysteria.

A languid laugh. "Man, you sell good shit, huh?"

"Shh." I laid a finger against her broken lips.

Her head tipped up and jerked from side to side. She shook.

I grinned.

I snatched up the pillow with my left hand and slid the Kimber out of my holster with my right and fired through the pillow, straight at the motherfucker. A second time. A third. The girl's muffled shriek strained against the tape over her mouth.

Mole's right eye erupted with a gush of blood. His chest bled from the two holes I incinerated through him. His head dropped to the side, blood spilling in gushes onto the shag rug.

I put my gun away and slid my small knife from the side of my leg. "I'm getting you outta here. Don't scream. Don't run. You won't get far. What we don't want are the cops here." I cut the ropes at her legs, still straddling her. "You're gonna get up and get your pants and your shoes on, and we leave together."

She nodded, her chest heaving, and I cut the ropes on her hands. She scrambled off the bed and grabbed a pair of faded jeans off the floor. She yanked them up her legs and then shoved her feet into a pair of Keds that had been tossed in a corner. Her shaking hands tried to cover her naked chest. I took off my leather jacket and approached her. She shuddered but accepted the jacket as I put it around her shoulders.

She stumbled under the weight of the heavy leather, staring at the dead dipshit's body in the chair. I grabbed my empty packaging from the small round table at his side and stuffed it in my pocket. There was a medicine bottle on the table.

Filled with what? I flicked open the top.

Gold flakes and grains.

An old man who had been panning for gold just west of here had been murdered the night before at his motel room, his treasure stolen. I glanced at Mole's lifeless corpse.

Motherfucker.

"Has he been talking to anybody on the phone?" I asked the girl as I inspected the bottle. "Anybody else come here or know he's here?"

She sniffed and wiped at her nose. "He called his brother. They talked. They were going to meet up tonight and...and party." She let out a low wail.

I grabbed his cell phone from the table and slid the gold into the front pocket of my jeans. "Okay, okay. It's over. I'm going to take you out of here on my bike and get you safe, okay?"

Her head jerked. "I don't wanna go with you. N-no. No more, please! Please!"

"I'm not kidnapping you. I'm getting you home. What's your name?"

"J-Jill."

"Listen up, Jill. We're walking out of here, all natural. I'm gonna put my arm around you, like you're my girlfriend, okay? Just so it looks normal to whoever's watching. You keep your face down. Don't look at anybody. Don't speak to anybody."

Her round eyes darted to my wedding ring. "You-you're married?"

"Yeah. And my wife's waiting for me. But I want to get you out of here first, all right?"

She nodded, tugging my jacket closer around her. "All right."

My jacket swallowed her up. Only her reddish-blonde hair and pale face were visible from that swathe of black.

"We're gonna get on my bike and get the hell out of here. You got that? We'll get you some clothes and get you to a bus or a train or whatever. That guy's on his way. You don't want him to find you, do you?"

She shook her head. "No. No. Let's go. Let's go!"

"All right then. No yelling, no running, or we'll get stopped."

She nodded as she wrapped her arms around herself, the jacket hanging on her.

"Go into my inside pocket there and grab my sunglasses." She carefully fiddled with the jacket and found the Ray-Bans. She held them out to me. "You put 'em on. Your eye looks like shit. Don't want anyone seeing that right now. Also needs protecting on the bike."

She slid the glasses over her small face. The large sporty black lenses made her look like a drunken teen starlet, bracing for the paparazzi the morning after. "Thank you." Her voice squeaked.

"Let's get the hell out of here."

I opened the door and closed it behind us firmly, wiping it with the bottom part of my shirt. I slung my arm around her. She flinched for a second and then walked rigidly beside me. We got to my bike, and I took out my phone and called Boner, who I knew was nearby. I got him to deal with the remains of the dipshit Demon nephew. I'd never seen the asshat before, and I wasn't sure if he was an official prospect or no, but there were no signs of anything Demon Seeds-related in his motel room. Just that tattoo on his arm. I couldn't afford to get into it with the Seeds now. Vig and I had our little covert agreement going, things had to stay cool. That body had to disappear.

We stopped at a convenience store, and I got her a windbreaker, a Mount Rushmore T-shirt, and a toothbrush while she picked out something to tie her hair with. At a fast-food joint by the bus station, I got her a milkshake and a burger and a soda for myself while she hit the restroom to get cleaned up and changed.

She came back out, and I smoked a cigarette while she ate her food. Her eyes studied my colors while she slurped on the last of her chocolate shake.

"You're in a biker gang?"

"It's a club, not a gang."

"I thought you were gonna—"

"I know. That's what I wanted him to think."

"Right. Thank you. I don't know what I would've done, what would've happened."

"You don't want to know what would've happened, so let's not go there." I leaned over the table and swirled the ice in my soda cup. "What I do know is that you need to go home and stay there.

"Me and my friends came out here for a concert which I wasn't supposed to go to in the first place. My mom just got remarried, and things…changed. He's real strict. I was ticked off at him, at her, and I went anyway, deciding not to bother going home at all. Knew I'd get into trouble anyhow. At the concert, I went to take a pee, and *he* started talking to me. He grabbed me, and…"

"I get it."

She toyed with the straw and chewed on her lips.

"If you're mad at your mom and your new dad, try talking it out first. Don't just pick up and run and get sloppy while you're doing it. They want to keep you safe, and that's the best thing there is for a kid, especially a girl. There's plenty of what you just went through out there. Worse even. Maybe if you act grown-up, they might treat you that way."

She frowned. "You a dad?"

"Gonna be. I'm actually missing a doctor's appointment right now." I glanced at my watch for the hundredth time. The damn cell phone buzzed in my back pocket.

Grace was gonna have my head. Again. I had put the cell phone on vibrate only. I knew it was her, but I couldn't answer and lie to her. I just couldn't. Not now.

Jill bit her lip. "Oh, I'm sorry."

"Yeah, well, that's okay. There'll be plenty more. Got six months to go till D-day."

She crushed her empty milkshake container between her hands. "Thank-you seems kind of lame for everything you've done for me."

"We're good. You got to keep this under your hat though. Cops getting involved won't be good for any of us. I'm trusting you."

Her spine stiffened. "I won't tell."

I leaned forward over the small table. "You need to remember that they could come after us, Jill, and if they find you or me, it won't go well."

She nodded her head.

"Appreciate what you got. Make the best of it. You got lots of time ahead of you to make changes and choices. Take care of yourself. Girls got to do that because boys are assholes and don't know any better. Okay? And you need help dealing with all the hell he put you through, you go get it. Don't take it out on yourself. Trust me on that one."

"Okay."

"You do that for me, and we'll be square.

"I'm plenty grateful, believe me."

"Okay. I'll be keeping my eye on shit around here. Take your ticket, and stay on the goddamn bus. It's going to be crap, being home the first few days, but you suck it up. In the end, it's always going to be up to you to make it better."

She rubbed her arms. "Never thought of it that way. You ever run away from home?"

"Yeah, I did. No more though. One day, you'll stop wanting to run, or maybe you'll find what you didn't realize you were always looking for. No one had ever given me a second chance until I met a guy from this bike club. He showed me that you make your own luck, pave your own road through life, and I believe that. I'm living proof. It's up to you to to find a way or make one when you need to, Jill."

She nodded and exhaled as she stared at the bus that had just pulled up before us. We got up, and I handed her her ticket.

"What should I tell them about my face?" she asked.

"Blame it on a guy. You fought back. You did, didn't you?"

"Yeah, I tried."

"Of course you did. That's no lie then, right?"

Jill hiccuped on a breath. She threw her arms around me and gave me a quick squeeze. "Thank you." She let go of me and ran up the stairs of the bus. She jerked to a stop, turned, and jostled down the steps again. "Wait—your sunglasses!" She took off my shades and held them out to me.

"You keep 'em as a souvenir. I got my extra pair." I handed her the case from my pocket. "Keep them, so you don't forget."

She smiled for the first time. "I won't forget."

Don't forget, Jill. Don't ever forget.

EIGHTEEN

"DIG, WAIT!"

Grace's hands pressed into my sides, our signal that she wanted me to pull over.

One week later, we were out for a short ride on a late afternoon.

At that appointment that I had missed, her doctor had told her that she needed to stop riding until after the baby was born. She was starting to show now, her belly curving just slightly.

We had looped around Meager on the quiet country route through the sunflower farms. The rolling fields of towering yellow-and-green flowers proudly wavered in the wind, their colors glowing in the late afternoon sun, hailing us as we zoomed past. Clouds moved overhead like a steady herd of buffalo, their massive shapes creating pockets of shadow and light over the fields that seemed to roll on toward forever. A moody masterwork come to life.

We stopped at the side of the road, and Grace opened a saddlebag.

"Where are your extra pair of sunglasses? They're always here."

Instead, she found Mole's stolen gold and a couple of tiny sample diamonds from Vig's stockpile that I'd hung on to after I'd stashed them.

A fight. Raised voices. Bitter words. Even more bitter disappointment. I tried to convince her that things had been quiet, not to worry. Anything to wipe that disappointment from her face.

"It's never enough, is it?" she asked, her voice strained.

"I don't sit back on my ass and wait to get served. That's not me. How can you not want better for the club? For us?"

Her hand passed across our kid growing in her tummy. "We have better for us, don't we?"

The woman who never stopped believing in me suddenly doubted me. I saw it in the stiffening of her back, her lips smashing together.

I swung back on the bike. "Hop on, we're out of here." I started the engine, but she didn't move.

My eyes slid to her. "Babe."

"Coming," she said through gritted teeth, the clipped tone of her voice ticking me off.

I clenched my jaw. *This will pass. She's just being emotional.*

I didn't tell her about Mole and the girl. I didn't want her to know that filth, didn't want her to worry about the girl. Grace would find something to worry about. I let her chalk it up to greed between boys, an argument over money gone amok.

But this time, I saw resignation in her eyes. Me taking chances over a two-bit drug deal, me getting into bed with Vig to score big bucks without telling my brothers about it for the time being.

She stood there, staring at me, while I ran the engine.

Her face tightened as she tamped down the tears I knew were gathering behind those eyes. It was all over her face—a sadness that I would never be able to control or wipe away in her. It was new, this anxiety of hers.

I snapped at her, and she relented, shuffling over to the bike. But it left a bitter taste in my mouth, and I hated it.

Taking in a breath, I loosened my tight grip on the handlebars. "Grace."

Her shoulders dropped, and she ran her fingers through my hair. That soft shiver raced through me.

"Get on, baby." I kissed the side of her face, the faint scent of her shampoo rushing my senses, dispelling the heaviness inside me for a sweet moment.

She got on and settled behind me, her arms at my sides, where they belonged. My heart beat again.

"Your doctor said no more riding for you after this, right? So let's enjoy it."

We took off.

And flew down the road.

The pop and whizz of gunshots.

Burning, searing, cracking. Flying.

The insane force of my bike crushing me.

Grace? Where are you, baby?

My wildflower.

I couldn't yell. I couldn't see. I couldn't see *her.*

There. A shadow.

Those fucking diamonds. *Tell her where they are.*

"Get gone, baby."

Mom?

I saw Eve's face beaming at finally getting her driver's license.

I saw Boner's fierce eyes as we'd jumped from the roof of that nasty group home to dive into that full Dumpster down below, heading into a better life.

I saw a young Miller burying his head in Wreck's chest when he saw his own bedroom at Wreck's house for the very first time, clinging to his brother, sobs choking him.

I saw Wreck grinning at me, that faded red bandana over his head, his mirrored shades hiding his eyes but not his eagerness. His big body perfectly conformed to his chopper as we'd ridden fast through the pink light of dawn, side by side, toward a town called Meager that very first time that August morning.

"We're going to have a baby, Dig. I'm pregnant."

I saw...

I saw...

"Damn it! Stay with me, Dig!"

...those beautiful hazel eyes that had once called me back to life.

So fucking beautif—

PART II
GRACE

PRESENT

NINETEEN

I WAS EXHAUSTED, BUT I COULDN'T SLEEP. I was wound up tight.

Insomnia hadn't taunted me in a very long time. I hadn't had a lot of coffee earlier today either.

Tossing and twisting in bed, I piled the pillows in different directions, in a variety of combinations. Still didn't work. The soft buzz from the one glass of whiskey I'd had at the club had quickly faded, and my brain was on some sort of tedious trek. I hadn't had the patience for Jump and Alicia this evening, and I couldn't tolerate watching Suzi, one of the old ladies, drinking too much and spouting off because she knew her old man had cheated on her. My head had started to pound, and I'd left Miller at the club and come home early on my own.

Lying on my back, I rubbed a hand in circles over my middle, soothing my stomach. I hadn't been able to eat all day, and I still wasn't hungry, yet somehow my stomach was in knots. I inhaled a long breath through my nose and exhaled slowly through my lips.

Nope. Not helping.

I grunted and scrunched myself around the body of pillows. My aching eyes drifted through our moonlit bedroom and rested on our framed wedding picture, on Miller's smile. My eyelids sank.

"Honey, I'm home."

Miller soft laugh broke the quiet of our dark room. The slide of a leather belt and the clink of a buckle. He let out a deep breath, and a light thud followed. He flopped down next to me, the mattress dipping under his weight.

A taut long arm slid under the layers of bedding and wrapped around my middle, pulling me into his naked body, his warmth seeping through my flesh. I burrowed back against him as he buried his face in my neck. Pushing my hair out of his way, he dragged his lips across my skin, inhaling, nuzzling. He pulled me in tighter, nestling me between his legs. Insistent fingers slid under my camisole and found a breast, taking it prisoner. I squirmed under his urgent touch, his tequila-laced breath hot on my skin. His one hand fanned my middle and snuck underneath my thin cotton shorts.

But I was somewhere else. In a dream? Wakeful but not. In the middle of feeling and sensation, warmth flaring through me, tossing me. Something shuddered inside me in the opposite direction of the pleasure my husband was summoning from me.

"Miller." I sighed as I took his one hand from my breast and kissed his long fingers, the skin salty, thick, durable.

He cradled me in his embrace, and I burrowed back into his body, pressing my fingers into his arms.

"You smell good," he murmured.

"I took a shower when I got home."

"What am I going to do with you? My old lady goes home early from a party, leaves me hanging. Then she takes a shower. I wanted to lick tonight off you." His lips nuzzled the side of my neck.

"Hmm." I squiggled my ass against his erection. "I didn't leave you hanging," I murmured.

"Yes, you did, baby. I cannot function at these club get-togethers anymore without you."

"How the mighty have fallen."

He only laughed and nipped at my shoulder with his teeth. "It's just that, now that I quit smoking, I need to hold on to something. My fingers got to keep busy, or I'm in danger of slipping." His fingers skimmed between my legs. "Headache gone?"

"Not really." I let out a soft moan.

"You need something more. I can think of a few things. Doctor's in the house." His tongue lashed my ear.

My hand covered his as it dragged through the sleekness between my legs, tingles of warmth shooting through me. "This is good, baby."

"That's not the adjective I wanted to hear. Give me that mouth."

I turned my face toward his, and he kissed me. I surrendered to being consumed like a cold beer on a sweltering August afternoon. He twisted me on my back and tugged my shorts out of the way, his tongue searing my skin as it journeyed down my body. My legs fell open for him, my one hand sifting through his smooth straight hair as his fingers dug in my behind.

Taylor Swift's "Shake It Off" ripped the seam of his lips against my flesh, snapping me back to reality. My nephew, Jake, had put that ringtone on my phone. I didn't like it much, but it would make him laugh so hard that his little belly shook every time, and he'd break into a frenetic dance move. I couldn't deprive him of that—or myself.

Miller groaned. "Who the fuck is that? It's past three o'clock in the morning."

My neck tensed instantly. *I had been waiting for something all night, hadn't I?* The tension in between my eyes, in every joint, in the pit of my stomach that Miller's kisses had alleviated for a few sweet moments flared anew. My palm hit the night table until it touched the cold smooth rectangle that was my phone.

Did something happen to Jake? To Alex, his dad?

I twisted over in bed and squinted at the small screen, the green light punishing my eyes.

My lungs froze.

Laura.

I hit the Receive call button.

"Grace! Grace! I'm sorry! So sorry!"

My pulse raced. I clutched the phone to my ear. "Laura?"

"I don't know what happened. Everything's been going great and then…"

No.

No!

"I'm at the hospital."

No.

"What ha—"

"I had these shooting pains, and there was bleeding, and…we lost the baby, Grace. I'm so sorry…so sorry," Laura sobbed.

My body went lax. The phone was taken from my cold fingers.

"Laura? It's Miller. What's going on? Oh. Uh-huh. How—right." Heavy exhale. "Yeah? You okay? All right. Take care. We'll talk soon. Yeah." He threw my phone across the bed, another horrid heavy exhale forced from his nose.

The bedding fell from my body, and the chilly night air swept over my heated skin as my face sank into my hands.

How do you have a miscarriage when you're not even pregnant?

How do you feel the pain of losing your child, the fruit of your body, and not be there, not witness it, not feel that cutting pain jar your own insides?

I had felt it once before, but so much had been going on around me then, so much else to cry over.

Now my soul was ripping. Everything…smothered.

But I didn't care about me.

"Miller?" My hand stretched out in the dark and slid up the curve of his smooth back.

Over five months ago, Miller and I had woken up one special morning before the alarm had even gone off.

We kissed and held each other. I wanted him inside me so badly, but I knew that would happen later—after this morning was done. Instead, I poured myself into making him come, my naked body pressing into his from behind. My very clean hand worked with his very clean hand on his throbbing cock to release his pleasure and, most importantly, his cum into a laboratory cup, so we could rush it over to the clinic. My lips had nuzzled his skin, my pelvis squirming against the bunched-up tight muscles of his rear. His rough choke of breath signaled his climax as his body tensed for a split second. In the very next instant, his hard long cock had pulsed, spilling forth its seed into the cup I held before it, making sure not one thick spurt would be lost. His fingertips pressed painfully into my flesh as we both watched our little fountain of life.

"Close the lid quick," he mumbled between short breaths.

I giggled. "I got it. Don't worry." I slapped the lid on the plastic cup, twisted it firmly into place, and then put it on the night table. "There."

We both stared at his liquid DNA. My gaze went back to my beautiful husband, hot as hell, with his longish black hair seriously mussed, his broody dark eyes still puffy with sleep, his muscular body flexing underneath mine. I pushed him back onto the mattress.

He grinned, squeezing my hips. "Babe, what are you doing?"

"I want some, too," I whispered.

His lips parted as I slid down his body and took his cock into my mouth. I lavished his now relaxed length with slow long licks, my hands stroking his massive thighs, as I sucked him clean. His eyes blackened as he let out a hiss of air, his hips flexing against my mouth. I released him and rose over him, planting a languid kiss on his lips.

"Let's go, Flies as Eagles."

He let out a rumbly small laugh. "Yeah, let's go." His one hand palmed a breast, the other slid down my ass. "After, we're gonna come right back here and fuck for the rest of the day. Three days of abstinence really sucked balls."

My pelvis rocked against his, and he let out a groan. "It definitely did."

We got to the clinic with our precious package and handed it to the nurse, who officially labeled it in front of us with our name. My hand wrapped around Miller's arm at the sight.

My and Miller's bodily offerings would now be introduced to each other in a laboratory. The doctor would raise his baton, the orchestra would begin playing, and our particles would dance the dance of life under observation. My thoroughly examined and approved eggs were patiently awaiting their suitors just beyond the doors of the clinic's reception area where we stood.

The nurse rose from her seat, our cup in hand. "Okay then, we'll let you know how it goes."

We watched them both disappear behind that door beyond our reach.

Six embryos had come to life that day. Two had later been implanted in our surrogate, Laura. One of those had failed within days, and the other that had taken root inside of her was now gone, failing its epic mission.

Gone.

"You can try again."

The words I didn't want to hear from my doctor. Hadn't planned on hearing.

Dreaded hearing.

I crossed my legs, clutching my suede bag tighter on my lap, hoping the softly textured surface under my fingertips would distract me. Miller's hand closed over my thigh. He stared at me from his seat to my right. I could feel that stare in every cell of my body.

My useless body.

I nodded and forced a quick smile, squeezing down the grief welling inside me and hoping that would assuage Dr. Carollton's concern.

"Good," he said, going back to his paperwork.

One down, one more to go.

My husband's concern would be quite another.

"We don't know the cause of the miscarriage?" Miller asked.

"No. Sometimes, these things happen in the first months."

A lot just happens.

If my mother were here, she would shrug her shoulders and say, *Just wasn't meant to be.*

Those smug, hollow words signified nothing but somehow managed to make the bearer of them feel good and trudge on. I despised the phrase.

Screw that.

Miller shifted in his seat. "Laura had never had a miscarriage before though?"

"True. I just got this report from her doctor. She had a D and C done right after." Dr. Carollton glanced at Miller. "It's a procedure akin to an abortion. And the good news is, there was no sign of genetic defects in the cells."

I gritted my teeth. My forty-three-year-old eggs were able to produce a nonchromosomal-defective human being. *Kudos, missy.* My gaze remained pinned to the toe of my right boot digging into the thin beige carpet on the floor.

Cells. Material to be scraped, prodded, examined. Dumped.

My and Miller's baby was now only a collection of cellular matter. Our test-tube alchemy of love and determination had not been strong enough to endure the nine-month journey of gestation in a foreign uterus.

Because I don't have a uterus.

Miller's hand squeezed my leg. "That's good," he murmured.

I glanced up at the doctor and nodded. I went back to staring at my boot twisting in the carpet.

"It's very, very good," the doctor continued. "Finding another gestational surrogate shouldn't be a problem. Once you do, you won't have to go through the IVF process again, Grace. We have three more embryos ready to use."

Oh, yes, my three popsicles. Ready for shipping and delivery at a moment's notice.

"Right," came Miller's tight reply. His one arm swept over my shoulders. "Grace? Anything else you want to ask the doctor?"

I shook my head. "No."

Dr. Carollton closed our folder, tapping it on his desk. "I will wait to hear from you once you find a new surrogate, and we'll go from there. Sound good?"

Sure, I'll just go find a new surrogate, like finding the right paint color for my living room or a new perfume to suit my mood. No problemo.

I got up from my seat and watched a somber Miller shake Dr. Carollton's hand. Only two weeks ago, we had been laughing and smiling and circling dates on our calendars.

Now this…

This nothingness.

This wait-and-see ho-humness.

My gut knotted. I slid my sunglasses down over my eyes as Miller steered me through the waiting room full of almost a dozen waiting women. Their expectant and anxious faces pressed in on me. Others glanced up from their magazines, tablets, and cell phones, appreciatively eyeing my husband up and down.

Once outside, he took my hand in his. "Babe, it'll be all right."

"Yeah," I said softly. If I said anything more, I would burst through the cracks already visible on my crumbly dry surface.

"You want me to call the lawyer and ask him to contact those agencies again?"

"No, no. I'll take care of it, honey." So didn't want to discuss this now. Nope. "You're going to go back to work, right?"

"No. I'm not leaving you on your own today." His hand rubbed mine, his dark eyes clouding over. He pushed back his hair behind his ears.

"Miller, you should go. You've got to finish those two bikes and that Ford before the rally next week. You don't have to babysit me."

"Babysit you? Shit, Grace. I just want to be here for you."

I chewed on my inner cheek. "That's what I'm saying, Mill. You don't have to do that."

He touched the side of my face. "Hey, our baby didn't make it, for fuck's sake. And you want me to go back to business as usual? How the fuck am I supposed to do that? I can't."

His eyes were glassy, the harsh angles of his face set. I had done this to him, put that sadness there.

Me and my happily ever after dreams.

I hugged him, tightly wrapping my arms around him. "Okay," I mumbled into his chest.

He rubbed my back. "Let's go get something to eat."

"Baby, what I meant was, I don't want you to worry about me. I'm okay. This was a risk to begin with. I knew that."

He kissed the top of my head and lifted my chin to face him. I forced a slight smile.

"You want to try again, right?"

My insides winced. There it was. Need. Hope. Fucking hope all over his beautiful face and in the suddenly soft tone of his deep voice.

"Yeah," I breathed. "Of course."

TWENTY

IT WAS THE FOURTEENTH DAY after the great Miscarriage Revelation.

I was pretending to be doing well, handling it, getting on with it. I had them all fooled—Boner, Dad, my friend Lenore, Dee, Alicia.

Even Miller.

I put down the teacup, the ginger flavor much too spicy for me, and sank down on the small sofa in Lenore's lingerie boutique in town. My fingers fiddled with my silver and leather bracelets as Lenore arranged new corsets on a tree branch–shaped display stand. I didn't want to appear cold and unfeeling, but I wished time would speed up, so I could clock in the requisite hour with my friend and then leave. Nope, not even shopping and girl time was helping.

My knuckles were still scarred from my last scrape down this road. My body felt as heavy as lead in the small lemon yellow sofa. Not even shopping earlier at Pepper's Boot Shop or Lenore's amusing chatter had done anything to distract me or lighten that load. My eyes glazed over as I scanned the provocative lingerie surrounding me in the boutique.

"Hell, honey, with a surrogate, you don't have to feel the crap side of pregnancy—the foot swelling, the back pain, the inability to move, all of that. Some women are into it, and some of us definitely aren't. That would be me. I didn't find that fun at all. Let's not talk about the belly tire that lingers long afterward." She patted at the curve of her lower belly.

I smiled. "I wouldn't have minded any of that, fat feet and all."

"Shit, I'm sure you wouldn't have. I'm sorry." Lenore rolled her eyes at herself. "I didn't mean anything by it. You know that, right?"

"Of course I know that." I leaned my head further back against the sofa. "I'm sorry I'm being such a drag."

"Don't be ridiculous. This stuff isn't easy."

"It isn't. I know that I should just be grateful that I could afford this whole process and I was able to give it a try."

"Grace, you feel angry? Feel it. You not being able to have kids is not your fault. That accident and the surgery you had to have—"

Let's not go there now. Whose fault anything was and is. Blah, blah, blah.

"I know," I said. "Really, I'm not feeling that I'm-a-barren-wasteland anger."

"Oh, don't talk like that."

"I guess it's this helplessness in the face of technology. I'm glad that I at least had a few good eggs to give."

Lenore's eyes brightened. "Exactly right."

"It's just strange, what a mechanical process it is. You have no control over it. You put your faith and trust in the hands of doctors and lab technicians." I stared down at the tiny herbs floating in the teacup.

Lenore folded piles of tissue paper into a neat stack and set it in a box. She pursed her lips. "How's Lock doing?"

I shrugged as my gaze flitted over the new delivery of high-cheek silk panties, frilly-trimmed satin panties.

"Grace, I wasn't going to say anything, but he called me yesterday, looking for you."

"What?" My face heated.

Lenore nodded. "You weren't answering your phone, and he thought that maybe you and I had hit an exercise class or gone out for lunch or something."

I waited for more. Lenore waited for a response from me. She'd be waiting in vain.

She held my gaze and tilted her head. "I told him that you'd been cutting out on cardio, and I hadn't talked to you or seen you here in a while." She propped the box on the floor by the cash register counter. "Grace, what the hell? Should I have covered for you or something?"

"Of course not. There's nothing to cover."

"Well, he wasn't happy. But it was the truth." Lenore sat down next to me. "Are you two okay?"

"Yeah, sure." I sat up straight.

Time to leave.

She eyed me. "Ah, so very convincing." The tone of her voice pricked at my skin like a newly sharpened pencil. "Where the hell have you been then? I've been calling you, too, if you've noticed, but you don't pick up."

"I'm sorry, Lenore. I've been moping. Things got busy with getting Jake ready to go stay with his dad. I went into Rapid a couple of times, did some shopping for Jake. He's growing so fast. He needed new jeans and PJs. And sneakers, too. Alex doesn't have much time for shopping, never mind laundry."

Since Miller had had a full calendar of appointments and deadlines last week, Boner had insisted on driving me and Jake up to Williston. I had been looking forward to alone time with Jake in the car, just the two of us singing along with his CDs and being silly, and most definitely alone time on the way back. Maybe doing some wandering before I went home. Something. Instead, I'd gotten Boner-chatter, as I liked to call it—an endless stream of remarks and observations and him driving my car way too damn fast. At least he hadn't insisted I chatter back. After the second hour, I'd managed to fall asleep, which was good because sleep had been eluding me lately.

Lenore pressed a hand over mine. "Lock loves you, Grace. Maybe if you just opened up to him? He can take it, I'm sure. Don't doubt that. That man's got a big heart for you."

"He does. And I just ripped a hole right through it," I whispered.

Her eyes widened suddenly. "What?"

I stood up, clearing my throat. *I have to get out of here.* I didn't want to discuss, analyze, or rehash any of this anymore. I just wanted it all to fucking go away. I had come today because, yes, I had been a lousy friend. Lenore had been trying to reach out to me since the miscarriage, and I hadn't responded. I wish I had come to her beautiful boutique today just for a spot of shopping or to have a laugh with her like I'd done the week before, trying on new nighties. But, no, not this. Not now.

The usually pleasant vanilla-and-mandarin candle scent stifled my nostrils. The colorful racks of silky tendrils, otherwise known as lingerie, hanging in the exotic small space did not entice or amuse me. Instead, they taunted me. Their playful, naughty promise of sex was supposed to make you feel good, feel close to your lover, and get you pregnant—the ultimate end game, if Nature had her way. Not me though. Not me. So many women fussed with all kinds of birth control for years to not make that baby. Just like I had once upon a time. For years. And years.

Cosmic joke.

I slung my suede bag over my shoulder. "I'm going to go."

Her eyes narrowed at me. "Where you off to?"

"I thought I'd take a walk before I head home. Window-shop down Clay Street. I've been wanting to check out that new pottery shop," I lied. My gaze darted out the glass front door at the gray fullness in the sky.

She chewed on her lip. "Honey, I'd go with you, but I've got these deliveries coming now, and I've got to be here."

"That's okay. You've got a business to run."

She squeezed my upper arm. "You call me if you need to talk. Anytime. Day or night, you hear?"

"I will. Thank you."

"Here, take these. Try 'em. I keep selling out." She stuffed several packets of nail decals in my handbag.

I let out a strained laugh. "As long as they're not hearts or Hello Kitty, I'll give them a try."

"Rhinestone chips. A little bling does a girl good." Lenore gave me a kiss on the cheek and shot me a wan smile as I waved good-bye and shut the door behind me.

The bartender at Pete's parked another full glass of whiskey in front of me.

"I didn't order another one, Randy. I haven't finished this one yet. But if you insist." I gulped down the last of my whiskey and reached for the fresh glass.

Randy wore a dark scowl on his thin face. "It's from that guy over there."

He raised his chin to my left, and I turned my head in that direction.

No way in hell.

"Grace, Grace, Grace."

"Sam?"

He raised his hands in the air. "Oh, yes, ladies and gentlemen, she actually remembers my name." A hand descended on his chest. "I'm touched, darlin'."

Sam Tremont—a former beau from Texas, a civil engineer who had a thing for motorcycles and who could afford to indulge in his hobby. He'd walked into the Harley dealership that I managed one afternoon, and I had tried to talk him into buying a bike. He hadn't bought the bike, but he had asked me out. We had lasted a little bit over four months. Kind of a record for me back then.

Still the same sassy look in those dark blue eyes as his mouth twisted into a smug sexy grin. There was now a hint of gray along the edges of his reddish-brown wavy hair, and it suited him.

I smiled, raising the glass of whiskey in his direction. "Thank you, kind sir."

His head tilted at me while he, no doubt, waited for a response to his sublime appearance as if he were doing me a favor by gracing my hometown and me with his presence. "Fancy meeting you here." He bent over and planted a kiss on my cheek, a hand squeezing my arm.

A different cologne, something crisper, greener, rose in the air between us.

"What the hell are you doing here?" I asked him. "If I remember correctly, you once declared that you would never set foot in the Dakotas again. They were too boring for you and your big, fat fancy BMW. What was it—'a whole lot of nothing that goes on forever'?"

He laughed and slid onto the barstool next to me. "Jesus, Grace, you are never going to let me forget that, are you?"

His smooth Texan drawl washed over me just like the liquor warming my throat and easing my insides. Yes, I used to enjoy the way he spoke. A lot.

"Never." I raised my glass and took another long gulp.

He laughed as he shook his head at me.

What had I seen in him?

An arrogance that I'd found exciting and intriguing, an arrogance that hadn't required stroking from me. It had been fun to go along on its high and mighty ride for a little while there—until it'd gotten annoying.

"Shit, it's been…how many years since I've seen you, and you still remember that? After everything else we had, that is the one thing that stuck, huh?" He drank from a longneck, his steely eyes remaining on me.

"Well, not the only thing," I shot back, quirking an eyebrow.

"Oh, all right then!" He laughed, his sapphire eyes lighting up. "Phew! My sense of manhood is still intact."

"But it is why I broke up with you, if you must know."

"Get real. You liked that bike, BMW or not."

I rolled my eyes at him, and we both laughed.

He scooted his stool closer to mine. "Did you come here after you dumped me? By the way, I came looking for you at the store and your apartment when I got back from that Hawaiian vacation I'd gone on by myself, but you were long gone. You gave up that for this?" His gaze darted around the tired bar before landing on me once more.

I smirked. I was sure he hadn't stayed on his own for long at that deluxe resort. "I went to Seattle, then I came here. This town is where I was born and raised actually, so watch what you say." My fingers trailed around the rim of my empty glass.

"No kidding." He waved Randy over and signaled for a refill for me. "Are you living here now or on a visit? You've got a sister here, right?"

Indeed I do, but she's in the ground. I rubbed my throat. "I'm living here now."

Randy poured the amber liquid in my glass and frowned at me before he stepped away. I ignored him.

Sam clinked his longneck with my full glass. I raised it.

"Well, it's very, very, very good to see you again."

I let out a small laugh, shaking my head.

"You look good, Grace."

We drank.

"Thank you. So do you." I turned away from his intense stare and nursed my drink. "What are you doing in South Dakota?"

"My friends wanted to see Mount Rushmore on the way to Devils Tower, so we organized a little expedition." He leaned in close to me. "I got rid of that BMW bike and got myself that Harley you'd told me I needed to have."

He brushed my hair off the side of my face and planted a kiss on my cheek. I burst out into laughter.

"You impressed?"

"No." I put a hand on his chest and shoved him away.

"You should be impressed, hon. Pissed me right the fuck off, the way things ended between us. In a big way." He sucked on his beer again and licked his lips dry.

"Oh, come on."

"Did so, Grace."

"If you say so."

"I do. Drink up now." He raised his beer bottle once more and waited for me to raise my glass. "Here's to random encounters."

My grip on my glass tightened. "What?"

"You and me, hon. Here in South Dakota. Amazing, huh? It's gotta be—"

Taylor Swift shrilled from my phone, and I grimaced. "Hold that thought, Tremont."

I glanced at my phone on the bar top. Lenore checking up on me. I hit the Ignore button on the screen and set the phone to vibrate only. His gaze followed my hand.

"Nice diamonds." He took my hand in his warm one and inspected my rings. "Splurge on yourself?"

"I got married." I peeled my hand out of his and looked away from the glare of my gorgeous eternity bands sparkling in the light from the hanging lamp overhead.

His body went rigid. "Jesus, I could barely get you to commit to a weekend away, let alone a Hawaiian vacation. What the hell happened? Bump into an old boyfriend, and he dragged you off into the sunset? I'll bet he had the right bike, huh?"

I didn't respond.

He drank more beer and edged closer to me. "So then, what brings you to this bar in the middle of the day? Woman like you—a married woman, no less—drinking on her own?"

"A lady doesn't tell her secrets." My phone vibrated.

Sam raised an eyebrow, a smirk creasing his lips. "Yeah, that's what I liked about you, Grace. Always a lady, even when you're being a cold hard bitch."

I scoffed. "Well, thank you very much, Mr. High and Mighty."

"You're welcome very much." He clinked his beer against my whiskey glass with a wide grin on his face.

I swallowed my drink, staring at him. "I seem to remember, you were quite a flirtatious asshole. Couldn't say no to anything with huge tits. You and your huge ego were a pain in my ass in the end."

"Well, honey, when you're not getting the attention you need from the woman in your bed, you start looking elsewhere."

"Really? What *you* need, huh? Well, lover boy, when you're unable to be honest in that bed of yours, you pay the price."

"Honest? Did you really just say *honest*?" He roared with throaty laughter, slamming a hand down on the bar top.

"Yes, I did." I saluted him with my glass.

"What the fuck is going on?" a dark-haired woman with flashing brown eyes butted in between us.

"Excuse me? Who the hell are you?" Sam asked, his eyes narrowing.

It couldn't be. It was.

I would recognize those huge almond shaped brown eyes and that bitter scowl anywhere. "Tania?"

Tania Reigert—my best friend from high school. Fellow Meager native. Fellow escapee of said town.

"What the hell are you doing here?"

"I live here."

"Since when?"

"Today." She shot a frown at Sam. "Who the hell are you?"

"Sam Tremont. And you? Should I ask, or are you going to shoot me?"

"Tania," she replied, a sour look on her face. She then shot it back at me. "He fucking cannot be the new husband."

"Excuse me?" Sam's eyes lit up.

Tania only ignored him. "Grace, say it isn't so."

"How do you know about my husband, for God's sake?" I asked.

"Meager has paparazzi, my starlet. Were you unaware?"

"Ah, your sister. I bump into her at Erica's coffee place a lot. Wait, and her husband came to the shop recently, looking at bikes. Not sure how serious he was though."

Tania rolled her eyes. "Fred on a bike? He wishes. What a poser. Penny told me about you getting married to another Jack."

Sam slammed his beer on the bar top. "A Jack? What the hell is a Jack?"

"He's not just another One-Eyed Jack, Tania. Don't start with me. Are we just going to pick up where we left off years ago? Because that is truly going to piss me off, and I'm not in the mood today."

"Okay." Unruffled, Tania turned back to Sam. "And I repeat, who are you?"

Sam grinned as he waved his empty beer bottle at Randy. "Grace and I know each other from way back. I was just passing through town and bumped into her here at this delightful bar."

"Hey, it is a delightful bar. Watch it, jerk," I said.

My phone jiggled on the bar top, quivering on the polished wood surface like a fat bumblebee stuck on its back. I let out a heavy exhale.

"Are you gonna answer your goddamn phone?" Sam asked.

"No, I'm not. That okay with you?"

One of Sam's eyebrows quirked, his lips twitching. "More than okay with me."

Randy slid a new beer in front of us. Sam winked at me, clinking my glass with his fresh bottle. "Shit, Grace. Were we ever this straight with each other before?"

"I don't think so, but at this moment"—I shrugged—"I can't say I remember."

"Shame, darlin'." He laughed, and I shoved his arm and laughed too.

"Could I have a Miner Red Ale," Tania asked Randy.

Randy immediately went to the tap and poured out the richly colored local microbrew. He slid the foam-topped glass toward her.

Tania settled on the barstool on my other side and wedged into our conversation like mortar between bricks. The three of us sat and talked for over an hour. Or was it two? We kept drinking. Sam's buddies came over—two of whom I knew, and the other I didn't. They told funny stories from their trip up from Texas, and we laughed. It was fun, and it felt good. Tania stood vigil over me, picking up guard duty of her bestie right where she'd left off, even though that was many, many years ago. We played a sloppy game of darts, and Tania and I returned to our stools at the bar.

"What the hell are you doing here?" I asked. "How long has it been? I can't even remember."

"Maybe all that booze did something to your brain cells."

"Shut up."

"Last time I saw you was at your wedding—your first wedding, that is."

"Right. You took off after that without much of a good-bye."

"Yes, I'm sorry about that. I am."

"So? Did you find a super exciting new life beyond Meager?"

"Did you?"

I only laughed. *Where to begin? Sixteen years of a forced walkabout around the country? Laying low and living half a life? Nope, not in the mood for that conversation right now.*

Tania let out a sigh. "Oh, there's plenty of life out there but nothing too spectacular."

"That sounds like it deserves another round or two. What do you say?"

"I say, you've had enough."

"Nice. I haven't seen you in over twenty freaking years, and here you are, yet again, telling me what to do. You haven't missed a beat."

"The hallmark of a true friend. Penny also told me about your dad being back. And about Ruby. I was really sorry to hear about Ruby. How are you doing with that? No need to answer actually. Not too great, by the looks of it."

I shook my head. "Here she goes again."

"Come on. What do you want me to say? I haven't even gotten to Dig yet. But we'll save that rewind for another time. So, what's new, buttercup? New husband, good times, right?"

"Oh, no, no, no. No more me. You entertain me now. Let's hear it. This was the girl who wanted nothing more to do with her hometown, had big shiny plans for herself and her future, who shook her head at her former best friend's life course as—and I quote—'an old lady of a swaggering good-for-nothing biker.'" I batted my eyelashes at her. "Let's hear it."

"I'm sorry about that. You loved him. That should've been enough for me. He loved you, too."

I averted my gaze and signaled Randy for a Miner Red Ale. "Spill. What's doing with you?"

"I got married, too."

"Ah!"

"But I'm getting a divorce."

"Oh."

"At least I want one. He doesn't want one. Thinks I'm overreacting. That's a guy thing, right? That we're always overreacting? Fuck that. He's back in Wisconsin. I came home to help my sister get Mom settled into a rehab in Rapid for a couple of months. She fell and broke her hip. It's been a bit rough."

"Very thorough *Reader's Digest* version of the life update. I appreciate it."

"You're very welcome. It's my forte—multitasking, concentrating vital information, organizing heaps of junk."

"Hold on." I touched her arm. "Rae is in a rehab facility? Oh, shit no."

Tania's mother, Rae, was one of the most headstrong, independent women I had ever known.

"Exactly. Don't have a choice though. Her MS has been progressing fast, and she can't be in that house on her own. She fell in the kitchen and broke her hip two weeks ago, had surgery. Now there's lots of physical and occupational therapy ahead of her."

"I'm sorry. I didn't know. So much has been going on for me lately that I haven't had a chance to visit with her at all."

Randy brought my beer. "Could you get us two glasses of water?" Tania asked.

"Sure thing."

She glanced at me, leaning over the bar top. "So, let's hear it."

"What?"

"Why are you doing an impression of your mother while you've got a brand-new beast of a man at home? Hmm?"

"I'm not Janet."

"Uh-huh. Said the frazzled woman with whiskey breath at two o'clock in the afternoon."

I leveled my gaze on her. "I found out my gestational surrogate miscarried my baby two weeks ago. Does that qualify, Ms. Tania?"

"Oh, fuck yes," she whispered as she sank down on her stool. "Sorry. Gestational means, it was your egg, right?"

"Yes." I let out an exhale and raised my beer. "Time to find a new surrogate."

Randy set two glasses of water in front of our beers.

"Oh, okay. Do you want to find a new one and try again?"

"I'm not sure."

"Are you considering *not* looking for a new one?"

"Maybe."

"Was it such a bad experience? Did you two not get along or something?"

"No, nothing like that." I shrugged. "It was odd when she called me herself from the hospital in the middle of the night to tell me about the miscarriage. She was very upset. Crying, wailing. But it wasn't her baby. It was mine. I wasn't sure who I had to console first—her or Miller. Or myself."

"Oh, man. I'm so sorry." Tania threw an arm around me. She held me there, at Pete's bar, like only an old girlfriend could.

I sucked in a hiccup and straightened my shoulders.

Tania released me. "You don't want to do it again?"

"I don't think I can."

"I know plenty of women who've gone through IVF three or four or five times. But if you can't, if you don't want to go through that process again, you don't have to. It's there to serve you, you know."

I sat up straight, flexing my lower back. "I don't have to go through IVF again. There are a few embryos left to use."

"Oh. Well, there's a plus, right?"

"I guess."

"You sure sitting here, drinking by yourself, is a good idea? Sure isn't an answer."

"It's good for right now."

Tania covered my hand with hers. The warmth of her touch soothed me for a few seconds, but then heated into a prickle on my skin. I loved her for caring, for showing me she cared. But I had to be here now, here at Pete's.

I knew every inch of this place, and just the sound of that old cash register dinging and the slam of its drawer in the distance was like the delicious caramel aroma of my mother's apple crumble. Familiar. Comfortable. Cozy. The very polished wood, sawdust, and yeast smell of this decades-old institution I'd once run made me homesick for a lost time, a time when I hadn't been lost. When I had been the innocent me who breezed through her life, one foot in front of the other, who made certain to have all her ducks in a row, first as a young woman and then as a newlywed old lady.

It was a sweet time when I'd been blindly happy, a part of a solid relationship, a crew of friends, a part of my community. Working here, flying from the bar to the tables, making jokes, making split-second decisions, dealing with fights, hiring bands, counting cash, chatting about nothing and everything with the regulars, flirting with my husband. Simple, mindless fun. I wanted to breathe that air again. I wanted to remember that person who had functioned on hope and brightness, that person who had a willingness to believe.

I raised the beer glass before me and admired the red color of the ale. "I'm good. I don't want to go home just yet. This is good beer. I haven't tasted this flavor before. Good for them."

"Grace…"

"Tania, really, I'm fine. Just need to catch my breath. Okay?"

She frowned. "I'm sure your new husband wants to help you catch your breath. Why don't you let him?"

"You're wrong. *I* have to help *him*. I'm just not sure how." I forced a tight smile and returned my attention to my drink. "I'll figure it out."

Miller would look at me now with that sorrow in his eyes. Well, it was actually behind his eyes. He was good at cloaking it, hiding it, but I could see it. I could feel it around me like getting lost in a oversized sweater when first tugging it on. Your face would get stuck in the thick weave, and a stifling instant of dramatic panic would threaten. Then you'd claw your way out. I was stuck in the sweater. The stifling would be over in a minute, wouldn't it?

"I'll be all right, Tania. Always am."

"Yeah. Miss Self-Sufficient."

I slid my fingers up and down the smooth wet sides of my glass.

"Was the surrogate from here?" she asked.

"No, she lives in Sioux Falls," I replied.

"Oh. Well, I guess that's better than way the hell out of state or across the country."

I wiped my hair from my face. "We were lucky."

"You find her through a lawyer or—"

"Through a service actually."

"Oh. That's good. You know, if you decide to look again, I can help you with any of the paperwork or whatever. I don't want to interfere in your personal business, but if you need help with weeding through stuff—"

"It is a mountain to get through, a lot of details, decision-making. You get to thinking that simply because someone has a hobby you don't care for that it will negatively impact your child in the womb."

"Freaky."

"Yeah, it does get to be overwhelming." I rubbed my eyes. "I can't imagine having a surrogate who lives way out of state, so far away, but you don't have a choice if that's who you want."

225

"I can help with all that busy work. I'm your girl."

I turned my head in my hand and stared at her.

Tania had freaked out at my wedding with Dig—not only because she had worn a dress and heels while surrounded by so many raucous club members giving her the eye, but also because I had actually gone through with marrying my first love. It was hardly the dream-wedding extravaganza we had once fantasized about as little girls together, giggling under the covers during one of our million-something sleepovers or as teenagers lying back on the grass in her backyard, staring at massive super-cell cloud formations swirling over us instead of doing our algebra homework.

After hoping that my Dig fascination would peter out and die after living the harsh reality of the club lifestyle, Tania had given up and accepted the inevitable. Finally marrying Dig had maybe worn down our friendship at the time. After the wedding, Tania and I drifted apart. Months later, she'd picked up and left. The odd note or holiday card had followed, but after I'd left Meager, we'd lost track of each other.

But she was here now. And I'd enjoyed every gripe and remark she made this afternoon. Yes, I had missed her. A lot. Tania just wanted the best for me. Tania, I knew with absolute certainty, had my back and not any kind of agenda. She had been my escape and refuge from a home gone mad with her family's open door, her and her mother's sharp humor and brash observations, often bossy tactics, and tight deep hugs. She loved me.

I gave her a weak smile. "Yeah, you are my girl, aren't you?"

The taut lines of her face softened. "I am."

Our eyes met in a mental gal-pal hug.

Her gaze darted over my shoulder. "Oh, looky. Time to say good-bye to your former fuck buddy."

"Shut up, Tania. Never thought I'd lay eyes on him again."

Tania took a sip of water. "Let's hope it's the last time."

"Well, ladies, this certainly has been fun." Sam wedged himself in between me and Tania, sliding his arms around us.

I bristled, a cold shiver spiking down my back, a holdover from my old-lady days. If ever a man who was not my old man—most especially if he was not a One-Eyed Jack—touched me or even got too close, no matter how casually, my alarm button would go off and my radar shield would go down. I shook my head at myself and kicked my reaction aside.

"We've got to get a move on here. We planned on spending the night in Deadwood to check out the casinos and the re-enactment of Wild Bill's dead man's hand." His voice trailed off as he studied my watery eyes.

"Yeah, you definitely cannot miss that," Tania muttered.

He ignored Tania. His fingers rubbed into my shoulder and up into my neck. "You want to come with us, Grace? Hang out. Just have some fun. 'Cause, to be honest, babe, looks like you could use it."

"Sam, I am not lacking in the fun department. It's just been a pretty bad week or two."

He ran a finger down my jaw. "You sure about that, babe?"

"She's positive," Tania said, shrugging off his arm.

"All right then." He glanced at Tania. "How about you, Ms. Tania? You up for showing a group of Texans around Deadwood?"

"Fuck no."

"Yeah, truly a shame." Sam squeezed my shoulder, and then his hand slid down and stroked my upper back. "Offer stands, Grace. We'll be at the Bullock if you want to let off some steam. No obligations, no questions asked. You don't feel like going home to that husband of yours, baby, you don't have to."

"The fuck you say."

A sudden hush filled the bar. My eyelids slid closed at the raw anger in the deep voice I knew so well. Sam's hand on me stilled.

Tania pivoted on her stool. "Now *that's* gotta be your old man!"

Sam let out a choking noise from the back of his throat and removed his hand from me. From behind the bar, Randy fidgeted and swallowed.

"Yes, that's him," I said.

"That's your cue to leave, Sammy," Tania said in a sour voice.

I glanced up at him. "Bye, Sam."

"Have a nice road trip," Tania continued. "And I'd advise, you should find an alternate route on your way back to Texas, if you know what I mean. I'd watch it in Colorado, too. There are One-Eyed Jacks there as well."

"One-Eyed who?"

Tania chuckled. "Best get going now."

"Yeah." Sam frowned, his eyes glued in the direction of the doorway.

I still faced the bar. Out of the corner of my eye, I could see Sam's friends gathering their jackets and shiny helmets and hustling toward the exit.

"Goodbye, Grace," muttered Sam.

I raised my head and focused my strained vision on the reflection in the side mirror of the bar to see a towering and very wired Miller clad in ripped jeans and a white T-shirt smudged with oil. His large dark eyes looked fierce from behind a curtain of raven hair, the colored prisms of the late afternoon sunlight glaring around him, as he filled up the doorway, standing perfectly still.

Tania slid my phone down the bar to me. "I called your hubs on your cell, so you know."

"I don't like being thrown under a bus, so you know."

"You were dragging this shit out. That is not the Grace I know."

Miller's gaze was drilling lasers into my back. I tucked my phone in my bag.

Tania strode over to Miller. "She needs to wake the fuck up."

"You Tania?" he asked.

"Yes, I am. Spank her if you have to." Tania marched out of Pete's, the door swinging behind her.

I took in a breath and wiped a hand across my mouth. Heavy booted footsteps drew closer, and my breath caught. His chest rubbed against my back, fusing his body heat with mine, as his long arms framed me, his hands planted on the bar top. His warm breath was like steam on the side of my face.

"Babe, what are you doing?"

"Hanging out. Bumped into Tania."

"Who was the dick hanging over you? Took everything I had not to bust in that pretty face of his."

"Old boyfriend from Texas. Passing through with some of his friends."

Miller picked up my beer glass and drained it before slamming it on the bar and pressing his chest into my back. "Oh, yeah? He didn't know you were living here?"

"How would he know that?"

He tilted his head. "Long as he's not passing through *you* on his way out of town."

My ribs squeezed together. "Is that what you thought?"

I finally turned to face him and was met by his simmering dark eyes. Wounded eyes. Of course they were. Instead of going to the movies or meeting a friend for lunch or going shopping for clothes, a new lipstick, a wok, another surrogate, I had instead chosen to sit at a bar in the middle of the day to drink, to wallow, to think and rethink the same old groove line. Alone. I'd been disappearing every afternoon for the past two weeks after putting in a few dutiful hours at the shop. And today, I'd let myself be entertained by a former lay, and Miller had gotten to witness it.

Dizziness erupted in my head. My heartbeat turned sluggish, transforming my once happy buzz into some sort of numbing potion, weighing down every limb. I lowered my head. A grown woman yet I was flailing. A disappointment.

Add it to the fucking list.

"Randy, what do I owe you?" asked Miller.

"Nothing. That Texan paid the tab."

Miller let out a harsh exhale. "Let's go," he muttered against my hair.

I nodded, and he pushed back away from me.

I pulled myself up from my stool as I shot Randy an it's-been-fun-but-it's-time-to-pay-the-piper smirk, much to his horror. I strode out of Pete's with Miller behind me. Our black GMC truck was double-parked out front, the hazard lights clacking on and off. The locks blipped, and I opened the door and climbed in. The truck rocked as Miller dived into the driver's seat, slammed the door, and shoved the truck in gear.

Tania stood outside Pete's, her hands at her waist, watching me. I turned my head and stared straight ahead as we sped off.

Miller unlocked the front door of our house, and I dumped my bag by the door as I kicked off my boots. He shoved the door closed behind him.

"This has been going on for days now. I call, and you don't answer. Or when you do, your voice is flat. That evil flat tone that I despise because it means you're shutting down, not functioning on all optimum levels. That you're somewhere else, dragging yourself through the mud."

His sharp tone made me stiffen as I headed into our bedroom. I opened a drawer and grabbed a pair of yoga pants and a long-sleeved T-shirt.

"That you are choosing—you hear me, Grace? You're choosing to deliberately blow me off. Some girlfriend of yours I don't know calls me on your phone and insists I get my ass over to Pete's because you need saving from yourself. And I find you there, laughing and getting up close with some asshole ex-hook-up of yours."

"Uh, no. He is an ex-boyfriend. *You* are the ex-hook-up."

Miller stilled, his eyes tightening, his rigid body emitting powerful gamma rays. "Let me make this real simple for you."

I bit the inside of my cheek, glanced up at him and waited, my insides churning.

"What the fuck?"

I ripped off my blouse. "I'm sorry."

"You're sorry?"

"Yes. I'm sorry. Sorry I've been uncommunicative. Sorry—"

"You going to go down a list of the obvious now? Save it."

My face heated. I tossed my blouse in the wicker basket in the corner.

"What is it, Grace? You gonna tell me what's eating you, or you gonna keep walking around in a daze?"

"Daze? I'm not in a daze."

"Bottom line, I want to be here for you, but you're not fucking interested."

"I am interested. I'm just…off." I didn't bother with the T-shirt. I took off my bra and threw on one of Miller's zipper hoodies that had been lying on a chair by the bed.

"You're full of shit."

"Aw, thank you, honey."

He folded his arms across his chest, his jaw harsh, his eyes flashing. "What do you want me to say? I can't believe you would've done anything with that guy, or am I way off?" He stood still, his chest rising and falling.

"Don't be ridiculous."

He scowled. "You sure as hell haven't been open to me the past two weeks. You think I don't know when you're pretending to be asleep?"

I clenched my jaw as I unbuttoned my jeans, teetering. I pressed a hand on the bed.

"Because even when you're asleep"—his deep voice wound around me, squeezing me—"with one touch from me, you're taking me in your arms, kissing me, opening your legs for me."

My head shot up. "Uh, I'm so sorry for that, too. Let's go." I kicked off my jeans with ferocity. "Come on, let it not be said that I don't fulfill my wifely duties." I climbed over the bed on my knees, and I unbuckled his belt and undid his jeans.

"Who was that fuck at Pete's?" he said through gritted teeth, staring down at me.

I slid my hand over his erection. His jaw clenched as I tugged his black underwear down.

"That was a guy I dated for a few months in Dallas."

His cock stood erect against his abs, and I wrapped a hand around his hard shaft.

"And so there aren't any unanswered questions hanging in the air, yes, we've slept together. He's on a bike trip to Wyoming with friends and happened to stop in at Pete's for a drink on his way through town."

"Did you enjoy your chat?" His voice was low, jagged.

I cupped his balls with one hand and stroked his dick with the other, squeezing tightly. "Sure did." I took his cock in my mouth and sucked hard—no niceties, no preludes to victory.

"Grace"—a scowl darkened his face—"stop."

My eyes met his burning ones as my teeth grazed his rock-hard length, and he let out a long hiss, his face tightening. Both his hands fisted in my hair as I fucked him with my mouth, faster, deeper. Cold sharp need built inside me as his hips began to shove against my face. My fingers tightened around his balls, and he let out a grunt.

"This what you want, baby? This what you want?" he muttered through short breaths.

My gaze flicked up at him. Yes, this was what I wanted. Not emotional gazes, not understanding hugs or sweet words. Just this raw, base—

"Goddammit!" Miller hoisted me up and flipped my body over on the mattress.

He pulled my legs down so that my feet touched the floor, and I collapsed onto my forearms. Raising my hips and ass high, he drove his cock inside me, and I gasped loudly at the shock of his harsh entry, my body jerking in his tight hold.

"I'll give it to you." He pounded inside my slickness. His one hand held down my hip, the other gripping a shoulder, as he rammed his body into mine. "You like that? This what you want?"

"Yes!" I gasped loudly in between each forceful slam of his body into mine.

"He had his hand on you."

"He's nothing."

"What were you gonna say to him, huh? Before I spoiled your fun," he bit out through gritted teeth.

"I was going to say, 'thanks for the offer, but only my husband makes me come.'" I squeezed my eyes shut at the building wall of burning mind-stuttering pleasure, groaning loudly as it towered over me and shattered all at once.

Miller grunted, his fingers biting into my hips as he buried himself deep inside me. He pulled his slick cock out of me. The wet slap of its exit was so anticlimactic, so mundane, signaling the return to our unhappy reality. My insides hollowed out at its loss, and that vibrant throbbing of my body evaporated. He flipped me over. His hands fisted in my hair as he leaned over me, one knee on the bed.

"That what you wanted? You feel better now?" A shadow drifted across his features.

I turned my face away.

He released my hair, his breathing choppy. "You got to say it, Grace. Just say it. Say you blame me. Say you hate me."

My heart sped up in my chest as I raised my face from the soft fabric of the deep-purple comforter. "What?"

"You're going through this again, this loss, because of me."

I raised my head. "No, no, Miller. No—"

"You're trying to bury it, to relieve me of it, but you can't. So, you end up at a fucking bar, drinking alone. Been doing that the whole time now?" He stood up over me.

I raised myself up on my shaky arms. "Miller, I made us do this, and it failed."

"For God's sake, Grace. You didn't make me. And you had nothing to do with that miscarriage! Nothing. Did you not hear the doctor? Our embryo didn't have any genetic problems. Maybe the doctor didn't implant it right. Maybe Laura's cycle was off, or her insides reacted funny. Maybe…who the hell knows?" He raked a hand through his black hair. "Hell, it could've been a combination of maybes. We don't fucking know!"

He pulled up his underwear. The waistband of his boxer briefs snapped loudly against his firm flesh, and I flinched. He shoved his legs in his jeans.

I curled up on the bed, squeezing my damp thighs together, my hands tucked under my head.

"Grace?"

"You just came inside me, and all that spunk has got nowhere to go or be contained, nowhere to attach itself to. I'm all scooped out inside."

His hand froze on his zipper.

"I brought an idea to the table, but I still can't deliver. I made your heart jump with hope, but I couldn't make good on it. I let you down, dragged you down. I couldn't leave well enough alone, and now I've marked you, marked us, in a new way."

My breath caught at the strained look on his face. His mouth hung open. He was unwilling to utter the denial that hung on his lips, for it would be a lie, wouldn't it? His brows had transformed into a ridge, a dam straining against the hurt.

I averted my gaze. "I've disappointed you. And I hate that," I whispered.

"Babe, we're trying. There's nothing wrong with that. It's a process. You don't have to worry about me."

"Of course I have to worry about you! I'm your wife."

"Okay, you want to worry about me. Here goes." His hands hung on his hips. "This isn't just about you. I lost that baby, too. It might not have been in your belly. It might have been hundreds of miles away from us, but goddamn it, that was my sperm in there with your egg that helped create that baby."

"It was a girl!"

The lines of his tan face tensed. "What?" His shaky voice shrunk.

My heart stabbed.

"Laura called me a couple of days after the miscarriage, after the tests came back. Turns out our baby was a girl. She thought we'd like to know."

Laura's call had put a different spin on my raw but controlled grief. Once her words had penetrated my brain, suddenly, I had known I was kidding myself. That embryo had had an identity. It had been real, a being bursting with my and Miller's DNA. But that bursting forth had ceased. I'd hung up the phone and plunged into a black pit of mourning for the three of us all over again.

I had been trying not to think about the baby as an actual *baby* too much until we'd hit the four-month mark, but that desperate notion had been crushed.

Miller swept the hair from my face. "Why didn't you tell me?"

Because it would've destroyed a little piece of you.

My finger traced a line down his chest.

"Grace, tell me."

"We would've given her your grandmother's name like we wanted to."

"Babe—"

I dug my finger in his chest, trembling. "We lost our Kim."

He swept me in his embrace, holding me, cradling me. "Shh."

My body shivered as I inhaled his earthy scent mixed with the musky heat of his skin. I didn't deserve Miller's exquisite understanding or his quiet strength, no matter how badly I wanted it. A scream rose in my throat. Nausea swirled in my gut, and I stiffened in his arms, pushing against him like a savage animal clawing free from a trap, my hair catching in my eyes, my mouth.

He shook me. "Stop it."

I gritted my teeth. "Don't tell me how to feel."

He pulled my face back, his one hand gripping my skull, his eyes blazing into mine. "I wouldn't dare. But that shit's not what I feel, not what I see. This isn't over yet, Grace. It doesn't have to be. It's fixable."

I squirmed in his arms, our choppy breaths mingling. "Fixable?"

"Ugly, isn't it? Just plain mean. But that's the dinner being served. It's sour, and it doesn't taste good, but there's no menu for us to choose from. We deal. We fucking deal. But we can't deal if you're determined to flip out and push me away. It only works if we're together on this."

"Fixable?"

"Yeah."

"Men always want to fix things."

"That's right. We do. This one's a bitch though. Yeah, Laura lives so far away, and we weren't there to witness it or help her or our kid. That was a part of us inside somebody else who was out there in the world, far away. I don't know what to do with that. Honestly, I don't. But I am trying. Grace, losing our daughter does not make me mad at you. It makes me mad but not at you. Frustrated but, again, not at you." He let out an exhale and released his grip on my head. "Did you start looking for another surrogate?"

I shook my head.

"Why not?" He brushed the hair from my face.

"Is that what you want?"

"Don't you? You just gonna give up?" He stared at me, his fingers lingering on my lower lip. "You're giving up, aren't you?" He released me and stood up. "Oh, man. Okay." His gaze shifted, his lips curling in.

Was it disappointment? Dismay? In me or the situation?

God, I hated this.

He rubbed the back of his neck. "This is too much. This is the second time for you," he said. "Going through it once was bad enough, but twice? No. I just wish you had come out and told me how you were feeling rather than all this hiding, this jerking away."

"I'm not jerking."

"Oh, yeah?" He stared at me, his lips in a firm line, his jaw set. "It's getting a little difficult for me to breathe with the bullshit in the air. I think I'd better go. My lungs will thank me. They've gotten sensitive since I quit smoking."

He turned his back on me, and my heartbeat kicked into overdrive. I jumped up and grabbed a long sinewy arm.

"No, don't go. Miller, please."

He released a long breath, his eyes holding mine. "You've been drinking every day this week, haven't you?"

Found out. I chewed on the inside of my cheek and didn't reply.

"I know you have. Haven't said a word. But it's been two weeks. Two fucking weeks. *This* is what's frustrating me, making me angry, Grace. And now I'm concerned. You need to think about what you want and how you want it. Don't ever forget you're your mother's daughter and Ruby's sister."

My face heated. "I'm not them!"

"No, you're not. But you gotta be vigilant about your inherited tendencies. All I'm asking is, you take it down a notch, starting now."

"And if I don't want to?"

His dark eyes pierced mine, and his body stiffened, towering over me. "We got three weeks until Jake comes back to us. You need to come up with a better answer before then."

My shoulders sank. He was right, so very right. My depression, my negativity stank.

"You need another prescription, then let's get one."

"No. After all those hormones, I don't want any more pills in my life, and—"

He gripped my jaw. "You need me to tie you to the bed until you decide what to do?"

I didn't move a muscle.

"Yeah, I'm thinking you do. You've been disrespecting yourself and your cunt all this time, and I'm gonna make you regret it."

Icy needles tracked up my spine at the iron tone in his voice, and I jerked against his hold on me but his grasp only tightened. A warning. A dare. A push.

"I thought you were leaving," I said.

"No. This is a much better idea." He yanked the zipper down the hoodie, revealing my bare breasts, and I let out a gasp. "If my words haven't gotten through to you, woman, my cock and my tongue will take over." His hard gaze held mine. "Take it off."

I tugged the hoodie off my shoulders and arms. It dropped to the bed at my side. He wrapped an arm around my waist and pulled me close to his body. His fingers sank into my pussy, swirling through the sensitive, wet flesh.

My chest constricted at the menacing look in his eyes, growing more intense with every harsh stroke.

"I'm gonna suck and fuck every ounce of negativity right out of this pussy," he rasped.

The sticky wet sounds of his fingers working me filled the space between us. I groaned, my legs wobbling.

"You been keeping it from me, and your pussy likes my mouth and my cock, doesn't it, Grace?"

I nodded, my breathing choppy. "Uh-huh." My eyes were pinned to his.

He kissed me, a demanding kiss, a this-is-what-I-want-and-you're-going-to-give-it-to-me-right-the-fuck-now kiss. His lips detached from mine, snatching any fragments of resolve I had been clinging to.

"Your pussy *needs* my mouth and my cock, doesn't it, Grace?" The hard line of his jaw grazed my forehead.

"Miller—"

He pushed me down on the bed. "Hands over your head," he ordered.

I complied, and one of his hands clamped down on my wrists.

"I don't like hearing you disrespecting your pussy. Ever," he said, his lips inches from mine, his knuckles rubbing over my clit. "Your pussy is my cock's home, my spunk's home. It's fucking mine, and it gets wet when I want it to, doesn't it?"

His deep hypnotic voice dragged his desire through my quickening blood. His heavy gaze and his fingers fine-tuned me to what he knew I needed and overwhelming my senses. Satisfaction was now stamped across that determined beautiful face.

"Yes," I breathed.

"And I make it come hard, don't I?"

My pulse raced, my insides hot and thick. "Oh…damn…"

"Don't I?" His fingers moved faster, sliding down and sinking inside me once more.

I pressed my head back into the pillow. "Will you just fuck me!"

"Answer the question." He tightened his grip on my wrists, his eyes narrowing.

"Yes! All right?"

"I think your friend Tania had a point." His broad chest rubbed over my aching breasts as he released my wrists and moved down my body, his tongue flicking over a hardened nipple.

"Wh-what?"

His hands squeezed my ass hard, and I gasped. My heart pounded in my chest at the growling sound that escaped his throat.

"Not going back to work this afternoon." He moved further down my body, nipping my flesh as he went, his smooth skin scalding mine. "Too much work to do here."

He cocked my knees and slowly nuzzled kisses down a thigh. His fingers hooked inside me, churning that rhythm that my body knew and craved. A unique rhythm that Miller had composed just for me. My back arched, and I cried out, cried out at his unforgiving assault, cried out for him to give me more, cried out to forget.

His mouth drove in between my legs, and I was lost.

TWENTY-ONE

A TALL CARDBOARD CUP of Meager Grand Cafe hazelnut latte landed on my desk at the shop. My gaze darted up.

Boner.

"Oh. Yum." I flipped open the thick plastic cover and took in the rich roasted aroma of my favorite coffee. "Good morning, and thank you very much."

His brows slammed together. "Nice disappearing act lately. You expect me to dance around that or some shit? I ain't one of your girlfriends."

"No, you aren't." I blew on the aromatic hot brew and sipped.

He pushed the piles of orders and bills I had been going through to the left and sat on the side of my desk. "I'm guessing the caveman routine at Pete's didn't go so well. Judging from the vibe inside the shed and in here, it's looking like another chilly gray-storm-clouds-on-the-horizon kind of day."

"Miller's not in a good mood this morning? You'd think he would be after…"

"Leave out the TMI on my brother. He's less black than yesterday but not good. Tense as a fucking tire iron. Yesterday sucked around here, so you know, with you being MIA yet fucking again. He kept giving me those razor-edge hard stares as if I knew where the fuck you were and what you'd been up to. Gotta say, I was happy that I did not have to lie to him about his own old lady, but then again, I was fucking pissed because I did *not* know what was up with you or where the fuck you were."

I sank back in my chair, nursing my hot coffee. The words on endless repeat in my vocabulary fell from my lips, "I'm sorry." I did owe it to Boner.

He exhaled a gust of air. "I'm sorry, too, babe."

I gave his arm a squeeze and went back to my latte.

Boner rubbed his fingers down the surface of the desk. "Lock's been worried about you. Mind's on you all the time. Had a huge important meeting yesterday with that rich rancher from Montana."

"I know. He didn't tell me how it went."

"How it went? Well, Lock was champing at the bit during the whole hour-long discussion about fixing up the dude's latest finds at some auction, getting 'em ready for two different car shows across the country. This is a big account, baby. One of his biggest so far. This could really put him on the map with a different level of clients."

"I know that, Boner. Who do you think set up the appointment? Me."

"Ah, so you do give a shit then?"

"What's that supposed to mean?"

"Get your head out of your ass already. That's what it means. He's your man, and he's worrying about how you're taking all this shit. He's upset about you and the miscarriage. And in the middle of it, he gets a call, hoping it's you, I'm sure, but no, it's Tania, who he doesn't even know. She's jamming on about finding you drinking alone at Pete's and hanging with some Texans and how he needs to get his ass down there. I offered to go instead, but he wouldn't let me."

"He didn't finish the meeting?"

"Oh, he did. Tight-lipped, all business, and then he made his apologies and took off. Left the rancher with one of the boys to go over the FAQs. His head was not in the game though, where it should have been."

My jaw stiffened. "I'm bad for business. Should I go apologize to everyone inside?"

His bright green eyes narrowed at me. "All I want from you right now is the goddamn truth. Don't care how fucking ugly it is. That's the way it's always been between us—except, of course, for all those years you took off and did your and Vig's thing."

"You ever gonna give me an inch over that? You know how it was."

"'Course I know how it was. Fuck that. This is different shit, plain and simple. You got your old man worrying about you while you're drinking alone at Pete's and hanging with some Sunday rider you used to have in your bed. What the fuck?"

"Oh, Jesus." My head fell back against my chair. "Don't tell me. Tania."

"I bumped into her at Erica's just now." He sucked on his double espresso. Boner was a coffee connoisseur, and lately, he had been drinking nothing else but Erica's coffee house brew at least five times a day. "She told me all about it."

"I bet she did."

"That chick has not changed."

"I still don't know if that's a good thing."

He shrugged. "I can still remember her practically spitting at me the first time we met."

"She was concerned about your bad influence on me."

He made a face as he swallowed the last of his coffee and pushed his long brown hair back behind an ear.

"What?"

"Her brother's with Flames of Hell."

"Are you kidding me?"

Boner shook his head. "For years now."

"First of all, I'm shocked that boy is still alive."

He smirked. "Yeah, right."

"Second of all, Flames of Hell?"

Tania's baby brother, Drew was ten years younger than us. He'd been a hyper handful who transformed into an anarchic slacker by the time he was in high school.

"Yeah. He's been with the Flames for a while now," said Boner. "Anyhow, this time, she gave me a hug and a kiss when she spotted me, and then she dragged me over to a table."

I let out a laugh. "Oh, yeah?"

"She's looking good, mellowed out some." He made a face. "Emphasis on *some*."

I grinned.

"Look it. My point here is that me and her are two of your oldest friends in this town, and we ain't letting you slide through this shit with a glass of booze on endless refill in your hand." He tossed his empty coffee cup in the small trash can at the side of my desk.

I sank back in my chair and sipped my warm frothy liquid heaven. He leaned into me, his long hair falling in my face.

"Don't do this now, babe. You've got everything in the palm of your hands. You are living a fucking blessing. Everything you ever wanted. Everything that Dig ever wanted for you." My eyes flared at him, and he clamped a hand on my shoulder. "I get that you're hurting, but this is not the way." His lips brushed the side of my face. "That man in there loves you with everything he is. Deal with your shit before it deals with you. We both know how that goes."

I put my cup down on my desk and slid upright in my chair. "I've got work to do."

His jaw tightened. "Why Pete's?"

"What do you mean?"

"You know what I'm asking. Why you been drinking at Pete's? There are plenty of other places to go. Nicer places for women on their own, let's say. Even your own house or Lenore's. Why only Pete's and alone?"

My eyes darted to the front lot where Miller was going over custom detailing on a customer's Charger. Purple and gold stripes.

"Grace?"

At the sharp tone in his voice, my head jerked to face Boner, his use of my real name still odd to me. Once Miller and I had gotten married, he and the club had officially put Sister to rest. She'd belonged to another man, another era.

If only emotions and feelings could be dealt with so efficiently

I swallowed. "Pete's was where I told Dig no."

Boner's eyes narrowed at me.

"After waiting and hoping he'd come around, one night at Pete's, out of the blue, he told me he wanted us to go for it, to have a baby. He'd finally relaxed his ass about all the monkeys on his back. He said to me, 'Let's do it,' and I told him no."

"Why did you say no?"

"I was a busy girl. I was the big cheese running Pete's, and I was working here for Wreck. I was having my good time, being an involved old lady, enjoying my moment of having it all together." I stacked the bills into a neat tight pile. "We had just gotten married. We were fixing up that house. That night, we were fooling around in the office. He had the most peaceful, beautiful smile on his face, and he asked me, 'Baby, you happy?' A mundane simple question." My hands smoothed over the pink, yellow, and white papers. "But not for him. Not typical. He didn't dwell on how he was feeling or what he was feeling."

"He just was, or he wasn't."

"He gave me that beautiful special moment, and I took it for granted. I crumpled it like an old grocery list on a piece of scrap paper, kicked it down the hall, and stumbled along without looking back. He told me he wanted to make a baby, and I asked him to wait. Wait at least another year or two, wait until I had my fill of career moves and responsibility-free good times. Before a baby could cause a…disruption."

"You were busy. You two were having fun. That don't mean—"

"There isn't any perfect time! That's something we convince ourselves of when we're young to justify anything. Boner, if I hadn't said no that night, we could've had our baby, and I'd be whole inside."

"Are you fucking kidding me? That's nuts!"

"Why?" My voice got louder. My throat constricted. "Maybe Dig would've still gotten killed by that jerk when he did and I still would have ended up in the hospital myself, but if I had agreed to getting pregnant that night at Pete's, I would've had our kid, and my insides would probably still be intact. I'd be able to give Miller a baby now." My throat clogged. "It all changed on a dime in Pete's. I did that."

"Grace—"

"We can blame Dig for losing his shit and killing Mole and putting himself at risk, and he did. He did that for fucking nothing—over a drug deal gone south. Got him killed a week later in the name of revenge. But what I had done? Blowing him off in that moment when he'd been sharing a piece of his joy with me that night in Pete's? That had changed everything. I'd delayed our happiness. I'd deprived Dig of that family he wanted so badly, needed to have so damn bad. Maybe we would've only had it for a couple of years, but he would've had it. He would've known what that felt like. He'd needed that wholeness, and he'd wanted that from me. I'd wanted to give that to him." My gaze moved back outside. Miller was hunched over the hood of the Charger. "Like I want to give it to Miller now. Instead, I'm fucking with his head. I'm some piece of work."

"Oh Jesus, stop it."

"I love Miller, Boner. I really do."

"I know you do."

"He doesn't deserve this mess I'm giving him. I thought this was a sure thing. The minute they'd told us our parts and pieces were good, that it was a go, I thought…I really thought…"

"Baby, don't…"

"I made this mess," I whispered, wiping at my eyes. "I don't think Miller had given having a kid too much thought before I brought it up. He'd shrugged off that kids weren't in the cards for him a long time ago, and he'd put it aside, buried it, forgotten it. I came along and had these big dreams and wishes for us, and in wanting to please me, he climbed on my bandwagon."

"And he's happy to be there."

"My point is that now he's dreaming those dreams, too." I lowered my voice.

"Why wouldn't he be? He loves you. You two are solid—"

"It's more than that. It's like he's reconnected to a piece of himself that he'd put away a long time ago. That's huge. He had bolted down that door, and I went and tore that goddamn door open."

"You're making a life together, Grace. You just wanted to make that life more beautiful. There's nothing wrong with wanting that, babe."

"He trusted me with all this, and I adore him for it, but—"

"Lock's a big boy. He will figure this out. What the hell are you thinking? That you betrayed that trust?"

"Yeah, that's it." My scalp prickled at his words, at the truth of it all seeping through me. "I do. I've been selfish, and I've let him down. He was fine with the way things were, more than fine. I feel like I took away a puzzle he just finished and broke it apart, rearranged the pieces, tossed them in his face. I've made everything confusing again."

"That's crap."

I crossed my arms and watched Miller laugh with the Charger customer. "You know what the worst part of all this is? I've disappointed two very fine men. That is some track record. So, there comes a point when you have to shut it down. You'd think I'd learned my lesson by now. Obviously not. I did this and all for selfish reasons," I scoffed. "I wanted to work. I wanted to have fun. I wanted to be the one to give them the family they deserve. Me, me, me."

"Grace—"

"Who the fuck do I think I am?" I gritted my teeth.

"You need to calm the fuck down."

"Fuck you!"

He pulled me into his arms and held me tight. "Shh." My fists pounded his back.

His chest heaved. "I miss him so goddamn much. So fucking much. I'll never have a brother like Dig again. But I had to close that book, or I would've gone crazy, right along with you. You remember that, don't you? Almost took those pills with you that night." My fists uncurled, my hands pressed into his back, a sob escaping my throat. "I can tell you, he'd be so fucking pissed off if he could hear the shit spewing out of your mouth right now."

His hands cradled my face. "I get you're feeling like you're in a whirlpool here, but you're not being fair. That boy out there? He needs you. It's been a rough long road for him. He needs a soft place to lean on. You are that place for him. You promised to do that in that church, didn't you? Both of you in those fancy clothes, gold rings on your fingers."

I nodded.

"You're an open wound right now. But you need to be open to Lock. He's good at being tough and hard, but you got under that, you got inside him, and now you're a part of him. You gotta prop him up now. He was there for you, stood by you with all that Vig shit and Butler crap. Now you be the cushion Lock needs. And if the way he needs that soft from you is by caring for you, and I suspect he does, then you let him care for you. Let him in, woman."

"He is in."

He pulled away just a bit and flattened a hand over my heart. "Let him be there. You be grateful for what you've got. God gave this bounty to you. You don't let go in the thick of it. You make sure it thrives."

My body went slack in his grip. "Sixteen years, I did things to keep my sister safe. I did it. And all that was brushed aside by cancer. She died anyway, Boner. I couldn't do anything about it."

"Don't go there."

"Why not? No matter what you do, no matter how hard you try, that road will never curve the way you want it to."

"If it did, that wouldn't be a fun ride, now would it?"

"Dig was right," I whispered.

Boner gripped my chin and leveled his gaze at me. "Don't start with that shit now. It used to piss me off. It's true to a certain degree, but it's how you deal in between the random hits that counts. The way you deal with each *fuck you* hurled at you. How you look that motherfucker in the eyes is the key to what kind of person you are. You either shoot first or you crumple or you run. It's up to you."

I wiped at my eyes.

"I got something for you," he said, pulling away from me.

He held out his open palm. The silver of a ring I knew so well shone against his hand. Dig's favorite ring. The .44 caliber revolver chamber ring. An ancient artifact of my past.

"You have it? I thought for sure he'd been buried with it. You gave me his club ring when I left town."

"Figured you needed a piece of us when you left. Piece of him."

A lead weight pressed down on my chest, making it hard to breathe, as Boner raised the ring before me.

"This one, he never took off. It was a part of his hand. Did you ever wonder why?"

I shrugged. "He loved his rings. He always had them on."

"This one was different."

There was something in the grim quality of his voice, a crisp edge, a clarity. I took in a small breath as Boner placed the ring in my palm. I never thought I'd see it or touch it again. The silver was smooth and battered, almost soft, if a hard metal could even be characterized in that way. My fingertips pressed into the grooves and ridges of the .44 caliber revolver chamber. My heart beat tripped.

This ring was a relic of the lost civilization of Dig Quillen, and it was now in my hands almost two decades later. Was this what archeologists felt like when uncovering objects in forgotten tombs? Precious. Sacred. The ring hummed in my grasp.

"You saved it?"

"I got to the scene first after I got your call. I was there on that blood-soaked road before Trey and all the rest of the cops got there. You were unconscious. Dig was dead. I went to him. Blood everywhere. His one arm had practically gotten twisted off by the force of the bike landing on him. I grabbed the rings off those fingers—one for you and this one for me. I wanted it with his blood on it. We'd gotten this together on our way to South Dakota. That was when we'd promised each other and ourselves that there was no going back, not ever. You ever see the inside of that ring?"

I shook my head.

"Look," he whispered.

My hand shook as I held the ring up to the light.

Aut viam inveniam aut faciam

"Is that Latin?"

"*I will either find a way or make one*," Boner rasped.

I swallowed down the knot in my throat and stared at him.

"That was an oath to himself to never forget and to always forge ahead."

"He couldn't let it go."

"Would you be able to?" Boner's gaze glittered.

I shook my head. "No, I wouldn't."

"Me neither," he breathed. "This ring was his call, his pledge of vigilance."

"Well, you live by the sword, you die by the sword. That's what happened to Dig. That's what *he* made happen, Boner. I don't want this ring."

"What?" His eyes widened at me.

"He didn't have to kill that punk at that motel. Dig brushed it off to me like it was just another day at the office, and of course, it was for you all. But his one moment of crazy, for whatever reason, during a simple transaction led to all this for us—living in a world without him in it."

"That's all true, baby. I was the one who went and cleaned up that mess for him. I know. But I have no doubt that piece-of-trash did or said something that was over the line to make Dig react that way. I never questioned it. Still don't. I see you do though."

Boner took three steps closer to me, his boots banging on the tile floor, his green eyes hard. "Dig was a brave and smart man, and I think you need to remind yourself of that kind of bone-chilling bravery, that take-no-prisoners reflex. He did not cower. No matter the pain burning his insides, he never cowered." Boner curled my cold fingers over Dig's ring. "Take it. Wear it. And you do what needs to be done."

"I sure don't need to kill anybody."

Stupid.

Boner shook his head. "No, you're trying to make a life here, and that's rough that you didn't get what you wanted the first time out. Try the fuck again. What makes you so fucking special in the scheme of things? Why should you be any different?"

I could barely see his face through the blur.

"What the fuck do I know?" His voice softened. "But I do know, Dig wouldn't have wanted to listen to this outta you either."

"No, he dealt by daring shit to come find him."

A slow smile tipped his lips. "That's right."

"Made him feel in control, didn't it?" I wiped my eyes.

"Maybe. But I've learned control is one big fucking illusion, baby. What I do know is that you can't sit back and let shit ride you." His jaw stiffened. "That's not what we do."

I sniffed in air as he wiped at my face with his warm fingers. "You get back up on that bike. If memory serves, took you a while to get used to handling a hog. But you stayed on that saddle, didn't you?" He raised an eyebrow at me. "Look, if it's too hard, if you think it's gonna break you—the way you got broke the last time—then don't do it."

My breath hissed. "Nothing will break me like that again. I won't let it. I've got too much to live for now." I pushed the gun-barrel ring over my thumb. Dig's battle cry of mindfulness and determination, settled over my skin.

Boner wrapped a hand around my neck and planted a kiss on the side of my mouth. "See that it don't."

I buried my face in his shirt, my fingers curling in the worn cotton at his sides.

"You getting boogers on my new shirt now?"

I softly punched his chest. "That's a new shirt?"

"You're such a stuck-up fashion bitch, you know that?"

"I have to go shopping for you again."

I pinched his side, and he only laughed.

"Fuck no."

"I don't know why I bother telling you. I'm on it. Today."

TWENTY-TWO

"GRACE! LOOK AT YOU, DARLING!"

"Good to see you, Mrs. Reigert."

Tania's mom wrapped me in her arms in a deep hug.

"Well, it's not good to see you here, I have to say. We should be in my kitchen, around a huckleberry pie and a strong pot of coffee. But no. We're here in this lovely rehab center."

"Mother! At least you have your own room." Tania's jaw jutted out, and she let out a heavy sigh.

"True!"

"I miss your kitchen. That does sound good!" I murmured. "I'm sorry I haven't been by to see you lately."

"Ah, honey." Rae took my hand in her warm one. "You're a newlywed girl. You've got a lot on your plate. Unlike some."

I glanced up at Tania, who shook her head and looked away.

"Yeah, I'm only running my own business, looking into relocating to assist my needy mother."

"We've already discussed that. You don't need to do that. I'll figure something out with Penny." Rae's lips smashed into a thin line.

Rae Reigert had been like a second mother to me for many years, even before I had lost my own. I'd spent so many nights sleeping over at Tania's, either from wanting to or just plain having to, in order to escape my mother's tirades over my sister's antics or after my mother had died so that I could escape the new antics Ruby and her wild crowd would get up to at our house. Our father had left us, and after our mother had died unexpectedly in a car accident, our house had become a crash pad for Ruby's latest boyfriends and a number of One-Eyed Jacks and their women. Although it had been fun at first, definitely different and freakishly liberating, part of me had only wanted to be a normal kid in a normal home.

Tania's house had been the opposite of mine. Rae was an extremely clean and fantastically organized housekeeper. She had been the receptionist at one of the local dentist's offices for years, and with her extra pocket money, she had kept her house decorated with the latest finds, according to the seasons and the holidays. The refrigerator had always been packed, and stews and roasts, with plenty to go around, had filled the house with their delectable aromas. There had been a warmth about their house that was severely lacking in my childhood home, a warmth I had secretly craved for years. I had sworn that, one day, I would achieve that for myself.

I had finally created that stable, warm home with Miller. *That wish had come true.*

Rae rubbed my hands in between both of hers, and I pushed away all my uptight crazy thoughts and focused on her soft brown eyes.

"Come on now. Come sit and tell it to me, all of it. Oh, what's this ring, Grace?"

"It was Dig's. His best friend saved it and gave it to me yesterday."

"Boner?" Tania asked.

"I didn't know he'd had it all this time. It was Dig's favorite. I assumed he'd been buried with it. It's a nice surprise to have it again."

"Kinda creepy," murmured Tania.

"For God's sake, Tania!" Rae made a face at her daughter.

"I caught the silver bug from him."

"I remember one ring he had was the head of a wolf," said Tania.

I nodded. "Good memory."

"Tania and I gave you a hard time when you were with Dig, didn't we?" asked Rae. "And I'm sorry for that, but we were worried about you. We had seen what happened to Ruby back then. We didn't want that for you. But you were happy. You made a life with him. That should have been good enough for me."

"Thank you, Rae. Yes, we did make a good life together." My thumb absently rubbed over the smooth silver of Dig's ring.

"Life pushes on though, doesn't it? Even if we don't want it to." Rae exhaled. "Now, I'm stuck here, but you're home again. So glad you came home." She chuckled. "Guess you needed a local boy, one of our own, to find your happy."

"Yes, I think you're right."

"Tell me everything. Is he as brutally handsome as I've been hearing?"

"That's your first question, Mother?"

"Why not? We're all ladies here." Rae winked at me. "This is my visit with Grace, not yours, Tania. You probably know all the juicy details already, but now it's my turn."

Tania smirked. "Actually, I don't think I know everything."

"Tell me, dear," said Rae.

"Miller is handsome—"

"Very handsome," chimed in Tania. "And very tall. And dark, too."

"Yes, he's all of that."

Rae pursed her lips. "Is he good to you, baby? That's what's important."

"Yes, Rae." I laughed. "He's very good to me. I love him very much."

"I hear his car-and-bike business is doing well. I'm so glad. You deserve nothing but the very best, good girl like you. You didn't deserve what happened to you before. Oh, those bad boys. We do our best to love them, but no matter what, trouble does find them."

"Ma!" Tania's eye's flared.

"She's right, Tan," I said.

"Correct me if I'm wrong, but the new husband is a bad boy, too," Rae said.

I let out a small laugh as Rae held my gaze.

She nodded. "If you love him, Grace, he must be a good man, bad boy or not. I'm sure you tamed him just a little bit though, hmm?" Her eyes were still that rich amber-flecked brown that I remembered so well. Those eyes used to look at me with a mixture of affection, concern, and pity, but now they beamed at me, full of pride and delight.

"I hope you didn't tame him too much!" Tania laughed.

"No, I definitely have not," I replied.

"You don't want me to stay home, Ma, and find my untamed happy?"

"You got a husband in Racine, Tania. Or have you forgotten?"

Rae was not a fan of her daughter's separation or divorce, it seemed.

Tania crossed her arms over her chest. "Why don't you show Ma those pictures, Grace?"

"Of course!" I took out my cell phone and went through my photographs that I had shared with Tania the other day. "Here you go."

Rae swiped through a shot of Miller and Jake polishing a bike at the shop, another one of them watching a football game on TV, and the two of them sharing a blanket with their hair standing on end, both their faces twisted in shock and anger over a lost opportunity at a touchdown. There was also one of me and Miller laughing while we danced at Dead Ringer's a couple of months ago on a night out with Judge and Dee, who had come down from North Dakota.

"Miller certainly is a hottie!" Rae blurted.

Tania and I burst into laughter.

"Isn't that what they say nowadays?" Rae grinned. "We used to say 'cute' or 'good looking' or 'sexy' in my day. Oh, and Jake looks just like Ruby. Imagine that." Rae handed me my cell phone.

"He's something." I tucked my phone in my bag. "He's coming back to stay with us in a couple of weeks while his dad is on another business trip up north, checking on oil wells. Maybe I'll bring Jake by for a visit. Would you like that?"

"Of course I would! How wonderful. My grandchildren come for visits all the time."

"Penny's two boys have really grown up fast. I've seen them in town," I said.

"Haven't they though?"

Tania moved toward the window and tugged open the curtains, letting in a stream of bright sunlight. "Don't forget about your granddaughter, Ma."

Rae lifted her face and then averted her gaze back down to her blanket. "I haven't forgotten, Tania. I just try not to think about her 'cause that only leads to a mountain of worry with no end in sight."

"I'm sorry?" I asked.

"Drew has a daughter," Tania said.

"Really?"

Tania nodded. "We haven't seen her yet. We haven't seen him in years actually. He doesn't really communicate with us anymore since he joined the Flames of Hell a while back."

"Oh. I'm sorry to hear that."

"I don't even want to hear that name!" said Rae. "My son has his own ideas about how to live his life. I can't say I agree with them. And to know a child is in the middle of all that, I can only imagine what the mother must be like." Rae pursed her lips. "Let's change the subject. Tania mentioned something about a surrogate?" Rae asked, a stiff smile on her lips.

"Ma!"

"I tried going the gestational surrogacy route," I replied.

Rae frowned. "You tried?"

"She just miscarried, Ma."

"Oh, Gracie. I'm so sorry!"

"Thank you."

"Well, I know it must be upsetting. I had a miscarriage myself, my first pregnancy, but then I went on to have three without any problems. You never know unless you try. Seems like lots of women are doing it these days. It's a real blessing. You should try again." Rae patted my leg.

"Well, that's your opinion, Mother," added Tania.

"It is. But I feel that, if a woman chooses to put herself through all that, she must have been extremely determined to begin with." Rae's eyes held mine. "Don't tell me, girl, that there isn't a small part of you that doesn't want to try again. You don't want to let this opportunity go to waste, hmm?

I smiled weakly at her.

A knock on the open door had us turning our heads.

A nurse's aid smiled at us. "Hi, Mrs. Reigert."

"Hi, honey," said Rae. "Girls, this is Casey. She makes life for me bearable around here."

"Hello, Miracle Worker Casey," said Tania.

Rae exhaled a long breath. "That's my daughter Tania."

"Hello," Casey replied. "The nurses are coming around with everyone's medication now." Casey took Rae's water pitcher to the trolley she had by the open door.

"Is it hard to find a surrogate?" Rae asked. "Where do you look?"

"There are agencies and lots of networking websites nowadays," I said.

Casey reappeared, the water jug refilled. "If you don't mind my saying, I have a friend who did it once, being a surrogate. She's a registered nurse at Vista Pines, down the street. She had a really positive experience, both pregnancy-wise and legally from what she told me."

"See?" said Rae. "Is she available now for another go?"

"Oh, Ma. Really?" said Tania.

"What's wrong with asking? How else are we going to find out? You have to network."

Casey put the plastic jug of water on the bedside table. "She's actually pregnant with her own baby right now."

"Good for her," I murmured.

"I could ask her for you though. She must know people."

"That'd be nice," said Rae, quirking an eyebrow at me.

Tania rolled her eyes and mouthed, *Sorry*, to me.

I shrugged.

"Okay then. I'll be back after your medication, Mrs. R. It's your shower day today, remember?"

Rae's eyes widened. "Oh, good! Thank you, dear."

Casey waved at us on her way out the door.

"Well, that's our cue to go. You got work today, Grace?"

"No, I took the day off."

"Oh. I have an idea."

"What is it this time?" asked Rae.

"Grace, how about you come with me on a little business trip?"

"A business trip?"

Tania was a professional "picker," an antiques dealer who scoured people's basements, attics, garages and barns hunting for forgotten treasures to restore and sell.

"I have a lead on a pick just across the border in Nebraska—if the beast men can spare you, that is." She smirked at me.

"When?"

"Now."

"Now?"

"Some tiny town just past Chadron."

"Chadron's not far. You two should go and have fun," said Rae. "But watching Tania burrow through some hoarder's mountain of dirty junk might not be too entertaining."

Tania groaned. "Oh, Ma."

A road trip. A girl getaway, like we used to do when we were younger without a care in the world, other than coveting yet another tube of lip gloss. A cooler full of flavored iced teas and chocolate bars in the backseat, our favorite music on cassettes, and getting out of work early with enough money for gas and booze. There would be no men hovering or treading lightly with me, not being able to look me in the eyes for fear of intruding or of the sadness or the crushed hope they might see.

Everything still looked the same at the store, the shop, the club, the supermarket, home, yet nothing was the same. I'd been functioning on automatic and felt guilty for feeling bad and felt bad for feeling guilty. Not even Miller taking me hard or very tender every night could tear through that tight web I had spun around myself. But he certainly tried.

"Grace...take me in all the way, baby. All the fucking way," he'd growled against my skin last night as he'd gripped my hips, thrusting deep.

I had taken him in. I'd surrendered to his high, a high like no other, but in the back of my heart, I'd felt that ping, reminding me that I wasn't worthy of his pleading or his urgent lovemaking. His mouth, hands, cock had all worked feverishly to give me a raw bliss that would make me forget, make me let go, make me fly. Yes, I'd seen bright stars last night, but I'd shut my eyes against the glare.

I grinned at Tania. "I'm game. Let's go."

TWENTY-THREE

"SO, WHAT ARE YOU AFTER ON THIS PICK?" I asked Tania.

We whipped by the *Nebraska...the good life* sign as we sped over the blacktop through the open stretch of arid prairie.

Her hands slid down the steering wheel. "Whatever I can find, basically. You never know. From old toys to gas station signs to old bicycles."

"Well, I'm on strict orders to look for a specific list of vintage Harley and Indian bike parts."

"This guy is a notorious hermit. I've heard about him from two sources, but trying to pin him down on the phone from Wisconsin has been challenging, especially when he doesn't answer his phone most of the time. Now that I'm here, I had to come see him myself. I'm glad you came. This is good."

I laughed. "Will he let us in, you think?"

She grinned. "Oh, he'll let us in."

"As long as he doesn't aim a shotgun at us, we'll be fine. I left my gun at home just so you know."

"Now she tells me," quipped Tania.

"How is business anyway?"

"Pretty good actually."

"You have an eye for this sort of thing, don't you?"

She glanced at me, grinning, and then went back to the road. "Yes, I do."

"I'm glad you're doing something you love. That's getting more and more difficult to do these days."

"I love it. I love the search, and I love connecting a client with something unique or something they've been looking for for a long time. I also love running my own show."

"I'll bet. You remember Wreck, Miller's brother? He ran the shop at the club."

"Yes, of course. He had all that eagle memorabilia."

"A huge collection, and a lot of other automotive-related material. I used to try to organize it for him, but it was pretty overwhelming. His house, where we're living now, used to be jammed with stuff. A lot of it, Miller got rid of. But a lot is in storage. Would you be interested in taking a look?"

She glanced at me, eyes blazing. "Hell, yes."

"I need to ask Miller, see if he wants to part with any of it. But it's just been stored away for a long, long time. Wreck traveled around a lot. If he saw something he really liked, he bought it. You never know what you might find."

"I want in, Grace. Talk to the hubs and let me know."

"Will do."

"You know, I've been thinking, with Mom in rehab for a while and not being able to live on her own anymore, that I should move back. Penny's got her kids, and Drew is AWOL, so she's got me."

"Back to Meager? Really?"

"Yeah. I have inventory I could bring over here and open my own shop in town. Rents are still reasonable, and some interesting new stores have opened recently. I'd like to get in on this Meager renaissance. I like the new hipster spirit in our little town."

"Tania, that would be amazing!"

"I poked around in this lingerie store on Clay Street the other day.

"Lenore's Lace?"

"Yes. Whoa! What didn't she have?"

"Lenore is a good friend. She has a gorgeous shop."

"A funky lingerie store in Meager. Never in a million years…"

"I still remember when all we had was the feed store and Dillon's, the five-and-dime."

"Dillon's!"

"Erica's coffee house is beautiful, don't you think?"

"Yes! And she has really good coffee."

"Amen." I sucked down the last of my second latte from Erica's that we had bought after we left the rehab earlier. "I just checked out this new pottery shop, too. She had some nice pieces."

"Oh, yeah? Such a relief to see Pepper's is still there."

"Oh God, Pepper's! Best boot shop ever. Tania, he has two shelves now devoted to women's fashion boots. I think I actually saw pink and turquoise leather when I was last there."

"No way!" We both squealed and erupted into snorty laughter.

"Tania?"

"Yeah?"

"What's going on with your husband? You haven't talked about this divorce at all."

"There's not much to talk about, babe. Just…no. I want out." Her jaw clamped down, and her brows slid together as she went back to concentrating on the road.

Another time, I would have pushed it further. But now, I, too, only wanted to enjoy the easy feeling of simply hanging out with my old friend.

Forty-five minutes later, I was comparing the map of Elk, a tiny hamlet just past Chadron, with Tania's scribbles in her notebook, trying to find where this Herman Grant's property began or ended and might or might not be. I was now ready to throw the map and the notebook out the car window. We tried asking for directions at a gas station, but we were met with blank stares and mumbling. Tania returned to the dirt road we had explored on the third go-around about town.

"I'm going to take a left here. It says right, but we went right last time and got stuck up that hill that led nowhere."

"Go for it," I replied, my head lolling back against the headrest.

Ten minutes later, a long gate made of splintered gray wood appeared in the distance.

"Grace, look." A faded carved wooden sign hung on the edge of the gate. "Grant."

We both sat up straighter.

"I'm going to park here, and we'll climb over. What do you say?"

"Let's do it."

Tania reversed her Yukon away from the gate and parked it on the side of the rocky path. She shoved the map, her papers and notebook along with my wallet in her messenger bag. I tucked my cell phone in my back pocket and stuffed my handbag under my seat, hiding it from view. I hopped down from the truck and closed the door. I glanced in the side mirror and smoothed over the skin under my eyes with my fingertips as Tania locked the truck.

"Well, there's no *Private Property* or *No Trespassing* sign, so…" She shrugged.

Tania toed her boots into the slats of the fence and heaved herself over it. I followed, and she steadied me by the arm. I jumped down on the other side. We were in. We trudged up the road winding up a small hill. Our boots crunched over the gravel and small rocks. The occasional bird circled in the pale gray sky, rays of sun struggling to break through.

Eventually, the hill evened out, and up ahead, rusted shells of decades-old automobiles dotted the overgrown wild grasses like oversized bugs. As we weaved our way between them, a row of aluminum shacks became visible in the distance leading up to a dilapidated small wood two story house. Before us was a field littered with towering piles of rusted gadgets and devices, unrecognizable thingamajigs and bits, sinks, metal piping, signs for stores—several for a local dairy and others for gas stations, luncheonettes and a beer brewery—long since gone, a huge marquee from an old movie palace. It was a junkyard, a museum *au naturel* that time had forgotten. Weeds and brush wound their way in between the piled scrap, coiling and knitting it together to the land. Rambunctious, ugly, and perversely organic.

Tania was entranced, standing still amid the chaos. Her face was flushed, her eyes scanning the property, up and down, as she reveled in the discovery of this field of yet undiscovered gold. Her entire body was at attention as if she were listening to the eerie call of textures and shapes scattered before her. She unclipped her mini flashlight from her bag, which she'd removed from her shoulder, and wordlessly handed to me. I dropped the thick nylon bag, crosswise, over my body, adjusting it.

I smiled to myself as she moved carefully through the piles of scrap crap. Tania searched and hunted through an endless series of piled high traffic lights, old cola vending machines, kerosene oil tank pumps and dispensers. On some innate instinct, she knew where to linger, her fingers skimming surfaces, investigating, turning the objects over, trying to read old labels, engravings, searching for brand names, dates, assessing rust and decay, wiping away dirt. There was so much stuff that it truly boggled me how anyone could live this way and want to preserve it, but I knew the human mind could convince itself of anything. At the end of the day, this was Grant's personal creation, his unique universe.

"Oh, look at this!" Tania hovered over an old Esso gasoline pump.

"How old is that?"

"Has to be from the early forties at least. Collectors love them, and they use these on film sets, too. Beautiful." She took out her phone and took photos of it. "Oh God, there's another one."

"I'll go see if Mr. Grant's around?"

"Yes! Good idea."

I meandered through the field of glorious junk, hoping to find anything that remotely resembled the parts that I knew Miller and Tricky, his car repair specialist, were after. I passed a fallen wall of rusted iron gates from a bygone era on the side of one of the shacks. The door hung open, and I peered inside. The hairs on the back of my neck stood on end. No wild critters jumped out at me—not yet at least. I stepped inside.

The late morning sun filtered through the dank space, revealing an undisturbed army of worn objects crammed throughout, thick particles of dust and debris floating everywhere. Rusted bicycle frames stood, stacked in rows. Tens of old railroad lamps crowded one side of a table. I tugged open the door wider to let more light in, and a long line of bike lights on a shelf along the wall greeted me. My fingers roamed over the damp cold metal of an old motor at my side.

I bent over it.

How the heck am I going to tell if—

My phone rang, and I slipped it from my pocket.

Boner.

"Hey—"

"What the fuck are you doing in Nebraska?"

"What? I came down with Tania on a shopping expedition for her store and—"

"Get the fuck out of there now!"

"What the hell are you talking about? How do you—"

"Listen. There's shit going down between the Flames of Hell and the Blades, and I don't care if you're hanging at McDonald's or the local police station. It ain't good. Get Tania, and get out!"

"Nebraska's a big state."

"You're in Flames territory, Grace. Does Lock know where you are?"

"Not really. He went on a scouting trip early this morning, and I couldn't reach him when Tania and I got on the road a couple of hours ago."

"Fuck!"

"How do you know where I am?"

"How the fuck do you think?"

"Of course. Stupid question," I retorted. Knowing my husband and Boner, I was positive they had put a tracking device on my phone a while back—just in case.

A scraping sound arose by the bicycle frames and behind a large telephone operator switchboard. My stomach hardened.

Ugh. Possums? Raccoons? Rats?

A shiver needled up my back as I retreated, straining my eyes for any quick movement over the junk heaped on the tables and the sagging shelves.

"Grace? I'm less than two hours away from where you are. You hear? I'm on my way!" Boner's voice buzzed in my ear.

Disconnected.

What the hell?

Metal creaked and groaned from across the packed room. My body tightened, my gaze darting everywhere. If the wild critters weren't enough, there were now opposing MCs on the warpath.

So much for the carefree getaway.

I moved backward toward the open door. Muffled sounds, a rustling, came from that same corner. A soft murmuring sound. No scurrying of ratlike creatures. *No, that sounds like a…*

I held my breath as I shoved back the metal door further. Light streamed in the shack, illuminating the crowded interior. A pair of glassy eyes peered at me from the far wall. My heart jumped in my throat as I strained to see clearly. The soft babbling sound grew louder. I blinked. A toddler, a little girl not more than a year old was stretched out on a blanket playing with some sort of toy, her legs kicking on the ground. Her one foot was tied by a rope to the stand of an oversized beater from a bakery.

"Oh my God!" I blurted.

The child's head turned, and she squinted in the light now flooding that corner of the shack. A wail broke from her lips, her little hands reaching out to me. Adrenaline shot through me as I shoved junk out of my way to get to her. My heart pounded wildly as I slid to my knees in front of the little girl with a dark blonde mop of hair. What the hell was she doing here? What kind of monster had tied up a baby and abandoned it?

My one hand tucked into the messenger bag and closed over my key chain that had my old Swiss Army knife on it. I sliced through the rope attached to her one foot, and the little girl's face broke into a huge smile. Her legs flexed and kicked against the floor again.

"Hold on. Hold on, honey. Almost there."

I tugged on the frayed rope as she yanked her leg free.

"There you go. Oh, sweetie!" I lifted her and tucked her into my embrace.

Her little fists grabbed at my hair.

"Who did this to you?"

Two blue eyes pierced mine as if they understood the gravity of my question. Her face was cold, her diaper full.

"We've got to get you out of here now."

I jerked my cell phone out of my pocket and messaged Boner *9XX*—as in, this is a dire-emergency-so-get-your-ass-over-here-now 911. It was our code from the old days, and it remained my reflex reaction in an emergency. He'd said he was on his way. He should know that something was already up before he stepped in. I couldn't be sure if this was Mr. Grant's doing or someone else's, but if there was one thing I'd learned, it was not to take any chances and prepare for the worst. I hit the Send button and tucked the phone back in my jeans.

"Okay, baby. Let's go. It's chilly in here. Oh, yes, it is."

I held her close, and she immediately wrapped her tiny arms around my neck yanking on my hair, her tiny fingers pinching at my neck.

"That's it." Tucking her closer into my chest, I raised myself up and turned.

The wood table to the left creaked and groaned. I froze.

"Where the fuck do you think you're going?" a male voice growled at me from the shadows.

TWENTY-FOUR

"STOP RIGHT THERE, BITCH," he seethed.

I stumbled back at the hard glint of a gun pointed at me. In the rays of light glowing through the shed, I saw the figure moving forward. My body stiffened.

Creeper.

Welcome to my nightmare.

His eyes sunken, his teeth bared like a desperate animal's, he was slumped against the wall, the gun in his hand trained on me. After news of him working with Vig had broken open last year, the disgraced One-Eyed Jack had left the club's North Dakota chapter and gone underground. There had been a charter-wide APB out on him ever since.

"Aw, ain't this something, huh, Sister? You and me, fuckin' meant to be." He cackled, his headful of straggly dark hair thrown back.

My heart thundered in my chest.

A sneer soured his face further. "This is turning out to be my lucky day. I'm gonna enjoy this."

Yeah, he still hated me—and with good reason.

I swallowed hard. "What the hell is going on?"

"You're holding my goody bag."

My stomach churned. "You kidnapped this little girl? Are you insane?"

"Oh, it's just been a few hours. We been having fun. She took a nap. I tripped out."

"What the hell, Creeper? What is going on with you?"

"You missed me, huh?" He laughed. "After the fun we had with Vig last year?"

The One-Eyed Jacks had been searching for him for payback ever since that night last year when he had aligned himself with the Demon Seeds, I tried to end my business arrangement with Vig, and Creeper had threatened to rape me to make a point.

My phone rang. *Damn it.*

A thousand needles pricked my throat.

He smirked at me. "Give me your phone."

"Creeper—"

"Give me your fucking phone now!"

I handed him my phone. "Is it Half-Breed calling his lady love?" He glanced at my phone. "Ah, no. Mr. Boner. Fascinating. He knows you're here?"

"No."

Creeper smirked as he dropped the phone to the ground and jammed the heel of his boot into it.

Motherfudgemycake.

"Grace? Are you in here?"

Tania.

"I think I found an Indian gas tank. You need to come see and tell me if—what the hell?" Tania froze in the entryway of the shed, the light streaming in around her figure as if she were a celestial Wonder Woman.

If only.

Creeper yanked at me, twisting me around in his grip, and shoving his gun against my head. The baby yelped and began to cry, and I cradled her head. The stink of his sweat, musty clothing, and bad breath overwhelmed me, and I grit my teeth.

"Get over here, or I shoot her," he spit out.

"What the fuck?" muttered Tania.

"Move! Now, bitch."

Tania shuffled inside a few more steps. "Grace, you okay?"

"Shut it, and get inside!"

Tania stepped farther inside the shed, her eyes widening at the sight of me holding the child.

"Get on your knees."

She scowled at him, and fell to her knees. He shoved me closer to Tania until we stood in front of her.

He studied her. "I like your friend, Sister. Don't fucking move. Creeper released me and secured a plastic tie around Tania's wrists.

"Jesus. Why are you doing this? Why did you take someone's little girl?" I asked, my hands stroking over the baby's back as she pleaded with me to make this all better, her pouty cheeks wet, her whimpers getting louder, her full lips spluttering.

"You know this jerk?" Tania asked.

Creeper chuckled. "Me and Sister got history."

Tania's face tightened. "Well, isn't *Sister* the lucky one?"

"Watch your mouth, or I'm gonna shut it by shoving my dick all the way in it."

"Then I'm going to have to bite it off."

"Aw! This should be loads of fun." He muttered, stroking the side of her face with his gun.

She clenched her jaw.

"Me and Sister got unfinished business. Last time I saw her, she shot me in the leg and took off on my bike," he said.

Tania glanced at me. "Good for her."

Creeper let out another squawking laugh. "Man, this day just got a fuck of a lot better. We're gonna be here for a while. I have Pop-Tarts for the kid. Maybe she'll share with y'all." He hitched the gun under Tania's chin. "You're up first, bitch."

"Let them go, Creeper. Take me," I said.

"Oh, I'll take you, honey. Have no doubt. But I need the kid."

"What are you talking about?"

"Collateral."

"That's a big word for you, isn't it?" muttered Tania.

"Fuck you," said Creeper, kicking her in the stomach.

Tania grunted, doubling over.

"Stop it!" I shouted.

"No way, whore. I like this party we got going on here. I got time to kill while I wait to hear from Catch."

Tania's face froze.

"Who's Catch?" I asked.

"The Flames of Hell piece-of-shit daddy."

Tania only nodded at me.

Oh, shit.

Catch must be Tania's brother, Drew.

Tania drew herself up onto her knees. "What about that Pop-Tart?"

Creeper let out a small laugh. "Aw, you're gonna have to work for it, honey."

Needles raced across my skin at the sardonic tone in his voice.

"And what does Catch have that you want?" I asked.

"I gave him information, and he owes me. Owes me big time. And has he paid up? Fuck no. Prick thinks he can get what he wants from me and try to kill me? Get rid of me? Me? No fucking way."

The zip of his jeans buzzed through me like a chainsaw. Tania's eyes widened.

His dirt-stained fingers gripped her chin, tugging on it. "Open up, bitch."

Tania smirked. "Fuck no. I want a Pop-Tart, not a cocktail weenie."

Creeper smacked her hard, and Tania crashed to her side. My lungs burned, and I held the baby tighter against me.

"You've always got something on somebody, don't you?" I said. "You're still working an angle wherever you go. Can't ever be faithful to any one thing or any brother."

He pivoted around facing me, his face twisting into a snarl. "What the fuck do you know about brotherhood?"

"A hell of a lot more than you ever will."

The baby started wailing, her hands thumping on my arms. She squiggled in my tight hold.

"Oh, yeah? Just for that, I want both of you on your knees, mouths open. Like a good old-fashioned train but just for me. I'll start with your mouths, and then your asses go in the air, ladies. Fuck yeah." He jammed his gun into the back of his jeans, muttering to himself, and shoved the other hand in a pocket. He moved towards me, a sharp grin on his face, his hand pulling out a plastic tie.

"Put the kid down," he said.

"No."

Tania lunged at Creeper, head-butting his torso, shoving him forward. Creeper grunted, his head banging into a rusted metal table, his body sprawling on the small patch of dirty cement floor. Two large metal typewriters perched at the edge of the table teetered and toppled over him. He howled and cursed.

I ran to the doorway and propped the baby up by the open door, out of the way of the junk and the rest of us, and I dashed back to Creeper who was struggling to raise himself up on all fours. I reached for his gun hanging from his jeans, and his one arm shot out at me.

"Grace!" shouted Tania.

Creeper yanked me down, and I crashed into the typewriters. "Ow!"

His loud grunt filled the air as his other hand grabbed my arm and he flipped me over, kicking his gun away. His hands dug into my arms, and he hurled me against the table. Pain exploded through my back. He shot up and lunged at me, seizing me by the collar of my jacket, lifting me to my legs, shaking me.

He grimaced, his lips curling. "Fucking bitch." He slapped me hard.

My skin stung, my head swinging. I struggled for air, staggering in his tight grip, my knees giving way.

The baby screamed and cried. Tania pushed up on her feet, kicking out a leg, ramming it into Creeper's back. He groaned, his back bowing, his grip on me easing slightly. I relaxed in his hold, and my right knee shot up, slamming into his crotch. He gasped— his eyes bulging, his body seizing—and he let go of me. My fingers stretched out and grabbed on to the handle of one of the old metal railroad lamps on the edge of the table behind me. I swung it out, banging the side of his head. Creeper flew back, crashing into shelves full of oilcans, sports trophies, and commemorative beer steins, all of it cascading down over him. A stack of thick wooden doors slid down like oversized dominoes.

"Jesus!" muttered Tania. "Cut me loose!" She raised her arms behind her.

I glanced at the baby, who was crying, slumped over, but she wasn't crawling around. I darted to Tania and cut the tie around her wrists.

"You okay?"

She frowned, rubbing her irritated skin. "Yeah, I'm okay." She marched toward the door and lifted the little girl in her arms. "Shh…baby, everything's fine now."

"Catch is Drew?"

"Yes. This has got to be my niece," Tania muttered, a grimace marring her face before it softened. "Hi, baby girl!"

The girl cried.

"Yeah, my thoughts exactly. Let's go, Grace, before he wakes up. I have to call my brother."

"Hold on." I stepped over Creeper, found his gun, and took it. Sliding the safety, I tucked it inside the messenger bag.

"Shit, my battery's dead. Yours?"

"He trashed it."

"Great. Just great. We're going to have to go to the Flames."

"Fuck."

"Exactly."

"Have you ever been there before?" I asked.

"It's not far."

"That's not what I'm asking, Tan."

Tania headed out of the shed her arms firmly around the baby's squirming body. "I know."

"You have a baseball cap or something?"

"Huh?" Tania glanced at me as she shoved the Yukon into park.

My mouth dried as I stared at the tall wire fence bordering a two-story warehouse that stood alone in a barren clearing, like an industrial fortress, with a line of bikes parked out front.

"Why?"

"They might recognize me. I mean, they probably won't. But why take chances? The baby here doesn't want to let go of me, so it looks like I'm going to have to come in. I think it'd be better if this was a One-Eyed Jack-free event. Of course, Drew might..."

"I'll take care of my brother." Tania stared at me from her rearview mirror. "Look in one of the seat pockets."

I tucked my hand in the seat pocket in front of me and found a black Chicago Bulls cap. I put it on and adjusted the sunglasses on my nose.

Tania sighed. "Ready?"

"No."

"Super. Let's go."

I took in a breath of air as Tania swung open the back door for me. We had stopped at a mini market and bought a couple of jars of baby food along with a pack of diapers and wipes. The little thing had been grateful for the food and the cleanup, and she'd shown it by clinging to me and cooing.

A heavyset prospect stood at the gate and glared at us, his tattooed arms crossed. "Ladies? What do ya need?"

Tania put her hands on her waist. "Hi. I need to see Catch. Is he here?"

The man's head tilted. "That's his kid."

"Yeah. I'm his sister Tania. I found his little girl. Is he here?"

He raised a finger at us and whipped out his cell phone. "Bro? You got a sister?" His gaze swept over me and Tania. "Yeah, she's here, out front. She's got your kid, man." He pressed a button, and the gate jerked open. He motioned at us, but then he stopped me. "Who are you?"

"She's a friend of mine. Maddie."

Oh, brother.

He twisted his lips. "Yeah, stop right there." He patted us both down. Of course, I had left Creeper's gun in the truck. "Go ahead."

Tania touched my arm, and we moved past him and headed toward the main door, which was open.

I stroked the baby's back in an effort to maintain my own cool. Dig had been on a run with the Flames when Wreck got killed. Dig had been convinced that working with them was a good thing. I really couldn't remember if they had ended things on a good note or not, but I didn't think Jump had anything to do with them now.

A tall dark-haired Flame with large brown eyes charged toward us. Drew was the spitting image of Tania.

Catch, my brain stammered.

He had grown much taller since the last time I saw him, but he remained that lanky hyperkinetic creature he always had been as a boy.

"Tania? What the fuck?"

"Becca!" A harried blonde came zipping around Catch before screeching to a halt in front of me.

The baby's eyes widened for a second, and she immediately burst into tears. The blonde scooped the little girl from me, and I crossed my arms against the sudden chill sweeping over my chest. She smothered the baby in kisses, and the baby's tiny hands wrapped around her mother's neck, her head dropped against her mother's chest. My heart tripped.

"Tania? How the hell did you find her? What are you doin' here? What the fuck is going on?"

"I've been home with Ma for about a week now, and I came down here today with my friend Maddie on business." She gestured at me, and my lips tightened into a firm line. "We found your daughter in this shed on the property. We also found the guy who was holding her."

"Where is he?"

"Gr—Maddie knocked him out, and we got out of there real quick."

Catch stared at me. I lifted my chin under the glare of his scrutiny. A stream of Flames filed into the cavernous room where we stood, forming a semicircle around Catch.

"Was it Creeper?" asked Catch through gritted teeth.

"I don't know. We didn't have a chance for a formal introduction." Tania made a face. "The name certainly fits. He was a bit of a freak show."

"Motherfucking Jack," he muttered.

My jaw clenched even tighter. Tania's back stiffened.

"This is all your fault!" the blonde shouted. "I'm so over this shit with you!" She approached Tania. "Thank you. Thank you so much," she glanced at me, "both of you."

"You're welcome," Tania replied.

I offered a slight smile and a nod of my head.

Time to go. Time to go. Time to go. Time to go.

"Did you call the cops?" asked Catch.

"No. We asked him why he had taken the baby, and your name came up. I would've called you, but my battery died, and I don't know your number by heart."

"Appreciate it, Tan."

"Of course."

"Why don't you two take a load off and tell us where you found the kid and more about this guy, so we can catch up with that motherfucker?" a voice rose from behind the Flames that had gathered in the room.

My body bent to the side, compelled to find the voice's owner. My stomach cramped at the sight. A tall, broad-chested man with deeply grooved scars over both his cheeks barely covered by his trimmed beard and mustache stood before us. Tattoos twisted up both his arms, and one slithered around his neck. His black hair was peppered with gray. The one and only Finger strode toward me and Tania. A president's patch was stitched on his colors.

Dig had told me the horrid story of how Finger had gotten his road name. With his facial scars (an F on each cheek) and missing digits, the newly baptized Finger had returned to the Flames of Hell a changed man, to say the least. Ruthless, cold, and single-minded, he had in recent years transformed his club into a highly respected and feared 1% organization. His facial scars gave him, an otherwise handsome man, a spectacularly sadistic look.

Tania shifted her weight, her previously steady demeanor suddenly unsteady. "Hey."

His large brown eyes took her in, a slight smile flashed over his thin lips. "Tania." His voice was a warm rasp. "Been a long while."

"Yeah." Her voice got quiet.

You have got to be fucking kidding me.

Another man moved forward from behind Finger.

Holy, holy, holy hell. My hands pressed into my sides.

Butler.

What the hell was he doing here with the Flames?

He tilted his head, holding my gaze, and my pulse skidded. He didn't move a muscle, only his lips pressed together. It'd been almost a year since I last saw him. I sucked in a deep breath as I took in the waves of pale blond hair framing his rugged face, the long line of his angular nose, and the distinctive square jaw covered in gold scruff. Butler was all contoured muscle filling his old leather jacket and worn jeans, ending in massive engineer boots. His face was slightly fuller, smoother, not pinched and worn as when I had last seen him. Only one piercing in his brow remained from all the jewelry he used to sport on his face and in his ears. I slowly released my breath. I was relieved to see him, but I wasn't sure this was so good either.

Catch's baby mama reemerged from another room just beyond the front hall where we stood. Two bags were slung over her shoulders, and the baby was in her arms.

"Where you going?" Catch hollered after her.

"Are you joking? I am out of here, once and for all. I am so done. Done!"

"Babe, come on now. It's over."

"Over? It's never over!" She let out a shrill laugh.

"You need time to settle down? Take it. Nothing's over though."

"For God's sake, Catch! Let's be real for a change. This has been over since before Becca was born. But I stuck it out. You were supposed to be watching your daughter while I was at work! You! But no! Instead, you had one of your whores doing it while you were out. Unbelievable. I'm getting out of here, out of this shithole town, and—"

"And where you gonna go?"

"I—"

"Yeah?"

"Why don't you come home with me?" Tania said, her voice sharp, even, demanding consideration.

The blonde spun around and faced Tania, her lips parted.

"Sounds like a plan," Finger said.

Was he keeping the peace or just fed up with the soap opera?

Catch's eyes flared. "To Meager?"

"Why not?" Tania said. "There's plenty of room at Ma's house, and she could use the company once she gets out of rehab. She was just saying how she wanted to get to know her granddaughter. I'm living there now, too, helping her out, but someone needs to be with her full time. If you're up for that sort of thing."

She smiled at Tania. "Yes, I am. Oh my God! Yes! Thank you."

Catch's face stiffened. "Tania—"

"Sounds like a fine plan," said Finger, his eyes drifting over me and Tania.

Finger was certainly done with this drama.

Catch shot his girlfriend a harsh look. "How am I gonna keep you safe when you're not here?"

"Like you kept us safe before? Give me a break!"

Finger eyed Catch, his hands slung on his slim hips. "Time to move this along, man."

Catch swallowed, his hard eyes glowering at his sister and then snapping back to his soon-to-be ex-girlfriend.

The young woman's posture was rigid, her eyes red. She must have been in her late twenties, maybe early thirties, but there was the desperation and resolve of a mother at her wit's end. I didn't blame her one damn bit. I admired her for it.

She glanced at Tania. "Thank you. I really appreciate this. God, you don't even know me!" She kissed the side of her daughter's face.

"You're welcome," replied Tania.

Catch jerked his chin toward the door, and his girlfriend rolled her eyes. She brushed past me, and little Becca reached out a chubby hand and nabbed my sunglasses from my nose. My hand snapped out and nabbed them right back. I slid them on my face once again.

"You okay?" Finger asked.

"Me? Yes, thanks." My lips tipped up into a quick grin.

"Long day, Maddie?" asked Butler, his eyes trying to penetrate the shield of my sunglasses. "Got a nice bruise there." My hand flew to my sore cheek. A muscle on the side of Butler's face pulsed.

"It's not every day you get held at gunpoint and your life is threatened by a ratty-ass biker, is it?" asked Tania.

Finger chuckled, the sound grating, stuck in his chest. Ominous.

"How 'bout you give me the details on this piece of shit, so I can head out after him?" Butler's familiar gruff voice had me digging my heels into the floor as he strode toward us.

"Sure," I mumbled.

Finger's stony eyes rested on me. "You know these two? Tania's from your parts."

"Yeah, we met years ago in Meager before I went up north."

Finger lifted an eyebrow as his gaze slid to Tania.

"Never seen this one before." Butler stared at me.

Tania shifted her weight. "Maddie came down with me from Racine last week to help me with my move."

Finger only nodded. The F scars on each cheek seemed to deepen on his skin. "Find out what these two know, and bring me that motherfucker." His iron gaze remained on Tania.

"Let's go, ladies." Butler gestured towards the main door. I slipped my arm through Tania's and tugged on her.

TWENTY-FIVE

"YOU REALLY GONNA GO TO SOUTH DAKOTA WITH MY SISTER?" Catch planted his feet in the pebbled weed-ridden yard. "You don't even know her, babe."

"Don't call me that anymore. Your sister is being very generous, and I for one am really grateful." She popped her head out of the backseat of her small red Honda where she was adjusting Becca in her car seat. "I'm going to get a life, Catch. The life I wanted to get when I broke up with you a year and a half ago. But no. I did the right thing. I stuck it out, stuck around that whole time because of our daughter, because of your promises."

Catch glared at Tania. "This is all your fault."

"Are you fucking kidding me?" Tania said, her voice low. "I just got here. If you can't be a responsible boyfriend and dad, that's on you, *Catch*. I'm offering the mother of your kid a way out of this mess, which by the way, happens to be *your* mess. Anyway, what's wrong with them coming to stay with me and Mom in Meager? Mom would love to spend time with her granddaughter, a granddaughter she hasn't had the chance to get to know, and so would I. Come on. They'll be much better off out of the line of fire."

"I can't protect them if they're in Meager, Tania."

"Oh, fuck off!" exclaimed the mom.

"Hey, you don't talk to me like that!"

The blonde spun around. "And you don't talk to us like we're idiot whores under your thumb. You got that? I know that's what you're used to, but that's not going to work here."

Nice. I was going to like this girl.

"Did you hear that, little brother?" Tania twisted her car keys in her fingers

"You know something? Right now, I only care that our daughter is safe and healthy." The young woman dug her hands in to her hips. "That's all. I don't even care that I'm about to pack up my worldly goods and leave the one place I've called home for three years." She swept her fingers under her puffy eyes. "I don't even care that I've wasted a long time now staying out here with you, that I put off doing all the things I've wanted to do—school, a better job. That's how important this is. Do you not get that? Really?"

"Babe." Catch ran a hand through his dark hair.

"Please." Her voice lowered, her heavy eyes meeting his. "Please. I can't do this anymore. I came here for you, Catch. But I have to leave for her."

Catch's head swung to the side as if she had hit him. His eyes darted at his sister. "This is on you now."

"Hell no. You're the dad. It will always be on you," Tania retorted.

He closed the passenger door of his ex's car. "You call me when you get to Meager. You hear? You fucking call me."

"I will," the young woman said as she climbed into the front seat and closed the door.

Butler finally emerged from the building and charged towards me. "Let's talk. Now."

Tania and I moved toward the gate with Butler at my side.

He moved closer to me. "You okay, *Maddie*?"

"Just groovy, never better," I muttered.

His eyes narrowed at me. "How bad did it get?"

"He tried to make it real bad, but we managed to knock him out," said Tania.

"You remember Tania?" I asked.

Butler glanced at her for a moment, and she grinned stiffly at him. "Yeah, I remember Tania." His eyes narrowed. "Lock know you're here?"

"No. I talked to Boner just before Creeper found me. He's on his way."

"You'd better get going. Tell me about Creeper."

We told him everything that had happened and where Grant's property was located.

I studied him as he checked the map on his phone. "What are you doing here anyway? With them?" I asked him.

He glanced up at me. "I'm not with them. I'm taking care of business."

His eyes were no longer the lively crystal blue electromagnetic forces I remembered them to be. They were contained. There was a grim edge to Butler now. Of course, there would be. He'd obviously wrestled with his drug addiction, and he had borne the pain and disappointment of his own choices in addition to mine. More importantly, he'd been spurned by the brotherhood he'd called home for so many years. He'd gone Nomad out of choice and necessity for the second time in his life. I hoped the One-Eyed Jacks would take him back—if he still wanted in, of course. But judging from all this, he was taking some sort of stand.

"Are you going after Creeper?"

"That motherfucker has been playing both sides of every fence he could hop on for way too long now. Been tracking him for months. With this little kidnapping stunt of his, the shit just hit the fan."

"Butler—"

He leaned into me, the aroma of wood, ash, and perspiration rising up between us. A heady blend of man. "I'm pulling the plug on that fan, babe."

My chest constricted at the deadly tone of his voice. His light-blue eyes glimmered in the glare of the afternoon sun across the high fences where we stood.

"Get home safe," he said, signaling to the prospect to open the gate for us. "Thanks for the info."

I held his gaze. "You be safe, too."

"And stay out of Nebraska, Grace."

"With pleasure," muttered Tania.

"Does the club know you're here?" I whispered.

"You going to tell Jump you saw me?" he shot back.

"No. No, I'm not." I raised my chin. "You do what you have to do. Are you okay though? Are you…"

A slight grin stole over Butler's lips, his eyes flashing. "Maddie, go." He turned and prowled away towards his bike.

Tania and I watched him tear out of the compound.

"I'm not having a delusional moment, am I?"

"Which? Take your freaking pick."

"Butler was here, right?"

"Oh, he was here all right."

"This is the first time I've seen him in almost a year."

"Really?" She glanced at me, her brow wrinkling. "He seems different from the Butler I remember. Sounds like I have some catching up to do."

"Yeah." I let out an exhale, not excited by the prospect of recounting my and Butler's tale of spying, betrayal, and stinging disappointments.

"I haven't seen him since your wedding with Dig. Is he some kind of outlaw bounty hunter now?"

"I have no flipping idea."

"Well, *Sister*, you can give me the Butler recap once we get on the road for home."

"You going to give me the Finger recap, too?"

She frowned.

Catch's ex pulled up in her car next to us. "I can't tell you how much I appreciate this. Really. Can you guys follow me to my place, so I can pack up my stuff before we hit the road?"

"Sure thing." I leaned down closer to her and smiled. "By the way, what's your name?"

She leaned her head back against the headrest, a smile on her tired face. "I'm Jill."

TWENTY-SIX

"WHERE THE FUCK HAVE YOU BEEN?" Boner's eyes bored holes into mine.

"My phone got—"

"I figured. I traced your signal to this property filled with all this fucking junk in the middle of nowhere. And who do I see? A couple of Flames casing the place. Do you know how worried I was? After they left, I checked it out, but there was no sign of you two, just your goddamn phone crushed to pieces."

Once we had gotten to Jill's apartment, I'd called Boner, who'd made it into town in the meantime. He'd come right over to Jill's place and met me out front.

"Explain. What the hell are you doing here?" He jerked his chin at the clapboard house behind me. "Who's this girl?"

"Catch's ex-girlfriend and baby mommy. I found her kid in the shed up there. Creeper had kidnapped the poor thing. We brought the baby back to Catch. But Jill, the ex, was in a rage about it, of course. Tania offered to bring her back to Meager to stay with her and her mom."

His dark brows slammed together, his green eyes piercing mine like arrows. "Back the fuck up. You went to the Flames' clubhouse? After I told you to get out of Nebraska, no less, and you just walked right on in there?"

"I had a hat on and sunglasses. I didn't do much talking. But Finger was curious about me."

"Holy fuck!"

"He and Tania seemed to know each other. That was interesting."

"I can't even go there now." Boner shook his head, his lips smashing together. "So, you're bringing this Flame's old lady home to Meager? Seriously? Catch must be loving that."

"He's not happy. But Finger was all for it." I moved in closer to him. "The best part was, Butler was there."

"Butler?"

"Yes. He covered, though, and acted like he didn't know who I was. He was with Finger and spearheading the Creeper chase. Have you heard from Butler at all?"

"Off and on. He lets me know that he's still alive, which is good."

"He doesn't want Jump to know that he's here. I promised him I wouldn't tell."

"But you're telling me?"

"Of course I'm telling you."

"How did he look?"

My lips tipped up. "Straight. Clean."

Boner dragged his white teeth across his bottom lip. "Good."

"He said the shit was hitting the fan, and he was going to pull the plug on that fan. You know what he's talking about?"

Boner crossed his arms and leaned back against his chopper, his face turning up to the gray sky. "I've been down here for days, dealing with the Broken Blades—or trying to at least. Their prez is being an asshole, as usual. Remember Notch?"

"Yes, I do."

"He's been getting into it with the Flames of Hell. Thinks he can play them at their own game. That kinda stupid comes with power. Seems Creeper was running go-between, doing odd jobs for both clubs. Think he got caught dipping in both pies though. Blades are not happy with him either."

"That's too bad."

"Us and the Blades worked together on this one deal a few months ago, but Notch pulled out at the last minute and sucked on Vig's cock for a while. Always the same game with the two of them. Notch tried to pull that shit with the Flames, too, so it's all one big happy shit pile. Can't go on much longer though. There's only so much territory to go around and the Mexicans have dipped their finger in every hole."

"And Butler's getting in between all that unhappy?" I let out an exhale.

"Nebraska was always the key for Dig, the key to standing up to the Seeds and the Russians a long time ago. For years, he worked on hammering out a kind of coalition of the Jacks with the Flames and the Blades, so we could work together to hold up our territories against outsiders. Our prez back then wasn't interested."

"Mick?"

"Yeah. Mick was more interested in what the Demon Seeds had going on out west, but Dig jacked that up for him. But when Dig got killed, it all went to shit—nobody talking to each other, everyone suspicious and striking out over anything, business never getting done. It was an endless circle of fire. Jump got it under control eventually, but things are splitting at the seams again.

"Maybe Butler's aiming to do something about it."

"Maybe."

"Boner, you have to reach out to him, see if he needs help, if...I don't know," I whispered.

Boner's chest expanded. "Butler remembers. My brother remembers." He rubbed a hand across his middle. "Fucking Nebraska."

The screen door burst open, and Jill trekked down the stone steps with a large black garbage bag stuffed with shoes, their heels and toes peeking out of the top. Tania came up behind her, holding Becca.

Jill dumped the bag next to her Honda. "Okay, we're finally done!"

Boner swiveled around, and his body stilled. It was just for a second, but I saw it. His eyes scanned over Jill once, twice.

He turned to me. "What's going on?"

"What? This is Jill. Jill, this is Boner, a good friend of mine from home. He happened to be in the neighborhood."

Tania rolled her eyes.

Jill's forehead wrinkled, her mouth hanging open for a moment and then cementing closed. Women usually reacted that way upon first seeing Boner. Discomfort. Apprehension. Fear. For me, Boner had always been my dark guardian angel. A little over six foot tall, he was lean and long-limbed, with dark hair just past his shoulders, dark brows, the beginnings of a beard, a slight mustache. A tightly wound tension seemed coiled inside him at all times, ready to spring, and if it did, you wouldn't know what hit you. Boner was a dark, volatile creature cut with doses of vulgar and dashing. A modern day gypsy, a contemporary buccaneer. Those bright piercing green eyes of his seemed to register everything about you, no matter if it was in plain sight, or hidden. There was no escape. He looked like he could sting, and if he did, there was a possibility that you just might enjoy the pain.

"You're Catch's woman?" he asked, his voice low.

"Ex," Jill retorted.

"Congratulations."

Her eyebrows lifted. "Thank you."

Boner stepped forward and grabbed the garbage bag, his eyes remaining on Jill. "Where do you want this?"

She licked her lips and pointed to her car. "Just in there, on the floor of the backseat. Please."

She tugged the back door wide open. Boner stuffed the bag on the floor of her crowded backseat as Tania fit Becca into her car seat.

"You okay?" Tania asked him.

"Yeah. Just want to head out. You all set?"

Tania nodded. "Yep. Let's get the hell out of here already."

"Yes, please!" I agreed. I put my hand in Boner's and tugged on it. "You okay?"

"Yeah, yeah." He jerked up the zipper of his leather jacket. "Fuckin' fed up with Nebraska."

"After I had Becca, it turned into an off-and-on thing with me and Catch. I shouldn't have dragged it out for so long though. But when there's a kid in the mix, it changes everything." Jill adjusted a white blouse on a hanger and hung it up in the closet in Tania's old room in Rae's house in Meager. "When he was around, he was an okay dad."

"Really?" Tania asked. "For years, my brother has barely been able to take care of himself."

"Well, she's a sweetheart. Look at her," I murmured as I stroked the side of Becca's impossibly soft cheek while she played with her My Little Pony doll in Tania's old twin bed. "Who wouldn't want to take care of her?"

I took Becca's tiny bare foot in my hand, my thumb running circles over her heel, as I watched her fingers pulling on the sparkly pink pony's hair, twisting it in the air. She giggled, her full cheeks rosy, her blue eyes dancing. She brought the pony to her heart shaped mouth and sucked on his snout.

I used to hover over Jake when he was this age, and Ruby would gently stroke my back then leave us on our own. Even when he napped, I would stare at him, nestling his tiny hand in mine.

Becca's face exploded into laughter, and she flung the pony across the room. I feigned shock and surprise with my hands flying to my face. She swung her legs, kicking, on the bed, and a little bud of wistfulness bloomed inside my chest, an aching flutter that I didn't mind at all.

"You have kids, Grace?"

My head shot up, and my face heated. "Uh...um, no. I have a nephew. He's five years old, almost six. He lives with us off and on."

"She's trying though," said Tania.

"Really?"

Tania told Jill my tale of surrogacy woe.

"Oh, I'm sorry." Jill brought the pink pony toy to her daughter, and Becca grabbed it, squealing. "But that's exciting. I mean, you're trying again, right? It'd be a shame if you..." Her voice trailed off.

I glanced up at her. "Jill? What is it?"

Her eyes were locked on my hand that was on her daughter.

"Your ring," Jill breathed.

"My wedding rings?" I asked, flexing my left hand out. "I love eternity bands—"

"No. That gun chamber ring."

"Oh." I touched the ring on my thumb.

"I didn't notice it today, with everything going on."

"It's been one hell of a day," murmured Tania. "Yet it's still not over, ladies!" She emptied a small tote bag on the bed, next to Becca.

Becca sucked in air, her eyes widening over the new treasures piled before her. Her hands sifted through the mound of costume jewelry, makeup, and hair accessories as if she were a pirate girl unearthing precious gems.

I twirled the ring on my thumb. "It was my first husband's ring actually."

"Your first husband?" Jill said.

"Yes. He died about seventeen years ago. I just got married again."

"And he's hot. Way hot," said Tania.

I made a face at her. "You never thought Dig was hot though, did you?"

"I sure as hell did, but I wasn't about to admit that to you. I was too busy trying to convince you that he wasn't the right choice for you. I'm such an idiot. But I know hot when I see hot."

"Oh my God. You still drive me nuts, just so you know."

Tania batted her eyelashes. "I'm thrilled to hear it."

I suddenly remembered the strange vibe between Tania and Finger. "That reminds me of a conversation we need to have."

"Oh?" Tania. "I'm going to go make some more tea." She slipped out of the room.

Jill sat on the bed next to me. "Your husband's name was Dig?"

"Yes." I turned back to Becca and marveled at the hairbrush she was trying to use on my hair. I leaned closer, and she banged the brush on my head. "Oh! Here, honey, like this." I put my hand over hers, and together, we dragged the brush through my hair.

Becca cooed.

"Do you need a new surrogate?"

"I'm not sure if I want to look just yet. It's a long process. My eyes glaze over from just thinking about it."

"How about me?"

My head jerked at Jill. "What?"

"I had a great pregnancy with Becca. No problems with my delivery. And I'm clean. I've been getting tested regularly. You know, with Catch at the club, I could never be sure what was going on."

"Jill…"

Coming here is really a second chance for me, Grace, a new beginning, and I want to do it right this time. If I'm going to be here, helping out with Catch and Tania's mom and around the house—which allows me to be home with Becca—I could be pregnant, too."

My brain cells stuttered. "I don't know what to say."

"Say yes. Grace, since I went to Nebraska, I've been working odd crap jobs, sometimes two at a time. I'm tired of being spread thin, always running around, and never having enough time for Becca. If I'm not going to have to do that for a while, why can't I do this for you as well? I've seen ads by agencies for girls to be surrogates all over the Internet and in magazines. Why not me? It would work out great for both of us." She shrugged her shoulders, a tight smile on her face. "Right?"

"You're serious?"

"Yes, I am. It'd give me more time with Becca, which I've been missing. I could get some studying done and save some money, all without having to work a regular job."

"You said something earlier about wanting to go back to school, right?" I asked.

"I wanted to get my degree in physical therapy. I have one year under my belt, and then I went part-time. I gave it up though to follow Catch. This would give me that time to prepare, apply to schools, save money for school. Then, after your baby's born, I could finally go back to school and afford it this time around. I'm sorry. I don't mean to make it sound like it's only about the money. I'd really like to be able to do something for you, considering everything you've done for me."

"I understand. At the end of the day, it's a legal monetary transaction. All the details would be covered in a contract."

"Right." Jill nodded, her eyes drifting over the items strewed over the bed. "I'd really like to help you. You saved Becca and made it easier for me to get out from under Catch. I haven't been able to think clearly about that in a long time. You and Tania are giving me a new start, and I'd really like to do something for you." That brief smile swept over her lips once more.

I didn't know what to say. It all made sense, didn't it?

"Refills, ladies." Tania put the tray with our mugs on the dresser. "What's going on?"

"Jill offered to be my surrogate," I replied. "Frankly, I'm sort of speechless at the moment."

Tania's eyes widened. "Holy shit. Really?"

"Really," said Jill.

Tania handed Jill a mug of tea. "Well, having you here in Meager would be—"

"Amazing," I said. "We could go to the doctor together. I can help you out when you aren't feeling well or tired."

"Massage her feet," said Tania handing me the mug of tea.

"Massage your feet, your lower back."

"Babysit Becca," added Tania.

"Yes, babysit Becca. I'd love that." I grinned. "Jill, I'm not quite sure what to say. Thank you. I'll discuss it with my husband tonight."

"Good." Jill exhaled and wiped at the edges of her eyes.

I chewed the inside of my cheek. "I don't want you to feel obligated. We just met. We barely know each other."

Jill sprang up from the bed and darted to her suitcase on the upholstered bench. "It's a good-timing thing for me." She shrugged her shoulders. "Really. It's perfect." She unearthed a stack of jeans from her suitcase.

Tania shot me a look. "Grace, are you trying to talk yourself out of this again?"

"No, it's just that…I guess I expected it to be harder to find someone else. I just want to make sure. Jill, we're talking about you carrying my baby for nine months, you being pregnant *again*. That's huge. A huge responsibility, and a huge bond of trust between us."

"And a huge belly," said Tania.

"Exactly," I said. "I need to be sure that you're completely comfortable with it. You're the one who offered, but…I don't know what I'm trying to say."

"Woo!" Becca sat up on the bed. Large black sunglasses teetered on her face as she rocked from side to side. "Mama! Mam!"

"Oh, those are way too big for you, honey!" I let out a laugh.

"Becca!" Jill said from across the room, her voice strained.

Becca tossed the light-brown case for the glasses at me, and it landed in my lap. I put my mug down on the night table and picked up the case.

My heart stopped.

My own handwriting from twenty years ago in faded ballpoint pen.

Shards of ice needled my neck, constricting my throat. My eyes riveted to the case, to my scribble.

"So you don't forget about me when you're on the road, which is most of the time."

"I always think about you. Never forget you, baby."

My fingers gripped the worn Ray-Ban case.

Those were Dig's sunglasses on Becca's face.

The extra pair.

The extra pair I'd looked for in his saddlebag but couldn't find the day he got killed.

My eyes shot to Jill. She was frozen to the spot, her face ashen.

"Who the hell are you?" My voice ripped through the room.

"Grace?" Tania asked, her eyes wide.

Jill remained still, her lips parted.

Becca reached up and pushed the glasses against my face. She clapped her hands together, giggling, and plopped back on the bed. A cry left my throat as I clutched them.

Jill's eyes sank closed for a moment. "I'm sorry, so sorry," she breathed.

My spine as well as my voice hardened "How do you have his glasses? You knew him?"

"Knew who?" asked Tania. "What the hell is going on you two?"

"These sunglasses are Dig's."

"I'm sorry," Jill mumbled once again, her face slack.

"What? What are you talking about?" Tania's eyes blazed at Jill. "Oh, no—"

"Dig never told you? You really don't know?" Jill asked. "I thought you knew."

My pulse raced, a cold sweat beading on my skin.

Jill's watery blue eyes met mine. "I met him. Once."

Tania scowled. "Holy shit."

Jill swallowed hard as she sank into the edge of the mattress.

My heart banged against my chest. *Where the hell was this going?*

"Whoa, hold up," Tania ordered. "You seem a little young to have—"

"I was fourteen at the time."

My heart skipped a beat.

Tania's eyes flared. "Ah, fantastic. Oh no, you don't. You just realized who Grace is, and you want to unload your guilt now? We do not need to go down your memory lane, Miss Biker Groupie."

"Go on," I said. "Tell me."

"Grace!" Tania snapped.

"I was kidnapped at the Deadwood Jam by a guy…a guy who turned out to be a thief and a murderer. He was a meth addict, and he tied me to the bed in his motel room. Dig showed up to sell him drugs."

"You're sure it was Dig?" Tania asked. "The One-Eyed Jacks? The skull with the sparkling star in one eye? From Meager?"

"Yes. I remember the logo, the name, the patches"—she gestured at the gun-barrel ring on my thumb—"that ring. I'd never been with a biker before. I remember everything about him."

I rubbed my hands down my face.

"Fuck me," Tania muttered.

"The guy who kidnapped me didn't have enough money to pay for all the meth he wanted." Jill pressed her legs together, her fingers entwining with her daughter's. "He offered Dig…he told Dig he could…" Her face reddened as she bit her lip.

Oh fuck.

"I understand," I said.

"I was tied to the bed. Dig came into the room and just stared at me. He came over to me, didn't say a word, and then he climbed on top of me."

Tania let out a hiss of air.

"He told me to keep quiet, his eyes, those golden brown eyes of his bearing down on me. I will never forget those eyes or his weight on my chest. I was so sure he was going to…but instead—"

"Instead, Dig killed him." The words spilled from my lips.

"Yes," Jill breathed, her watery gaze pinned on mine. "Dig distracted him by giving him the drugs to do, and then Dig made the guy think he was going to rape me," she whispered. "Dig shot him straight through the eye in one go."

"Oh God." Tania's hand went to her mouth.

"I really thought he was going to…you know. But it happened so fast," she whispered. "He pulled his gun out of nowhere and shot that bastard dead. Dig got me out of that hellhole. He bought me new clothes, food to eat, even a toothbrush, and a bus ticket home." Her eyes were round, glassy. "He waited with me for the bus. He took the time to talk to me and made sure I got on the bus. I'd noticed his wedding ring. He told me that his wife was pregnant, and he was missing a doctor's appointment with her." She bit down on her lip, her face crumpling. "That was you."

I nodded, my body sagging.

She cleared her throat. "He felt bad about it, and I felt horrible, but I was so grateful."

Becca climbed in her mother's lap and pulled on her hair. "Mam!" Tears spilled down Jill's face. Tania lifted Becca in her arms.

"He didn't have to save me, you know? He could've taken his money and left. In fact, he could've taken whatever he wanted and just walked away. The pizza delivery guy who had shown up before him sure didn't give a damn. He'd even stayed and played for a while. Left that bastard a free pizza in exchange." Jill wiped at her wet eyes.

"Jesus," whispered Tania.

"Your husband saved me. He saved my life. He killed to set me free. It was all so stupid. I wasn't supposed to go to that concert, but I'd lied to my parents about it. I'd stayed out late past my curfew anyhow and gotten drunk with my friends, and that guy had taken me. Your husband had come along, out of nowhere. He gave up being with you and your baby to save me and send me home."

"You did go home?" I asked.

"Yes, I did. I was scared, but my parents were thrilled to see me. I'd been missing for a couple of days."

I squeezed her leg. "Oh, Jill."

"Dig was right. He told me no one had ever given him a second chance until he met a guy from a bike club. That guy showed him that you could make your own luck, pave your own road through life."

My eyes squeezed shut. *Wreck.*

"Dig had said, 'It's up to you to either find a way or make one.' That's helped me a lot over the years whenever I've been tempted to feel sorry for myself or helpless."

My fingers lingered over Dig's ring on my thumb. *The Latin inscription.*

Jill touched my knee, her face brightening for a moment. "And that's what this is about for me, being your surrogate, me making my way. I've finally left Catch, left Nebraska after years of waiting, feeling stuck, feeling trapped, being annoyed. I wanted to believe things would change, that he'd be the man I wanted him to be. But he isn't, and that's okay. I've finally, finally faced that fact and accepted it. Everything that happened today made me see that." A tear slipped down her face. "Please, Grace. Please let me do this for you." She squeezed my knee. "It made Dig smile when I asked about you. That was when he told me about you being pregnant. He was excited about it. Seemed kind of nervous, too, but excited."

My vision clouded. I pressed my hands down my thighs. "I got really mad at him for missing that appointment. He'd promised to meet me at the doctor's office, but he never showed. I hadn't known where he was. I was upset. I had just gotten a cell phone for the first time, and I'd tried calling him, but he never answered. When he finally came home that night, I picked a fight with him over it because he wouldn't tell me the reason why he hadn't come or why he was so late in getting home."

Jill's eyes widened. Her face flushed. "We didn't. I-I—"

"No, I didn't think it was another woman. I figured it was some kind of club business, either petty or epic, but business was business. He'd been evasive in general during the prior two months, but he'd never broken a promise to me before, not really. He'd been excited about that appointment, too. He'd wanted to see the baby on the monitor. Hear the heartbeat."

Jill's eyes filled with water. "He made me promise never to tell—not my parents, not the police. Never. And I never did. I didn't want to get him in trouble. I was so grateful to him. He'd given me my justice. He'd made that happen for me. I didn't feel guilty at all about that asshole dying, not one bit. He probably got chopped up into bits and thrown in some hole. Still don't feel guilty. Does that make me a bad person?"

I shook my head as our fingers laced together.

"When I saw the pistol ring just now, I remembered his bravery, the sacrifice he didn't even realize he was making." She took in a breath. "I'm so glad and very grateful, that today, my baby was safe. That you and Tania are safe. That we're out of there." She shook her head, her face breaking into a smile.

"What is it?"

"When I first saw that ring on his hand, it kind of scared me."

My grin wobbled. "Me, too."

"He had a gun, a knife, a loud huge bike, and he wasn't afraid to use them. It's funny. He was everything my mom always warned me about in a guy, but if it wasn't for him...I always think about that. Pretty damn ironic."

I took in a breath. He had killed for Jill, but I knew Dig had killed for Eve, for his mother, his father. Killed for himself. That day—I knew it in my heart—he had also killed for me, clearing the way for our baby, our future, with one less dirtbag in it. I let go of Jill's hands.

She sighed as she brushed her hair from her face. "I went home. I worked on things with my parents. It was hard at first, but it was worth it. Then, not even a week later maybe, I saw on the news that a biker got shot and killed, and his wife was seriously injured. I prayed it wasn't Dig. But they showed his picture, mentioned his name. I was devastated. Just devastated."

"It was your kidnapper's brother who came after him."

"Yes. I read everything I could about the shooting. You were bleeding to death, but you shot him. You killed him. You know, I had been tied to a bed for over twenty-four hours. I hadn't known how to fight back. I'd been too scared. All I'd wanted was to die. Instead, Dig and your baby..."

"Jill, don't," muttered Tania.

Jill's back straightened at the sharp tone in Tania's voice. "I feel responsible for all that pain and loss you must have gone through. All because of me," she whispered, tears streaming down her face.

"Jill, he saved your life."

"But he risked his own and yours and paid for it in the worst way."

How could I explain to Jill that the sacrifice she felt Dig had made was actually the only decision he could have made? There was no other way for him. His absolute action was one of absolution and justice, pure and simple. Dig, the lone warrior, the avenging angel. I rubbed the gun-barrel ring on my thumb. Something shifted in my chest.

"I came to find you in Meager, about a month later, when I was able to get away. I went to the bike club, but I didn't get very far. They wouldn't talk to me. Your friend with the long hair and green eyes, Boner, was so mad at me."

My eyes widened at her.

"He kicked me off the property. Had me followed home. I promised myself that one day...one day, I would find you and tell you. I didn't know what I'd tell you or how I'd tell you. I was sure the other bikers knew all about it. That was why they'd blown me off. That was why Boner had been so pissed. They resented me, hated me. And I assumed you knew what had happened and that you hated me, too, but I didn't care. I needed to find you. To look you in the eyes, to thank you. To fall at your feet. Something." She shuddered, hunching over.

But I had nothing to give her. I was numb.

"Today, when I realized Becca was missing, taken, all I could think was that his bravery couldn't have been for nothing. That I'd failed him, failed my daughter. But then you came walking into the Flames clubhouse, holding my baby."

She held my gaze.

"Grace, I want you to know, I hate that the wonderful thing your husband did for me shattered your family. I hate that. But every night, I count my blessings that a drug-dealing biker showed up to that motel room that horrible day. Wasn't even a profitable deal. The idiot barely had any cash on him." She cleared her throat. "I'm sorry, Grace. So sorry."

She sagged against me, and I took her in my arms and held her.

"He saved me," she rasped.

"He saved you."

"He taught me to have hope for a better day. That it was my choice. That I could make that happen."

"It is. I had to learn that all over again myself. It took me years to learn it all over again," I whispered.

"What the hell were you doing with my brother then?" Tania asked. "You got bit by the biker bug?"

Jill sat up, pulling away from me. She rolled her eyes as she wiped at her face. "Yeah, I suppose." She picked up Dig's Ray-Bans from the bed. "I've kept these all this time."

"I had a pretty bad black eye and bruises on my face when he found me. He gave me his sunglasses to put on to get me out of the hotel and on his bike without attracting attention. I tried to give them back to him before I left, but he said I should keep them. He said he had an extra pair."

"He always kept the extra pair on his bike," I said. "These were his. The ones he was wearing when he was killed...they were the extras..." My body wavered. A cold sweat sprinted down my back, my chest constricted.

"Grace, you okay?" Tania deposited Becca on the bed, and her arms went around me as nausea swept through me. "Breathe, honey."

My lungs flattened against my chest. A stinging pressure seared me between the eyes.

I struggled to take in air.

"Lay her back. Let's get her feet up." Jill's even voice floated over me.

My body was extended, my legs lifted. A cold wet washcloth banded around my neck, and I shivered. The buzzing ceased, the blur dissipated, and the room clarified for me once more. A splash of cool water passed my lips. My fingers curled into the quilt and grazed hard metal.

I had forgotten my glasses at home on that last ride together with Dig. I had gone looking for the extras in the saddlebag where they always were. But that one time they had been missing, in their place, I'd found Mole's stolen gold and two of Vig's damn diamonds.

Dig had brushed off the whole confrontation with Mole to me like it was nothing but an irritation, an annoyance, a waste of his time, and I'd only scoffed at him. I'd known better. I had believed that his short temper and his arrogance as a defiant outlaw had gotten him into yet another club quagmire. *But that hadn't been the case, had it?* Here was a testament to his bravery, his determination, his I-must-do-this-or-I-am-nothing attitude. My fingers touched the cool black metal frame, closed over the smooth curve of the lenses.

Proof.

Testimony of his compassion, his pain, his deep and dark beautiful love, his brave buckled soul. Cold hard evidence of it in my very hands right now. How could he feel alive to me in a pair of ordinary scratched sunglasses that I held in my grip? My fingers tightened around the metal and glass.

All these years of my purgatory, he was rightly being worshiped and prayed for by a young girl I hadn't even known existed as her avenging angel, a noble and brave martyr to her salvation. And we—his brothers, his old lady—had done what? Blithely commended him as a martyr of that arrogance and devil-may-care attitude that had typified him.

I clutched the glasses to my chest.

"Never forget you, baby."

A moan escaped my lips. My vision swirled. A huge wave washed over me, pulling me under.

"I'm sorry! Oh God, I'm sorry." Jill's tiny voice seeped over me.

Becca cried out, shrieking.

"Grace!" Tania warbled from a distance.

A vintage radio losing contact.

Static.

"Never forget you, baby."

Nothing.

TWENTY-SEVEN

HEAT PENETRATED THROUGH MY CLOTHES, warming my flesh. My body was tightly clasped, my face buried in a firm warm wall, and the strong aroma of paint and damp skin filled my nostrils. Miller's skin. I pressed closer into him. A sigh escaped my lips, my muscles loosening.

"Hang on, baby. Taking you home," he said, his deep voice rumbling in his chest.

My eyelids cracked open. It was dark. Was it night already?

The gearshift of Miller's truck was gripped by a woman's hand, her pale skin illuminated by the glow of the dashboard and control panels. Whoever was driving was driving real fast. The drone of a motorcycle flared behind us. My pulse tripped. I rubbed my face in Miller's chest and let out a moan.

"Stop the truck!" Miller growled, his body tensing around mine.

We came to a swerving halt, the bike groaning behind us. I gulped for air as my head rolled back, my eyes straining to find his black ones. Had to.

There.

His large hand cradled my face. "Grace, you need to go to the cemetery? We'll go. What do you want, baby?" His hand swept to the back of my head.

I blinked.

Those eyes.

His molten beautiful eyes searched mine for an answer. I had an answer—there was only one—with all the certainty in my soul.

"Home." My voice creaked from my dry lips, my icy fingers curling into the worn cotton of his T-shirt. "I want to go home."

"Sweetheart," he murmured, the lines of his face softening, as he rubbed the back of my neck.

The truck jumped into gear, lurching forward. Miller's arms tightened around me, pulling me closer. I sank back into his chest once again, planting a kiss over his heart, and closed my eyes.

Within minutes, my body recognized the twisted turn and the jolts of the rocky dirt road leading to our house. The truck bumped to a stop, and the door jerked open. The motion sensor popped on the bright white lights. Miller held me in his arms and got us to the front door. I peeked over his shoulder. Tania and Boner stood in front of the truck, her holding both our handbags. The two of them were speaking, their faces drawn.

Miller set me down on our big sectional couch and immediately bundled me up in the large charcoal-gray wool throw. He brought me a glass of water and wrapped himself around me again, none too gently planting kisses on my forehead, as I took sips of the cold liquid.

"Better?" He wiped a strand of hair from my face. "You ready to tell me?"

"Is Boner still here? I need to ask him—"

"Right here," said Boner in the doorway, the sunglasses case in his hands.

Tania was at his side.

I sat up. "Did you know? Did he tell you what he'd done? Did he tell you why?"

Boner sat down on the coffee table in front of me, his knees rubbing mine. "I only cleaned it up after. He'd called me, told me he'd gotten into a scrape, and asked if I could grab a couple of brothers to get rid of any evidence and the body. And that was what I did. Didn't know about any girl. He never said nothing about it to me. I didn't question him about that shit, Grace. I trusted his judgment." His thumb rubbed over the surface of the Ray-Ban case in his hand.

"You'd met her back then."

He nodded. "It was a bad time. We had the cops and the Feds breathing down our necks. She showed up, and I kicked her out. I figured she was just another girl. Told her never to come back again. Told her to keep her trap shut about knowing him, never to mention you or the One-Eyed Jacks to anyone. Ever."

"You made an impression," muttered Tania.

"Yeah. She was a kid. I made sure I spooked her off. Had Dready follow her, and I kept tabs on her for a bit. Never any problems."

"You recognized her today, didn't you?"

"Yeah, I did." Boner gave Miller the Ray-Ban case. He leaned over me and planted a kiss on my cheek.

I sank back into the sofa, wrapping myself up in the throw again, and stared into the empty fireplace.

A hand squeezed my shoulder. "You need anything, Grace, anything at all, you call me." Tania turned to Miller. "Anytime."

"Thanks."

The door closed, and Miller's body was around mine again. His fingers found the silver ring on my thumb.

"Dig's?"

I took in a breath. "Boner had it. He gave it to me yesterday." I stretched out my hand in his much larger one. "Why did he keep it a secret from me? We got into a fight about the diamonds, the gold. I figured he'd killed Mole, but when I reacted—and I reacted badly—he didn't defend himself, didn't tell me the reason."

"It was something he needed to do, it went deep."

My head sank against Miller's shoulder.

"It was good, Grace. A very good thing."

"It got him killed."

"Yeah, it got him killed, and look what got my brother killed. Jack shit. Is Dig's a nobler death because he died for a good cause? Maybe. I don't fucking know anymore. Does it even matter in the end because the result is still the same? Both of them gone, ripped from their lives, from us."

He sighed and leaned his head against mine.

"I used to think that what was left was only what was in his coffin." I touched the Ray-Ban case. "But it's bigger than that, different than the things they actually left us—the bikes, a business, the houses, money."

He squeezed my hand. "How are you feeling about Jill?"

"She was afraid I'd hate her once I knew the truth, but I don't hate her. She didn't get Dig killed. If I hated her, it would negate Dig's decision, which was no decision at all—not for him. That had been his fight. It had been a burden to him, but it'd defined him. I only wish I could've helped him through it, made it better somehow. Maybe I should have pushed him more. I don't know. But look what he did for her—not only saving her from more rape and torture and probably death, but she also went on and had a life. Her own child. Got out of a bad relationship, stuck up for herself. She has professional goals, dreams."

"He inspired her."

"I think so." I curled up in Miller's arm and peeked up at him. "What better way to bring our baby into the world?" I whispered.

"What?" his voice softened.

"She offered to be our surrogate." My one hand rubbed over his chest. "I can't help but feel that somehow, someway, he's giving us this chance."

Miller kissed me lightly, his hands sifting through my hair.

"I like that, him giving this to us. Like he's watching over us somehow." I slid my forehead to his. "I love you, Miller."

"I know you do, baby." His warm hand moved around my neck.

"He felt so guilty about you when Wreck was killed," I said against his lips. "He was always hearing the sirens after that." I sucked in air and buried my face in his neck.

"Shh…" Miller rocked me in his arms, the firm muscles of his back rippling under my fingers. "I didn't hate him, didn't blame him or anyone else. It was just such a shock. You don't ever expect the earth under your feet to give way. It gave way for me that day."

I clung to him. "Boner gave me this ring to snap me out of my head mess. I wore it, and she saw it. That's more than good timing, that's…"

"Convergence."

I smiled as my hands raked through Miller's hair, and I rose up in his lap. "I can't ignore that. I don't want to."

"What are you saying?" His hands slid around my ass, pulling me into his body.

"I found you," I whispered, my hands cradling his face. "The very day I stepped foot back into South Dakota, I found you. Now, I found Jill. I found her when she needed me, and I needed her. Not all those years ago when I wouldn't have been able to listen to her without anger and bitterness. I wouldn't have been able to see it, understand it like I do now. Now."

Tears spilled from my eyes, and he wiped at them and licked them from my hot face. My mouth found his, our tongues seeking each other. I dug my fingers into his neck, and a groan escaped his lips.

"Grace." His hand dipped down the gap in the back of my jeans, sliding under the thin elastic of my panties, cupping my ass.

"Wait, baby. Wait."

"Ain't waiting." His voice was hoarse, his breathing short and choppy.

"I want to call Jill right now. She needs to hear from me, and I need to make sure she's okay. I want her to know that I'm grateful for her, that I'm grateful for what Dig did. I'd like to ask her to go to Dr. Carollton with us. What do you think?"

Miller stretched back and took in a deep breath, his lips twitching. He reached for his cell phone on the coffee table without disconnecting us, his head swinging up at me. "I'm good with it. You sure?"

"Very sure." I grinned. "Very, very sure. Ah, and then I have to tell you all about our little adventure in Nebraska."

His eyebrows slammed together. "I heard. Not happy. Creeper is a dead man."

"Baby—"

"That slime grabbed my old lady. Again. He's gonna pay, and I'm gonna make him pay."

"Honey, Butler was there—"

A muscle in his jaw tensed. "Yeah."

Still a sore subject.

His hands wrapped around my neck, his eyes narrowing. "I don't know what the fuck he's up to, but I'm glad he was there. If anything had happened to you, Grace..."

I clutched his shoulder. "Butler's out there on his own, cleaning up. He's got some sort of plan brewing in Nebraska with Creeper as his bargaining chip. He's leaving Jump out of the loop. You and Boner should have a little chat about it."

"Fuck."

My lips twitched, and he smirked.

"Love that grin." His thumb rubbed across my lips. "Missed it."

An ache careened through my chest. "I missed you," I whispered. I planted a kiss on the bump on his nose and then another along the scar down his cheek.

"Don't shut me out again, Grace. Don't hide from me. Not from me."

I hugged him. "I won't."

He pushed me back against the sofa, and I let out a huff of air.

"Baby, hang on. Let me call Jill. One sec. Please!"

He ignored me and unbuttoned my jeans, sliding the zipper down. My stomach dipped at the light touch of his fingertips. He let out a low growl as his hands snuck under my shirt, skimming my bare skin, making heady promises.

"Miller…"

His tongue lashed over our eagle and key tattoo on my tummy, prodding the satin trim of my panties. "Make the call, and make it quick, baby. I got to get inside you."

TWENTY-EIGHT

"THEY'RE STARTING NOW." The nurse smiled.

"Thank you." Miller turned to me and lifted his eyebrows.

I grinned as he took my hand in his and led me back to the small sofa in Dr. Carollton's waiting room.

In the two weeks since Jill's confession, we had gone to Dr. Carollton, and Jill had undergone all the appropriate tests. She'd passed them with flying colors. We'd trooped across the state to the lawyer's office in Sioux Falls to sign newly prepared surrogacy documents, arranging for payments and care and protecting all of us on this journey toward the birth of a new life.

Our new life.

It was finally happening. The transfer of our Flies as Eagles embryos into the hopeful safety of Jill's haven.

Tania waited with us, shuffling through every magazine in the office and on her phone checking in with Lenore who was babysitting Becca.

Miller's fingers suddenly tensed around mine.

A nurse stood before us. "It's done. She's resting now."

"Can we go see her?" I asked.

"Sure. Come with me."

"Go," said Tania, a smile lighting up her face.

With Miller's one hand at my back, we followed the nurse behind a closed door.

"Hey," Jill whispered.

I took her hand. "How are you doing? You feel okay?"

"I'm fine. It went great."

I placed my other hand over hers and squeezed. "Thank you."

She slightly shook her head against the table, her eyes filling with water. "I need to thank you, Grace. This is my answer, too. This giving back to him. To you."

"You picked a hell of a way," Miller said.

An hour later, Tania brought Jill home and had her tucked in bed.

Stopped at a red light, I raised myself up in the seat of the Harley and pressed myself against Miller's back, my mouth at his ear. He relaxed his head against mine.

"Can we go home first before we go to the shop?"

"What is it? You okay?" He raised his voice over the hum of the engine.

I only squeezed his middle. The light turned green, and Miller punched the Fat Bob into gear. We tore out of Rapid, speeding off for Meager.

Forty minutes later, I jumped off the bike and sprinted to the front door. My entire body was tingling with giddy energy. My heart raced as my key turned the lock, and Miller's big hand pushed the door open. He hustled me inside, away from the cool air, the sun's mild rays doing nothing to warm us. I threw the keys and my bag on the floor, flung my leather jacket to the side, and tugged his off his frame.

He let out a rumbly laugh. "Babe?"

"Make love to me. Now. Now that our baby is finding its home inside Jill, starting its life, getting cozy in its little nest, I want to make love for us and make love for our baby. He might not be in here"—my hands went to my tummy—"but he is, all the same. Fill me with us, Miller."

His face tightened, and he picked me up in his arms and brought me down the hall to our room.

He laid me on our bed, his eyes holding mine. My heart raced as he quickly peeled off his clothes, my hands stroking over his smooth firm flesh. I wanted him to strip off my clothing, to take me the way he wanted to, from start to finish, to be his. For this to be ours. He did just that and slammed into me without preface.

"Fuck, I love you," he murmured over me, his voice shuddering. "Love you, baby."

He slowly pulled himself out and rocked right back in even deeper. We both groaned loudly, our lips searching each other's. My hands slid to his face, and we held each other's gaze as his cock dragged out and slowly thrust inside me once again, savoring its home. My hips rose, pleading for every thick inch of him inside every inch of me. We ground into each other, our bodies lost in a fevered rhythm. His teeth grazed my shoulder, his groans filling my ear. I never wanted this to end, never wanted it to change, never wanted to not feel this, because *this* is what had made our baby.

Yes, there was some sort of holy coordination of past and present in the making of our child, but this, this was its essence.

Heat flooded my insides, need searing through my flesh, joy squeezing my heart. "I love you, Miller."

"Aw, Grace." His groaning with every slow, long thrust filled our bedroom.

"Yes, yes." My voice choked, my body on fire.

His one hand cupped a breast and squeezed it, kneading it. He held me, held me down, and I came, as he thrust deeper and faster, coming inside me. But I didn't want to let go of him, didn't want any kind of disconnect. I wanted to feel it all again, surge into him. Again. Until there was no Grace, no Miller. Just us.

I wriggled against the heat of his heavy body, my sensitive clit pulsating as my legs squeezed around his hips. His mouth nuzzled my throat as I rubbed against him, circling my hips frantically. My hands clung to the firm muscles of his rear, and he held himself still, murmuring filthy encouragements against my damp skin. He slid his index finger into my mouth, and I sucked hard on it as his molten needy eyes held mine.

"Fuck, baby." He took it away from me and drilled it into my rear.

I cried out, a harsh rush of pleasure detonating through me. "Oh!"

He chuckled as he nipped at my throat.

I tugged on his hair. "More," I whispered against the side of his jaw, down to his smiling lips. "Miller…more."

Two weeks later, I got a call from Dr. Carollton. I gripped the edge of my desk at the shop as his words penetrated. I held my breath as I tapped on the phone's screen, ending the call. The phone slid from my hands, clattering on my desk, and I ran through the door leading into the shop.

Boner's eyes widened at me.

Tricky raised his head from the interior of a car engine. "He's painting—"

I ran.

Miller peeled off the disposable togs he wore while spray painting. His dark brows lifted as he yanked the cover off his head, his hair sticking out of his man bun. "Babe?"

I lunged at him, and he stumbled back two steps, his arms under my rear.

"Jill's pregnant. We're having our baby."

His eyes flashed, and then he buried his face in my neck, lifting me higher in his embrace. There was victory in the tense squeeze of his arms around me. Humility and pure joy.

All of it burning with gratitude.

Even in this quiet, dusty town called Meager, in lives marked by slim offerings and harsh circumstances, there was still the opportunity for synchronicity, for the alignment of the stars in one's favor, especially when graced by the power of one man's love.

Dig had loved me well, both me and Miller, and that love and care was a living blessing, here and now. It touched our lives still, and in the most beautiful way.

For years, I had thought that love had ended in a blaze of regretfully hasty decisions, manly arrogance, hubris, but it hadn't. It burned bright and reached out to me still. I could feel it now shimmering through my heart as that muscle pounded wildly in my chest. It was a raw thing, elemental and undiluted, flowing from the deepest part of me and showering me and Miller with brilliant shooting starlight across our night sky. Dig had given us the gift that the three of us had once thought, at one time or another, we never deserved and could never have.

That piece of my heart that was Dig sang in my chest, bursting there.

Thank you, Dig. Thank you. Rest, my love. Be at peace. It's all good. So very good.

Miller's heartbeat raced through me as I pressed deeper against him, his breathing ragged.

"I love you, baby."

Life's random hits may have brought us pain, but they also gave us rare beauty, rare to lost souls like us. Like when a girl had taken a chance asking a group of bikers to save her sister at a keg party. Like when a tired man had decided at the last minute to stop for a quick drink at a bar on his way home and noticed a woman sitting alone, enjoying a glass of whiskey.

"Love you, Grace."

Yes, rare beauty for souls like us.

EPILOGUE

Dig

ONCE, I LOVED.

Once, I was loved, and I undid myself in her, in us.

I am air, a current whispering over her skin, the once-in-a-while irregular rhythm of her heart. I am there in her smile, her tears, in her humility, her disappointments, her hopes, her breath.

I have no explanation for it. I don't know how this works, but that's not important. What is important is that we are connected in some way—past borders, past geography, beyond flesh. We are passion and faith and hope that stretch and ripple across time. We are a flash, a slice, a crease through so many layers of experience all defining our reach, our imprint, our touch on each other.

Now, grief, regret, and remorse have no place. They can't take root any longer. Finally plucked from my spirit and hers, they're weeds that have withered, drifted away like the dried grasses of our land. That fog of regret has lifted and waned in that infinite sky.

I no longer drift.

I feel that release.

And I believe.

Yes, once I loved, and I was loved; an honor I regard with pleasure and satisfaction, not yearning. It simply is—that one single precious, truly good moment, that instant in time of loving her with all my heart and soul.

Once, I loved. I stumbled here and there, but I loved well.

It was definitive, remarkable.

My compass.

And that love did not waste away on a broken branch or diminish with my passing over. It grew and bore fruit beyond me, beyond my understanding even, into something worthier than my petty longings, my needs, my wants, or twisted desires when I'd walked the earth and rode over it.

It was once, yet I know now it will always be, always exist, this love. And that is the way it should be.

They both know. They feel it, too.

Extant. Grace would like that word.
What was once a wild heartbeat,
a falling tear,
a deep sigh,
an insistent touch,
an angry thought,
a delicious high,
a wild laugh,
a precious hope,
a hand in mine.
Once a whisper against skin
sweeps into the wind
and is no longer simply hers and mine,
it grows and multiplies and enriches all those around it.
It has survived random, chance acts of thoughtless brutality
and brutal thoughtlessness.
Not vaporized. Not destroyed.
It's proven us wrong after all.
For there is no fear in the face of this.
This is another sort of weapon. This is a wellspring.
Here is significance. Here is rare worth.
And it has set me free.
It's that strong, that bright, that true. Its vibrant colors will not
fade in the harsh rays of the sun.

OTHER BOOKS BY CAT PORTER

LOCK & KEY

WOLFSGATE

ABOUT THE AUTHOR

CAT PORTER was born and raised in New York City, but also spent a few years in Texas and Europe along the way. As an introverted, only child, she had very big, but very secret dreams for herself. She graduated from Vassar College, was a struggling actress, an art gallery girl, special events planner, freelance writer, restaurant hostess, and had all sorts of other crazy jobs all hours of the day and night to help make those dreams come true. She has two children's books traditionally published under her maiden name. She now lives in Athens, Greece with her husband and three children, and freaks out regularly and still daydreams way too much. She is addicted to reading, the beach, Pearl Jam, the History Channel, her smartphone, her husband's homemade red wine, really dark chocolate, and her Nespresso coffee machine. Oh, and Jamie & Claire Fraser and those Vikings...never mind. Writing keeps her somewhat sane, extremely happy, and a productive member of society.

Come Find Me Online

Facebook: www.facebook.com/catporterauthor

Website: www.catporter.eu

Twitter: @catporter103

TSU: www.tsu.co/CatPorterAuthor

Goodreads:
www.goodreads.com/author/show/8286871.Cat_Porter

Instagram: instagram.com/catporter.author

Pinterest: www.pinterest.com/catporter103

Email: catporter103@gmail.com

R&R Book Trailer: https://youtu.be/_F7jqiBbqLM

ACKNOWLEDGMENTS

I COULD NOT HAVE MADE THIS DREAM COME TRUE without a great many wonderful, supportive and very smart people who deserve my big hugs and my sincerest thanks:

To Jovana Shirley for your keen insights and for your patience, generosity, and the magical sweep of your editing and design wands.

Lots of hugs and kisses to Najla Qamber for yet another fantastic collaboration and for making my little ideas a breathtaking reality.

To Billy Blue of Blue Bayer Design NYC for the use of your beautiful silver pistol ring featured on the cover and in my story and for your enthusiasm.

To Needa whose trust and friendship mean so very much. This book could not have come to fruition the way I wanted it to without your generosity and non-sugarcoated input, and our mutual devotion to keeping it real, yeah? To Jenn who is my rock, my hand holder, my oracle, Sister of my Heart. I shudder to think where I would be without you and all the laughter and the girly good times. To Natalie whose ancient forever love continues to keep me centered and on track after lo all these many years. To Alison for cheering me on and for your organizational skills on my behalf an ocean away. To Ellen W., Lena, DiDi, my Java Girl, Lorelei, Andrea, Jordan, Penny, Sue B., Tina, Evan—endless rivers of love for your friendship, support, laughter, and pearls of wisdom.

To my terrific beta readers Alison, Judy, Lena, Natalie, Needa, Rachel, Rose. Thank you for taking the time to help me with so much care and thoughtfulness. I appreciate each and every one of you and truly would be lost without you. A special thank you to Angela who after reading "Lock & Key" insisted on finding out if Grace ever got her baby (*"I must know!"*) to which I had initially rolled my eyes, and to the Goodreads member who remarked, *"I don't want to read a book about a dead guy."* Both of you spurred me on in a direction I least expected for this book, and I thank you for annoying me.

Huge thanks to Chas Jenkins and Rock Star PR for their support, guidance, and friendship while navigating the choppy seas.

Big smooches to all the Facebook book groups and fellow authors and reader friends for their support and enthusiasm and soooo much laughter. I've made so many wonderful new friends from all over the world on this book journey, and it never ceases to amaze me: Amy, Caroline, MJ, Paige, Tamra, to name a few. And a very special thanks to Angel Dust, Mary Orr, and MC Rocker Reader whose tireless work and devotion amaze me on a daily basis. (And Angel, our book trailer...heavy sigh, girlfriend!)

To the wonderful women of Guilty Pleasures, The Book Bellas, EDGy Reviews, I Love Book Love, Platypire Reviews, Cruising Susan, Book Reading Gals, Book Babes Unite, Shayna Renee's Spicy Reads, Perusing Princesses, and Totally Booked, among many, many others whose generous support and insights I cherish. I thank you and all the book bloggers who took a chance on my books, share their book love, and are even inspired to make their own teasers! The incredible, tireless work these wonderful women do on their blogs in the name of books and woman power mean so very much to me as an author and a reader and always will.

To my husband for his support and most especially to my three children who put up with my crazy at all hours and thankfully laugh along with me at that crazy, giving me hugs and gentle reminders to feed them and pick them up from school. You're my everything.

To my readers, this is truly nothing without you. Thank you for letting my words whisper in your ears and in your hearts. You make it all the sweeter. I love hearing from you on Facebook, Twitter, Tsu, and Instagram. Visit my Pinterest page where I have dedicated boards to "Random & Rare" and "Lock & Key" that I hope you enjoy as much as I do pinning them into creation. (Can't stop, that thing is addictive...) And please do leave a review wherever you may roam. All are very much appreciated and vital to a book's journey out in the big world.

xx, C